Caroline A⸳⸳⸳rso⸳ ⸳⸳⸳
garde⸳⸳⸳, unofficial tearo⸳ ⸳⸳⸳ ⸳⸳
of lovely cakes. Not necessarily in that order!
What Caroline loves: her family. Her friends.
Reading. Writing contemporary love stories.
Hearing from readers. Walks by the sea with
coffee/ice cream/cake thrown in! Torrential rain.
Sunshine in spring/autumn. *What Caroline hates:*
losing her pets. Fighting with her family. Cold
weather. Hot weather. Computers. Clothes shopping.
Caroline's plans: keep smiling and writing!

Born and raised just outside Toronto, Ontario,
Amy Ruttan fled the big city to settle down with
the country boy of her dreams. After the birth of her
second child Amy was lucky enough to realise her
lifelong dream of becoming a romance author. When
she's not furiously typing away at her computer she's
mum to three wonderful children who use her as a
personal taxi and chef.

Discover more at millsandboon.co.uk.

BOUND BY THEIR BABIES

CAROLINE ANDERSON

A MUMMY FOR HIS DAUGHTER

AMY RUTTAN

MILLS & BOON

First Published in Great Britain 2018
by Mills & Boon, an imprint of HarperCollins*Publishers*
1 London Bridge Street, London, SE1 9GF

Bound by Their Babies © 2018 by Caroline Anderson

A Mummy for His Daughter © 2018 by Amy Ruttan

ISBN: 978-0-263-93344-4

Printed and bound in Spain
by CPI, Barcelona

BOUND BY
THEIR BABIES

CAROLINE ANDERSON

MILLS & BOON

Special thanks to the Gibbs family, who were inadvertently so helpful with the medical elements. I'm so glad it all went well in the end!

And huge thanks to my daughter Sarah for the excellent source material in the form of her four delightful and often hilarious young children, who help me to remember just how challenging parenting can be!

I love you all. xxx

PROLOGUE

June

'HI, EM. I'VE just come out of Theatre and found two missed calls, and I tried the house phone and got no reply. Where are you? Are you OK?'

Jake heard a soft laugh, then a little gasp, and his pulse shifted a notch.

'Em? Talk to me!'

'I'm in labour, but I can't do this. I need you, Jake…' Another little gasp. 'I'm in Maternity Reception—'

She broke off breathlessly, the contraction obviously peaking, and his heart went into overdrive.

'I'll be right there,' he promised, and sliding his phone back into his pocket, he told a colleague to page the registrar to take over from him and headed for the lift at a run, his heart hammering.

Crazy. There was no reason for him to react like this. He was an obstetrician, for heaven's sake! He spent his life surrounded by women in labour, but this was different. This was Emily, his dearest, oldest, closest friend, and he'd promised he'd be there for her. Not as an obstetrician but as her birth partner, and that was much harder because it wasn't his place to be there, it was Pete's.

But Pete, her husband of eleven years, the father of her

baby, couldn't be here with her today or any other day. The man who'd had everything any man could want—everything he himself wanted—had lost it all for ever in a cruel twist of fate, and now all Emily had was Jake.

How could he possibly take Pete's place?

The lift was on a go-slow, and he drummed his fingers on the door, wishing he'd taken the stairs. *Come on, come on...*

The doors finally hissed open, and there she was, leaning against the window opposite and breathing with soft, light huffs.

'I'm here, Em, I've got you,' he murmured, and laid his hand on the small of her back and rubbed firmly, and she moaned softly and leant into him, rocking from foot to foot as he stared out into the darkness and waited for the contraction to ease.

The first hint of dawn was just appearing on the horizon, a thin sliver of grey pushing back the night. New day, new life...

'How are you doing?' he asked, when the huffing stopped and she straightened up.

'Awful.' She turned and met his eyes, her own pinched with fear as she took his hands and hung on. 'It's not due for two weeks, how can I be in labour? I'm just not ready, Jake.'

Which made two of them. 'Yes, you are. You know babies, Em. They come when they come, but at least you're here now and I didn't have a thirty-mile drive in the middle of the night to get to you.'

'Oh, don't! I thought you were being silly making me move in with you this week. I so nearly didn't come. I didn't think there was any need yet, and now I just can't believe it's happening.'

'I can, so I'm really glad you finally listened to me—

and you'll be fine,' he promised rashly. 'You're fit and well—'

'Don't give me that. I'm an obstetrician too, I know all the things that can go wrong, and fit and well's got nothing to do with it.'

'And you also know the odds, which are slim,' he said calmly, even though his heart was still pounding. 'You'll be fine, Emily. I'm not going to let anything happen to you or the baby.'

'You can't say that.'

'I can. I have,' he told her, mentally crossing his fingers, because this baby was her last link with Pete, and absolutely nothing could be allowed to break that link. 'Come on, let's get you upstairs and admit you. Can you walk, or do you want a wheelchair?'

'Walk. It's easier.'

'OK.' He led her to the lift, and somebody was holding the doors. Liv, one of their most trusted midwives, and he felt a surge of relief as he flashed her a smile.

'Hi, Liv. This is Emily—the friend I told you about? Em, Liv's a senior midwife and she's amazing.'

'And you're a smooth talker,' Liv said with a laugh. 'Hi, Emily, it's good to meet you. I'll come up with you, get you settled in. Want me to stay for the delivery?' she added to Jake, and he nodded.

'That would be great if you can,' he said, as Emily turned into his arms, gripped his shoulders and moaned softly. 'It's OK, Em. Just breathe, in and out, nice and light,' he coaxed gently, and felt the soft huff of her breath drift against the open V of his scrubs. 'That's it, well done, you're doing really well.'

'Two minutes forty,' Liv murmured, and he nodded. They were coming thick and fast. No wonder she was struggling.

The lift pinged, and the grip on his shoulders eased.

'Are we there?'

'Yes. Come on, let's get you comfortable.'

They felt like the longest two hours of his life, Em's contractions blurring into each other in an untidy avalanche punctuated by calm reassurance and steady progress reports from Liv.

He was so glad Liv had stayed with them. He trusted her, and in this situation he felt so out of his depth it was absurd, but Liv was calm and in control and she handled it brilliantly while he tried to stop being a doctor and did what he could to help Em.

He rubbed her back, he held her hand, he walked her round, he held her, rocked her, mopped her brow, and then at last he lifted up the squalling, slippery little body of her son and laid him against the bare skin of her breast, his eyes blinded by tears as he tucked a warm towel around the baby.

'Well done, Em. Well done. Clever girl.'

'What is it?'

'A boy,' he said, his voice catching. He swallowed hard and tried again. 'It's a boy.'

Her head was bent so he couldn't see her eyes, but he could see her fingers, the tender, sure curve of them over the baby's head, the loving touch of a mother soothing her baby in those momentous moments after birth.

She pressed her lips to the baby's head. 'Hello, little one,' she murmured, her voice a caress. 'Welcome to the world.'

He was quiet now, his eyes fixed on his mother's, tiny fingers curled around hers, and Jake's throat was so clogged he couldn't speak, but he squeezed her shoulder and she looked up at him and smiled, her eyes shimmering in the slanting light of the early morning sun.

'We did it,' she said softly, her voice incredulous. 'We actually did it.'

'No, you did it,' he said, his voice cracking. 'You've been so brave through all of this. Pete would be really proud of you.'

A tear slid down her cheek, and she gave a tiny nod and kissed the baby again.

'He's lovely and pink,' Liv said with a smile, and Jake stepped back and made room for her to do her job. His presence was redundant now, and he just wanted to get out into the fresh air and sort out his feelings, because they were all over the place and some of them had no business being there at all.

'Apgar score ten at one minute,' Liv was saying to the other midwife, and he turned to the basin and washed his hands on autopilot, his emotions flayed.

It was fourteen months since Matilda had been born last April at his old hospital on the other side of Suffolk, but it could have been yesterday. It was the only other time he'd been at what felt like the wrong end of a delivery bed, and he'd been shocked at how emotional he'd been when his tiny daughter had been put in his arms, and how much he'd instantly loved her.

He'd only just started here at Yoxburgh Park Hospital then and Jo had refused to move with him, but he'd been there for Matilda's birth, heard her first cry, been there to hold her, to bond with her, and he spent as much time with her now as he could.

It didn't feel like enough, but at least he was alive. At least he knew his precious, darling Tilly, and she knew him. Pete would never know his son. The nearest he'd got was a grainy ultrasound image of a tiny foetus taken shortly before he'd died. Now Em was alone, and her little boy would never know his father. That gutted Jake, but he'd always be there for them, whenever he could. He'd promised Pete, and that promise to a dying man was unbreakable.

He went back to Em and stroked her damp, tangled blonde hair gently. 'I'll see you later. Give me a call when you're all tidied up, and I'll come back.'

Her mouth opened—on a protest?—and then closed again, and she gave him a fleeting smile and nodded. 'Go and get a coffee or something. I'm not going anywhere fast.'

'OK. Look after them for me, Liv.'

He gave Em a smile no steadier than her own, shunted the door out of the way and went out into the corridor.

It was deserted, thankfully, because right then he just needed to be alone. He headed for the lift, strode down the corridor to the Park Café as it opened, picked up a cappuccino with an extra shot and went outside, sucking in the fresh air.

It was still cool, only seven o'clock, but it was going to be a gorgeous summer's day and he found an unoccupied bench and sat sipping his coffee in the slanting post-dawn sunshine, letting the tension ease out of him.

He'd been so tense at times during Em's labour—totally illogically because it had been utterly straightforward, but he had been, anyway. She'd been through so much with Pete in the last few years and he'd felt so responsible for her care and safety during her labour, so duty-bound to make sure that nothing bad happened either to Pete's baby or to Emily herself.

He'd worried until he'd heard that first cry, but not for the baby so much as for Emily and what it would have done to her if anything had gone wrong. If the baby hadn't made it...

He'd been much more detached about Jo when she was

in labour—partly, he had to admit, because he'd never really been in love with her. Not that he was in love with Em, not that he'd ever admit to, even to himself, and certainly not to her, although he'd come close to it years ago after the wedding of mutual friends. It was shortly after she'd met Pete, and after the wedding wound up they'd walked back to their hotel and she'd gone to his room for coffee and things had got a little out of control.

Maybe it was the champagne, maybe it was the music, maybe just the whole soppy romantic thing of it, but before he'd known what had happened they'd been on the brink of making love. Then her phone had pinged with a text from Pete, and it had acted like a bucket of cold water over both of them, stopping them in their tracks.

She'd fled to her room and they'd never mentioned it again in all these years, but it had been the moment when he realised the full extent of his feelings for her. Feelings she hadn't reciprocated, because she'd gone straight back to Pete the following day and he'd had to learn to live with it.

He'd buried those feelings for her so deep he'd almost forgotten them, but he still loved her deeply as a friend, and there was nothing he wouldn't do for her, or her for him. She meant the world to him. She was his best, his dearest, most loyal and honest friend, and he'd be lost without her.

Not that her honesty was always an asset. There were times you didn't want to be told you were being an idiot, but she'd never been wrong.

He'd met her in freshers' week, when she'd found him handcuffed to the railings outside university halls at six in the morning, stark naked and horribly hungover, next to a pile of dew-soaked clothes carefully placed just out of reach. She'd been heading out for a run when she'd seen him, and she'd found the key taped to the fence beside his clothes and set him free, but not before she'd lectured his ear off.

In between laughing herself silly.

He'd loved her from that moment, through all the ups and downs of med school, their first clinical placements—dammit, he'd even walked her down the aisle to marry Pete, knowing he had cancer, knowing how hard it would be for her, but knowing, too, that he had to be there for her no matter what.

And he had been. Still was, always would be.

His phone vibrated, and he pulled it out and read the text with a chuckle.

Safe to come back now. The messy stuff is over. In a side room.

He drained his cold coffee, dropped the cup in a bin on the way past and went up to see her.

She was sitting up cross-legged in bed breastfeeding the baby, and it hit him like a brick. Jo had never done that—said it didn't work for her, which had saddened him, but she'd made it clear that it wasn't his decision and in the end he was just grateful she'd gone through with the pregnancy at all.

He shoved the thought aside and pressed a tender, lingering kiss to Emily's forehead, breathing in the fresh scent of shampoo. 'How're you doing?'

'OK. I feel much better now I've had a shower.' She caught hold of his hand, squeezing it gently. 'Thank you for getting me through it. I was so scared.'

He wrapped his hands around hers. 'Silly girl. I told you I'd look after you, and I won't stop just because you've had the baby now. You know I'm here for you for as long as you need me, don't you? And I'm not just saying that.'

'Oh, Jake…'

Her eyes welled, and he leant over and hugged her carefully before detaching himself and stepping back, creating some much-needed distance. 'So, how's the feeding going?'

'Oh, he's a natural, apparently. He certainly knows what he wants and goes for it—that's good, according to Liv, although you could have fooled me,' she added with a wry smile.

He chuckled. 'It is good, and you'll soon both settle into it.' He dropped into the chair beside her bed and stifled a yawn.

'Tired?'

'A bit. Long night, with all this added excitement at the end of it, but see? I told you nothing would go wrong.'

Her smile faded. 'Nothing else, you mean? I suppose never getting to meet his father is enough. We were probably owed a break.'

'Yes, I think you were,' he said softly, then after a slight pause, 'Have you thought of a name?'

'Zachary—Zach. Pete liked it, and he always said if we had a boy he'd want to call him that, so I said I would. Zachary Peter, for him, and Jacob.' She smiled again and held his eyes. 'For my best friend.'

'Wow.' He swallowed the lump in his throat. 'That means a lot, Em. Thank you.'

'It's the least I could do. I couldn't have done this without you, Jake—any of it. You're the only thing that's kept me sane since Pete's cancer came back.'

'Don't be daft. You've been amazing. You've done incredibly well.'

'Hardly. I've just got through it one day at a time,

didn't have a choice.' She looked down at her baby, fast asleep now, and a little worried frown crossed her face. 'I can't believe I'm going to have to go back to work and leave him.'

He frowned. 'You don't have to worry about that now. You've only just had him. There's plenty of time.'

'I know, but it doesn't stop me worrying about how I'll juggle a baby and my job. I can't just ignore the future.'

He reached out and squeezed her hand. 'Don't worry about money, Em,' he said firmly. 'It'll sort itself out, and if it doesn't, I'll help you.'

'How? You're already supporting Jo and Matilda. You can't run three households, Jake, and anyway, it's not just money, it's my career. I'm the sole breadwinner, have been for ages, but I worked hard to get where I am and I can't afford to neglect it.'

He dug out a smile. 'We'll find a way. Just concentrate on the baby. He's the most important thing, and the only thing you need to worry about at the moment. The rest will sort itself out. In the meantime, I've got two post-op patients to see and then I'm done, so I'll go and get the house ready and come back for you.'

He made up the little crib he'd used for Matilda, put flowers in his sitting room to welcome her home, and went back with the car seat from her pram to find her ready to go.

'Here—have a cuddle while I put my cardi on,' she said, and he put the baby seat down on the bed and took Zach from her, settling him easily in the crook of an elbow and staring down at him with an odd sensation in his chest.

'Hello, little guy,' he murmured, his finger tracing the

line of his tiny nose while that annoying lump reappeared in his throat. 'Gosh, you're like your daddy.'

'That's what his parents said. I sent them a photo. I'm so pleased for them that they haven't lost all of him.'

And neither had Em. He swallowed the lump again and put his feelings back where they belonged, deep below the surface.

'Come on, then. Time to go home,' he said, clipping the baby into the seat, but his words echoed in the quiet room and he had to remind himself that, for them at least, his house wasn't home, and he'd do well to remember it.

CHAPTER ONE

The following April...

THERE WAS A tap on the door of the consulting room and it opened a crack.

'Mr Stratton? I'm sorry to interrupt but Mr Walker's in the Park Café and he needs you there straight away.'

Jake opened the door and frowned at the receptionist.

'So why do I need to go? I'm in the middle of an antenatal clinic—'

She beckoned him out of the room and lowered her voice. 'He's with your little girl. Her mother's disappeared.'

'Disappeared?'

She shrugged. 'That's what he said.'

'Right. Can you find my registrar, please, and ask her to take over? I need to sort this out. And tell him I'm on my way.'

His mind whirling, he apologised hastily to his patient and sprinted down the corridor to the café. He couldn't see anything at first, but he could hear Matilda crying hysterically, and he pushed his way through a crowd of onlookers and found Ben crouched down trying to soothe her in the buggy.

'It's OK, Tilly, I'm here,' he said. 'It's all right, darling, you're OK. Come to Daddy.' He undid the straps and scooped her up into his arms, her little body racked with sobs as he sat down on the nearest chair and rocked her against his shoulder.

'Dad-dy,' she hiccupped, burrowing into his shoulder, and he rocked and hushed her while he tried to make sense of it.

Ben sat down beside him, and he looked at him in confusion. 'I don't understand. Where's Jo, and why is Matilda even here?'

'I don't know,' Ben said softly. 'Jo said she recognised my name from my badge. She told me who she was, said she'd forgotten to put a ticket on the car and could I watch Matilda for a minute, and she hasn't come back.'

'When was that?' he asked, but Ben just shrugged.

'Fifteen minutes ago? She kissed her goodbye which I didn't really think anything of, but she looked a bit upset for some reason and when she didn't come back I started to wonder, and then I noticed this sticking out of the buggy so I rang the clinic.'

Ben was holding out an envelope and he stared at it blankly. 'What is it?'

'I have no idea. It's addressed to you.'

He took it, pulled out a folded sheet of paper, flicked it open and scanned the words in disbelief, then read it again, just to be sure.

I'm sorry to do this to you, but I can't look after Matilda any more. It's not that I don't love her, I do, and I'm sorry it didn't work between us, but I've met someone I really want to be with, and we're going travelling. I've always wanted to do that, and I know it seems selfish, but I have to do this for me,

*and I know she'll be better off with you than she
would with me.*

*She loves you to bits, and I know how much you
love her, and you can give her a better life than I'll
ever be able to. I'd like to keep in touch with her
and see her when I can, but please don't try and
contact me to talk me out of it. I know you would,
that's why I couldn't tell you to your face, but I
know this is the right thing for everyone, and I'm
really sorry about all the money.*

Love her for me.

J

Nothing else, except a key in the envelope. Ben held
it out silently, and he frowned. The key to her house? Of
course. With all Tilly's stuff in it. No doubt she'd left
already—and what was that about all the money? All
what money?

'This is crazy. She can't just walk out on Matilda. I'll
call her.' He pulled out his phone, rang her number and
got no answer. Great. He looked back at Ben.

'I can't get her. She's not picking up.'

'Do you want me to call Security in case something's
happened to her?' Ben asked, but Jake shook his head,
realising the futility of it as it started to sink in.

'No point. She's gone, Ben. She's left us.' He pressed a
kiss to his daughter's tangled, sweaty hair, his love for her
overwhelming him. 'It's just you and me, Tils,' he murmured, 'but that's OK, I'll look after you. Daddy loves
you. We'll be OK.' He kissed her again, and she burrowed
tighter into him, her little legs tucked up against his side,
arms tight around his neck.

'You need to go home,' Ben said softly.

'How? I'm in the middle of a clinic, and it's only

Monday. What about the rest of the week? I can't just walk out.'

'Don't worry about work, someone'll do your clinic today and we'll sort the rota out. Your daughter needs to come first. And I'll get Security to locate and copy all the CCTV images of Jo from the time she arrived to the time she left. Just in case you need them for any reason in the future.'

He nodded, the implications of Jo's actions beginning to sink in as anger took the place of shock. If she loved Matilda, as she'd said she did, then how could she just dump her like that, without talking to him first?

Because she knew he would have tried to talk her out of it. She'd been right about that. Right about him taking care of her, too, but how? How could he? He had a full-time job, with irregular hours and huge responsibilities. He couldn't just drop everything. It wasn't fair on his colleagues or his patients. And in any case, he had a mortgage to pay—assuming she hadn't totally emptied his bank accounts and put him into overdraft right at the beginning of the month. Was that what she'd meant? Panic swamped him for a moment, but he fought it down.

At least Matilda was all right, but what if she hadn't been? Jo had only left her with Ben because she'd recognised his name. If he hadn't been there, would she still have left her? Anything could have happened to her. Someone could have taken her—

He felt a wave of nausea and swallowed hard. 'Thank God you were here, Ben, but what if you hadn't been? What if someone had taken her?' he said, but Ben just shook his head.

'Don't go there, Jake. Just take her home,' he said softly, so Jake took the key from him and put it on his keyring, then made a quick detour to pick up his things from his office before heading off to sort out the chaos his life had just become.

The following morning he went to her house, but it was empty apart from the landlord's furniture and a small pile of Matilda's things—her clothes, her toys and books, a few birthday cards and half a packet of nappies all stacked in the hall. Oh, and the landlord, who was delighted to see him.

'She owes me two months' rent,' the man said bluntly. 'I told her yesterday morning I'd call today to collect it, but she's gone. That's all that's left, those things there of the little tot's. I'm just waiting for a locksmith. Apparently she was seen leaving yesterday afternoon with the child and a man in a battered old campervan, and the neighbours said he's been around a lot recently.'

Well, that fitted with what she'd said in her letter. Great. So not only had Jo dumped Matilda without warning, which was quite bad enough, she'd also defaulted on her rent—even though he paid her more than enough every month to cover that and her living expenses. And that was on top of her emptying his savings account yesterday morning—

'So who are you, then?' the landlord asked.

'I'm Matilda's father. I'm just here to get her stuff and I'm as much in the dark about where Jo is as you are.'

He folded his arms. 'Well, someone's got to pay the rent. I'll let you off one month because I've got the deposit and there doesn't seem to be any damage, but I want the rest.'

'That's fine, I'll pay it,' he said heavily. Frankly, a month's rent was the least of his worries. Her 'sorry about all the money' had made him check his accounts last night and find she'd stripped his savings account—not that there had been much in it, but there was nothing now. She must have got his bank details from his phone when he'd seen her last week on Tilly's birthday. That would teach him not to be so trusting.

Teach him a lot of things, but on the plus side she hadn't emptied his current account which meant he had enough—just—to pay the landlord and get through the rest of the month. He should probably be thankful for small mercies, but he didn't feel thankful. She'd no doubt sold the car as well.

Well, he'd have to pay the outstanding rent, but that was it. He certainly wasn't funding her travelling—or at least any more of it than he already inadvertently had, and he'd had to change all his passwords last night which was a real pain.

He put Matilda down and got out his phone to transfer the money to the landlord, and she toddled off, calling for her mother and looking puzzled.

'Where Mummy?'

He swallowed the lump in his throat and picked her up again. 'She's not here, sweetheart, she's had to go away so you're going to come and live with me all the time now, and I'm not going *anywhere*,' he said softly, propping her on the worktop while he dealt with the landlord, then he threw all the things Jo had left for Matilda into the bags he'd brought with him, scooped his daughter up again and walked out, seething with anger, disappointment, regret—a whole catalogue of conflicting emotions that had already kept him awake half the night.

Now all he had to do was talk to HR and work out how he was going to juggle his job and childcare commitments, but first he needed a friendly ear—and a shoulder to cry on?

No point in crying over spilt milk, even if it felt like Jo

had dumped an entire dairy on his head. But the friendly ear he could *definitely* do with.

Emily was trying to stop Zach spreading banana everywhere when her phone rang for the second time in quick succession. She nearly didn't answer it, but Zach had finished eating now, so she wiped her fingers and pulled the phone out of her pocket.

'Jake, give me a second. I'm covered in banana.'

There was a muffled laugh from the other end, and she turned on the speaker and grabbed the wet wipe that Zach was stuffing in his mouth. 'Don't laugh at me. You have no idea how far he can spread it. So, how goes it?'

Another laugh, this time wry. 'Not great. Look, I'm not far from you. Can I drop in and scrounge a coffee?'

'Yeah, sure. Jake, are you OK?'

'Not really. I'll tell you in a minute. Stick the kettle on.'

'Will do. Grab some milk, please? I'm almost out.'

'OK. See you shortly.'

The phone went dead, and she stared at it, then shrugged and handed Zach a toy to play with while she cleared up the sitting room and worried about Jake.

He'd sounded odd. Sort of taut, like he was about to snap, which was so unlike him. He was always so easygoing, so relaxed and unfazed by anything. Chewing her lip, she plumped the cushions, scooped up the washing she'd been sorting, dumped it back in the basket and went back to tackle the kitchen.

She'd just finished loading the dishwasher when she heard him pull up, and she opened the front door as he got out of the car with a shopping bag in his hand. 'That was quick,' she began, but then she saw his expression and the words dried up in her throat.

He looked awful.

His face was a mask, the tension coming off him in waves, and she pulled him inside, put her arms around him and hugged him hard.

'What on earth's happened?' she asked softly, and she felt the sigh shudder through him.

'Jo's dumped Matilda with me—well, strictly speaking she left her in the hospital café—and she's walked out of her life.'

Emily felt her jaw drop and she let him go and took a step back so she could read his eyes, and saw confusion and white-hot rage. 'She *what*? How? Why?'

His shoulders jerked in a shrug. 'Who knows? She's gone travelling, of all things. She left me a note in the buggy apologising. She's got a new man, apparently, and the landlord said they were picked up by some dude with a battered old campervan, so presumably that's him. God knows what she's done with the car I bought her. Sold it to fund the travelling, I expect, and she also owed rent that I had to pay, and cleaned out my savings account.'

'That's outrageous!'

'Tell me about it, but that's not what's making me so mad. Don't get me wrong, Em, I'm not thrilled, but it's only money. It's the fact that she just abandoned Matilda in the café that makes me so furious. Thank goodness Ben Walker was there. Apparently she saw his name badge and realised who he was, so she introduced herself and asked him to keep an eye on Tilly while she put a ticket on the car, and then she didn't come back. What if he hadn't been there, Em? Was she just going to rely on someone finding the envelope before something dreadful happened to her? What if she'd been abducted?'

He raked a hand through his hair in frustration. 'I'm so angry I don't know where to start, but she said she couldn't tell me because I'd talk her out of it and she knew this was the best thing for everyone. I suppose I should just be grateful she didn't take Matilda with her—oh, and the icing on the cake is she wants to keep in touch. Well, we'll see about that,' he added furiously, finally grinding to a halt.

'Oh, Jake,' she said softly. 'I'm so sorry. How is Matilda? Is she all right?'

Another shrug. 'I suppose. A bit unsettled but she's used to being with me so she's not too bad—yet. How she'll be down the line I have no idea. We've just come from the house and she was wandering round asking where her mummy was. I'll bring her in in a minute, I just wanted to tell you all this out of her earshot because I don't want to make it worse, but I had to unload before I blow a fuse. I know she's only just two but who knows what she's making of all this?'

'I can't imagine. Oh, poor little girl—and poor you! Bring her in and I'll make coffee. Is there milk in that bag?'

'Yeah, and a packet of giant triple-chocolate cookies, still warm. I need serious comfort food.'

'We'd better get started, then,' she said with a little laugh, and retrieved Zach before he crawled over the step and fell onto the path. 'Go and get her, I'll put the kettle on.'

She took the coffee through to the sitting room where Jake was perched on the sofa staring at the floor, Matilda at his feet building a tower with stacking cups while Zach watched her intently.

'Hey,' she said softly, and Jake looked up and met her eyes, his own filled with a worry that he wasn't even trying to disguise. At least the anger was gone, for now at least, but he just looked desperate and she wanted to hug him. She perched next to him and handed him his coffee and one of the gooey chocolate cookies instead.

'That's my second.'

'Who's counting? So, what are you going to do?' she asked, keeping her voice to a low murmur, and he shrugged helplessly.

'I don't know. I don't honestly know what I'm going to do. I'm on carer's leave at the moment but that's just crisis management and it can only be for a maximum of ten days, besides which we're short-staffed as it is, and I don't want to use the nursery. It seems wrong, when she's just been abandoned by her mother. What if she thought *I'd* abandoned her, too? What if she hates it? And anyway, I work crazy hours. She'd practically have to live there, and what about nights when I'm on call? The only way round it is to find a full-time nanny, and they don't grow on trees, and what the hell do I do in the meantime?'

'I'll come and stay,' she said without a second thought, and it shocked him into silence for a moment. Then he shook his head, the hope that she'd seen in his troubled eyes replaced by despair.

'No. No, I can't ask you to do that.'

'You're not, I'm volunteering, and it's nothing compared to what you've done for me since Pete died, not to mention the rest of the last twenty years. It'll get you out of a fix in the short term, give you time to think.'

'I've *been* thinking. I've done nothing but think since yesterday afternoon. There isn't an answer, Em, and this certainly isn't it.'

'No, not long term, of course it isn't, but I'm still on maternity leave until the middle of June, I'm not doing anything else and how much harder can it be to look after two babies than one?' she asked, lifting Zach up before he lunged at the plastic cups Matilda had carefully stacked and knocked them all down.

'Matilda's not a baby. She can be—'

'A two-year-old?' she asked lightly, raising an eyebrow, and he laughed despairingly.

'Yes. Exactly. And there are the practicalities, like I haven't got a cot any longer because she's in a bed.'

'I've got a travel cot for Zach, and we can buy a double buggy from somewhere if we need to, so I can take them out. It's not an issue, Jake, and it's not as if we haven't lived together before. We're both house-trained. I'm sure we'll survive. And you can get your life back on track and stop worrying about letting everyone down while you work out what to do next.'

'Really?'

'Really. I want to. Please, let me help you.'

He held her eyes for the longest moment, then let out a defeated sigh and nodded. 'OK. If I wasn't at my wit's end I wouldn't let you do this, but if you're really sure, it would be amazing. So—when are we talking about? Next week?'

She laughed. 'I was thinking today? My fridge is all but empty, and it seems like a good time to do it.'

His mouth twitched into what could have been a smile. 'I have to tell you my fridge isn't a lot better, but I can soon fix that. I'll take Matilda shopping and make the bed, and I'll see you later, if you're really sure?'

'That again?' She laughed, and he gave another crooked grin and hugged her with his free arm.

'I love you, Em, you're a star,' he said gruffly. 'You're such a good friend. I don't know how to thank you.'

Her heart hitched. 'You don't need to grovel,' she said lightly, but she wanted to curl up and cry, because he'd been amazing to her—more than a friend, really, more of a rock in her life, the only constant for the last twenty years, and especially since Pete's terminal diagnosis.

He did love her, she knew that, and she loved him, too. He was the best friend anyone could have and she'd do anything to help him, but she realised this would help her, too, because it meant she wouldn't be alone with her thoughts from the moment Zach went down for the night to the moment he woke in the morning, and she was so sick of being alone...

'You head on back, then, and I'll pack our stuff and see you later—about five? Then I can give Zach supper before his bedtime so I don't mess up his routine.'

'Five's fine. What does he eat?'

She laughed, her mood suddenly lighter for some reason. 'I have no idea. It changes from minute to minute. I'll bring stuff for him, I've got baby food and formula. It's the only thing I have got. And you know me. I eat anything.'

She was early, of course.

He'd been expecting that. Em was always early. Always had been, unlike him, although he had a golden rule of never being late. Just on time.

So although he'd been shopping and made the bed, the house was still a bit chaotic because he'd brought in Matilda's things and dumped them in the hall and they hadn't got any further. On the plus side, he'd borrowed a double buggy and another high chair from Daisy Walker, his clinical lead's wife, but on the downside they were in the hall as well.

She'd dropped them round on her way to pick up the older children from school, and she'd even given him a lesson in how to fold the buggy, most of which had gone clean over his head. He just hoped Emily could work it out, because he was damned if he could.

He moved it out of the way so she didn't trip over it, opened the front door and was handed a baby.

'Here, can you take him, I'll empty the car,' she said, and was only halfway down the path when Matilda tugged his jeans and frowned up at him.

'Baby down,' she said crossly. '*My* daddy.'

He crouched down with a soft, coaxing laugh. 'Of course I'm your daddy, Tilly. I'm just holding Zach for Emily. Say hello to him.'

'No.' She turned her back on him, folded her arms and tilted her head. 'I not.'

He stifled the smile and stood up, just as Emily came back with an armful of bags and the travel cot.

'What's up with her?' she asked softly, and he rolled his eyes.

'*My* daddy,' he mouthed, and she bit her lip and shook her head.

'Oops. Oh, well, she'll get over it. And so will he,' she said, taking Zach before he fell out of Jake's arms leaning over trying to reach her.

'Why don't I empty the car?' he suggested drily, and headed out of the door, leaving Matilda standing in the hall with Emily.

'Daddy!' she wailed, running after him, and he turned and caught her as she tripped on the step, lifting her up into his arms and holding her close as she sobbed against his neck.

His gut wrenched. 'Hey, little one, I was only getting Emily's things from the car,' he said gently, stroking her hair. 'Do you want to help me?'

She hiccupped and nodded, and he handed her a teddy that was falling out of the top of a bag, picked up the

bag and Emily's suitcase in his other hand and went
back inside.

Em greeted him with a raised eyebrow, and he
shrugged. 'As you said, they'll get over it.'

He just hoped she was right, because right then none
of them had a choice.

He came down from settling Matilda in bed and sorting
out the travel cot to find Emily ensconced on the sofa,
feeding Zach.

'You're still breastfeeding,' he said gruffly, stating
the obvious and floundering to a halt, the sudden wash
of conflicting emotions taking him totally by surprise.

She looked up and smiled, her face tender and mel-
low in the light from the lamp, and his heart turned over.
'He's still only a baby. He isn't ten months yet, and he's
going to be my only child, so I might as well carry on as
long as he wants to. It's only morning and evening, and
it means so much to both of us.'

'Hell, Em, you don't have to justify it to me, I'm heart-
ily in favour of you doing what nature intended, but you'd
talked about formula milk so I was just surprised,' he said
lightly, trying to ignore his crazy reaction.

Since when had breastfeeding been erotic?

'I'm going to put our food on. Cup of tea while it
cooks?'

'Please—decaf if you've got it?'

'Of course. I have enough trouble sleeping without
chucking caffeine into the mix.'

'Do you need a hand?'

'No, you're all right. You stay there with Zach.'

He headed for the kitchen, trying to work out what was
going on in his head. He knew what was going on in his
body, and it was entirely inappropriate and out of order.

Didn't stop it, though.

He turned on the oven, put the kettle on, braced his hands on the edge of the worktop and let his head drop.

He did *not* need this—this sudden and unexpected and unwelcome complication to a situation that was already complicated beyond belief. She was a widow, a vulnerable woman with a young child, putting herself out to help him. The last thing—absolutely the *last* thing— she needed was him turning weird on her. Protective he could cope with. Lust—no. Absolutely not.

He thrust himself away from the worktop, put the supermarket ready meal into the oven, then prepped the veg.

Not that opening a tray of pre-prepared sugar snap peas, baby corn and tenderstem broccoli took much prepping, but anything rather than go back in there while she was still feeding Zach. And that in itself was ridiculous. He spent his life surrounded by women in various stages of undress, was thoroughly familiar with their most intimate anatomy, saw new mothers breastfeeding on a daily basis. So why was he reacting like this now, and why with Emily, of all people in the world?

And there was no way—*no way!*—he was letting himself answer that question! It was a whole other can of worms, and he needed to get a grip. He wasn't an adolescent exploring and exploiting his emerging sexuality, he was an adult, more than twice the age he'd been when he'd first met Emily. Surely to goodness he'd developed a little self-control and discretion in all that time?

Not to mention common decency.

With a low growl, he pulled two mugs from the cupboard, made the tea and went back in, studiously avoiding looking anywhere near her chest. Not that he could see anything, anyway. She was being incredibly discreet and she'd obviously got it down to a fine art—

'I think there must be some kind of narcotic in breast-milk,' she said with a smile that sent his resolutions into a tailspin. 'It's like he's drugged, he's so heavily asleep.'

He hauled his eyes off the sliver of smooth, pale skin he could see above the baby's downy head as she tugged her top down. 'Will you be able to sneak him into his cot, or will he wake up the minute you let go of him?'

She gave a wry laugh. 'I'm guessing that was Matilda?'

'Yup. Every time.'

'Zach's usually all right. I might go and try if you don't think I'll wake her?'

'No, she should be fine. Go for it. The travel cot's ready.'

She unravelled her legs and stood up gracefully, and he gritted his teeth and dragged his eyes off the smoothly rounded curve of her bottom as she headed through the door.

What the hell was going on with him?

He picked up his tea, cradled the mug in his hands and blew the steam away crossly.

He was better than this. If ever a woman was off limits, it was Emily, and especially now. He knew that. It was just getting his body to listen that was the difficult bit, and right now it seemed to have gone stone deaf.

CHAPTER TWO

JAKE WAS HUNCHED over his tea when she went back to the sitting room. He looked deep in thought, and the thoughts didn't look happy from where she was standing.

'Thanks for getting the travel cot ready for me, he's gone down like a dream,' she said, and he glanced up at her, his eyes unreadable.

'You're welcome. I didn't know if you'd still want him in your room, but I thought it was better to be on the safe side as it's a strange place. We can always move him, I'm not short of bedrooms.'

'No, it's fine. I keep meaning to move him out, but—I don't know. I quite like knowing there's someone else there with me. It wards off the self-pity a bit.'

She knew her smile was wry, and his eyes locked with hers searchingly.

'Don't you mean grief?' he asked her, his voice gentle, and she shrugged.

'Same thing, really, isn't it? I miss Pete, but he doesn't miss me, he can't, and I'm sure he wouldn't miss the pain he was in, or the dread of what was to come, or the worry about how we were going to cope without him. He's spared all that now. It's those left behind who have to pick up their lives and carry on, so in many ways grief is just a selfish emotion.'

'Or an acknowledgement of the person he was, and the part he played in your life. It's OK to grieve, Emily.'

She smiled. 'I know, but I've done that. I did most of my grieving while he was still alive, because to be honest I never really dared to let myself believe he was cured when they gave him the all-clear, so when it metastasised there was a sort of horrible inevitability about it all. I think I always knew it was coming, and now it's just juggling the things that need to be done with the lack of support and practical help. Things like cutting the hedge and putting up shelves in Zach's room and all the other stuff that he used to do that I'm rubbish at.'

'I've offered to help,' he reminded her, but she didn't need reminding. She dropped onto the sofa beside him, tucked her arm in his and squeezed it firmly.

'And you *have* helped. You'll never know how much you've helped me, Jake. I wouldn't have got through it without you, but I need to toughen up now and get a grip. Time to return the favour, and I'm really sorry it's because of Jo doing a runner and turning your life upside down, but I'm here, I'm not going to run out on you, and I'll stay until you don't need me anymore.'

She held his eyes for an age, but then something flashed through them and he turned away, as if he couldn't look at her any longer, and shook his head.

'I can't ask that of you,' he said gruffly.

'Yes, you can—and by the way I rescued the supper. There was an interesting smell coming from the kitchen so I turned off the oven and opened the door a bit.'

He swore and leapt to his feet, and she followed him into the kitchen as he whipped open the oven door and stared into it.

'Is it OK?'

He pulled the dish out and inspected it. 'Debatable.'

He put it onto the hob and prodded at it with a fork, and she chuckled softly and peered over his shoulder at the bits of singed pasta sticking up out of a rather dark golden crust.

'Will we live?'

He grunted. 'Just about. There are one or two bits that might need ditching, but it won't kill us.'

She tutted. 'You're a slow learner, Stratton. I taught you to use an oven timer twenty years ago. I would have thought you'd mastered it by now.'

He gave a low chuckle, and she slid her arms around him and rested her head against his broad, solid shoulders that were curiously comforting. 'Thank you for everything you've done for me, Jake. I meant what I said, I don't know how I would have coped without you.'

She straightened up and slackened her arms, and he turned in them and gave her a brief hug, then reached for the kettle.

'You're welcome. Now go and drink your tea and put your feet up,' he said over his shoulder. 'I've got to steam the veg but that won't take long. I'll call you when it's ready.'

'Don't forget to time it,' she said with a cheeky little wink designed to needle him, and took herself out of range before he threw something at her.

He watched her go, the feel of her still imprinted on his body, front and back, then he closed his eyes and swore softly and comprehensively under his breath.

What was *wrong* with him?

He plonked the pan on the hob, poured boiling water into the steamer under the veg and laid the table, then stuck his head round the door. 'It's ready.'

'Good, I'm starving. So—what is this?' she asked,

poking at the slightly over-browned crust as she sat down at the table.

'Chicken, tomato and mascarpone pasta bake. And yes, I timed the veg,' he growled.

'Wonders will never cease,' she mocked, rolling her eyes, then stuck a forkful of the pasta bake in her mouth and moaned. 'Oh, that's really tasty. Good job I caught it in time.'

He opened his mouth to reply, and she raised both hands, her lips twitching at the corners, and he gave a soft huff of laughter and rolled his eyes. 'Why don't you just shut up and eat it before it's cold?' he said drily, and she smiled, stuck her fork into her food and then looked up at him again, her eyes almost luminous, her voice wistful.

'You know, it's really nice having someone to eat with, especially someone I can have a conversation with.'

He raised an eyebrow. 'Zach doesn't talk to you?'

It got a laugh out of her, although it was just a little one. 'You know what I mean. I love him to bits, but it's not the same as sharing a meal with an adult. It's a long while since I've done that, and even longer since someone cooked for me. Thank you.'

'My pleasure,' he said softly, grateful for the timely reminder that she'd only lost her husband less than eighteen months ago. Dragging his eyes off hers, he turned his attention firmly back to the food.

'What time do you start tomorrow?' she asked as he cleared the plates.

'Seven. I need to leave at quarter to.'

'So—will you see Matilda before you go? Does she know you're not going to be here all day?'

He sighed and propped his hands on the worktop, defeat in every line of his body.

'Not yet. I was going to tell her in the morning. I didn't want her worrying all night.' He straightened up and turned back to face her. 'Do you think that's the wrong thing to have done?'

She shrugged. 'I have no idea. I have to admit to being wildly out of my depth here, but I would imagine that the loss of her mother is going to affect her. She'll be missing her presence, the familiar surroundings—although she's used to you and to being here, so that's not an issue, but she doesn't know *me* very well, she's only met me a handful of times, and then there's Zach. She wasn't exactly overjoyed to see him and she probably won't be thrilled at being left alone with us.'

His shoulders slumped. 'No. I'm sure you're right. Damn, this isn't going to work, is it? It's too much to expect of either of you. I should never have asked—'

'You didn't, but you didn't really have a choice and we've already had this conversation. If you want to do something useful, you could shut up and put the kettle on. I could murder another drink before I go to bed.'

He gave a soft huff of laughter, walked over to her, pulled her to her feet and hugged her hard.

'Thank you for helping me out, Em,' he murmured, his head resting against hers. 'I don't know where I'd be without you. You're such a good woman, and the best friend I could ever ask for. I don't know how to thank you.'

She hugged him back, suddenly and shockingly aware of him, of the blatant masculinity she'd made a life's work of ignoring. 'Ditto. Except you're not a woman, obviously, but whatever.'

He laughed, and his arms dropped and he turned away.

'So, having cleared that up, tea or coffee?' he asked lightly, picking up the kettle, and she felt a tension ease that she hadn't even known was there.

* * *

He was right, it wasn't going to work.

Jake had only been out of the house half an hour and Emily was already at her wit's end.

Matilda *hated* her. Or, more exactly, hated not having her father there and not having Emily's undivided attention, either. Which meant she also hated Zach. No surprises there, then.

'Come on, Matilda, let's go downstairs and get some breakfast,' she coaxed. 'Shall we see what Daddy's got in the cupboards?'

'Want toast,' she said, after Emily had finally persuaded her to come down, so she put Zach in the nearest high chair and Matilda promptly burst into tears and tugged Zach's arm hard.

'My chair,' she sobbed, so Emily lifted the now crying baby out of the way and hooked over the other high chair, only of course he didn't want to go in it now, arching his back and screaming.

Stifling a scream of her own, Emily jiggled him on her hip, found the sliced bread that she assumed Jake had got for Matilda, put two slices in because Zach would be happy with toast, too, and then tried again with the high chair once he'd calmed down.

'There you go, baby. You stay there now, while Mummy gets your toast.'

'You not Mummy,' Matilda piped up, her voice wobbling.

Oh, lord. 'I'm Zach's mummy,' she told her, but she was starting to recognise that mulish look that meant Matilda wasn't having any of it. She crouched down to Matilda's level and reached out to touch her shoulder, but she jerked it back out of reach, her lip quivering.

'Not my mummy. Go 'way. Want Daddy.'

'Daddy's had to go to work, sweetheart. He'll be back later, you know that, he told you he would.'

'Want Daddy now,' she demanded, folding her arms emphatically in a curiously adult gesture that nearly made Emily laugh.

She stifled the urge. 'Darling, I'm sure he'd much rather be here with you, but he's had to go to work at the hospital. There are lots of mummies there with tiny babies, and he's got to look after them, but he'll come home when he's finished for the day, and he'll be back in time to put you to bed, you'll see.'

The toast popped up, and she crossed her fingers behind her back, straightened up and put the toast, the butter and some plates on the table then lifted Matilda into the other high chair. *Her* high chair.

'Don't want toast,' Matilda said, folding her arms again, but the defiant little gesture wasn't funny anymore.

None of it was funny. It was exasperating, worrying, and nothing to do with toast. It was all about controlling a situation that Matilda had been thrown into by her mother's sudden disappearance, and all Emily could do was damage limitation. And not having breakfast wasn't going to damage the little girl.

'OK,' she said easily. 'You don't have to have breakfast today if you don't want to. I can eat your toast.'

She ignored Matilda for a few moments, buttering the first slice, cutting it into fingers, handing one to Zach who grabbed it with both hands and stuffed it into his mouth.

'Mmm, yum-yum,' she said, but Matilda just folded her arms more firmly and stropped a bit more, and Emily let her, pretty sure hunger would cut in before any harm was done.

'Want honey on it,' Matilda said, caving in as Emily

handed Zach a second finger of toast and buttered the other slice.

'OK. I'll see if I can find any.'

Please, please don't have run out and not replaced it.

There was a smear at the bottom of the jar, but—hallelujah!—a new, unopened one behind it. She twisted off the lid, dug the knife into the smooth, unblemished surface and made a wish.

No prizes for guessing what her wish was going to be, but she smeared honey on the toast, cut it into fingers like Zach's and slid it across to Matilda.

'Say thank you,' she said, sure that Jake would have taught her that even if her mother hadn't, and maybe her fairy godmother was watching over them because Matilda stuffed the first bite into her mouth and mumbled, ''Ank you,' around it.

Round one to her? She certainly hoped so.

The phone rang for ages before Em answered it, and Jake was starting to worry when she eventually picked up.

'How's it going?' he asked without preamble.

He heard a sigh, then a little laugh that did nothing to reassure him. 'OK, I guess. I put Zach in the wrong high chair.'

He winced. 'Oops. I bet that was fun. She can be such a drama queen, and she's territorial at the best of times. You might be better taking them out, if you feel you can cope. It's a lovely day, the fresh air'll do them good.'

'Great minds,' she said with a tired chuckle. 'I thought maybe a walk? Feed the ducks, if there are any ducks to feed?'

'There are—there's a little park not far away. If you turn right onto the street and walk along to the end and cross over, there's an entrance to your left. It's got a lovely little playground, too, as well as the duck pond, and she likes it there.'

'OK. I'll give it a whirl and see how I get on. I can take the double buggy since you've got it. At least that's neutral territory.'

'Ah, rats! I meant to show you how it folds and un-folds, but to be honest I'm damned if I can remember. I'll text you Daisy's number so you can ring her if you can't work it out. She'll tell you.'

He heard her laugh, but it sounded a little off kilter and he guessed her day was turning out tougher than she'd expected.

'It's a buggy, Jake,' she said with exaggerated patience. 'I'm sure I'll be fine. How's work going?'

'Busy. They're very glad to have me back. Ben said to thank you for stepping in to help.'

She laughed. 'Tell Ben I'm not doing it for him, but happy to oblige. Oops, gotta go, Zach's in the fireplace.'

He heard a clatter and a howl before the phone cut off, and he squeezed his eyes shut and tried not to imag-ine what might have happened. The fire tongs and poker were his most likely guess. Oh, well. Hopefully he'd just had a fright. And as for Tilly—

'Mr Stratton, have you got a moment?'

Tilly would be fine. He slid his phone back into his pocket and went back to work, putting Emily and the children firmly out of his mind.

Three days and a thousand small obstacles later, it was obvious to both of them that Matilda needed much more of her father than she was getting. And probably less of her, Emily thought despairingly.

It all came to a head late on Friday evening, when he'd been caught up in Theatre with a tricky post-partum haemorrhage and Matilda refused to go to bed until he got home, despite all Emily's best efforts. She wouldn't even let her change her nappy and put her in pyjamas. She just sat on the landing and cried.

'Want Daddy,' she sobbed, so Emily took her downstairs to the sitting room so they could wait for him, but she was inconsolable. She didn't want a story, she shied away from cuddles, and by the time he came home at nine Emily was on the point of phoning him.

They were in the hall by now, Matilda prostrate on the floor and still sobbing, and the moment he was through the door she scrambled up and clung to his legs, and the anguish in his eyes was awful to see.

He scooped her up, hugging her close and rocking her, and Emily went into the kitchen and left them to it, because she was sure her presence wasn't helping. She'd been at her wit's end all day, and seeing the little girl so distraught had been horrible, but he was home now and maybe he could calm her down.

Was it her fault? Maybe. She'd done her best to handle an impossibly difficult situation, but Matilda was only two, her mother had deserted her—how was the poor little mite supposed to react? She was just upset, but it was so hard to deal with and it was upsetting Zach, too.

It wasn't doing a lot for her, either. She sniffed hard, swiped away the tears she hadn't realised she'd shed and yanked open the fridge door. She'd been trying all day to find time to cook, but every time she did anything there was another incident with Tilly.

She'd bitten Zach, she'd pushed him over, she'd gone into the study and pulled all the books off the shelf—

The crying had stopped—finally—and she heard Jake's quiet tread on the stairs as he carried her up to bed. Not that she expected it to work.

Why on earth had she volunteered to do this? It wasn't helping anyone, especially not Matilda. Was it her fault? She didn't know enough about Tilly—had she inadvertently upset her by doing something wrong, something Jake would never have done? How was she supposed to know?

And then there was Jake himself, her friend, the person she was helping out—or trying to, but this close proximity was stirring up feelings that had been dormant for years. She was suddenly so aware of him, of his physical presence and blindingly obvious sex appeal, but this was Jake, for goodness' sake! She'd known him for years, he hadn't changed, so why now? Was it just her sexuality reawakening after all this time, and if so, why pick on Jake, of all people?

She slashed at an onion, and then dropped the knife with a yelp and squeezed her finger hard. Blood leaked out and ran down her hand, and she went over to the sink, turned on the tap, stuck her finger under it and gave in to the tears that had been threatening all day.

'Em?'

She was standing at the sink with her back to him, holding something under the running tap, and he went up behind her and squeezed her shoulders gently.

'I'm sorry, Em. This is all my fault. I should never have agreed to you doing this—'

'Rubbish. It's not your fault, it's mine.'

'No, it isn't. It's her mother's fault. She's a little girl—how could she just leave her? Of course she's upset. Don't blame yourself.'

'That's easy to say, but I do. Everything I do upsets her. I should be able to comfort her, but she doesn't want me, she wants you, or her mother. And she just won't let me comfort her. She hates me, and she hates Zach, and it's just not working—'

He leant in closer, and then saw blood all over the sink and reached past her and turned off the tap. 'Em, what've you done?'

'Isn't it obvious?' she said, and he let out a sigh, put his hands on her shoulders and turned her round.

'Let me see,' he said gently, taking a handful of kitchen roll and resting her hand in it. 'Let go?'

She released the pressure, and blood welled rapidly in the wound before she pressed it again with her thumb.

'OK. Well, at least it's a nice clean cut, not too deep, and it won't need stitches. Just a firm dressing and it should be fine.'

She nodded, and something wet dripped on his hand. He tilted her face up and shook his head. *Tears?*

'Oh, Em, don't cry,' he pleaded softly. 'I don't need two of you doing it, and Matilda's fine now, she was just exhausted. She's gone out like a light.'

'She's been crying for ages. She wouldn't go to bed without you, I couldn't even change her, I couldn't do anything—'

'Oh, Emily. Come here.' He pulled her in against him with one arm, the other hand cradling her wounded hand in its nest of bloodied kitchen towel. He could deal with that later, he'd had far worse to worry about today, and so had she. For now, all she needed was a hug, and she turned her head into his shoulder, gave a ragged little sob and slumped against him.

It was the first time he'd seen her cry since Pete's terminal diagnosis, when she'd just discovered she was pregnant. She hadn't even cried at his funeral, and it was so unlike her that it gave him a real and unwelcome insight into just how bad her day must have been with the children, and he was swamped with guilt.

'I'm sorry,' he sighed. 'You're right, this isn't working. I'll phone Ben and tell him I can't do it anymore. I'll have to find another way until she's more settled.'

'Such as what?' she asked, pushing herself away and swiping roughly at the tears. 'Put her in nursery? That won't be any better. It was just a bad day, Jake. Anyway, it's the weekend now and you'll be at home. Maybe that'll help her to get used to me, to the whole situation. She just needs time to adjust.'

'I can see that, but I'm worried about now, before she's adjusted, if she ever does. It sounds as though today was awful for all of you, and what happens if it's still as bad on Monday, or the day after, or the week after that? I can't ask this of you, or Matilda. She obviously needs much more time with me than she's getting.'

'She does, and Zach needs me, too, but you have to work, Jake. There's no way round it. Life costs money and something's got to give. We all have to compromise. We just have to find a compromise that works, and in two months' time I'm going to be in the same boat and I have no idea what I'm going to do either.'

He pressed his lips together, let out a sharp sigh and let go of her hand. 'Here, let me dress that, then we'll order a takeaway and sit down and talk about this calmly.'

Half an hour later her finger was dressed, she had a glass of a nicely chilled Aussie white in her hand and they were sitting down to a selection of steaming takeaway cartons, the contents mostly chosen because they were fork food.

And now she'd finally stopped wallowing in guilt and self-pity and re-engaged her brain, apparently it had come up with a brilliant idea. Now she just had to sell it to him.

'So, I might have a solution,' she said.

He paused, his fork halfway to his mouth, and gave her a sceptical look. 'There isn't a solution.'

'There could be, if you'd consider a job share.'

He put the fork back down and stared at her as if she'd grown two heads. 'Who with? And anyway, that doesn't help with the nights and weekends. It wouldn't work.'

'It might,' she said slowly, suddenly desperate to convince him, 'if it was with me and we shared the child-care.'

There was a second of silence while he absorbed it, then he shook his head. 'No. I couldn't ask you to do that, Em, especially after today. It's not fair on you or Zach and you've got enough on your plate without taking us on. What I really need is a nanny, but it'll take time to find one and I don't have time. You're right, she wouldn't have been any better in a nursery. Probably worse, in fact, because she wouldn't have been in familiar surroundings. She's just testing you.'

'Well, she certainly did that, but she doesn't need me to tell her where the boundaries are, she needs you.'

'She needs consistency, but that isn't the point. The point is it upset you, and it's too much to ask of you when you've got your own problems—and anyway, there's no way we could job share, you live too far away.'

'Not if I move in here,' she said, and held her breath.

His eyes widened in surprise, and she could almost hear the cogs turning. 'Here?'

'Yes, here,' she said, gesturing around her at the huge kitchen dining room that ran from front to back in his double-fronted Victorian semi. 'Your house is massive, Jake. There's tons of room.'

'Em, it's a heap. I only bought it because I thought it would make a fantastic family home, but then Jo changed her mind and I ended up running two households, so I haven't had the money to sort it out. It's just a millstone round my neck and if it wasn't such a wreck I'd sell it.'

'Rubbish, it's a fabulous house, a fantastic family home, as you said. It just needs a lick of paint.'

He sighed. 'It needs much more than that. It's just tired from one end to the other. I was going to put an en suite next to the main bedroom, refit the bathroom, refit the kitchen, change the carpets, repair the roof— at the very least the whole house needs a coat of paint, and then there's the garden which has been neglected for years—it's endless.'

'That's cosmetic,' she pointed out. 'There's a down-stairs shower room. I could use that. And you have five bedrooms, so even if we take two, you'll still have a spare for visitors. And there's your study, which is big enough to be another sitting room, so we don't even have to share that if you don't want to.'

His brow furrowed, the worry evident in his eyes. 'It's not that I don't want to share with you, Em, that's not an issue, we were housemates for years, but we're not at uni anymore. We're adults, parents, and anyway, you don't want to leave your house. You shared it with Pete for so many years, you can't walk away from that just to help me out. You'd be giving up so much.'

She would, but she wouldn't let herself think about that. Not now. Pete was gone, but Jake was very much alive, and he needed her. And she needed a job.

'It's just a house,' she lied, 'and believe me, my mo-tives for suggesting it aren't entirely selfless. I need a job as much as you do, but the reality is we both need cover for nights and weekends and random shift patterns, and that's going to be really difficult to manage without live-in help, but if we lived here together that would solve it, and it would also mean taking a cut in salary was more viable for both of us because we'd be paying out much less in childcare and only be running one household. And it needn't be for ever. A couple of years, maybe a little more? Five, even, and who knows where we'll be by then? You might have met someone you want to marry, someone you love, someone who loves Matilda. But for now, it would solve both our problems. We could make it work, Jake.'

He stared at her for the longest moment, hope flaring in his eyes, and then he dug around on his plate with his fork, moved the food around, then looked back at her again searchingly.

'Are you serious?'

'Yes, I am. Why not? I want a part-time job with consultant pay, and you think nannies don't grow on trees? I've networked my butt off the last couple of months and there's not a glimmer of part time or a job share anywhere in our field at the level we're at. Well, there's a staff grade post in Cumbria, but that's miles from everyone I know and miles from Pete's parents, and they have a right to share in Zach's life. They've already lost their son. I can't take their grandson to the other end of the country, it's not fair. And in the meantime I have to earn a living and make appropriate care arrangements for my child, and so do you. Think about it, Jake. You'd be working part time, so you'd have time with Matilda, I'd have time with Zach, we'd both be working at consultant level—it's a win-win.'

He scrubbed a hand through his hair and searched her eyes again. Goodness knows what he was looking for, but she didn't think he'd found it because he shrugged and looked away and his eyes were bleak again, the flicker of hope she'd seen in them extinguished by defeat.

'I don't know. It's a lot to think about, for both of us, and we can't make a snap decision. Come on, let's eat this while it's still hot. I'm starving and I didn't get time for lunch and I can't think clearly on an empty stomach.'

She reached out and laid a hand on his, suddenly afraid he was going to spend the rest of the night finding reasons why it couldn't work, and for some reason she didn't really understand she was desperate that he shouldn't do that. 'Just don't dismiss it, Jake. Don't close your mind to it. Promise me you'll give it serious consideration.'

He nodded slowly. 'OK. I promise. Right, food. Do you want the last of that rice, or can I have it?'

Jake stared up at the ceiling, his eyes tracing the cracks in the Victorian plasterwork, seeking out the peeling paper at the edge by the window where the roof had leaked last year. How could he ask Em to give up her lovely home and share this place with him and Matilda? Never mind the job thing…

Enough. He needed to sleep. He turned out the light and rolled onto his side, bashing his pillow into submission, but it didn't help. Nothing helped, and his mind was still churning, struggling with the concept of a job share with Em.

Could they do it? Would it work? Or would it put such an unreasonable strain on their relationship that it would destroy it? Because it wouldn't just mean sharing the job. He'd be sharing his home, his child, his entire life with Emily. Could they honestly make it work?

He didn't know, but sleep evaded him and he lay awake for hours turning it over and over in his mind without coming up with anything better—or anything else at all.

He knew they could live together, they were already

doing it, and they were coping, even if he did spend hours every day slamming the door on his lust. They'd squabble about stuff and she'd complain about his untidiness, but there was no malice in it. But was it fair on Emily to ask her to leave the home she'd shared with Pete?

No, but then the whole situation was unfair. It wasn't fair that Pete had died and left Emily widowed and Zach without a father. It wasn't fair that Jo had walked out first on him and then on Matilda, and almost bled him dry in the process.

None of it was fair and they had no choice but to deal with the hand life had dealt them, but the children weren't coping, and that was the root of the problem. Matilda didn't really know Emily. How was she feeling being left with her every day? Not great, if today was anything to go by, but would Zach fare any better when it was the other way round? And how would he feel, looking after Zach? Looking after his own daughter, come to that?

He'd never anticipated being a full-time father, but it was just an extension of what he'd already been doing, with Zach chucked into the mix for good measure.

Could they manage to make it work, juggling the childcare between them? It was an awesome responsibility. Was he up to it? Was Emily?

He had no idea, but short of finding a nanny in the next few days he was out of options. It had to work, they had to make it work, and the first thing he was going to do tomorrow was run the idea past Ben Walker, and see what he thought of it.

He wasn't even going to consider what he'd do if Ben said no.

CHAPTER THREE

BEN DIDN'T SAY NO—well, not a flat-out no, at any rate, and maybe even tending towards a yes.

He was on call that weekend and already at the hospital when Jake sent him a text at six-thirty saying he needed to talk. He rang straight back, and didn't turn a hair when Jake suggested they meet on the benches outside the Park Café before eight on a dewy April morning. He didn't even mind that Matilda was with him, sitting on the damp bench between them eating a little muffin from the café for her breakfast. He listened carefully without interrupting until Jake ground to a halt, then pulled a sort of 'maybe' face and nodded slowly.

'Would you consider taking on a bit more? Because we could really do with a female consultant, but we also need more consultant time in general and getting someone for just one or two days a week is impossible. If you could manage another two or three sessions between you and a share of weekend and night cover, the Trust might look on it very favourably, especially if I lean on them,' he added with a grin. 'You'd end up overlapping for a day, but you'd probably want to anyway for continuity. The only real difficulty I can see is the night cover when you're on call. How will you deal with that?'

'No problem. We'll be living together, which makes us much more flexible.'

Ben frowned, his face concerned. 'When you say living together…?'

'Not like that, we're just friends,' he said hastily.

Ben's eyebrow quirked sceptically. 'You'd have to be very good friends to make that work. Are you sure you know each other well enough? It's a lot to take on, Jake, and if this job share relies on your domestic situation and it breaks down—'

'It won't break down,' he said firmly. 'We've house-shared before. I've known her for over twenty years and I can't think of anyone else I'd contemplate doing it with. Let's face it, we both have a very strong vested interest in making it work. And if it really got on our nerves, we could divide the house into two flats. Heaven knows it's big enough.'

'Well, that's true,' Ben said with a wry smile. 'And how long are you thinking this would last? A year? Two? Ten? Because there are implications for your future, for your pension, for your career progression. It's not trivial.'

'I know. I realise that, so does Emily, but to be frank, Ben, we'd don't have a lot of options and this is far and away the best idea we've come up with for either of us. Can I talk to her about the extra sessions and come back to you?'

'Of course. What sort of start date were you thinking of?'

'As soon as possible. I can't mess about like this for ever, it's not fair on you or Matilda or my patients, and Em needs an answer, too, because she's coming to the end of her mat leave and she needs to get a job sorted soon.'

Ben gave a wry smile. 'Good, because juggling the rota is frying my brains. Look, go and talk to her and let me know what she thinks. Obviously you'll have to jump through all the official hoops, but nobody's in the business of making this any more complicated than it has to be and if you want to go ahead I'll do everything I can.'

He nodded. 'And until then? Because yesterday was a really tough day for Emily and the kids, but I'm so conscious of letting you down if I take more time off and I'm just torn in two.'

'Of course you are,' Ben said quietly. 'Anyone would be, and I do understand, but don't worry about it. We all need this sorted out one way or another very quickly, but I'm sure it can be done, subject of course to interview and your joint proposal ticking all the necessary boxes. We'd need to be sure it would work before we could agree to it.'

He closed his eyes briefly, felt some of the tension leak away and gave a quiet laugh. 'Of course. And thanks for being so reasonable. I'm really sorry about this.'

'Don't be. Stuff happens, Jake, it's all part of life's rich pattern. The trick is to learn to roll with the punches. Go on, take Matilda home, talk to Emily and get back to me.'

Her phone rang while she was swiping porridge from every accessible part of Zach's high chair.

Jake. Of course.

'You have a gift for calling me when I'm covered in gloop,' she said drily. 'How did it go?'

'Well, I think. He's going to talk to the Trust. We're just on our way home. I'll tell you more then.'

So it could be happening. She put the phone down and carried on wet-wiping, a funny little hitch in her chest. And not in a good way.

Ridiculous, because she had to work, she *wanted* to work, and this whole thing had been her idea, so from that point of view it was good, but he'd been right about her house. She already missed it, missed having her familiar things around her like a security blanket, even if she'd denied it yesterday. It wasn't for ever, though, just until the children were a little older so they could go into full-time childcare without being irreparably damaged.

And that time would come. She couldn't imagine Jake wanting to work part time for ever. He was too much of a career doctor to want to take a back seat, and then she could go back to her own house, or sell it and move on. There was no hurry now, though. She could let the house in the meantime and see how it went. She didn't have to sell it and burn all her boats.

Not yet.

They took the children to the park and pushed them side by side in the baby swings while she listened to what Ben had said.

'There's a lot of official stuff. We'll have to submit a joint application for the job share, outlining how we'd split the workload, and we'd both have to be interviewed so they can be sure we've thought it through, but in the meantime Ben's going to run it by them because it's an opportunity to gain a few more sessions of consultant cover each week, so actually he's really on board with it, especially as you're a woman. And it means we'd both earn more if we did the extra hours. Would you be up for that?'

'Yes, I don't see why not. It all sounds really positive,' she said. 'And in the meantime I can look after the children so you can get back to work at least most of the time, and we'll just have to rub along somehow. It'll give them time to settle into a routine, and you'll know Tilly's safe even if she's not overjoyed with the situation.'

'And if the Trust says no?'

She shrugged. 'Then I'll have to look for another job or go back to my old one, and you'll have to put Tilly into childcare, but let's just hope it doesn't happen.'

There was a long silence, punctuated by the creak of the swings, and then he said, 'Are you absolutely sure you want to do this, Em? Because I don't want to set this all up and then you change your mind because it's too big a commitment or you want your own space back—or even your old job, because it'll be gone, so it has massive implications, especially for you. If we can do this, it'll be great, but I want you to be absolutely sure before it goes any further because there's no way back to where we are now, for either of us.'

She met his eyes, read the conflicting emotions of hope and concern, and shut the lid on her doubts.

'I am sure,' she said, to convince herself as much as him. She owed Jake so much, and if she could do this for him and make it work, it would go at least some way towards repaying him. She wouldn't even think about failing, because it wasn't an option. It couldn't be.

His eyes held hers. 'Honestly?'

'Honestly,' she said, her voice firmer now. 'If the Trust says yes, I'll move in with you properly and let my house, but in the meantime Zach will have a chance to get used to you before I need to leave him. Don't worry, Jake. We'll get there.'

'We could split the house, if you'd rather. It's easy with the bathrooms, I'll just use the shower room, but if you want your own floor, or a separate sitting room—'

'I don't. If you do, just say the word and we can sort it out, but as I've told you, I like the company.' She smiled at him. 'And sure, you've got a few irritating habits, but I'll just have to turn a blind eye to those.'

'Irritating habits?'

His voice was indignant, but his eyes were smiling, and she stretched up and kissed his cheek and felt it dimple under her lips. He smelt of soap and Jake with a hint of chocolate muffin, and there was something vaguely disturbing about it.

'Don't worry. I'll soon get you trained,' she quipped, and gave Zach's swing another little push while she tried to work out why her heart was beating just that little bit faster.

He downloaded the job-share protocol and applications forms from the Trust intranet once the children were in bed, and after they'd finished eating they sat at the dining table scrolling through all the endless pages.

'I *hate* this kind of stuff,' he muttered, as if she was having such a great time.

'Whereas I just love it,' she mocked, rolling her eyes. 'Do you have a copy of your timetable?'

'Yeah, I'll print it and we can squabble over who does what. And don't even think about dumping me with all the routine gynae.'

'It says in the protocol—' she began, but he threw a pen at her and disappeared to the study, leaving her grinning. She'd forgotten what fun he was to be around, even when he was grumpy. Forgotten what fun *was*, even, but her enduring memory of their time at uni had been laughter, and Jake had been at the centre of that, always.

It seemed so long ago now...

She was just reading through *Points to consider when becoming a job-sharer* when he came back, dropped three copies of the timetable and a packet of highlighter pens down in front of her and opened the fridge.

'This calls for wine,' he said, and sat down again with

two glasses, the bottle they'd started last night and a giant packet of hand-fried crisps.

'Right. Let's do this.'

Three hours, the entire packet of crisps and most of the bottle of wine later, they'd thrashed out a workable time-table that gave both of them what they wanted, shared out the tasks equally and wouldn't let any of the patients down, and they'd built in capacity for another three sessions.

He sat back, let his breath out in a whoosh and gave her a high five.

'Sorted. Now all we have to do is write a load of appropriate twaddle about how well we've thought it through and what makes us think it's not going to crash and burn.'

She chuckled and stood up. 'Not tonight. Come on, let's watch a bit of mindless TV and go to bed. It'll still be there tomorrow and we won't sleep if we don't have a break from it.'

She was talking sense, but a huge part of him wanted to sort it now, because he knew it wasn't twaddle and Ben had made it perfectly clear how important it was.

'I bought chocolate earlier,' she taunted, heading for the sitting room.

'As if we haven't just eaten enough rubbish. What sort?'

'Oh, it's healthy. Fruit and nut. Two of your five a day—*and* it's dark chocolate, which is positively good for you,' she said over her shoulder, and he dropped his pen, stood up and followed her.

'There could be disadvantages to working with some-one who knows me quite so well,' he growled, plopping down onto the sofa beside her and picking up the TV re-mote. 'Hand it over, then.'

* * *

He was up at five to fill in the application form, putting his case for wanting to job share and how he saw it working for the patients in his care, and he heard the stairs creak and Emily walked in in her pyjamas, hair tousled, one cheek rosy from having slept on it.

And looking as sexy as hell.

'Tea?' she asked, and he nodded, his head draining of coherent thought.

'Please. With caffeine. Why are you up?'

'To help you? I heard you go downstairs, and I had an idea you'd be doing this while the children are still asleep.'

He gave a wry grunt. 'Absolutely. If we can, I want to give it to Ben today for his thoughts so we've got time to tweak it before he puts it to the Board tomorrow. Are you OK for me to go to work tomorrow, by the way?'

'Of course I am. I have to be. It's the new reality, Jake.'

She filled the kettle and came and sat down next to him, the drift of warm, Emily-scented air and the crazy pyjamas doing nothing for his concentration.

'I'm a bit worried we might have a timing problem. I have to give eight weeks' notice if I'm not going back to my old job after mat leave, which means by the end of next week, but if I hand in my notice there and they say no to the job share here, I could end up with a break in my continuous NHS employment and have to give back my maternity pay, and I just don't have the money.'

He stopped thinking about her pyjamas and let his breath out on a long, low whistle.

'I hadn't realised you were so near the end of mat leave, but you're right, that could be tight. I'll make sure Ben knows, but as we don't have a female consultant or anyone wanting to do more sessions, it's a golden opportunity for them and they'd be mad to turn us down because some women really need a female doctor. It'll take the pressure off our female registrars, and I can think of at least one patient I've seen in the last week who I'd want to hand over to you for just that reason and I'm sure there are others. We just have to sound convincing.'

He sat back and stretched out his shoulders. 'Has that kettle boiled yet? This is making my head hurt.'

He went off to see Ben later that morning, armed with their draft proposal and suggested timetable split, and she girded her loins to deal with another joyous day of tantrums from Matilda, but there were none—or at least not on the scale of her previous efforts.

Instead she ate her breakfast nicely, then lay on the floor with Zach and built a tower of cups for him to knock down, and built it again, and again, and again, and every time he knocked it down she giggled, and so did he.

Emily was stunned, and when Jake rang in the middle of it, she held the phone out so he could hear.

'Is that Zach laughing?'

'It's both of them. It's delicious. I don't know what's got into them, but I'm all in favour of it. Have you spoken to Ben?'

'Yes. He's taken it all away to read through a bit more thoroughly, but he seems more than happy. He was talking about the Board contacting your referees before they interview you, so you might want to OK that with them before tomorrow.'

'I've done it—or at least the ones I could get hold of. I've emailed the CEO but my clinical lead's going to have a word. He was brilliant, so supportive. They've been amazing to me, and I feel bad about not going back, but—I just feel this is right for both of us.'

'You and Zach, you mean?'

'No! You and me. Well, and the children, on current form, but I won't hold my breath,' she said with a laugh. 'Any ideas what I should do with them next when this all falls apart?'

'Matilda likes cooking. We make rock buns sometimes. It's hard to ruin them.'

She chuckled. 'What, even for you?' she teased.

'Very funny. I'm on my way, but you'll find everything you need in the cupboard next to the fridge. Don't eat them all before I get home.'

'You know what? It's a gorgeous day. Why don't I make a picnic instead and we could go to the beach? They'd love that, and maybe what we all need is some time together just having fun.'

'That's a brilliant idea. Want me to pick anything up?'

'Sandwiches? I think we've got everything else.'

'OK. I'll see you shortly.'

She was right, the children had a wonderful time on the beach, and so did they.

They found a nice flat area in the shelter of a breakwater and had their picnic, then they built a sandcastle just below the high-water mark where the sand was still damp enough to stick together.

'It needs a moat,' Emily insisted.

'Of course it does, why wouldn't it?' he said wryly, knowing what was coming, so he rolled up his jeans as high as he could and took a bucket down to the sea and got predictably drenched by a freak wave.

'It's not funny,' he told her, trying not to laugh, but Matilda thought it was hilarious and little Zach joined in, and then when they'd all finished laughing at him they decided—they being Em, of course—that it would be fun to bury him in the sand.

'Really?'

'Really. Lie down and stop fussing. You know you want to.'

So he dug out a hollow and lay down in it obediently and let them cover him in sand. It was damper than he'd realised, though, and by the time he broke free and stood up, he was plastered in it.

'It'll fall off when it dries,' Em said cheerfully, and handed him a bucket. 'Why don't you go and rinse your hands and feet and bring some water up so we can rinse our hands, too, and then I think it might be time to go. They're getting tired.'

'I'm not surprised. They've shifted about a ton of sand between them.'

'They had help.'

'I noticed,' he said drily, but he went and fetched water, more cautiously this time, and then they cleared up all the toys and the remains of the picnic and set off.

The children were both fractious by then, so they decided to go for a walk to let them sleep in the buggy.

Zach was gone in moments and it didn't take Matilda long to join him, so they went round the point past the sea defences and followed the sea wall along to the harbour, falling into step as they strolled along.

The sea was quiet, the silence broken only by the sound of their footsteps and the soft slap of the waves on the shingle, the stones settling with a little whisper as the waves receded. Out at sea some gulls were wheeling over a fishing boat, and they could hear the faint putter of its engine in the distance.

'Gosh, it's beautiful. I can see why you love it here,' Emily said with a sigh, and he grunted softly.

'Jo couldn't. She flatly refused to live here with me, even though she hadn't said anything negative when the job came up and I started looking at houses, and then of course it was too late, I was committed to the move and there was nothing I could do about it.'

She turned her head so she could see his face. 'Do you think she really hated it and didn't want to live here, or didn't want to live with you because she'd realised she didn't love you? You're old enough to be pragmatic, but she's not, she's still young enough to be dreaming of a happy ever after, which is probably why she's gone off chasing rainbows with the dude in the campervan. And maybe you moving here just gave her an out?'

He sighed and scrubbed a hand through his hair, dislodging the sand that had finally dried in it. 'I have no idea. Maybe. I knew she was a bit of a hippy at heart, but I wouldn't have said she was manipulative so I think you could be right. She was probably just out of her depth. You know she nearly didn't have Matilda? She said at the time she wasn't ready to be a mother, and judging by the way she walked off last week and left Tilly without a backward glance, she was right.'

'So, what did your parents say about that?' Em asked curiously. 'I take it you've told them.'

He laughed, but there wasn't a trace of humour in it. 'Nothing new. My mother told me it was no more than I deserved, and my father gave me another lecture on contraception and what he called my indiscriminate sexual habits— What?' he asked, shooting her a dirty look when she laughed.

She tried to straighten her face. 'Well, it was high

time someone said it,' she pointed out. 'You're a bit of an alley cat, Jake.'

'I am *not*!' Her eyebrows shot up, and he frowned. 'Seriously, Em, I'm not, at least not anymore, and I have no idea how she got pregnant.'

'You need me to explain?' she said, and then stopped walking, mostly because she was laughing so hard she couldn't breathe.

'I didn't mean it that way,' he growled.

'So what did you mean?' she asked when she could speak. 'Because you can't have been that careful or she wouldn't have got pregnant. Was she on the Pill?'

'No, and we *were* careful! We used a condom every single time, and as far as I know none of them failed— not that it's *any* of your business,' he added, glowering at her and trying not to laugh.

She wasn't even trying. 'Well, clearly one of them failed—or else she sabotaged you.'

'Why would she do that?'

She fell into step beside him again, giving him a dis- believing look. 'Oh, come on, Jake. You're a good catch.'

'So why didn't she catch me? Why not insist that I marry her? God knows I offered.'

'She didn't need to. You were supporting her anyway, and maybe by then she'd realised she didn't love you.'

He shook his head. 'No, she's not like that. She's not organised enough to be premeditated.'

She stopped walking again and turned to look at him, thoughtful now. 'I don't know, Jake. She stole your money and defaulted on her rent, so she obviously planned that. And if she said it was an accident when she got pregnant, you'd believe her. Accidents happen all the time, and people get carried away in the heat of the moment and fall into bed without thinking. It has been known, and it wouldn't be the first time you'd done it.'

She knew that all too well. She vividly remembered the time they'd come really, really close to making love...

'Can we *please* stop discussing my sex life?' he muttered, and she wondered if he was actually blushing or if it was just that he'd caught the sun.

'Well, at least you have one. I can't even remember what it was like,' she said with painful honesty.

'Ah, come on, Em, you and Pete were married for years!'

'And most of the time he was too busy trying not to die,' she pointed out.

All trace of laughter was gone from her voice now, and Jake stopped walking and pulled her into his arms with a ragged sigh, resting his cheek against her hair.

'Ah, hell, I'm sorry, Em,' he murmured apologetically. 'I shouldn't have said that, it's none of my business. It must have been so tough for you both, living on a knife-edge throughout the whole of your marriage.'

She eased away from him and started walking again, somehow uncomfortable talking about Pete while she was standing in Jake's arms. 'Not all of it. Some of it was OK, especially after he got the all-clear, but I always knew in my bones it couldn't last.'

'So why did you decide to have a baby if you thought he was going to die?' he asked, finally asking the question that must have been bugging him ever since she'd told him she was pregnant and Pete was dying.

She sighed, her shoulders lifting in a little shrug. 'Because I thought he would live to see it. Pete had always wanted children, so had I, and my clock was ticking. He'd banked some sperm as soon as he was diagnosed, before he had the first chemo, so it was sitting there waiting, and I felt if we didn't get on with it I'd have left it too late and missed my chance, but I never dreamt it would be over so soon for him. That was a real shock, when he went downhill so fast and I realised we'd left it too late.'

'It must have been. Do you regret it?'

'What, marrying Pete, or having Zach?'

'I meant having Zach,' he said, although he must have wondered if she'd regretted her marriage to a man she'd known was probably dying, but maybe he felt he'd been intrusive enough.

She smiled down at the sleeping baby snuggled up in the buggy, her heart filling. 'Not for a single second. It hasn't been easy, and I've often been scared that I couldn't cope, but no, I've never regretted it. He's the best thing that's ever happened to me. Well, apart from you, of course, but that's different.'

She flashed him a smile, and he reached out and took her hand and squeezed it, but he didn't let go, just kept her hand there in his as they strolled along side by side, their fingers loosely linked.

It was only when the path narrowed again that he slipped his hand out of hers to go on ahead with the buggy, and she curled her fingers tightly into her palm and felt oddly bereft.

Jake rang her on Tuesday morning to say he'd had an email inviting him for interview at nine-thirty on Thursday.

'Gosh, that was quick.'

'It was. Ben promised he'd hustle it. Check your emails,' he said, but she was already doing it and her heart was racing.

'Yes, they want to see me at ten-fifteen. And they said allow until one. Ouch.'

'Mmm. I think that's because they want us one at a time, and then together.'

'Can you get the time off?' she asked, hooking Zach out of the bottom pan drawer and sliding it shut with her leg. 'Because taking these two to an interview could be interesting, although we'll need cover for the joint interview anyway. What are we going to do about that?'

'I'll sort it with Ben—he'll need cover, too, and I'll talk to the nursery,' he promised. 'I spoke to them about Matilda the other day, and they had some capacity then, so hopefully they can squeeze them in. Right, got to go, I'm due in Theatre. In fact, why don't you come up here and talk to the staff at the nursery anyway, because this is for Zach, too, and it might give the children a chance to get familiarised before we have to leave them there—assuming they still have space.'

'And failing that?'

She could almost see him shrug. 'Then I'll ask Ben's wife Daisy if she can help out for the interviews as a one-off. She's lovely and Tils knows her, but in the long term we may have to find somewhere else.'

'OK. I'll take them up there now and see. I'll text you the answer.'

She spent the next hour at the nursery, and although Matilda dragged her everywhere she wanted to go, she did at least explore the garden and have a go on the play equipment, and Zach seemed happy in the sandpit so long as Emily sat on the edge. Then she found the water trough, and that was it.

'Right, Tilly, we need to go now and see the ducks,' she said, and to her amazement Matilda shook her head.

'No. I playing.'

She was pouring water from one container to another

and getting utterly drenched, but she seemed totally content, and Emily pulled out her phone and took a picture and sent it to Jake.

Hallelujah! he texted back, and she smiled.

Hallelujah, indeed. For now, at least.

Predictably Jake rang her in his lunch break to find out more.

'It was great,' she told him. 'I saw Caitlin, she said you'd spoken to her, which was really useful because I didn't have to explain anything in front of the children.'

'How about security?'

'It's excellent, and they seem to have wonderful facilities. And they have space, which is a miracle, apparently, but someone's just left so we got lucky.'

'What did Matilda make of it at first?'

'She was a bit wary, but after she'd found her feet a little she loved it, and so did Jake. We played for ages, and the other children seemed happy, which was good to see. I've been quite worried about it because I've never left Zach with anyone except Pete's parents, and that's only been for an hour or so to have my hair cut or go to the dentist, but I don't think I need to worry about him at all or you about Matilda.'

'No, thanks for sending me that photo, it's delicious.'

'It is, but I had to drag them away. Neither of them wanted to leave. I had to bribe them with feeding the ducks.'

He chuckled. 'Yeah, the ducks can be quite handy. Well, that's brilliant. Thanks. So are we all set for Thursday?'

'Yes—except I need to go home this evening and grab something to wear for my interview that might not be a total disgrace. I can do that after you get home once they're in bed.'

'OK. I'll try not to be late.'

It was only a flying visit to collect some clothes, because all she'd brought with her was a few pairs of jeans and an armful of tops, and that wasn't going to impress anyone. Not that she had much at home to choose from that would still fit her since she'd had Zach, but there had to be *something*.

She parked on the drive, went in and shut the front door, and then stood for a second while the silence closed in around her. She realised it was the first time she'd been alone in the house since Zach was born, and it felt odd. Odd, and strangely unsettling. And, to her surprise, although the house she'd shared with Pete for so long was familiar, it didn't feel like home. It just felt wrong somehow, so she raided her wardrobe and left without lingering.

'That was quick. Did you find what you wanted?' Jake asked her when she got home—home?—and she nodded, going into the sitting room and perching on the arm of the sofa.

'Yes, I suppose so. It'll do.' She frowned at the television. 'Are you seriously watching *Titanic*?'

'Oh, I was just killing time till you got back, really. There's not much on.'

'*Titanic* made you cry.'

'It made you cry, too, if I remember rightly,' he reminded her drily.

'Surely not.' She peered at the bag beside him. 'Is that popcorn?'

'It might be.'

She felt her mouth twitch and bit her lips to trap the smart retort. 'What flavour?'

'Wasabi and ginger.'

Her mouth dropped open. 'You're kidding,' she said, and his eyes crinkled.

'I'm not, they do make it, but it's salted caramel.'

She couldn't help the laugh. 'I knew you wouldn't eat anything that weird. Give me five seconds to change and I'll be back. I'll have tea, please—and don't finish the popcorn!'

She ran upstairs, grinning and ignoring the muttering she left behind, and by the time she was back in her PJs there were two mugs of tea steaming on the coffee table, *Titanic* paused on the television and Jake with his hand back in the bag of popcorn.

'Hey, get out of that, we're sharing, remember?' she said, dropping down on the sofa beside him and reaching for the bag.

'Say please.' He held it out of reach, laughing, and she lunged across him, trying to make a grab for it and digging her elbow into his ribs by accident.

'Ouch! Get off me!' He laughed, holding the bag further out of reach, but she made another lunge for it and grabbed it victoriously, and their eyes met and something weird happened.

They froze, eyes locked, and for a paralysing second she thought he was going to kiss her, but then he removed his hand from the bag and looked away, and she retreated hastily into the corner with the popcorn, wondering if her cheeks were as red as they felt, and he picked up the remote without a word and restarted the movie.

'Popcorn?'

What, and risk another highly charged wrestling

match? He'd only just got his body back under control. But the bag was just there, so he dug into it and took a handful.

'I hate this bit,' she said, when the ship started to list and fill with water, and she wriggled up against his side, her hand tucked through his arm as if nothing had happened.

Another layer of torment? He could still feel the warm softness of her body under his hands, feel the silk of her skin, smell the scent of her as she'd squirmed giggling against him.

How was he supposed to feel? To act? She might be just a friend, but she was a beautiful woman. Of course he'd noticed, but apart from that embarrassing blip fifteen years ago he'd spent twenty years ignoring it, keeping the lid firmly on the box.

And she'd either done the same, which he doubted because she frankly wasn't that good at hiding her feelings, or she'd genuinely felt nothing more for him than friendship. Well, not in that way, anyhow, and even if she did there was no way he was ripping the lid off the box at this point in their relationship, not with so much riding on it.

He felt her head settle on his shoulder, then after a few minutes, as the story came to its inescapable and heart-rending end, her grip on his arm tightened reflexively and he heard a tiny, stifled sniff.

'You're a softie, do you know that?' he said, resting his head against hers, and she pulled away and sniffed harder, grabbing the remote from the table and turning the television off.

'You're such a hypocrite. You snivelled just as much as me in the cinema.'

'I was nineteen, and anyway, it's sad!'

'You were a softie,' she told him, swivelling round to look at him. 'And you still are!'

'I am not!'

'So what's this?' she asked victoriously, lifting her hand and touching a finger to the outer corner of his eye. She lifted it to her lips, flicking her tongue out to taste it, and he stifled a groan. 'Tears, Stratton! Actual, real tears! So don't you go giving me grief!'

She was just there, mere inches away, hands on her hips and laughing at him while her eyes still sparkled with her own tears, and the urge to lean in and kiss that sassy smile off her face nearly finished him.

But not quite.

He took her by the shoulders, eased her away from him and stood up, sending a shower of popcorn crumbs onto the carpet. 'Right, enough nonsense, it's time for bed,' he said briskly. 'I've got a long day tomorrow, and we need to rehearse our interview technique in the evening.'

'Really?'

'Yeah, really. Come on. Bedtime.'

He reached out a hand and hauled her to her feet, then just because he couldn't help himself he reeled her in and hugged her.

Just briefly, just enough to mess with his dreams, but they were probably going to be X-rated anyway after that wrestling match over the popcorn. Dammit. He let her go, screwed up the empty bag and picked up the mugs as she headed for the stairs.

'I'll see you in the morning,' he said, and flicked off the light and went into the kitchen for a quiet moment alone to gather his ragged composure and have a stern word with his heart, because the tears she'd seen in his eyes had had nothing to do with the film and everything to do with his feelings for a woman he couldn't allow himself to love.

Not if this job share was going to stand the slightest chance of working.

CHAPTER FOUR

THEY SPENT WEDNESDAY evening interviewing each other, thinking up all the horrible questions they could be asked and trying to answer them coherently.

How would they divide their time? What if it didn't work? How about sick leave, holidays—would they cover for each other on an overtime basis? Did they have an agreement to share the tasks equally and equitably? What if one of them wanted out? Medical questions, too, because Nick Jarvis, the husband of Liv who'd delivered Zach, had been grilled by Ben when he'd come back to work here the year before and he'd warned them not to expect Ben to play nice.

'Enough!' she said, jumping to her feet and clutching her hair when midnight was looming and her head was ready to explode. 'If we don't stop talking about this, I'm going to be awake all night and I won't be able to string two words together. It's bad enough that I'm going to look like a bag lady.'

He started to laugh. 'Don't be ridiculous! Why will you look like a bag lady?'

'Why? Because none of my decent clothes fit me properly now—and I can't even remember when I last wore a skirt.'

'So wear trousers.'

'I can't get into them either, they won't do up because I've changed shape and put on weight. The only thing I can get into is a stretchy pencil skirt I had when I was first pregnant, and a jacket that won't quite meet. And frankly, Jake, that's not adequate!'

He laughed again, but his eyes were tender and made her feel strange. 'Em, you're gorgeous. You couldn't look like a bag lady if you tried—'

'Don't patronise me! I don't look gorgeous, and I certainly don't look professional. At the outside I'll get by.'

'Hey, you'll be fine,' he assured her, serious now. 'They want to talk to you about the job, not check out your dress sense.'

She growled under her breath. 'It's not about them, it's about *me*. I need to feel professional and well presented to give me confidence, and I've worn nothing but stretchy skinny jeans and baggy tops covered in baby goo for the last nine months!'

'Oh, Em.' He laughed softly, and getting to his feet, he pulled her into his arms and hugged her hard. His chest was broad and solid, and the scent of his skin drifted over her, warm and familiar and oddly disturbing.

'You'll be great,' he murmured, his low voice rumbling in his chest beneath her ear and adding to the disturbing sensations. 'Don't worry. It'll be fine, you'll wow them. Now go to bed. I'll wake you in the morning so you've got time to get showered before I have to leave, OK?'

'OK.'

He let her go, the warm, safe embrace broken, and she kissed his cheek and went up to bed, too tired to worry any more. What would be would be, and worrying wasn't going to make a blind bit of difference.

* * *

Jake watched her go, then stared sightlessly out of the window into the night.

He hoped he'd managed to reassure her, but there was nobody to reassure him, and so much—*so* much—was hanging on these interviews.

Tomorrow had the potential to change the entire course of his life. He just hoped it would be for the better—for all of them.

His mind churning, he tidied up the kitchen, turned out the lights and went upstairs. Her bedroom door was open, the light on, and as he walked past it to check on Matilda he saw her sitting up in bed in those cute pyjamas that made him think of things he had no business thinking about.

And it didn't help that she was feeding Zach.

She patted the mattress beside her, and he went in and perched on the edge of the bed.

'What's up?'

'I'm just nervous. It will be all right, won't it?' she asked, a worried frown puckering her forehead. 'It has to be.'

He shrugged. 'I hope so. We're well prepared. We can't do any more than we have.'

'No, I guess not.'

She eased the sleepy baby off her nipple, and he looked away hastily, his eyes falling instead on a small double picture frame on her bedside table.

'Could you hold him for me, please? I need the bathroom and then I need to change his nappy.'

'Sure.' He stood up and took Zach from her, his eyes drawn again to the photos under the bedside light as she left the room.

They were both pictures of Em and Pete, but they were

very different. The first had been taken on their wedding day, laughter shining in their eyes; the second looked like a selfie, with her propped up beside him on a bed, Pete holding something on his chest. He peered closer, and the little blur became clear.

'Oh, Em,' he breathed, emotion clogging his throat. The only image Pete would ever see of his son, his twelve-week scan photo, was resting on his heart. Em must have been taken the selfie on the day of the scan, less than a week before Pete died.

He stared at it silently, the image blurring. It was so cruel, so unfair. He'd promised Pete on his deathbed that he'd look after Emily and the baby and keep them safe, and he said it again now, his mouth moving silently as Emily came back into the room.

'Thanks,' she said, taking the now sleeping baby from his arms. She put him down on the bed, then turned back to Jake as he stood up and slipped her arms round him and rested her head on his chest with a sigh.

'We will be OK, won't we, Jake? We can do this, can't we?'

He dragged his eyes off the photo and tried to stop thinking about the feel of her body against his. 'Of course we can, and it'll all be fine, one way or another. Go on, go to bed, get some sleep.'

Her arms tightened briefly and then, as if the hug wasn't enough to finish him off, she tilted her head and touched her lips to his cheek. Her scent curled around him, the soft touch of her skin, the warmth of her lips, the fullness of her body pressed against him not helping at all.

He dropped his arms and stepped back, blew the sleeping baby a kiss and walked to the door. As he turned to shut it, the photo caught his gaze again.

He closed the door, checked Matilda and went into his own room, shutting the door firmly between him and temptation.

What on earth had he let himself in for? And he'd told *Emily* to be sure she was doing the right thing? If it hadn't been for his promise to Pete, he'd tell Emily he couldn't do this and he'd find another way, but he couldn't, because he'd promised to look after her and her baby, and she needed this job share every bit as much as he did. He'd just have to grit his teeth and get on with it.

Assuming they got the job share, which they wouldn't if he didn't get some sleep so he could think straight tomorrow.

But sleep was a long time coming, because every time he closed his eyes he saw the haunting image of a dying man, chiding him for his hypocrisy.

Nick had been right.

The interviews were thorough, rigorous and didn't cut either of them any slack, but somehow they got through them, and after the joint interview they were sent out so the board could discuss the results.

There was a small waiting area with chairs grouped around a low table with a pile of magazines on it, and as they sat there Emily rested her head on his shoulder and sighed.

'I hope I didn't let you down,' she mumbled. 'I didn't know what they wanted from me half the time. I probably talked rubbish.'

He slid his arm round her shoulders and hugged her. 'It can't have been any worse than mine, and I thought we did all right in the joint interview.'

'By a miracle.'

'Well, maybe we're due one,' he said, the photo of Pete on her bedside table all too clear in his mind.

'Hope so. A lot depends on it. I spoke to Pete's parents while you were in there, they said if the children didn't get on at nursery they'd have them on Wednesdays for us.'

'Wow. That's a big commitment.' Not one his own parents would be able or willing to make, he knew that. They'd made their feelings perfectly clear and had very little time for him or their granddaughter.

She shrugged. 'They're lovely people, and I think they'd like it, but they live on the other side of Bury St Edmunds and it's a long way. Further now than it was, so it isn't really feasible.'

'Let's wait and see. It may not even be necessary—oh, here we go. Chin up.'

He retrieved his arm as the boardroom door opened, his legs suddenly like jelly as he got to his feet, but Ben was smiling as he beckoned them in and the CEO told them that their application had been successful and the job share was theirs.

'We were very impressed with the amount of thought you'd both put into it, and the meticulous planning of your schedule, and also your willingness to be flexible and add extra time. So if you want to go ahead, I'll inform HR and they can start working on the contracts, and we look forward to welcoming Mrs Cardew to the hospital.'

'Thank you—that's amazing,' he said, not knowing whether to laugh or cry, and beside him he heard Emily sniff and let out what might have been a sob of laughter.

'Wow. Thank you—thank you so much,' she said, her voice wobbling a little. 'I won't let you down. *We* won't let you down.'

* * *

She waited until they were out of the room and walking along the corridor before she let out a tiny whoop and hugged him. '*Yessss!* We did it!'

'We did,' Jake said with a laugh, hugging her back, 'and I'll make sure you don't regret it.' He glanced at his watch. 'Shall we grab a really quick lunch? I'm in Theatre this afternoon and I ought to go and see my patients first, but I've got half an hour. Are you OK to pick up the children without me afterwards and talk to the nursery about having them every Wednesday?'

'Yes, of course I am—and definitely yes to lunch,' she added, suddenly aware that she was shaking all over. 'I think my blood sugar's a bit low. I couldn't eat breakfast and I'm starving.'

'Me, too. We'll go to the Park Café and get a sandwich and a coffee. We can celebrate properly later.'

They walked into the café and he headed for the grab-and-go chiller. 'Are you sure a sandwich and coffee's OK?'

'Of course it is,' she said, and took a sandwich out of the chiller, just as one of the café staff hailed Jake from behind the counter.

'Hello, Mr Stratton. How's your little girl? I felt so sorry for her. Is she all right?' the woman asked, and Emily realised that this must be where Jo had left Matilda, in the middle of this busy café right off the main hospital thoroughfare where anyone could walk in.

'She's fine, Sue, thank you,' Jake was saying. 'She's doing well and we're all sorted.'

'Oh, good, I am glad. Cappuccino with an extra shot?'

'Please, and a decaf cappuccino, as well.'

He added a bar of chocolate and paid the bill, and they

headed out through a set of doors that led to an outside seating area.

There was an open barrier around the outside, just a few low screens to indicate the café area, but beyond it was the park, which was open to the public and without any security, and Jo had left Matilda here? She was even more appalled. Compared to the security of the nursery, this was terrifying—

'I can't believe it she left her here,' she said, shocked. 'What if Ben hadn't been there? Anybody could have wandered in off the park and just wheeled her away, and who would have stopped them? No wonder you were so angry!'

He nodded. 'I know. Don't worry, I know. She could have just brought her up to Maternity, where she would have been safe. Maybe she would have done if Ben hadn't been there, but she should have spoken to me, handed her over, done it properly, not just dumped her like she dumps everything when she realises it's not what she thought it was going to be.

'That was exactly what she did with me when she changed her mind and decided she didn't like Yoxburgh after all and didn't want to live here. Too cold, too windy, too far from her friends. And apparently I was too obsessed with my job, which I can understand, and you're probably right about her holding out for happy ever after, but—to leave your own daughter like that? I could never do that, and for the life of me I can't imagine what I saw in her.'

She smiled wryly at him. 'It's not rocket science, Jake. You were lonely, and she was there. And I've seen photos, she's lovely.'

'No. No, *you're* lovely,' he said emphatically—so emphatically that she felt her eyes widen. 'Honest and straightforward, decent, kind, thoughtful, considerate, and you'll put yourself out for a friend.'

'Well, of course I would—'

'No, not of course. Not like you have. For God's sake, Emily, you've just given up *everything* to help me. That wouldn't have occurred to Jo. Sure, she's pretty, but she can't commit to anything, not even her own daughter, and as soon as the going gets tough, she's off. I don't suppose she even stopped to work out how I was going to juggle caring for Matilda with earning a living so I could put a roof over her head. She just—*went*.'

'Did you ever look at the CCTV?'

He shook his head. 'No. Ben got them to create a copy of the recordings, just in case I want to take her to court, but as I don't have a way of doing that it doesn't seem relevant, and anyway, I haven't exactly had time. Besides, what's it going to tell me? Nothing I don't already know.'

'No, I guess not. I'm so sorry it didn't work for you.'

He threw her a bitter smile. 'Don't be. It's not your fault I had such a massive error of judgement, but Matilda's fine and so am I, and thanks to you and this job share I can see light at the end of the tunnel. And for what it's worth, you're beautiful. Right, coronation chicken, BLT or half each?'

The doorbell rang at eight that evening, and it was Ben, with a bunch of flowers and a bottle of Prosecco.

'Just to say well done and to welcome you to the team,' he said, kissing Emily's cheek.

'Are you sure it's not to apologise for grilling us like kippers in the interviews?' Jake asked drily from behind her, but Ben just shrugged.

'Got to be done,' he said with a wry smile, 'and you both came out of it very well, so I wouldn't let it worry you. Anyway, I won't hold you up, I just wanted to give you these. And Daisy says if you're ever at a loose end, either of you, she's always looking for another adult to talk to, so give her a call and you can have a play-date with the children. And she does mean it.'

'I might well do that,' Emily said. 'I've heard so much about her. And thank you, for the flowers and the Prosecco, but most of all for doing so much to make this happen. We're both really grateful.'

'My pleasure. I should give you a guided tour of the hospital, really.'

She smiled. 'I've sort of had one. Don't forget I road-tested the facilities when I had Zach, so it's not a totally unknown quantity. And I'm sure Jake'll help me find my feet.'

'I'm sure he will. And I really hope this works for you both, because you've obviously thought it through very thoroughly, so it deserves to. And any problems, any time, my door's always open. And I mean that. If you need help, ask.'

He kissed her cheek again, shook hands with Jake and went out, and Jake looked from her to the Prosecco.

'Shall we celebrate?' he asked, and she thought of all the things she'd given up—her job, her friends, her house...

No, not her friends. Jake was and always had been the only friend who really mattered to her. And the house wasn't hers, either, it was hers and Pete's. It had felt like a prison at times, but it had also been her sanctuary and she'd thought losing it would be hard, but when she'd gone there the other night it hadn't felt like home any more, as if that part of her life was done.

And this—this was her new life, here with Jake and yet not with him. It was odd, unsettling, a little confusing, but it wasn't for ever and Jake was making sacrifices, too. It wasn't a one-way street—

'Em?'

Putting the negatives aside and concentrating on the very many positives, she looked into Jake's serious, searching eyes and found a smile.

'Yes,' she said at last. 'Yes, let's celebrate.'

He popped the cork, poured two glasses and handed her one. 'To the future,' he said, and she lifted her glass.

'To the future,' she echoed, and shut the door firmly on the past.

It took until the end of the following week to sort out the contracts and shuffle patient appointments to accommodate their new arrangement, and in that time Jake moved all his stuff from the bathroom to the downstairs shower room, decorated the bathroom and started on the room that would be Zach's, ready for him to move into.

It was just a quick coat of paint, but it made him feel slightly better about the sacrifices Em was having to make.

'You don't have to do this for me,' she said, bringing him tea after she'd fed Zach and settled him for the night.

'Yes, I do.' He put the brush down, got off the ladder and took the mug from her. 'I want you to feel at home, and I've been in your home, and it's beautiful, and this place is a mess.'

'It's a glorious mess. Our house is dull in comparison.'

Our house.

He looked away. 'I didn't think it was dull. I thought it was lovely.'

'It is, but it hasn't got the high ceilings or the original fireplaces or any of the other things the Victorians were so good at.'

'What, like the rattling windows and the leaky roof and the fact that the floor's slightly wonky in the kitchen because the back of the house has sunk?'

She grinned at him. 'It's all part of its charm.'

He snorted. 'It's nearly summer, Em. You wait till the winter. You might want to reassess when the wind's shrieking off the North Sea and pouring in round the edges of the window frames.'

'Oh, you paint such a glorious picture! We can wear thick jumpers and snuggle up under fleecy blankets. And anyway, fresh air's good for you. So, what can I do?'

'Keep me company,' he said, trying not to think about snuggling up with her under a fleecy blanket. 'Cutting in round the edge is boring.'

'Want me to roller the walls?'

'Be my guest,' he said, so she joined in and they finished Zach's bedroom together, and all the time he reminded himself that it should have been Pete doing it. Pete painting their baby's bedroom with her. Pete snuggling up with her under a fleecy blanket—

'Right, we're done. I'm going to wash this lot before the paint ruins them.'

'Want a hand?'

'No, you're all right,' he said, suddenly feeling the need for space, because it was beginning to dawn on him that, for the next several years at least, he was going to be sharing every detail of his house, his work, his life with another man's woman.

The woman he loved, he finally admitted to himself. The only woman he'd ever really loved, the woman he wanted with all his heart. How the hell had it taken him so long to work out how much she meant to him? All those wasted years—and now he'd be living and working alongside her, with her and yet not with her, and it was going to be way, way tougher than he'd realised...

The contracts signed, they went to her house that weekend before she started work on the Monday, and while the children played on the floor with Zach's toys, Jake dismantled the cot and loaded it into his car, together with all Zach's clothes and toys and all the baby equipment she hadn't already taken over there. While he did that she packed up all the food in the kitchen, throwing out the dregs of packets, the oddments of jam and chutney in the fridge, the last few bags of green tea that had been all Pete would drink in his last days, lurking in the back of the cupboard behind some out-of-date coffee beans.

She held them for a moment, pressing them against her chest. She was trying to be strong, but it was so hard, and so cruel, and yet it seemed so long ago, as if it had happened to a different self—

'How are you doing?'

She dropped the tea bags in the bin on top of the coffee beans, tied the top of the bag and lifted it out of the bin. 'I've finished the kitchen. The fridge is auto-defrost so I'll just leave it on. The oven could do with a good clean but I'll get an agency to do that before the tenants move in. I've still got to pack up all my clothes in the bedroom.'

And Pete's, she realised, and then suddenly it was all too much and she turned and rested her head on Jake's chest. 'Can you do something for me? Can you take the children home with you? I've just got some things I have to do here before I can leave.'

He tipped her head up and stared down into her eyes searchingly, his own filled with concern. 'Are you sure you want me to leave you, Em? You don't want me to stay and help?'

She nodded. 'Yes, I'm sure. You can't help me, Jake. It's something I have to do on my own.'

He nodded slowly and stepped back. 'Give me anything else you've got ready to take, then, and I'll put the kids in the car and take them home.'

Ten minutes later he was ready to leave, and she put her arms round him and hugged him. 'Thank you.'

His arms closed around her, holding her tight. 'Don't thank me. You're doing this for me,' he said, his voice gruff, 'and I can only imagine what it feels like to pack up your life like this. So don't thank me, Em. Just promise me that when you're done here, you'll drive home carefully.'

Home...

His eyes searched hers again, and she nodded. 'Don't worry, I will. Zach's already lost his father. I'm not going to let him lose his mother.'

'Good. Call me when you leave.'

And then, out of the blue, he caught her chin in his fingers, bent his head and brushed the lightest, sweetest kiss on her lips. 'Take care, my love,' he murmured, and then turned on his heel and walked away.

'You, too,' she called after him, but it was too late, his car was gone. Too late to call him back, too late to put her arms around him again and kiss him back, to ask him to stay just a little longer to help her do this thing she had to do.

No. She had to do it alone, had to bring down the curtain on the last part of her life with Pete, and as she closed the door behind Jake, she'd never felt so alone in all her life.

It was hours before she got back, by which time the children were in bed and he'd rebuilt Zach's cot in the bedroom he and Em had painted. He didn't know where she'd want any of the things, so apart from the food which was obvious he stacked everything in Zach's new room and left it for her to sort out.

In the time since she'd phoned to say she was leaving, he'd thrown together a meal for them, and he was about to call her when he saw her pull up outside and get out of the car.

He opened the door and she walked into his arms, hugged him hard and stayed there with her head on his chest for the longest moment.

He waited it out, trying and failing to know how she must feel. He had no idea what it must be like to close the door on a house where your whole marriage had been played out to its tragic end. All he could do was what he was doing, holding her until she was ready to let go, and then he stepped back and smiled at her warily. 'OK?'

She nodded. 'OK. The car's full, but most of it's for the charity shops. Pete's clothes—'

She turned away, heading upstairs and going into her bedroom, presumably to see Zach, and he gave a heavy sigh and went out to the car to check that it was locked, then came back in and boiled the kettle.

'I hope you aren't making me tea.'

He laughed at her tone. 'No, it's for the pasta. There's a nice crisp Chablis in the fridge, and I've made a creamy seafood sauce to go with it. I just have to heat it through.'

'Sounds wonderful. Thank you—for everything.'

'Stop it, Emily,' he said, putting a glass of Chablis down in front of her and dropping into the chair opposite. 'You've had a tough day, on top of a tough—well, how far back do you want to go? Ten, twelve years? More? You don't need to thank me for cooking you a meal.'

Her eyes welled. 'I don't—want to go back, that is. I

need to move on, Jake. Yes, it was sad clearing up the house, but it was only the last bits. I'd already done a lot, and it's time to move on, to start the next phase of my life. As you said the other day, here's to the future. After all, it's all we've really got, that and each other, and we're lucky to have that.'

She picked up her glass, tilted it towards him in a bitter-sweet toast and took a sip. 'Mmm, lovely.' She looked up again, her eyes clear now to his relief. 'Thanks for putting Zach to bed. Was he OK?'

'Yes, he was fine. I gave him a bottle, and he gave me a bit of an old-fashioned look and then downed it.'

She laughed, and the sound sparkled in the room and drove away the shadows. 'That's my boy,' she said, and took another sip of her wine. 'So, tomorrow I need to buy at least another skirt and a few tops for work before Monday. Is there anywhere round here I can do that?'

The first day of their new contract, they dropped the children into nursery for a couple of hours so that Jake could introduce her to everyone, hand over some of his patients to her and give her a quick guided tour.

'Bit of a heads-up on your antenatal clinic this afternoon,' he said while they were in his office going through the paperwork she'd need. 'Brianna Owen, incompetent cervix. It's very short, so I haven't been able to put in a stitch. I've been treating her with progesterone pessaries from sixteen weeks but she's had a lot of problems and I've been keeping a very close eye on her and she's booked herself into the clinic and I don't know why. Anything you're not sure of, ring me and check, because I don't want anything to go wrong for her. It's all in the notes, but speak to me if anything's changed.'

'Will do. Keep your phone on you,' she said as he was leaving, and he laughed.

'Really? You needed to remind me of that? Of course I'll have my phone on me, but you'll be fine. Just go for it, and trust your judgement. You know what you're doing.'

And then she was on her own, conscious that if she did anything wrong, quite apart from any repercussions for the patients, the buck stopped with them both so it wouldn't be just her career on the line, it would be his, too.

Which meant that taking on the job share had been a huge leap of faith for him. Either that, or he'd been so desperate that he was past caring. Whichever, she was determined not to let him down, and it seemed there were plenty of others there to make sure she didn't.

She'd met some of the staff on the labour ward and they'd given her strict instructions to ask if there was anything she needed to know or couldn't find, and there was always someone in range to help.

Then to her delight Liv, the midwife who'd delivered Zach last year and who was off on maternity leave herself, popped in with her baby daughter and gave her a hug.

'Welcome to the team! Nick told me you were starting today, and I just had to come in and see you. How are you?'

'I'm fine, I'm well, and you've had a baby! She's beautiful. What's her name?'

'Isobel—Izzie.'

'Oh, that's such a pretty name! I've always loved it.'

'Me, too. Oh, I'm so glad you're going to be working here. We've all been really worried about Jake. He's been juggling Matilda and his job ever since she was born and he's done so well, but just recently with Jo walking out like that…'

'Well, you don't need to worry any more, I'm here now,' she said, and then added ruefully, 'and I'm really pleased for you that you've had a baby, but on a purely selfish note I was so looking forward to working with you. You were just wonderful when I was in labour, but at least now I've had a chance to thank you for the way you looked after me.'

Liv hugged her. 'You're more than welcome, Emily, and it was a privilege to share it with you. So how is Zach? He must be nearly a year old now.'

'Gosh, you even remembered his name. He's fine. We're both fine, settling in with Jake and hopefully this is going to work really well for us all.'

'Oh, I'm sure it will,' Liv said with a laugh, 'not least because it's high time we had a female consultant, so you'll be hugely popular with everyone! Talking of which, I'm sorry, I've got to go, I've brought cake in for the girls and they're expecting me. I'll make sure they leave you some. Have fun.'

Fun?

She wasn't sure it was fun, but by the end of her first day she'd followed up the patients Jake had handed over to her first thing, checked the blood test results of one and arranged a scan for another, discharged a couple of post-op patients in gynae and survived most of her first antenatal clinic, all without contacting Jake.

And then she saw Brianna Owen, who'd been booked in for a check-up as she'd been worried over the weekend, and the first thing she did was ask for him.

'I'm afraid he doesn't work on Mondays now,' Emily explained, 'but he has another antenatal clinic on

Wednesdays if you particularly want to see him. We're working alternate days and sharing the caseload, so anything I find I'll report to him and vice versa, so if you want to switch to Wednesdays from now on you're welcome, but I think I should see you today anyway if you don't mind, as you've obviously got some concerns.'

'Oh, no, that's fine, I don't really want to wait. I don't think I should. I've had a few twinges and a bit of an ache over the weekend that comes and goes. That's why I'm worried.'

And it was not what Emily wanted to hear, because she was only twenty-nine weeks and the last thing she needed was to go into labour just yet, but before Emily called Jake she wanted to know more about what was going on.

She gave her a reassuring smile. 'OK. Well, let's have a look at you and see what we can find. It might be nothing, but I'll take some swabs to check for infection, because that can sometimes happen with the pessaries, and it could potentially set off contractions, and I'll also take a sample of fluid from close to your cervix to test for foetal fibronectin. That's a protein that acts like a kind of glue that holds the baby in place in your uterus,' she explained. 'If the glue's starting to break down, it'll show up on the test, and if it doesn't show up, then we don't need to worry about it, but if it does then it could be an indication that you might be going into premature labour, so I just want to rule it out.'

'Does it hurt?'

'No. Not at all. It's a simple painless procedure rather like a smear test, and we can do it here and get the result in a few minutes, and then we'll have a better idea of what's going on and what to do next. Is that OK, Mrs Owen? Are you happy with that?'

'Yes—and please, call me Brie. Only the school kids call me Mrs Owen. Or Miss, which I can't stand!'

'OK, Brie it is,' she said with a laugh. 'Just lie back and relax for me, Brie. This won't take long.'

Fifteen minutes later she had the result, and she rang Jake from another room.

'Hi. I've just seen Brianna Owen, she's had a few contractions, so I took a swab to check for infection and I also did an fFN test and the results are back and it's slightly elevated, so I want to admit her and do a cervical scan and put her on steroids while we wait for the swab results to come back. Her urine was clear so it's not a UTI.'

'What's her gestation now?'

'Twenty-nine plus three.'

'Right. Ouch, Tilly, don't climb on me, darling. Yes, do admit her and I'll see her first thing tomorrow. If she's got an infection it might be triggering contractions. But definitely go with the steroids—ow, Tilly, no. Get down, that's enough. And can you put her on nifedipine, please, to suppress the contractions, just in case?'

'Sure. I was going to do that. Are you all right there?'

He gave a strangled laugh. 'I'm fine, but I'm being trampled by my daughter and I'm not convinced it's doing anything for my fertility.'

'Oh, dear. Well, have fun,' she said, trying not to laugh, and she went back to Brie to report her findings and break the news that she was going to be admitted.

By the time she got home it was after six, and as she walked in she could hear the children splashing in the bath, so she kicked off her shoes, ran upstairs and changed into jeans and a comfy T-shirt and went in to join the fun.

'Em, Em, I got bubbles!' Matilda squealed, and Zach slapped his hands down on the water in excitement and drenched Jake. Not that it mattered. Judging by the look of the floor it wasn't the first time.

He swiped the water off his face and gave her a searching look. 'So how did it go?'

'Fine. I want to talk to you about Brie, but that can keep. How've you been?'

'We've had a good day, haven't we, kids? Tilly, why don't you tell Em what you did today?'

'We saw baby ducks,' she said, bouncing in the water and threatening to slosh it over the side of the bath and capsize Zach. 'And I got bubbles!' She scooped some up and dumped them on Zach's head, and she'd hardly opened her mouth before Jake chipped in.

'Don't worry, they won't hurt his eyes. Right, time to get out now.'

'No!'

'Yes, if you want a bedtime story.'

'No! I not getting out!'

'Oh, yes, you are,' he said with a laugh, and scooped her out, kicking and giggling, while Emily rescued Zach from the tidal wave of bubbles, a long-forgotten warm sensation curling round her heart...

CHAPTER FIVE

HE TUCKED MATILDA up in bed and read her a story, then another one, then sang 'Twinkle, Twinkle, Little Star' three whole times before he was allowed to leave her. Not that it was anything unusual, far from it, but because they were putting the children to bed simultaneously his attention wasn't divided, and she took full advantage of that.

'Again.'

'No, that's enough now. Come on, snuggle down with Teddy and go to sleep.'

'I not tired,' she lied, yawning, and he kissed her cheek and tucked her duvet round her and her teddy as her eyes drifted shut.

She was asleep before he reached the door, and when he came out of her room Emily was still busy with Zach, so he went down to the kitchen and finished off cooking their meal while she settled him for the night.

He could hear her singing softly overhead, and the gentle, homely sound brought a lump to his throat.

Somehow, out of the chaos of Pete's untimely death and Jo's defection, they'd come together and created a little makeshift family, and against all the odds, it seemed to be working.

Far from hating Zach and being jealous, it seemed as if Matilda was enjoying the baby's company. Jake was, too. Zach was a sweet baby, full of sunny smiles and incredibly easygoing, and for the first time in years he felt truly happy.

Happy for himself, happy for Matilda and happy for Emily and Zach, too. Sure, he didn't have everything he wanted, but he'd settle for this any day. Now all he had to do was make sure it lasted.

The floor creaked overhead, and when he heard Emily's soft tread on the stairs he dished up and took the plates over to the table.

'All settled?'

'Yes, he went down like a lamb. I thought he'd be really clingy, but he wasn't. How did you get on today?'

'Great. Tilly seems to love having him around and they were both as good as gold. It's probably a one-off, mind you, but I'll take it for now,' he added with a grin.

She smiled back at him. 'Well, we'll see how I get on tomorrow. I'm not holding my breath,' she said, then pulled out a chair and pointed to the plate in front of it. 'Is this mine?'

'Whatever, they're both the same.' He put two glasses of water down on the table and sat down opposite her. 'So, what about your day? And most specifically, how was Brie?'

'OK. I went up to the ward to check on her before I left, and she seemed all right. Resigned, I think, but happy that I was taking it seriously.'

'Yes, I am, too. I've been worrying about her. Did she tell you she'd had shingles a few weeks ago?'

'Yes, and I saw it in the notes. It must have been the icing on the cake for her.'

'Absolutely, but she had an antiviral early on from her GP so it wasn't too bad, I don't think, and it shouldn't affect her pregnancy, it just made the situation even more miserable for her. It could well have been brought on by stress. She's found this very hard to deal with, and she's been terrified she's going to lose the baby.'

'Well, I don't think she's about to do that imminently. Her cervix is still nicely closed and I only felt one contraction and it wasn't anything to worry about, so they might just be Braxton–Hicks', but with the raised foetal fibronectin I think her chances of going to term are slim to none.'

'Did you tell her that?'

'Not in so many words, I thought I'd leave that to you. I explained that the nifedipine was to calm her contractions and could be quite effective, and we were giving her steroids to mature the baby's lungs as a precaution, but I didn't want to worry her unduly and she didn't seem surprised. I told her you'd be in tomorrow and would come and see her first thing and talk it through.'

'Yes, I will, she's top of my list. Did she mind seeing you instead of me?'

Emily shrugged. 'I'm not sure. I explained about the job share and told her she could see you at your Wednesday antenatal clinic in future if she'd prefer, but she didn't say any more about it. It may not be relevant anyway if we can't stall her contractions. You might want to repeat the fFN test and see if the level's gone up overnight.'

She ate a forkful of food and made an appreciative noise. 'Oh, wow, this is really tasty. How did you make it?'

He grinned. 'Well, I could lie, but actually it's a supermarket dine in for a tenner job because I thought the day might be complicated enough without cooking from scratch. And yes, I set the timer,' he added, his grin turning into a wry smile.

She bit her lip, but laughter was bubbling in her clear blue eyes and there was nothing she could do to hide it.

'So is there a pud?' she asked, finally regaining control of her mouth.

'Uh-huh. And wine, if you want it.'

'No. Not on a school night,' she said.

'It's not a school night for you, you're not at work tomorrow. I am.'

'But that's not fair, and I don't want to drink alone.'

He shrugged. 'Suit yourself. It'll keep. So, was it a good day, all in all?'

She nodded and put her fork down for a moment. 'Great day. I saw Liv and met her cute little baby, and you know, she even remembered Zach's name.'

'She would. She's amazing—such a good midwife and we really didn't need to lose her, but I'm very pleased she and Nick got back together and they've got a baby now. She's so much happier, and so is Nick. They're a great couple and I think they've had quite a tough time, although they don't talk about it.'

'Maybe we could have them round for dinner,' she suggested, and he nodded.

'Yeah, we should. There are all sorts of people I ought to have for dinner, people who've been amazing to me since I started here. Ben and Daisy, especially. We should have the four of them together.'

'Really? You guys will just talk shop.'

'And you girls won't? Liv's a midwife and Daisy's an obstetrician, too, you know.'

'Is she? So why didn't Ben ask her to do the extra sessions they were looking for?'

He laughed. 'He did. She said no. They have four young children and I think she likes being a stay-at-home mum.'

'I can understand that, but I have to say I really enjoyed today, even though it was exhausting. Using my brain, interacting with adults, being in a professional environment—I didn't realise how much I'd missed it.'

He laughed again, a little wryly. 'I can't tell you how glad I am to hear you say that. I was worried something would go wrong and you'd hate it and want out.'

Her eyes widened in surprise. 'Why would I hate it?

He shrugged. 'I don't know. I just thought you might.'

'No. No, Jake, I love it. Relax. Actually, no, don't relax, not yet. Dish up the pud and let's take it through to the sitting room and slump in front of the TV and chill. My feet are killing me.'

She heard him moving around before six the next morning, and crept downstairs to get a cup of tea to start the day just as he emerged from the downstairs shower room, damp hair on end and his robe hanging open, giving her a perfect view of his naked body.

'Well, good morning. Trying to impress me?' she teased, and she wasn't sure but he might have coloured slightly as he snatched the sides together.

'Sorry. I wasn't expecting you to be up yet. Is everything OK?'

'Yes, of course it is,' she said, trying to drag her mind out of the gutter and wondering how red she'd gone. 'I'm just thirsty. I didn't get much time to drink yesterday and I woke up with a bit of a headache. Are you off shortly?'

'If that's OK. I want to check on Brie Owen before I do anything else.'

She nodded. 'Of course it is. I hope she's all right. Can you let me know?'

'Sure. Are you putting the kettle on? I could murder a coffee.'

'Was that an order?' she asked, and he gave a soft laugh and rumpled her hair on the way past.

'Take it however you like. I'll have it in the travel mug,' he said over his shoulder, leaving her in a disturbing waft of soap and man that she'd come to associate with him.

She heard the stairs creak as he went up, and shut her eyes, but the image was still there, tantalising her. He'd filled out since she'd found him handcuffed to the railings outside halls. Well, he would have done, of course he would, in twenty-odd years, but that unexpected glimpse of his fit, toned and *very* masculine adult body had caught her with her guard right down and she was shocked by her response.

It was almost visceral, a clench of need in her gut, a longing to reach out and touch—and that was never going to happen! Not now, at least, with so much at stake, and she'd had her chance and lost it years ago after Kat's wedding when they'd ended up in a clinch in his hotel room and backed away from the precipice in the nick of time.

It was just after she'd started dating Pete and he'd sent her a text that had slammed the brakes on both her and Jake, and then a year later Pete had been diagnosed with cancer and she'd ended up marrying him because she couldn't bring herself to leave him. Not then, with the odds stacked against him when he'd needed her support. But that didn't make her blind...

She pressed her hands to her scalding cheeks for a moment, downed a glass of water to rehydrate her clearly addled brain and gave herself a stern lecture while she put the kettle on, found the ground coffee and warmed the cafetière.

People joked all the time about sex-crazed widows, and there was no way—*no way*—she was turning into one! This was *Jake*, for heaven's sake! Her friend. Not her lover. Not her boyfriend. And certainly not someone for a casual one-nighter.

Although they'd almost gone there that once, and the memory of the awkwardness that had followed when they'd come to their senses and pulled away from the brink had never left her, although it had long been buried.

Until now...

She heard the stairs creak again, and pressed down the plunger and slid the pot towards him as he came into the room.

'Here, your coffee.'

'Aren't you having any?'

She shook her head, but she couldn't quite meet his eyes, and she realised he wasn't looking at her, either. 'I'll go back up in case Zach cries and wakes Matilda. Don't forget to ring me when you've seen Brie.'

'OK. Thanks for making the coffee.'

'You're welcome. Have a good day.'

She tiptoed up the stairs, listened for the sound of the front door closing and watched him from his bedroom window as he walked briskly down the road towards the hospital, travel mug in hand.

He turned the corner and went out of sight, and she sat down on the edge of his bed, her fingers knotting in a handful of rumpled bedding. *What was she doing?* With a stifled scream of frustration, she fell sideways onto the mattress and buried her face in his duvet.

Mistake. She could smell the scent of him on the sheets, warm and familiar and strangely exciting, could picture that glorious nakedness stretched out against the stark white linen, a beautiful specimen of masculinity in its prime—

She jack-knifed to her feet. This was crazy. What on

earth had happened to her? They'd been friends for years, and now all of a sudden this uncontrollable urge to sniff his sheets?

She stripped the bed, took the bedding downstairs and put it in the washing machine before she could be any more ridiculous. Then she topped up the cafetière, poured herself a coffee and sat with it cradled in her hands while she tried to talk sense into herself.

They had to keep this platonic. So much was riding on it—their mutual careers, if nothing else! They had to be able to work together, both at home and in the hospital, and there was no way anything could be allowed to derail that.

And the children—they had to make this work for the children, especially Matilda. Poor little girl, losing her mother so abruptly. The last thing she needed—any of them needed—was this fragile status quo disrupted for anything as trivial as primitive, adolescent lust.

It wasn't fair on any of them, and she'd embarrassed herself enough fifteen years ago. She wasn't doing it again.

No way.

She was standing at the kitchen sink with her back to him when he came down from changing out of his work clothes.

'You made my bed.'

He couldn't read her face but he thought she stiffened a little.

'I thought it was time I did something useful around the house, and your room was such a mess, so I did your washing.'

He frowned. It wasn't that much of a mess, and she'd

been there for three weeks now and she'd never felt the urge to do it before.

And anyway, he'd only changed the sheets a few days ago. Still, he wasn't going to argue with her. Instead he thanked her and picked up a tea towel and dried the saucepan she'd been washing up.

'You don't have to do that,' she protested without looking at him.

'It's not going to kill me,' he said calmly. 'So how was your day? I'm sorry I was so late back.'

'That's all right. We had a good day. We went for a walk along the prom as the tide was going out, and they puggled about in the damp sand and got messy and had fun, and then I cleaned them up and we walked home and made rock buns.'

'Did you save me one?'

'Matilda did. It's in that cake tin there.' She pointed with a sudsy finger, and he dried the last things she'd washed up and opened the tin.

'Yup, that looks like one of hers.'

'What, squashed and overworked?'

He chuckled. 'That would be the one. So where are the ones you made? They might be safer.'

She tipped out the water, dried her hands and reached for another tin. 'Here—but don't spoil your appetite. I've cooked us a curry.'

'Nothing will spoil my appetite. I'm starving. I haven't stopped all day.'

'How's Brie?' she asked, finally turning to look at him. 'I got your text earlier. Has anything changed?'

He shook his head, his mouth full of Matilda's rock bun—eaten out of duty. He was looking forward to one of Em's.

'No, she's fine. She did have an infection so I've kept

her in. She on clindamycin now and she's still having the nifedipine to suppress the contractions, and we can review her tomorrow, but at least she's finished the course of steroids and there's been no change in the fFN level. Shall I put some rice on?'

'No, it's done, it's all ready. I did it while you were changing. Let's eat. I'm starving, too. You can have the rock buns later.'

By some sort of tacit agreement, they got through the evening without any of their usual teasing and banter, and she wasn't sure if she was imagining it, but he didn't seem as inclined to hug or touch her.

That was unlike him. He was given to spontaneous gestures of affection, always had been, and he'd hugged her so often in the past few weeks, but tonight it was as if he knew they needed to keep their distance.

Or so she thought, but then, when they were going up to bed, he paused on the landing and dropped a kiss on her cheek.

'Sleep tight,' he murmured, his breath teasing her hair, and then went into his own room and shut the door maybe a little more firmly than usual.

Then again, she might have imagined it, because the following morning he seemed to be back to normal, and the status quo was thankfully restored.

He went in before her to do the labour ward round, and she joined him on the prenatal ward after she'd dropped the children at nursery.

Typically, because the previous two days had gone so well and they'd started to take it for granted, Zach was clingy and had to be prised off her, and Matilda threw herself down on the floor and screamed.

'Just go, they'll be fine,' Caitlin said firmly, so she handed them over and fled, tears welling in her eyes.

She knew Caitlin was right, but Zach's little face—

When she reached the ward, Jake took one look at her and frowned. 'Em? Are you OK?'

She sniffed and shook her head. 'Not really. The kids didn't want to go to nursery. Tilly screamed and Zach wouldn't let go—'

'Hey, hey, come here.'

His arm curled around her, and he steered her into an office and shut the door. 'Come on. They're all right, you know that. They'll be fine.'

'I know, but I just felt so mean leaving them. They're so little, Jake, and Zach's just—'

'Zach's fine, and so's Tilly. They'll be all right, you'll see. Caitlin'll send you a text any minute now.'

Her phone pinged in her pocket, and she pulled it out and gave a slightly damp laugh. '"Both fine," she read. "M cried for thirty seconds and Z is having a cuddle and smiling." And don't say told you so.'

'Told you so,' he said, just for naughtiness, and with another hug, he left her to sort her face out and went back to the ward to wait for her.

After they'd done the prenatal ward round she went to do a busy gynae clinic and he was in Theatre with an elective list with a couple of emergencies tacked on the end, and when they met up again they discharged Brianna Owen because her contractions had subsided and she was stable.

They went their separate ways again, arranging to meet up for the labour ward round after his antenatal clinic, at the end of his day. Or at least, what was supposed to be the end of his day, because she was supposed to be on call that night and then working the following day, but he'd decided to take the night for her.

'It's easier than trying to convince Zach to have a bottle if he wakes at three in the morning and wants his mummy.'

'He doesn't often do that.'

'Often enough,' he said, and she felt guilty that he'd been disturbed.

'I'm sorry.'

'No, don't be, he's just a baby and he'll grow out of it, but he was a bit sad this morning when you dropped him off and he needs his mummy to put him to bed. And don't apologise for him, he's a lovely little chap. He's normally so sunny.'

'I know, but he can be a bit of a nightmare in the night.'

'Nobody's perfect,' he said, and then added with a grin, 'Well, not many of us, anyway.'

She gave him a look, and he patted her cheek and walked off chuckling, and she couldn't help but laugh.

'You look happy. Is it going well?'

'Oh, hello, Ben. Yes, it is, touch wood. So far nobody's howled with protest at having me instead of Jake, anyway.'

'How are the kids, talking of howling with protest?'

She laughed. 'How did you guess? They chose this morning to have a paddy about nursery, but apart from that it seems to be going OK.'

'Great. While I've got you here, Daisy's been on at me to invite you both round for a meal. Do you want to have a chat with Jake and work out when would suit you?'

'We were only talking last night about having you two and Nick and Liv. That might be easier, if you have a regular babysitter you trust, because Zach might get a bit funny with a stranger, and I don't think Jake would want to leave Tilly so soon with someone she doesn't know. Why don't you all come round to ours?'

Ours? Not Jake's? Really?

'Sounds good. I tell you what, talk to the others, see if you can come up with a date and we'll go from there.'

'Great. Right, I'd better go, I've got a few new admissions to check and we have to do another ward round before I leave. But I'll talk to him later and get back to you.'

It was much, much later by the time he came home, because there'd been three emergency admissions and he'd been in Theatre or doing post-op checks until eleven.

She was dozing on the sofa when he came in, and he flopped down beside her and stuck his feet up on the coffee table.

'How's tricks?' he asked tiredly.

'Fine. They both went down OK, they seemed fine at nursery and there wasn't a tear in sight. Have you eaten? I saved you supper but it'll need to go in the microwave.'

He shook his head. 'No, I haven't but I'm too tired to bother. Don't worry about it.'

'I'm not worried. Stay there, I'll get it. I've been asleep for hours.'

He turned his head and watched her go as she wandered into the kitchen in those altogether too enticing pyjamas, with the predictable result. He obviously wasn't tired enough, he thought disgustedly, and dragged himself to his feet and followed her.

'I can do that—'

'It's done. Shut up and sit down, you're fine. Drink?'

'Oh—water, please. I feel as dry as a desert and I just know my phone's going to ring.'

He drained the glass, dug his fork into the pasta dish

she'd reheated for him and rolled his head on his shoulders as he chewed.

'Neck ache?'

'Nah, I've just been crunched up in Theatre trying to stem a bleed. I'll be fine.'

He could feel her eyes on him. 'Maybe we should share the nights? Because it's not like either of us can lie in the following day, not with the children.'

'I'll be fine. There's a question mark over one of the women in the labour ward, but the midwife in charge of her is red-hot, so I'm hoping I won't have to go back in, but I've told her to ring me if there's a problem.'

He scraped the plate clean, pushed it away and rolled his shoulders, wincing.

'Come here,' she said, getting up and walking round behind him. He felt the warmth of her abdomen behind his shoulders, the soft press of her breasts against the top of his head—and the firm dig of her thumbs in his shoulder muscles.

'Ow—ow! Ah—you're evil. Oh, that's good. Oh, yes, just there. Ouch—'

'A long illness, bravely borne,' she murmured sarcastically, but then she took hold of his head, rested it back against her and massaged the back of his neck with firm, upward strokes, tunnelling her fingers through his hair and working on his scalp muscles.

'Oh, that is so good,' he groaned. 'I'd forgotten about your massage skills.'

'Probably traumatic amnesia. Better?'

'Much better. Thank you.'

'Don't thank me, just go to bed while you can.'

'No point. I know she'll ring.'

'And if she doesn't? Don't be daft, Jake. Go to bed and grab some shut-eye while you have the chance.'

'Yeah, you're probably right. Only one problem.'

'It's upstairs?'

'Exactly.' He got to his feet, pulled her into his arms and hugged her wearily, his head propped against hers. 'What's it like to be so clever?' he mumbled in her ear.

'I thought you were the perfect one?'

He gave a grunt of laughter and stepped away from her while he still could. 'I wish. Right. Bed. And what do you bet me—?'

Rolling his eyes, he pulled his ringing phone out of his pocket. 'Hi, Kath. Do you want me to come in?'

'No. She got up and walked round, and the baby shifted and we have a lovely healthy little boy, so unless anyone else needs you, you can go to bed.'

'Oh, I love you. Thanks, Kath. I'll see you later.'

He slid the phone back into his pocket, grinned at Em and punched the air. 'I'm off the hook. I get to go to bed. Yay!'

'Right, well do it, then, before someone else gets in on the act.'

'I will. I'll just clean my teeth and I'll be up. Thanks for the neck massage—and the supper. It was really tasty.'

'Any time. I'll see you in the morning.'

She leant in and dropped a kiss on his cheek and he reeled her in for a hug, resting his head against hers again as he had before, taking a moment to enjoy the feel of her body against his, too weak-willed to push her away. He was exhausted, but letting go of her meant losing all that warmth and softness, and he didn't want to do that—

'Jake, you're falling asleep on your feet.'

'Mmm.'

She eased out of his arms and tilted her head to kiss his cheek, just as he turned towards her. Their lips collided, and with a muffled groan he lifted one hand and cradled her head as his mouth found hers again.

Her lips parted under his, opening to give him access to all that warmth and sweetness, his tongue seeking hers out and finding it—

She pulled away a fraction and he followed her. 'Em—'

'Jake, no. Stop. We can't do this.'

'Why?'

'Because it's a bad idea, you know that. Come on, you need to go to bed. You've been up since the crack of dawn and you're drunk with exhaustion.'

Was he? Or was he drunk with the sweetness of her mouth, the softness of her body, the promise of all that could follow?

He dropped his arms and stepped back. 'You're right. I'm sorry. I don't know what I'm doing. Go to bed, Em. I'll be up in a minute.'

She headed for the stairs and he watched her go, her scent lingering in the air behind her. It would be so good to follow her up, to crawl into bed behind her and pull her back into his arms and fall asleep with her hair in his face and her body pressed against his, warm and soft and yielding—

'Get a grip,' he growled under his breath, and headed for the shower room and then his own bed. Not that there was any way he'd sleep, with her scent in his nostrils and the feel of her still imprinted on his body...

He crawled onto the mattress, hauled the duvet up over himself and was asleep in seconds.

CHAPTER SIX

HE DIDN'T GET any more calls that night, and she managed to get out of the house without seeing him. She left him a note on the kettle telling him to ring her if there was anything he wanted her to follow up on, and he called shortly after she arrived at work.

'Em, hi. Everything OK?'

'Yes, as far as I know. I'm just heading up to the ward. I'll let you know if I'm worried about anything.'

'OK.' There was a pregnant pause, then a sigh. 'Look, Em, I'm sorry about last night. I wasn't really thinking.'

No, neither was she, but she'd done nothing but think ever since—about him, about the feel of his mouth on hers and his body pressed against her, about what they might have been doing, about why it was a bad idea when at the time it had felt like such a *good* one...

'Jake, you're fine, forget it,' she said softly. 'I haven't given it a minute's thought.' More like hours, but he didn't need to know that and it was best to forget it.

'Sure?'

'Sure. Right, I'm on the ward now. I'll ring you if I need to.'

'OK. Take care. I'll talk to you later.'

She slid the phone back into her pocket, pasted a smile on her face and walked into the ward.

* * *

After she'd followed up on his emergency admissions she spent the rest of the day at work settling more into her routine and getting to know the staff better.

She rang him a couple of times to confirm a treatment protocol for a patient with epilepsy in the high-risk prenatal ward, but they kept it professional and by the time she'd finished writing up the notes she'd managed to convince herself that it was just a blip and they'd be fine about it.

Luckily the day's work was mostly fairly standard—a forceps delivery, a C-section for a woman too exhausted to continue and a query appendix that turned out to be a ruptured ectopic sent up from the ED.

She discharged three post-op gynae patients and a C-section, did a stack of admin in between ward rounds and went home to find Jake lying on the sitting room floor covered in cushions with Matilda and Zach bouncing on him, although Zach was getting quite a lot of help from Jake.

She stood in the doorway and laughed at him, and he turned his head, a wry smile on his face.

'Hurrah, it's the cavalry,' he said, ending on an '*oof*' as Matilda landed on him a bit more firmly.

She stifled a chuckle.

'Would you like rescuing?'

'I'd love rescuing. They're monsters, aren't you, kids? Little horrors!'

'I not a little horror! I a fairy princess!' Tilly said indignantly, and tried to straighten her drooping rainbow-coloured wings. They were upside down and bent out of shape, but Tilly didn't seem to care, and Emily whipped out her phone and took a photo.

'That's one for the family album,' she said with a

laugh, and then met Jake's eyes startled amber eyes as she realised what she'd said.

'Sorry—I didn't mean that the way it sounded—'

'It's fine,' he said softly, his eyes warming, his gaze tender. 'And actually, I thought it sounded rather good.'

It did. Very good. Rather like the kiss. *Too good to be true?*

Emily looked as stunned as he'd felt, and then a little awkward as she lapsed into silence, her eyes sliding away from his as if she couldn't look at him any longer. A slip of the tongue, or a deeper, hidden meaning?

He didn't know, but what with that and the kiss last night, he was suddenly finding it really hard to breathe.

'Can you take the baby?'

She lifted Zach off his chest and he rolled to the side, dumping Matilda in a pile of cushions and fairy wings as he unravelled himself and stood up.

'So, how was your day?' he asked, trying to keep his voice normal and failing miserably.

Her laugh sounded a bit off-kilter, too. 'Less fun than yours, I'd say. Certainly no fairy wings. Where on earth did you find them?'

'Oh, a shop in town. She's been nagging me for weeks. I finally did something about it. Right, little ones, time to get ready for bed, I think,' he added, clutching at normality.

'Want Em.'

He blinked at Matilda. 'Darling, she's only just got back from work and she wants to put Zach to bed.'

'You put Zach. Want Em.'

'Why don't I put them both to bed?' Emily suggested, and he shrugged and gave in.

'OK, if you're sure. I'll start cooking our supper.'

'What, rip the film off the top of a ready meal and bung it in the oven?' she teased, but he didn't rise to it because it was so often true and anyway, he didn't feel like banter. Not now, not after that...

'No, sorry, you're going to have to put with my own concoction,' he said, without elaborating, and went into the kitchen, leaving her to it.

He'd bought the ingredients for a stir-fry, and he spent the next half-hour chopping and shredding and slicing, all the time listening with one ear for the sound of her voice reading a story, singing a lullaby, crooning softly to the baby as he fell asleep in the bedroom overhead.

One for the family album?

In his dreams...

He left early for work the next day, and once the children were up and dressed and breakfasted, she asked Matilda what she wanted to do.

'Ducks,' she said promptly. 'And playground.'

'OK.' It seemed like a sound enough plan, and although the forecast wasn't great it was shaping up to be a lovely day, so they piled coats and wellies and a bucket and spade into the buggy just in case and headed off to the little park around the corner.

They fed the ducks a sprinkle of bird food—not bread, because that wasn't good for them or the pond—and then she spotted some new baby ducks that must only recently have hatched.

'Oh, look, Tilly—baby ducks! Shall we count them? One, two, three—'

'Five, 'leven, two.'

OK, so Tilly couldn't count yet, but she had fun trying and they finally established that there were five fluffy brown ducklings paddling around with their mother.

Zach squealed and flapped with excitement, and Matilda crouched down with her bottom stuck out and her hands on her knees, fairy wings askew, watching them intently while Emily looked on with a smile.

She heard the wheels of a buggy approaching, then it stopped right beside her. 'Emily.'

It was a statement, not a question, and she turned to look at the pretty dark-haired woman who'd spoken her name. She had a baby boy a little younger than Zach asleep in a buggy, and she was smiling and holding out her hand.

'I'm Daisy Walker—Ben's wife.'

She took the outstretched hand. 'Hi—how...?'

'The double buggy? I've walked a few hundred miles behind it, I'd know it anywhere! And anyway, I know Matilda. It's lovely to meet you at last. I've heard lots about you, all good before you ask!'

She laughed. 'Well, that's a relief, since I seem to be holding Jake's career in my hands as well as my own.'

'Oh, gosh, don't worry about that. Ben thinks you're brilliant and so do I, because he kept putting pressure on me to go back to work again and I really don't want to! I'm having way too much fun with Harry. Hello, Tilly. I love your fairy wings.'

'Daddy buyed them,' she said, and turned straight back to the ducks.

'Did he? Good for Daddy.' She bent over and looked into the buggy. 'So this must be Zach. What a pretty baby. He's got gorgeous eyes.'

'They're his father's,' she said quietly. 'Every time he looks at me, I see Pete. It can be a little disconcerting.'

'But lovely,' Daisy murmured, her smile understanding.

'Yes. Yes, it is lovely. He was very easygoing and

good-natured, and Zach's the same, which is just as well since Jake has to look after him for at least two days a week,' she added with a wry grin, which Daisy returned.

'Yes, it does help. Ben's daughter Florence from his first marriage spends quite a lot of time with us, and she's a darling, but he's never forgotten what it's like to be a single parent or how hard it can be on the child, and I think that's one of the reasons he was so keen to help you and Jake with the job share. So, what are you doing this morning?' she added with a smile. 'Do you have plans?'

She laughed. 'Only heading for the playground if I can drag Tilly away from the ducklings.'

'Well, good luck with that! Do you fancy coming back to mine for coffee? It would be lovely to have a bit more of a chat and get to know you. We only live round the corner from you and Liv's coming over at ten-thirty with Isobel. I gather she delivered Zach.'

'Yes, she did, and she was brilliant. I bumped into her briefly the other day but I'd love to see her again.'

'So—coffee?'

Emily felt the inexplicable urge to cry. Daisy holding out the hand of friendship to her made her realise how much she'd missed her old friends and colleagues, and she'd hardly seen them since she'd been on maternity leave.

Time to make new friends?

'That would be really lovely. Thank you.'

Ben and Daisy lived in a big Victorian house similar to Jake's, but filled with the evidence of a busy family. A huge American fridge-freezer plastered in pictures held up by fridge magnets, multi-frame photos of them all on the walls, a small dropped sock lying on the stairs, probably a refugee from the washing pile—it was warm, homely and very welcoming, and she loved it.

Loved spending time with Daisy and Liv, too, while Tilly entertained herself with Henrietta's dressing up box and the babies crawled or lay kicking on the floor between them.

Then Daisy broached the subject of dinner. 'I'm glad I've got the two of you together, because we said we'd like to have you and Jake over for dinner, and then I gather from Ben that you'd suggested we should all come to you instead, which seems a bit unfair.'

'It's not unfair, we'd been talking about it the night before, and we'd love to have you all. It's tricky with the on-call rota and babysitting, I know, but it would be great if you could manage it.'

'I'm sure we can, but it was our idea, too, so why don't you do the main course, and we'll bring the starter and the dessert and we'll do it that way. Agreed?'

'I'll do the dessert and bring a cheese board,' Liv offered. 'Any preferences?'

'Chocolate,' she and Daisy said together, and then laughed.

They ended up staying for an impromptu lunch of hummus and vegetable sticks followed by another slice of Daisy's apple cake, and then Liv had to go for a health visitor's appointment and Emily left straight afterwards.

'Thank you so much for inviting me this morning,' she said, giving Daisy a quick hug. 'It's been lovely getting to know you both, and I'm really looking forward to our dinner. I don't know anybody in Yoxburgh apart from Jake and the few people I've met at work, and I hadn't realised how lonely I was.'

Daisy frowned. 'Well, we can't have that. There are lots of us with young families around here, and we're always happy to get together. Don't get me wrong, small people are lovely, but it's good to have an intelligent conversation with an adult,' she said with a laugh. 'Leave it with me. A group of us get together on Tuesdays with our little ones. Is that a work day for you?'

'No—no, it isn't, but won't they mind if I muscle in?'

'Absolutely not. I'll give them a call, and in the meantime I'm always around, so don't be lonely. There's no need.'

'Thank you.'

She hugged her again, then walked briskly home, conscious of the huge pile of Jake's ironing she'd been ignoring. She'd done most of it, but he must be running out of shirts by now. If the children had a nap…

'I had an interesting case today,' he told her that evening as they sat down to eat. 'Her first labour went wrong and she ended up with an emergency section, so she's going for an elective section and because it was so traumatic for all of them she wants this one to be as natural as possible, so she wants a skin-to-skin Caesarean. I've scheduled her for next Wednesday because I thought you might like to be in on it.'

Her eyes lit up. 'I'd love to! It's fascinated me for ages but I've never seen it done. Have you done many?'

'Quite a few. I'd do them all like that if I could, but the parents have to be up for it and it has to be a low-risk case with no clinical reasons for not doing it, so it's not that common, which is a shame because the outcome's better for everyone. The babies seem so much calmer, and so are the parents, and it's almost like a normal birth. Very gentle, very calm, the parents can watch the baby being eased slowly out, they're the first people to see the sex of the baby, and then we use delayed cord clamping just like in a vaginal delivery, and lift the baby up onto the mother's chest straight away, and many of the babies start feeding immediately—I'm a huge fan of it, and the parents really appreciate it, too, especially if they've had a traumatic delivery in the past.'

'Gosh, I can't wait to see it. They didn't do it at my last hospital, they thought it was too risky.'

'I know, but you've met Ben. He's all about innovation and pushing the boundaries, and he jumped on this when they rolled out the trials. And talking of Ben, I gather you and the kids spent the day with Daisy.'

'Yes, we did,' she said, a smile lighting up her face. 'It was great. I was beginning to feel a bit isolated, but Daisy wasn't having any of that and she made me feel so welcome.'

'I told you she was nice, and I'm really glad you got on. I've been worried about you not having any friends round here.'

'Well, you don't need to, I get the feeling Daisy's going to take me firmly under her wing and introduce me to all her friends, so I'm fine. Oh, and we talked about dinner. We just need you guys to sort out the date.'

He nodded. 'OK. I'll get on to Ben and Nick and we'll find a time that works. Are you all done, or do you want more?'

'No, I'm stuffed, I had too much cake at Daisy's as it is. I'll be like a house.'

Not a chance, he thought. She'd been too thin in the aftermath of Pete's death, and it was only now that she looked back to normal. Sure, she had curves, but they were healthy curves—and the less he thought about them, the better, he thought, and put their plates into the dishwasher.

* * *

The following morning Emily announced out of the blue that she was going to take Zach to see Pete's parents for the weekend, which left him alone with Matilda.

It was only what they'd been used when Jo was still around, but although they did everything they'd normally have done, there was something missing, and he felt curiously lost, as if he'd been cut in half.

Which was ridiculous, and he told himself that countless times as the hours slowly ticked away until her return.

And then when she did come back, Tilly ran to greet her with a huge hug and a kiss, and Zach reached out to him, arms flapping in excitement.

'Da-da,' he said, and he felt the air leave his lungs in a great whoosh.

His eyes flew to Em's, and she froze, stopped in her tracks by Zach's reaction. And then he said it again, more urgently, leaning over and reaching out to him, and Jake lifted the baby into his arms and cuddled him close, his eyes filling.

'Em, I'm sorry,' he breathed, but she shook her head and smiled, her own eyes filling, too.

'It's his first word,' she said, and then turned away, unable to speak any more. He reached out and wrapped his spare arm around her, drawing her into the hug, and felt Matilda wriggle in between their legs and hug him, too.

Another one for the family album? Except there was no one to take the photograph, but they didn't need one, the memory would be etched on his heart for ever.

He gave Em a little squeeze, let her go and kissed Zach's head. 'Hello, little guy. Have you had a good weekend with Granny and Grandpa?'

'Da-da,' he said again, and grabbed Jake's cheek.

'Ouch. Gently.' He prised the chubby little fingers carefully off his face and searched Emily's eyes. 'Are you OK? Has something happened? You look a bit shaken.'

She gave a fractured little laugh. 'I am a bit. We passed an accident on the A14 on the other carriageway. There were lots of emergency vehicles there, it looked quite nasty. It's good to be safely back.' Her eyes found his again, the blue turning to storm clouds. 'Jake, we need to talk later.'

He frowned slightly. 'OK,' he agreed. 'Have you eaten, or does Zach need supper? I was just about to feed Tilly and there's enough for two.'

'That would be lovely. Could you do it for me? Would you mind? I need to put some washing on for tomorrow.'

'Sure.'

What on earth was going on?

He had no idea, but he wanted to find out, and he wasn't going to wait any longer than he had to.

He'd made a pie with the leftover chicken from the roast he'd had with Matilda, and after the children were in bed he'd dished up and put it in front of her, but she wasn't hungry, the image of the car accident too vivid in her mind.

And the way Zach had reached for him, calling him Dada...

She put her knife and fork down and met Jake's searching eyes.

'What's up?' he asked softly.

'I've been thinking about the children. Spending time with Pete's parents, seeing the accident—Jake, dreadful things happen, and I'm worried about the babies. What if something happens to one of us? Jo's all but given Matilda to you, you have no idea where she is, she hasn't been in contact once—who could look after Tilly if you died? And Zach—if anything happened to me, I know Pete's parents would have him in a heartbeat, but they're getting older, his mother's got arthritis in her knees, his father's had a triple bypass, and by the time we left they were exhausted. They're nearly seventy, and there's a very good chance they won't be around by the time he's in his teens, or at least not in any position to care for him. What then?'

He nodded slowly. 'I know. Stuff happens, and it's easy to say it happens to someone else, but it doesn't always. One of our team had to leave because his wife had got cancer and they needed to be near family, but they're lucky to have them. My family couldn't help. My parents were old when they had me, and they don't know Tilly because they've cut themselves off from me, and my brother's in America. It didn't matter until now, but as you say, Jo's dropped off the face of the earth and I have no idea how to contact her. My texts haven't been delivered, my emails have bounced—it's like she never existed and I'm not sure we'll ever see her again, so I have to think about the unthinkable.'

'And?'

He shrugged. 'I have no idea. I've got friends, but the only person I'd really want to look after her is you, and that's too much to ask.'

She could feel her smile was crooked, but there was nothing she could do about it. 'Not if I asked the same thing of you.'

Her words hung in the air between them, and after an age he sucked in a breath and looked away.

'You'd trust me to look after Zach?'

'Of course I'd trust you! I'm trusting you now, aren't I? You're doing it already, and I am for you, but we're both around. What if one of us wasn't? Zach was miserable all weekend.'

He nodded slowly. 'So was Tils. It was like something was missing. So what do we do?'

She shrugged a little helplessly. 'I don't know. I think we need to talk to a solicitor, because I think it needs to be something formal and witnessed—I don't know. Legal guardianship? How does that work? And what about Jo? Could you make me Matilda's legal guardian while she's still alive? And what about our properties? I haven't looked at my will since Pete died, and I need a new one. Things are very different now.'

'I know. I know nothing about it, but I agree, we need to find out, and we need to put something in writing that will give the children protection for the future. And of *course* I'd have Zach, without a second thought. I love him, Em. He's part of the family, and so are you. You were right when you took that photo. It *is* one for the family album—and I know it's a little unconventional and very early days, but I feel like we *are* a family, and I wouldn't want it any other way.'

She felt her eyes fill, and put her hand over her mouth. 'Oh, Jake—neither would I.'

'Good. So let's eat this before it's stone cold, and then we can draw up some kind of a plan, and tomorrow I'll make an appointment to see a solicitor as soon as we can fit it in, because you're absolutely right, we need to do this, and the sooner the better.'

Monday was busy—very busy on the labour ward, and with a full antenatal clinic in the afternoon.

Brie Owen came back for a routine check-up, and everything was stable, to Emily's relief. She was now over thirty weeks, a critical marker, and Emily sent Jake a text to tell him Brie was doing well because she knew he'd be thinking about it.

A message pinged back straight away, to thank her for the update and telling her he'd made an appointment to see a solicitor on Friday at four.

It would be tight for him to finish by then, she knew, but maybe he'd come to some arrangement with one of the others to cover them. She'd need to book the children into nursery, as well. She'd have to find time to do that.

She did a final round in the labour and high-risk ante-natal wards, then went home, turning the key in the door and walking in just as Jake was ushering the children out of the bathroom and towards bed.

'Emmy,' Matilda shrieked, and she ran up the stairs and scooped her up and hugged her. Zach was flapping in Jake's arms, and she took him, too, and followed Jake along the landing with the children clinging to her like baby monkeys.

'What a lovely welcome,' she said with a huge smile, and he rolled his eyes.

'Tilly's talked about you non-stop. I don't know why I bother,' he muttered, but his eyes were laughing and his warmth and good humour wrapped around her like a blanket.

'Here, let me take her off you before you drop her,' he said as Tilly wriggled, but Zach lunged at him with a shriek of 'Da-da!' and he caught him just in time.

'What about Mama?' Emily said, rolling her own eyes. 'Talking of not knowing why we bother...'

He gave a soft snort and took Matilda from her, dropping a kiss on Zach's head before handing him back, his affection for the little boy so evident it made her well up again.

'Right, little man. Bedtime,' she said firmly, and took

him into her room and shut the door before she made an idiot of herself and cried in front of Jake.

They had another of the 'dine in for ten pounds' meals for supper, because Jake had taken the children to a nearby farm park for the day and he'd been too busy to think about food, and afterwards she filled him in on her day so he was up to date before he went to work in the morning.

He disappeared into his study then, and she curled up on the sofa with the book she'd been trying to read for months.

He emerged a little after ten and plonked himself down on the sofa next to her. 'What are you reading?'

She handed him the book and he glanced at it and frowned. 'Blimey. *The Theory of Everything?* That's a bit impenetrable.'

She laughed. 'Tell me about it. Pete read it after we watched the film and said it was great, but I can't understand a word. I loved the film, but the book's utterly defeating me. I didn't realise our minds were so different.'

'No. There again, I'm not a physicist so I wouldn't hope to understand Stephen Hawking, but I loved the film, too.'

They talked about films then, the films they'd loved, the ones they'd hated, the ones that had made them cry, and then he yawned hugely, unravelled himself off the sofa and announced that he was going to bed.

'Sounds like a good idea. I'm having coffee with Daisy and her friends at ten tomorrow, and I've got a few things to do before then—like the rest of the ironing. I don't suppose you've done it?'

He snorted. 'In what spare minute? Don't worry, I'll do it tomorrow before I leave.'

She was already awake when she heard him stirring

at six, so she quietly followed him downstairs, took the iron out and had just finished the first shirt when he came into the utility room, hair still damp, dressed only in a pair of trousers, his bare and well-muscled torso tantalisingly close.

'Are you just showing off again, or did you want this?' she asked drily, holding out the freshly pressed garment and hoping he couldn't see her heart thudding in her chest through her pyjama top.

He snatched the shirt out of her nerveless fingers and thrust his arms into the sleeves. 'You're a saint! Have I told you how much I love you?' he asked, hugging her briefly against that broad and very solid chest. He smelt of soap and freshly laundered shirt and raw, animal male, and her heart went into overdrive.

'Don't mention it. The bill's in the post,' she said drily, her pulse slamming in her throat as she pushed him away with a strangled laugh.

When had she fallen in love with him?

Because she had, she realised in shock. Hook, line and sinker, and she had no idea what to do about it, so she did the safest thing.

She turned her back on him and picked up the next shirt before Jake could see what she was sure must be written in her eyes…

CHAPTER SEVEN

COFFEE WITH DAISY and the others was friendly, slightly chaotic and full of laughter.

And, when they realised she and Jake were not only job-sharing but house-sharing, a great deal of thinly veiled curiosity.

They were in the garden of the lovely clifftop home of Annie Shackleton and her paediatrician husband, Ed and their two sets of twins. Em had met him when Zach was born, and also again in the maternity unit over the neonates, and she could see him instantly in the boys. Kate Ryder was there, too, with her little daughter Isadora. Her husband Sam was an ED consultant, as was Connie Slater's husband James, and their two were milling about in the throng of little people.

It was Annie who made the first comment when Emily explained their domestic situation.

'Gosh, that's brave,' she said, and Emily shook her head.

'No, not at all,' she lied. 'We've known each other for so long we're like brother and sister, and it's working really well.'

'But don't you miss having your own home?'

That was Kate. Emily had met her husband Sam only

yesterday in the ED, and she was beginning to realise what a closely knit community she'd joined.

No secrets there, then. She gave a faint smile.

'Of course I do, but it's where my husband died, so in some ways it's nice to be able to leave that behind and move on.'

Kate coloured slightly. 'Oh, Emily, I'm so sorry, I had no idea. That was really thoughtless of me.'

'No, it wasn't. You weren't to know—and you're right, Kate, it was tough at first, but I've been looking after Matilda for weeks now, so I've had time to get used to it, and I've let the house now, anyway, so it's irrelevant.'

'You're so brave,' Annie said, coming in again. 'It must have taken so much courage to do what you've done and go into that job share. It's such a massive long-term commitment.'

'It is, but I was looking for a job share anyway, and sharing the childcare *and* the job with a very old friend makes it so much easier. At least I know I can trust him absolutely.'

'That makes sense to me,' Connie said. 'I married my best friend, who was also my first husband's best friend, and it was a bit awkward, at first. Neither of us wanted to rock the boat and it took us a while to work it out, but actually it was easier in the end just because we knew each other so well.'

Which struck a chord with Emily. *If only they could get to that point...*

'It would probably be easier for you if Jake wasn't quite so hot, though,' Kate said, chipping in again with a grin, and Emily hoped her cheeks didn't burn as much as she felt they had.

'Honestly, he's just a friend,' she lied, and she wasn't sure who she was trying to convince, them or herself, but they were all teasing Kate now about Sam and asking how she'd even noticed another man when she was married to the hospital hottie, and thankfully it drew the attention away from Emily.

'Anybody want more coffee?' Annie said, getting to her feet and bringing the conversation to a close, and to her relief they moved on to other topics and their attention was diverted away from Emily and Jake and the intricacies of their relationship.

'Ready?'

Emily nodded, buzzing with anticipation. 'I can't wait. I've wanted to see this for so long.'

They were dressed in scrubs, gloved and gowned and ready to go, and their patient, Lucy McGovern, was lying on the theatre bed as the anaesthetist checked the epidural, her husband beside her holding her hand.

'OK, we're good to go,' the anaesthetist said, and Jake shot Emily a grin and went over to them.

'Right, let's put you all out of your suspense, shall we? Are you both ready for this?'

'Definitely. I can't wait,' Lucy said.

'Sure? You can change your mind, it doesn't make any difference. It's only when we're ready to drop the drape—'

'I don't need a drape,' she said. 'I'm a vet, James is a farmer—we're not squeamish and we both know what's going to happen. We're just really excited and can't wait to meet the baby.'

'OK, well let's do this, then. Can we have masks, please?'

Someone put them on, and Jake turned to Emily. 'Want to start?'

She shook her head. 'No. I'll just watch, if that's OK with you? Just in case there's anything different.'

'There's nothing different, except you need to deliver the head first instead of whatever the presenting part is. Go on, you lead, I'll talk you through it.'

She looked at Lucy. 'Are you OK with that?'

'Of course, if Mr Stratton is?'

'I'm quite happy, and you should be, too. She's a neater surgeon than I am.'

Emily wasn't at all convinced that that was true, but she appreciated the vote of confidence as she swabbed the skin and made her careful incision under the watchful gaze of Lucy's husband.

'That's great. OK, now, you need to find the head, which can be a bit tricky. Can you feel it?'

She worked her hand around the baby's side, sliding her fingers underneath the head. 'Got it.'

'OK, now gently coax it round—that's lovely. Then wriggle it out a bit and keep supporting the head—OK, Lucy, here we go. Can someone prop the bed up, please?'

'Oh, can I touch it?' Lucy said, lifting her head to get a better view.

'Not just yet,' Jake told her. 'Wait till it's nearly out, so you don't contaminate the site. It won't be many seconds.'

The baby squirmed and wriggled, its little face screwed up as Emily found first one arm and then the other, and it coughed and mewed and then let out a wail.

'Oh, hello, baby,' Lucy murmured, her voice choked with emotion. Emily could feel the baby's head in her hands turn towards that familiar voice, tiny arms flailing.

'OK, this is when mum gets to do what comes naturally,' Jake said, his eyes creasing in a smile. 'Lucy, can you give a little push, please, to help the baby out?

That's great. Em, lift the baby up towards Lucy—and there we go.'

'Oh—oh, James, look! It's a boy! Oh, baby, come here—!'

She reached out her hands and Emily lifted the baby into them and laid him on the bare skin of Lucy's chest.

'Congratulations,' she said, her eyes welling a little. 'He's beautiful. Oh, Jake, that was amazing!'

'Wasn't it? I love it. And you see we don't clamp the cord until it's finished pulsating—and did you notice the fluid draining from the baby's mouth as you delivered the head? So we don't need to whisk the baby away to suction it and get the respiration going, there's no crying, just a little wail and then look at them. So much better.'

She turned her head and looked at Lucy, James and the beautifully pink baby, warmly snuggled on her chest under a heated towel and a layer of bubble wrap, and she realised the baby's eyes were fixed intently on his mother's face.

She lost focus then, the moving little tableau blurring, and she sniffed and blinked hard and turned back to Jake.

'So what happens now?'

'Now we carry on. The cord's stopped pulsating, the midwife's clamping it, James will probably cut it, and we do exactly what we would normally do, only with a touch of the warm fuzzies,' he added, his eyes crinkling over his mask.

She laughed at that, shook her head at him and turned her attention back to finishing the job.

The 'warm fuzzies', as he'd put it, stayed with her for the rest of the day, and they talked about it again that evening after the children were in bed.

They were sitting in the garden on the bench under

the climbing rose that cascaded over the fence, and the heady scent was intoxicating in the warmth of the summer's evening.

'I can't believe I've finally seen a skin-to-skin section. Thank you so much for letting me lead,' she told him for the hundredth time, and he just laughed and hugged her.

'My pleasure. Anything that helps you do your half of the job in the same way as I would makes me happy.'

'What, because you don't trust me if I don't do it the same way?' she said, giving him a stern look, and he laughed again.

'Of course I trust you, but at the moment we've got patients coming through who I've been caring for all along the line, and we need to make sure that their expectations are met. That's why liaising every day is so important. So what's on the agenda for you tomorrow? Anything you're worried about?'

She shook her head. 'I don't think there's anything that we haven't discussed, but tomorrow evening we need to sit down and work out what we want to say to the solicitor on Friday afternoon. I've asked the nursery if they can have them until six, and they've agreed, so we just need to sort ourselves out. How are you getting away early?'

'Nick's covering me till six and then he'll hand over to my registrar. He's on till midnight and then I'm on call for the weekend. Right, I can't sit here all night, I've got stuff to do.'

'Anything I can help with?' she offered as they went back inside, but he shook his head.

'No, you're fine. Don't wait up for me, you've got a busy day tomorrow. I'll see you in the morning.'

'OK. Sleep well.' She put her arms round him and hugged him, and he hugged her back, holding her silently for a long and speaking moment, then he let her go and stepped back out of reach.

'Sleep well, my love,' he murmured, his lips brushing hers, and then he went into his study and closed the door with a quiet but definite click.

The next two days flew by, and before they knew it they were sitting in front of the solicitor explaining their situation.

Only maybe not clearly enough, because after they'd finished talking, he frowned and said, 'You know, a great deal of this would be taken care of if you were married instead of just cohabiting. Marriage provides a lot of legal protection and makes the issues of paternal responsibility and inheritance a lot more straightforward.'

They stared at him in stunned silence for a second, then they spoke simultaneously.

'We're not—'

They stopped and looked at each other, and Jake shook his head and turned back to the solicitor.

'We're not cohabiting. We're house-sharing, job-sharing, childcare-sharing. We're just friends. Marriage isn't on the agenda in any way, we just want to secure the children's futures.'

The solicitor looked confused. 'Ah. Sorry, I must have misunderstood. In that case, I think I'll have to do a little research and see what I can come up with to give the children the best protection, because these are very unusual circumstances and I haven't come across them before. You also need to consider your wills, if you haven't done anything about them since you had the children.'

'Um—I haven't changed mine since my husband died and I had the baby, so it's now all totally irrelevant,' Emily said, her mind still stalled on the word 'marriage'.

'Mine, too,' Jake added. 'There've been a lot of changes for all of us, and we're only just settling into this but we thought some advice would be a good idea. It seems it's not before time.'

'No, indeed,' the solicitor agreed. 'Look, leave it with me for now, I'll see what I can find out and I'll get back to you, but it's a pity that marriage isn't an option.'

'It's not,' Jake said firmly, and got to his feet. 'Thank you for your help. We'll wait to hear from you.'

They walked out of the building and headed back towards his car in silence, but that didn't mean her thoughts weren't tumbling, and she would have given the world to know what was going on inside Jake's head.

Marriage?

To Emily?

His heart was pounding, his emotions so tangled he didn't know what to think, but there was no way Emily would agree to marry him. She'd only lost Pete eighteen months ago, for heaven's sake! No way was she ready for another relationship—and neither was he. Not after the fiasco with Jo.

No. It was a crazy, ridiculous idea, and he needed to put it out of his head. Right now.

No matter how tempting it sounded…

He didn't mention it again, apart from a fleeting, 'Well, that was awkward,' as they got into the car.

'We'll have to see what he comes up with,' she said, and got a monosyllabic response for her pains, so she gave up.

He was clearly not even going to consider it, and she couldn't believe she was, either. She'd just come out of the fog of emotions that had surrounded her for most of her marriage to Pete, and the last thing she needed was to do anything hasty.

Not that twenty years of friendship could be described as 'hasty' under any circumstances, but they had that, a solid, long-lasting friendship that had sustained both of them through some incredibly difficult times. There was no way she was going to do anything to compromise that. Far too much was riding on it, and it would be fool-ish—so foolish—to jeopardise it.

But there had been that kiss, and it wasn't an isolated incident. Was it such a crazy idea? She didn't know, but the idea wouldn't leave her alone.

Jake was on call from midnight, and his registrar rang at eleven-thirty as he was dozing on the sofa.

'I've just admitted someone who needs urgent sur-gery, but it's not going to be quick. Are you in a position to come and take over now?'

'Sure. I'm on my way,' he said, stifling a sigh. He went up and tapped on Emily's door and opened it a crack, and the landing light slanted across the room and fell on the photo of Pete. He shifted his eyes to Emily, who'd propped herself up on one elbow giving him a perfect view of her cleavage.

Dammit, her room was a minefield. He hauled his eyes up to her face.

'I've got to go. Don't expect me back soon,' he mur-mured.

'OK. See you later,' she whispered back, and Pete's eyes challenged him across the room, as if he could read Jake's mind.

He shut the door, ran downstairs and let himself out. Hopefully it would be a nice, busy weekend and he wouldn't have time to dwell on what was never, *ever* going to happen.

Be careful what you wish for.

He heard the landing floor creak and his bedroom door open.

'Can I come in?'

'Yeah, sure.' He propped himself up and scrubbed the sleep from his eyes, and she came and perched on the edge of the bed. 'What's up?' he asked.

'Nothing, but you've been so busy all weekend we haven't had time to catch up, so I don't know what's happened and what's going on in the wards. Do you need to fill me in before I leave? Anyone I should be worried about?'

He shook his head to clear it as much as anything. Was it really Monday already? 'No, not really, I don't think. A couple of gynae emergencies, they're on the ward and one of them might need discharging but review them and call me. Otherwise all obstetrics and they're done and dusted.'

He yawned hugely and she tutted. 'What time did you get in?'

'Oh, I have no idea. Three something? What time is it now?'

'Six-thirty. I've fed Zach and he's gone down again, no sound from Tilly. You might even get a lie-in.'

He gave a hollow laugh and fell back against the pillows.

'In my dreams.' He yawned again, and felt the mattress shift as she stood up.

'Hope you get a lie-in. I'll see you later.'

He felt the air shift, then the brush of her lips against his cheek.

'You need a shave,' she murmured, a thread of laughter in her voice.

He opened his eyes and stared up into hers, and they looked soft and luminous, her smile tender. It would have been so easy to reach for her, to pull her down into his arms and kiss her—

'Call me if you need me' he said, his voice suddenly gruff. 'I've got my phone on me.'

'OK.'

The door closed and he rolled to his side, hoping for a few more minutes' sleep, but there was a faint scent lingering in the air, delicate and tantalising, and although he slept again, he woke from a dream that was confused, explicit and definitely X-rated.

He rolled out of bed, headed for the shower and turned the thermostat firmly to cold.

Poor Jake.

He'd been on the go all weekend, and he must be exhausted. She felt guilty for waking him, but she just hoped the children slept in long enough to give him a few more minutes.

At least it didn't sound as if there was anything too critical for her to know about, and she was glad she'd left early. It gave her time to study the notes, talk to the night staff and do the ward rounds before the daytime routine started.

She arranged the discharge of the gynae patient he'd talked about, went round the high-risk antenatal ward and checked that the mother with epilepsy was still stable, then checked in on the labour ward, but everyone was OK and there were no imminent problems.

It was eerily quiet—unlike the weekend, she thought wryly, and then of course it all kicked off, and she was called to the labour ward for a woman with twins who'd insisted on a natural birth.

'I'm worried,' the midwife said, coming out into the corridor to talk to her. 'She's got a lot of fluid in there, and neither of the babies is head-down and engaged, so when her membranes rupture one or both cords are likely to prolapse, and I can't talk her out of it. She just says we're overly risk-averse and we should let her follow her instincts, but mine are screaming at me and I know more about it than she does.'

'Well, I'll happily have a go, but I'm not convinced I'll be able to make her listen and we can't force her to have a section.'

'Unfortunately. Don't get me wrong, I'm totally pro natural birth, but my gut feeling is that this lady is going to have a very bad outcome if we don't intervene. And we have no notes. She walked in off the street—she says she's here on holiday but nobody in their right mind would go on holiday thirty-seven weeks pregnant with twins, so I don't believe her and Ben Walker's in Theatre. He's our twin specialist but as I say, he's busy.'

She contemplated phoning Jake, but he was exhausted, there were the children to consider and anyway, it was her job. Except...

'Let me try Ben,' she said. 'Stay with her, I'll see if I can find him. What's her chorionicity?'

'Mono-chorionic, di-amniotic.'

She nodded. 'Well, that could be worse, at least they're not both in the same membrane. I'll look for Ben, you call me if there's a problem.'

She tracked him down as he was coming out of Theatre. 'Can I have a word, please? It's about a twin delivery.'

'Ah. OK. Fire away.'

She filled him in on what he knew, and he phoned his registrar, left him in charge and followed her back to the labour ward, just as Emily's phone rang.

'Right. Her membranes have ruptured, and the first twin's a transverse lie. Luckily the cords haven't prolapsed and the first baby's amnion seems intact, but she wants the baby turned.'

'Not a prayer,' Ben said flatly. 'Do you want to tell her, or would you like me to?'

'I'll do it, but I'm happy to let you explain why. She might take it better from the expert.'

He snorted softly, but just as she'd expected, his charm and gentleness and his obvious expertise wooed the patient, and she agreed, still reluctantly, to have a section.

'I so wanted a natural birth.'

'I know, but there's no way that baby's turning, and it can't come out sideways. There are laws of physics and that would flout most of them, but at the moment your babies are strong and well, as far as we can tell, and they'll be fine, and there might be a way we can make it better. Have you heard of a natural or skin-to-skin Caesarean?'

She hadn't, but she jumped at it when he explained, and Ben turned to Emily. 'Are you all right with me taking this or would you like to do it?'

'I'd love to do it but I don't really have time. If you do, then go for it. She's got confidence in you. That's all that matters. I'm not worried about my pride. I just want those babies safely delivered and I've got an antenatal clinic that technically started twenty minutes ago.'

'Leave it with me, then. I'll let you know how it goes.'

She thanked him, wished the woman well and headed down to the antenatal clinic.

Although she would have loved to be there for the

twins' delivery, she didn't want to hand the clinic over to her registrar because Brie Owen was due in again, now thirty-one plus three weeks and hopefully still stable, and she wanted to see her, partly to be certain that everything was going well, and partly because she knew it was the first thing Jake would ask.

'How's Brie?'

She dropped her bag on the kitchen table, folded her arms and laughed, which confused him. He paused the sweeping, leant on the broom and frowned at her.

'What? What did I say?'

'Nothing. I just knew you'd ask—I nearly sent you a text, but I thought I'd wait and see how long it took for you to crack. And you stuck it out even though I've run really late—well done, you! And she's fine, before you ask again.'

She was eyeing him critically now, her head tilted slightly to one side and a tiny frown pleating her brow.

'What now?' he asked.

She shrugged. 'You look exhausted. Have the children been a nightmare?'

'No, they've been as good as gold. I'm just bushed. I didn't sleep very well—'

'What, for the whole three hours you had?'

He laughed tiredly. 'That would be them. Are you hungry?'

'Starving. It was all ticking along nicely, and then a visitor to the town came in off the streets in labour with twins, and she flatly refused a section, which messed up my lunch plans.'

He frowned at her. 'Did she need one?'

'Not at first, but neither head was engaged, she was mono-chorionic, di-amniotic, and then her membranes ruptured and the first baby was a transverse lie, so I called Ben in and he talked her into it by offering her a natural Caesarean. I tell you, if I hadn't already been late for my antenatal clinic I would have been in there like a shot, but I wanted to see Brie, and now I'm kicking myself because doing it with twins would be the icing on the cake.'

He chuckled and went over to her and gave her a hug. 'Chin up. There'll be another chance. Ben's the local guru for multiple births, and we get lots through the unit. All is not lost.'

'No, I'm sure it isn't, and I probably don't need to be practising on twins.' She gave a tired sigh and eased away from him. 'I'm sorry I'm so late, I had to take someone to Theatre for a tricky perineal repair after my clinic. How long have the babies been in bed?'

'Half an hour? They weren't any trouble. Tilly was shattered and went out like a light, and Zach was asleep before I got him in his cot. I haven't had time to cook, though. I've been sweeping up sand all through the house.'

'Sand?'

'Yes, sand. Buckets of it. We spent the afternoon on the beach and they came home plastered in it. It's been a gorgeous day.'

She looked out of the window at the sun, slowly dropping down the sky. 'So I see. I totally missed that. It could have been pouring all day and I wouldn't have noticed. Do you want me to cook?'

'No, I want you to pick up the phone and order a stonking great Chinese takeaway while I finish sweeping the floor. One of those set meals for two—and some sticky ribs.'

Em rolled her eyes at him. 'You are such a student.'

He leant on the broom again. 'No, I'm not, Em, I'm just tired after the weekend from hell, and the children haven't stopped all day, and I'm starving and knackered. That's all. We can have real food tomorrow. I've done an internet order. Just don't give me grief, please, not today?'

Her eyes softened and she hugged him, and his insides turned to mush.

'Hey, it's fine, I'm with you all the way,' she murmured. 'I can't be bothered to cook, either. What's the number?'

'I'll find it in a minute,' he mumbled into her shoulder. 'Just stay there and let me hold you. I could do with a hug.'

Except he didn't just want a hug. He wanted much, much more, and it was getting harder and harder to deny it...

The rest of the week was slightly more orderly, but it was the children that she found so fascinating. They'd really gelled, and Tilly was so good with Zach now. It was touching, but what really got to her was Thursday evening. She'd just she got back from the hospital and heard them in the bath, and when she went in Jake looked up and said, 'Zach, Mummy's here!'

And Tilly beamed and said, 'Mummy!' and her heart turned over.

Jake looked at her, looked back at Emily and blinked. 'Did I hear that right?'

'She's telling Zach,' she said, her heart thudding. 'She calls me Emmy.' But even so, just to hear it brought tears to her eyes and she had to turn away.

'Em?'

'I'm fine. Give me a minute. I just need to change.'

She went into her room, shut the door and leant back

against it. With the children in the bath she was safe in there. There was no way he'd leave them, and it would give her time to get herself together, and remind herself that she *wasn't* Matilda's mother, and never would be.

Not even her stepmother, as things stood. They had an informal arrangement, and she was just *in loco parentis* when Jake wasn't around, as he was with Zach, but she'd been letting herself live in a little bubble of loveliness, pretending it was all going along so well when all the time she wanted more.

Much more.

She wanted Matilda to have the security, the confidence, the *right* to call her Mummy—although that should properly be reserved for Jo, but where was Jo? Had she forfeited that privilege? Could you ever forfeit the right to your child? What if she came back and took Matilda away again? It would kill Jake, she knew it would, and it would mean everything they'd done was for nothing.

She could hear Zach shrieking with laughter. Jake was probably tickling him or blowing bubbles on his tummy or some such silliness.

He called him Dada now, all the time.

Her eyes flicked across the room and landed on the photos of Pete. Pete when he was well, Pete when he was dying. And those eyes, the eyes he'd given his son, stared back at her solemnly.

What would he make of this, their odd little family formed out of necessity and mutual support?

'Oh, Pete. What do I do? Where do we go from here?'

There was no reply. Of course there was no reply.

She took off her work clothes, threw them in the laundry bin in the corner and pulled on her jeans, then went back to join in the fun.

CHAPTER EIGHT

A LETTER FROM the solicitor came on Friday, in a big, fat envelope addressed to both of them.

She put it on the table in the kitchen dining room, the centre, or so it seemed, of negotiations over their 'arrangement', and it haunted her all day.

What did it say? She had no idea, but she didn't feel it was right to open it without Jake. And of course, he was late.

He was often late, and so was she, which simply underlined how critical their arrangement was, how important their give and take and mutual commitment was to keeping this whole complicated thing afloat.

If they weren't living together, it simply wouldn't work, but did it need more than that? More security, more certainty, more guarantees?

Because there were no guarantees on life itself, she knew that from bitter experience.

She made supper, a creamy fish pie topped with root vegetable mash, with a rainbow of freshly prepped veg ready to go in the steamer, and she waited.

The hands on the clock crawled round, and finally she heard his key in the lock and went to meet him.

'Hi. You OK?'

'Yeah. I'm sorry, I should have rung you but I haven't

had a second. I had to go down to the ED. A pregnant woman was involved in an RTC, and she went into a coma and I had to do an emergency section. I've only just got away.'

'Oh, Jake, that's awful. How is she? And how about the baby? Is it alive?'

He nodded, but his eyes were strained. 'Yes, they both are, just about, but it's not great. I had to do it in the ED because she was crashing, so he's in NICU now, and she's in ITU on life support but it's not looking good, and all because a drunk driver shot the lights. Her partner was driving and he's absolutely distraught, but there was nothing he could have done. It's just tragic.'

'Oh, Jake.'

She put her arms round him and hugged him, and he rested his head against hers and held her tight for a minute before dragging in a breath and dropping his arms.

'Something smells good.'

'Fish pie. It's ready to go. Go and wash your hands and I'll cook the veg.'

'So, what's this?'

'It's from the solicitor. I haven't opened it.'

He slit the flap open with his finger, pulled out the stack of paper and she sat down beside him down to read through it.

It outlined the legal position of married and unmarried cohabiting couples, and also described a 'living together agreement' which could apply in their case, but it seemed incredibly complicated and unwieldy and didn't really move them a great deal further forward.

The main things that came out of it were that they weren't legally next of kin if they weren't married, and although Jake had been granted parental responsibility

for Matilda as soon as she was born, there was no way
Emily could become Matilda's legal guardian in the event
of Jake's death without Jo's consent as long as she was
alive, although apparently more than two people could
have parental responsibility, so she could always apply,
although it might not be granted. She couldn't, however,
adopt Tilly if Jake died unless Jo could be found, although he could, of course, adopt Zach if Emily agreed.

'Did you follow any of that?' he asked, and she shook
her head.

'Not entirely,' she admitted, so they read it again, but
it didn't get any better once they'd fathomed the ins and
outs.

'Well, we'll just have to make sure we don't die,' Jake
said with a shaky laugh, pushing the stack of papers
away.

'Or we could get married.'

Her words hung in the air, and he let the silence stretch
until her nerves were at breaking point.

'Are you serious?'

'Absolutely. It means we don't need a living-together
agreement, which might overlook something that happened down the line that we hadn't thought about, and
it means as my spouse you'd have parental responsibility for Zach so his future would be secured, and I could
apply for parental responsibility for Tilly. If we're married, they're more likely to consider that.'

He closed his eyes briefly, then looked up at her again,
his gaze sober and searching.

'You seriously want us to get married?'

'Why not?' she asked. 'We're already living together,
sharing the house, sharing the job, sharing the childcare—why not? It needn't change anything, it just makes
it a more legally binding, formal arrangement, gives you

parental responsibility for Zach and would tie us more firmly together as a family. And it's not as if there's anybody else in the pipeline for either of us.'

She reached out and took his hand, gripping it firmly. 'Jake, Matilda called me Mummy again today, and I didn't know what to say to her, but Zach calls you Dada all the time and he *needs* a father, and Pete can't be here for him—'

Her eyes welled, and Jake freed his hand and got up and walked away.

'That's emotional blackmail, Emily.'

She leapt to her feet and followed him, getting in front of him so he had to look at her.

'No! No, it's not, it's the truth! Pete died, Jake! It happens. Look at your lady in ITU, with her baby in NICU and a partner in bits! It happens, it happens all the time. You can't legislate against it, you can't change it or avoid it, all you can do is mitigate its effect. And that's all I want to do. It doesn't have to change anything.'

'Of course it would change things.'

'Why? Why does it have to? It's a legal arrangement, nothing more, and it can last as long as necessary.'

He turned away again. 'So—you're suggesting we just carry on as we are?'

Was she? It wasn't what she wanted, but if that was what it took to secure her child's future, then yes. 'Why not?' she asked again. 'It's working for us, isn't it? And, more importantly, working for the children, and that's what matters most. It would just make it better. At least think about it, Jake.'

He propped his hands on the edge of the sink and stared out of the window, and she waited while the silence stretched on and on.

The sky was streaked with gold, the sun all but gone,

and as they stood there the colours turned from gold to purple to grey as the last of the daylight faded.

And then he turned and looked at her, his eyes shadowed so she couldn't read them.

'OK,' he said, and for a moment her heart leapt, but then he went on, 'I'll think about it. I'm not making any promises, but I will think about it.'

It was *all* he thought about for the next several days.

All weekend, with Zach crawling all over him and kissing his face and calling him 'Dada', his chubby little face lighting up if Jake went into the room. Tilly calling Em alternately 'Emmy' or 'Mummy', almost as if Jo had been wiped from her memory.

Was that a good thing? He hadn't heard a dickybird from her in all the weeks she'd been gone, and that was worrying. He only had parental responsibility for Matilda because he'd made sure of that when she'd been born. He'd had to, because they weren't married, and it was the first thing he did after registering her birth and making sure his name was on her birth certificate, but Emily would have no say if he died.

She could apply to have parental responsibility, although Jo's agreement would be hard to secure given she seemed to have dropped off the face of the earth, and obviously that application would have more weight if they were married, but was that a good enough reason to do this?

Of course it was, he realised heavily. He owed it to Tilly to make sure she was safe, and nothing was more important to him than that.

And Zach. He couldn't have loved him more if he'd been his own son. He'd been there for his birth, he'd grown to love him over the months since, especially since they'd moved in with him. He'd do anything in his power to protect him and keep him safe, too, but—marry Em, in the way she'd outlined?

God, he wanted to. He wanted to so much, but not like this, not with nothing changing and them carrying on as they were, because he loved her, and there was no hiding from it any longer, no pretending they were just very dear friends. He loved her and wanted her with all his heart, and not being able to tell her, to show her that, to hold her, make love to her, share his feelings, grow their family—could he do that?

Live a lie, every day for the rest of his life?

It would kill him, but the last thing he should do was come clean and tell Emily how he really felt, because there was far too much at stake for him to upset the status quo.

But how could he stand up and make those vows when he knew it was just a legal arrangement for the children? Was that really a good enough reason for marriage?

And round and round and round it went, until he was ready to scream.

Then on the following Wednesday it all came to a head, because he had a text from Ben to say that tests on the woman who'd been involved in the car accident on Friday had confirmed brain stem death and they were discussing organ donation with her partner.

Her poor, distraught partner. Not to mention the baby—

'Jake? What's up?'

He was standing near the lifts staring out blindly at the car park when Em spoke, and for a moment he couldn't answer.

'Jake? Jake, what is it? What's happened?'

He turned his head and her face came into focus, her blue eyes scanning his worriedly.

'She's brain dead,' he said, his voice expressionless. 'The woman in a coma. The transplant co-ordinator's discussing organ donation with her partner as we speak.'

Her face crumpled. 'Oh, Jake. I'm so sorry. What will happen to the baby?'

He shrugged. 'I don't know. He might not make it anyway, it's touch and go, but if he does, her partner's going to have to fight to be allowed to keep him because he's not the baby's father, apparently. He doesn't have automatic parental responsibility, and he told me the other day that she doesn't have a will. God knows what he's going to do.'

'Oh, Jake. Do you need to go and talk to him?'

He shook his head.

'No. No, she was one of Ben's patients, so he's got Ben with him, he doesn't need me.'

He straightened his shoulders and gave her what he knew must be a rather crooked smile. 'So, how are you getting on? Any problems?'

'No. I've just been to see the lady with twins who Ben delivered. Apparently she chose to come to Yoxburgh when she was in labour because she knew we'd got a multiple birth specialist and her own hospital were very risk averse.'

He grunted. 'She obviously isn't. That was a pretty risky strategy.'

'I think Ben pointed that out to her when she confessed, but she's singing his praises. She loved her natural Caesarean, said it was amazing, and the babies are both doing well. They're like peas in a pod—identical boys.'

'They'll keep her busy, then.' He glanced at the clock on the wall above the lift. 'Have you got time for a coffee?'

'Just about. I hardly dare say it but there seems to be a lull.'

'Good. Let's go. I could do with something to eat before I start my clinic, and I haven't had a drink since ten.'

They grabbed a coffee and a sandwich from the Park Café and went outside, taking advantage of the late May sunshine.

There wasn't a table free, so they sat on one of the benches and talked about the patients in the high-risk prenatal ward, and then his phone beeped and he read the text and swallowed hard.

'What is it?'

His face looked drained. 'They've taken her to Theatre to harvest her organs.' He put his paper cup down, turned his head and met her eyes, his own as sober as she'd ever seen them.

'So that's that. The baby has nobody now. The father's not interested, her partner's not down as next of kin so he has no say in any decisions for the baby's treatment or his future—it's just a bloody mess, and I don't *ever* want that to happen to our children.'

He reached out and took hold of her hand, squeezing it almost painfully tight.

'Let's just do it, Em. Let's get married. Life's too fickle, too fragile to leave anything to chance. As you said, nothing needs to change, but at least this won't be hanging over us, all the what-ifs. We will have done everything we can for the children, and for each other. We'll sort our wills, decide what to do with our property, our bank accounts—all of it. Just in case.'

Her heart was thudding in her chest, but there wasn't a glimmer of anything but despair in his eyes, and the tiny shred of hope she'd cherished shrivelled and died.

She nodded.

'Yes. Yes, let's do it. As you say, it doesn't have to change anything.'

He held her eyes for an age, then nodded, let go of her hand and picked up his cup as if nothing had happened.

'I need to get back. I want to pop up to SCBU before I start my clinic. I'll see you later. Are you OK to get the children?'

'Yes, of course,' she said, her voice hollow. 'I'll see you at home.'

He nodded curtly and went, leaving the second half of his sandwich untouched on the bench beside her. She threw it in the bin and went back to work, feeling curiously flat.

She'd just had a proposal of marriage. It was supposed to be the happiest day of her life, wasn't it? But it hadn't been, either now or when Pete had asked her twelve years ago.

Then, it had been after his initial cancer diagnosis, and then, too, it had been after her initial suggestion.

'Let's get married,' she'd said. 'We'll fight this thing together. You won't be alone.'

He'd resisted at first, just as Jake had, although for different reasons, but when he'd eventually said yes, lying in hospital after surgery and facing a bleak future, his eyes had been as dead as Jake's had been just now.

She felt her own eyes fill.

Once—just once—it would have been nice to have someone propose to her because he loved her, passionately and irretrievably, for herself. Not necessarily on one knee, or in a fancy restaurant with a diamond ring hidden inside her dessert, or on a tropical beach under the rays of a setting sun, but for the *right* reasons.

Just a simple, 'I love you, and I want to be with you.

Marry me,' would be more than sufficient, but it wasn't going to happen, and certainly not now, now she was marrying Jake for all the wrong reasons—

No. Not the *wrong* reasons. Just not for the right ones, too. And she was old enough and wise enough to know that fairy tales didn't exist and there was no such thing as happy ever after, and she knew he did love her, in his way, but it would have been so *nice...*

'Emily.'

She turned and fished out a smile from the dwindling stock. 'Hi, Ben. I'm sorry about your coma lady.'

His mouth compressed. 'Yeah, me too. It's awful, but hey. That's why we're here, to pick up the pieces. Look, it probably seems a bit trivial, but I've spoken to Nick about dinner, we've looked at the on-call rota and we're either talking about this Friday, or Saturday in four weeks' time, if either of those are any good to you? Otherwise it has to be a week night.'

'Ah. I can't do four weeks, that's Zach's birthday, but as far as I know we're not doing anything this Friday. Do you want to go for that?'

'Sounds good. Are you two OK with seafood? Daisy wants to do her crab and crayfish thing, and we're bringing some nibbles as well, and she said Liv's doing the desserts and cheese.'

'Sounds gorgeous. And we both love seafood.'

'Great. Shall we say eight o'clock? Oh, and don't forget it's the ball the following weekend, so keep that free. I'll bring you tickets.'

Ball?

'What ball?' she asked, but he'd gone.

He felt flat, curiously deflated.

It should have been a moment of joy, but instead it

was all about safeguarding the children and mitigating against disaster.

Ridiculous. He was too old to be chasing romance, too old to believe in happy ever after, and she would have had a fit if he'd gone down on one knee—although what would he have said?

'Marry me so when one of us is hit by a drunk driver it's not a total disaster'?

Or the truth, 'Marry me, because I love you'?

No. It was what it was, and he just had to suck it up and get on with it, because at the end of the day there were worse things than being married to a funny, sassy, intelligent and beautiful woman, especially one who could put up with his untidiness and bad habits with—mostly—good grace.

So they weren't sleeping together. So what? He could live without sex, but he couldn't live without Emily, and this way he wouldn't have to.

Emily spent Friday fielding the children as she tried to prepare dinner for six.

Good job Daisy was doing the starter and Liv the dessert, or it would have been a disaster, but she'd stuck with simple and gone for chicken and mushroom stroganoff with wild rice and fresh green beans, because she could put it all together at the last minute and fit her prep in during the day as and when the children let her.

For once, and by a miracle, Jake was home on time, so he took the children upstairs and got them ready for bed while she cleared up the kitchen and started cooking.

He ran down half an hour later, shot through the shower and reappeared in a pair of beautifully cut chinos and a shirt she'd ironed the other day, and as he came over to her she caught the scent of his cologne, fresh and clean with the warmth of amber coming through to tease her senses.

'Right, I'll take over, you go and get ready,' he said firmly, rolling up his cuffs. 'What do you want doing?'

'Nothing, it's all under control. Oh, you could get out glasses and sort out which wine you want, and we could probably do with water glasses, too. Oh, and the pepper mill needs refilling.'

'Right. Go.'

He heard water running, then the sound of her hairdryer, drawers opening and closing, and by the time he'd finished laying the table and sorting out the wine and the pepper mill, she was back down.

'Do I look OK? I didn't have time to straighten my hair, so I just put it up out of the way. Is this dress all right?'

He ran his eyes over her, over the navy print with a flock of tiny white birds scattered across it, the wrap-over front with more than a hint of cleavage at the top, down to the asymmetric hem above smooth bare legs that ended in strappy, open-toed sandals showing off her painted toenails.

He dragged his eyes off them and up to her face, framed by fine blonde tendrils escaping from the tumble of curls she'd pinned up at the back of her head. Her eyes seemed bluer than usual, clear and bright, and she was wearing a touch of lipstick, just enough to tantalise him.

Was her dress all right? Definitely. She looked gorgeous, good enough to eat, and he wanted nothing more than to unpin her hair, peel off the dress and make love to her.

'It's fine, you look lovely,' he said, and wondered if his voice sounded as strangled as it felt. 'I thought we'd have

Prosecco to start,' he said. 'We should really tell them we're getting married, and I thought we could do it then. Make a bit of an announcement. What do you think?'

'I hadn't thought about it at all. We ought to tell Pete's parents, too. Perhaps we should go and we see them tomorrow?' She bit the inside of her lip thoughtfully, then nodded. 'Yes, let's have the Prosecco. Do it properly. I don't think we need to explain our arrangement really, do we, to any of them? I don't know if they'd understand. It might be better just to let them think we've changed our minds and want to get married for the normal reasons.'

Well, that wouldn't take a lot of pretending on his part. The difficult bit was going to be remembering that it wasn't normal. Anything but…

'We've got something to tell you.'

They were all standing in the kitchen, glasses in hand, and Jake slid his arm around her waist and eased her up against his side. All part of the pretence?

'We're getting married,' he said, and they all stared for a moment, wide-eyed, and then Ben shook his head and laughed.

'I knew it. I *knew* it! All that nonsense about just good friends—congratulations. I'm glad you've both come to your senses. I'm very happy for you.'

There was a chorus of 'Congratulations!' from them all, and Jake turned and looked down into her eyes and for a fleeting second—

Then his lips brushed hers, light as a butterfly's wing, and everyone moved in, hugging and kissing and back-slapping, while she smiled furiously and tried not to cry.

'Right, let's eat. I'm starving,' Jake said, and Daisy produced her canapés and they moved into the sitting room.

'I'm assuming you two are coming to the League of

Friends' Summer Ball, so I've brought you a pair of tick-ets,' Ben said, pulling them out of his shirt pocket and handing them to Jake. 'It's in aid of SCBU this year so put your hand in your pocket, Stratton.'

Jake looked at her searchingly. 'We haven't talked about it. It's—when? Next Saturday. Is that OK, Em? Can we go?'

How could she lie? The only reason she didn't want to go was that after their news got out—and it would—they'd be under the intensely curious gaze of all the women in the Tuesday coffee group, and their probably equally curious husbands, and she'd have to pretend that it was all hunky-dory when it actually wasn't. But she couldn't tell them that, and she couldn't lie and tell them they were busy, because they weren't, so she just nodded, sprayed on another smile and said yes.

It was a good evening.

If it hadn't been for the fact that his cheeks ached with pinning that smile in place, it would have been a great evening.

Maybe telling them they were getting married had been a mistake—or at least, pretending that it wasn't an 'arrangement'. If they'd been up-front about it, it would have been easier, but the lie had been told and they'd have to live with it.

Well, one thing was certain. They weren't lying to Pete's parents when they saw them tomorrow. No, make that today, he realised, checking the clock on the chimney breast before he turned out the kitchen light.

They were leaving right after breakfast in the morning, and the last thing they'd need was to come down to chaos so he'd sent Em to bed and spent the last half-hour clearing up the kitchen. Still, it was done now, and hopefully he'd be tired enough that he'd be able to sleep instead of lying there thinking about the soft, yielding warmth of Emily's lips as he'd kissed her.

Only fleetingly. He regretted that. He happily—very happily—could have lingered a great deal longer, but he wasn't a masochist and that way lay madness.

They were in Jean and Duncan Cardew's garden sitting in the shade of a pergola and sipping coffee after lunch when Emily finally made herself broach the delicate subject of their marriage.

'We've been talking,' she said, 'Jake and I, about the children—their futures, about what would happen to them if—well, I don't have to underline it, we all know life's not something to be taken for granted, but we've been to see a solicitor, talked through our situation and we've decided the best and safest way to secure the children's future is if we get married.'

'Married?' Jean said, her eyes widening. 'Oh, that's wonderful! Congratulations!'

'No, Jean, it's not like that,' she said hastily. 'Nothing's changed, nothing's going to change. We're still friends, that's all, nothing more. This is just for the children,' she lied, half expecting lightning to come out of nowhere and strike her down, or for her nose to grow like Pinocchio's, but neither happened.

Jean looked at her husband Duncan, looked at Jake, and frowned.

'Jake? Are you sure about this?'

'Absolutely. She's right, Jean. We're both going into this with our eyes open, and we know exactly what to expect. Neither of us has anyone else in our lives, and we're not expecting happy ever after, we just want to take care of our children as well as we can. That is and always will be the most important thing for both of us. It's just a legal arrangement, nothing more.'

Odd, how crushing those words were to hear. And Jean was giving Jake a strange look, as if she was trying to work out whether or not to believe him.

Then Zach started eating grass, and Em took the chance to escape from the conversation to rescue him.

Jake watched her as she scooped him up, fishing grass out of his mouth and making a game of it.

'She's a good mother,' Jean said quietly, as Duncan went to join them.

'Yes, she is.'

'Look, there's a butterfly—isn't it beautiful?' Duncan said, pointing one out to Tilly. 'Can you see that spot like an eye on its wing? It's called a Peacock butterfly.'

'I got butterfly wings.'

'I thought they were fairy wings?' Em chipped in.

'Butterflies *are* fairies,' she said with exaggerated patience, and Jean smiled tenderly.

'She's a sweet child. She's very good with Zach and she seems to get on well with Emily.'

'She does—well, she does now. At first it was a bit tricky, because her mother had just left her, but she's started calling Emily Mummy sometimes now. I don't know if it's because Em calls herself Mummy to Zach, or if Tilly's just switched allegiance, but we seem to have gelled into a real family, and it's all down to Em.'

'She's a good woman—and you're a good man, Jake. A very good man. You've always been good to her, but to take on this commitment—'

'We've already got a huge commitment, Jean. Our entire careers are now locked together. We're just extending that to our domestic situation.'

Jean sighed. 'But you're still young, and you're talking about a legal arrangement. Is that really what you want?'

'What more could I want? She's the kindest, fairest, most generous person I know. She's also without exception the biggest nag, but I can live with that.'

Jean smiled slightly, but she wasn't fooled. 'Yes, of course you can, because you love her. I can see it in the way you look at her when she's not watching you. Peter never did that. I know he was my son, and I don't want you to think I'm being disloyal, I'm not, I just knew him very well, but Peter leant on her very hard, and she let him, but I had hoped that now she was free she might find real happiness with someone who genuinely loves her for herself, and not for what she could do for them, but that's what she's doing. She's doing it all over again.'

He stared at Jean, shocked. 'Is that what you think *I'm* doing? Using her?'

'No. I know you're not, and she's not using you, although you're using each other, I suppose, but—Jake, does she know how much you love her?'

'Yes, of course she does. I tell her that all the time.'

'But not in the right way. Not in *that* way. She needs to know, Jake. You owe it to her and to yourself to tell her.'

He looked away, his eyes tracking back to Emily and the children, his throat filling with emotion.

'She's happy, Jean. Look at her—you can see she's happy. And it's enough for us. I don't believe in happy ever after anymore. I'm not sure I ever did, and I'm certain Emily doesn't—'

'Are you? Are you really?' She laid her hand on his arm. 'Don't close the door to love, Jake. It comes in many guises, and she loves you, too, you know.'

'Not in that way.' He swallowed and glanced at his watch. 'I'm sorry, we're going to have to leave you or we won't get back for the children's supper time and they've had a busy day.'

'You could feed them here before you go,' Jean said hopefully, but he shook his head.

'No, they'll just fall asleep in the car and then they won't go to bed when we get them home. I'm sorry to cut it short. We'll come for longer next time, maybe stay the night if that's OK with you? I know Em would like to.'

'Oh, that would be lovely—and if you wanted to go out, you know, for dinner or something, we could always have them both for a sleepover. Any time you like.'

'Do you really mean that? Because if you do, we're going to the hospital summer ball this time next week and we haven't arranged a babysitter yet.'

'Perfect! Drop them off on Saturday and pick them up on Sunday. It'll be a joy to have the children, and you'll have a wonderful time! I used to love summer balls. They're always such fun, and the music will get everyone up and dancing.'

Dancing. Damn. He'd forgotten about the dancing. It had got him into trouble at Kat's wedding, but the last time he'd danced with Em had been at her own wedding. Pete hadn't been well enough, but Jake had dragged her onto the dance floor and tried to help her forget that she'd just committed her life to a dead man walking.

So long ago, so much water under the bridge, but he'd never forgotten holding her as she swayed against him to the music, and it dawned on him too late exactly what he'd let himself in for.

As if this whole thing wasn't tough enough already, but there was one thing he knew for certain.

He couldn't tell Emily how much he loved her, because it would trash their finely balanced status quo and destroy everything they'd worked for. He'd just have to keep quiet, do a better job of hiding it and carry on as before.

He'd already hidden it for years. How much harder could it be?

CHAPTER NINE

'I DIDN'T REALISE you'd asked Jean if they'd have the children next weekend,' Em said as they drove away.

'I didn't. She offered to babysit, said it would be nice to have them for a sleepover if we wanted to go out anytime, so I asked her about the ball, and she jumped at it.'

She turned to look at him. 'Really? Well, that's a relief. I was wondering who we could ask, because I'm sure all the willing nursery staff will already have been booked, and I don't know anybody else.'

'That's what I thought, and I would never have suggested it if she hadn't sounded so keen to have them.'

She would be, of course. They missed Pete, and Jean had been angling to have his mini-me to stay for ages, but she'd never needed to take them up on it. But with Matilda as well?

'What about Tilly? Are you sure she's ready for it?'

He laughed. 'I'm sure she is, she'll love it. They'll spoil her rotten, and anyway, Jean offered and I didn't want to hurt her by refusing, and it gets us out of a hole.'

It also took away any excuse for not going to the ball, and Em felt a frisson of—what? Anticipation? Dread? Both, probably. She hadn't danced since her wedding, and apart from a very gentle sway with Pete, she'd only danced with Jake then, and she'd never forgotten the feel of his arms around her, his body so in tune with hers.

Was then when she'd realised how much she loved him?

Or was it just because she'd had way too much champagne to drown out the reality of what she'd done?

Then Jake's phone pinged, and he handed it to her.

'It's bound to be work. Can you see who it is, please?'

He told her the code—Zach's birthday, which left her feeling slightly odd. 'Nick Jarvis. Brie's been admitted—her membranes are leaking.'

He swore softly. 'How many weeks is she now?'

Em thought for a moment. 'Thirty-three today? Or yesterday? We've kept her going for four weeks, at least.'

'More than that. She was only sixteen weeks when I first saw her and without intervention she would have lost it then, so that's at least seventeen weeks, so that's pretty good. I'll go in and see her when we get back, if that's OK?'

He kept her going another three days, but then on Tuesday morning at five he had a call to say she was in established labour, so he told Em and went in, arriving just in time for the birth of Brie's small but healthy baby.

He rang Em at six forty-two. 'It's a girl, four pounds, perfect little thing. She's absolutely gorgeous and Brie and her husband are over the moon—' He broke off, feeling a little choked. 'She's going up to SCBU in a minute, but they're just having a cuddle first and everything looks fine. I thought you'd want to know.'

'Oh, I do, I'm so pleased! Give her my love and tell her well done and I'll come and see her tomorrow.'

He passed the message on, then went down to the café, got a takeaway coffee and a bacon roll and went back to work, still smiling at the outcome of what had been an uncertain and eventful pregnancy.

But they'd done it, they'd kept the baby where she belonged as long as possible, and it was all going to be all right.

The coffee group met at Daisy's that day, and predictably they were all agog about the engagement.

'Where's the ring?' Kate asked, and she just laughed it off.

'It's only just happened, we haven't had time and anyway, that sort of thing doesn't matter.'

Of course it mattered, no matter how much she told herself it didn't, but she kept that to herself, just another one of the lies she'd told them, and the talk soon switched to the ball on Saturday and what everyone was wearing, and she listened in mounting dismay.

'I haven't got a thing to wear,' she admitted. 'Nothing suitable, anyway. It sounds really dressy.'

'It is,' Daisy confirmed. 'Why don't you go to the boutique at the bottom of the hill just above the prom? It's brilliant. They had some gorgeous dresses in there the other day. In fact, why don't you leave the children here with us and go now?' she suggested.

'Really?'

'Really. Take the shoes you were wearing the other night, and knickers that don't give you VPL, and your best bra, and go for it.'

'Yes, go on, and bring it back here when you've found it. We all want to see.'

'No pressure, then,' she said with a laugh, but nevertheless she went, dropping into the house en route to grab the shoes and decent undies.

'I need a dress for a ball on Saturday,' she said, trying not to feel too frumpish next to the glamorous lady behind the counter.

'Are you Emily?' she asked with a beaming smile. 'I've had Daisy on the phone, she told me to expect you. Let's have a look, I might have just the thing. Did you bring your shoes?'

She got Jake to hang the dress from the curtain pole in her bedroom when he got home from work. It was the only place high enough, and she'd tried to reach by standing on the chest of drawers, but it was too far away.

'Wow, that's glam,' he said as he hung it up for her, and she laughed a little awkwardly.

'Yes, it is, so you'd better up your game, Stratton,' she quipped. 'I don't want to show you up.'

He rolled his eyes and left her to it, and on Saturday evening he lifted it down again and laid it on her bed.

The children were safely installed at the Cardews', and for the first time they were alone together in the house and it felt weird, as if the safety net that had hovered under them had been whipped away, leaving them dangling over an abyss.

She showered, dried her hair and at the last minute decided not to straighten it as usual but to run the curling tongs through it and pile it up as she had last week.

She applied her make-up with more care than normal, but her fingers were shaking and she splodged the mascara and had to blot it off with a cotton bud. Crazy. Her insides felt as if a zillion butterflies were having a party, and she stepped into the dress, pulled it up over her shoulders and then called Jake.

'Can you do the zip up, please?' she asked, turning her back to the door, and she heard the slight hiss of his indrawn breath as he came in, then felt the touch of his fingers, warm and—trembling?

'There. All done. Anything else?'

'No, that's all. How about your bow tie?' she asked, turning back to face him and catching a strange look on his face.

'It's fine. I gave up with the knots and bought a fake one. The cab'll be here in five minutes. I'll wait for you downstairs.'

She looked stunning.

Even more beautiful than she'd looked on her wedding day, and probably nearly as nervous, for some reason. He helped her out of the cab and squeezed her hand.

'Hey, come on, it's just a party. Let's go and find the others.'

They spotted Ben and Daisy standing with Ed and Annie and Sam and Kate, and soon Nick and Liv joined them, then James and Connie, and they went and found their table for dinner.

He'd been hoping they'd be split up at the table but whoever had been in charge had seated them with their partners, so throughout the meal his senses were bombarded with the sound, the scent, the warmth of her beside him. Her perfume curled around him, her laugh made him want to smile, and every now and then their bodies brushed against each other—a leg, an arm, her shoulder as she leant back against him and took a selfie.

'Another one for the album,' she murmured, her breath teasing against his skin, and he found a smile and turned back to Liv, just as the MC announced the start of the auction.

At least that gave him something to concentrate on

apart from her, but in no time at all it was done, the band struck up and the lights went down.

'Right, come on, everybody, let's have you on the dance floor,' Ben said, getting to his feet, but Emily looked oddly uncomfortable.

'Do you really want to?' she murmured, but Ben was having none of it, so they ended up on the crowded dance floor with all the others.

Which was fine while the beat was pumping, and there were all the usual songs to get everyone going, like 'YMCA', and he had to watch Emily waving her arms above her head and laughing when she got it wrong, which she did, repeatedly.

And then the tempo slowed, and she turned towards him and met his eyes and he was lost.

He opened his arms, she moved into them and his right arm closed around her. She could feel his hand against her back, his fingers touching her skin in the deep V above the zip. His other hand found hers and held it lightly, his fingers warm and firm and reassuring, and she moved with him, their bodies closing in on each other as if they were made to fit together.

His shoulder was just there, broad and inviting, and she rested her head against it and let the music flow through her, cherishing this moment, this rare opportunity to hold him, to feel his body against hers, his heartbeat under her ear, the solid warmth of his body so *right* against hers.

Except it wasn't right, it wasn't what he wanted, and if she had any sense she'd step away before she made a fool of herself.

The song changed, the mood romantic, the air heavy with the sensual words, and as he turned his head and bent it a fraction to suggest that they sit this one out, her head lifted and her eyes locked with his and blood roared through his body, deafening him to everything but his need for her.

They were right back where they'd been fifteen years or more ago after Kat's wedding, only they weren't in Brighton, and Pete wasn't going to be sending her a text to bring them to their senses. They were going home together to an empty house, and if he didn't pour cold water on this right now it was all going to go to hell.

He had to step away, to get off the dance floor and call a halt to this, but her eyes held him like a spell, and he was powerless.

'Em,' he breathed raggedly, and then his lips touched hers and he was a goner.

'Get a room, you two,' Ben laughed from behind him, and it broke the spell and he pulled away.

'Come on. Let's get out of here. I've had enough.'

They picked up his jacket, her bag, her wrap, and headed for the door, a careful space between them as they went out into the foyer of the hotel.

'Can you walk in those shoes or shall I call a cab?' he asked, his voice gruff, but it was a miracle he could speak at all, and he was relieved when she shook her head and said she could walk.

Thank heavens for that. There was no way he wanted to hang around for a cab at almost midnight on a Saturday night, and maybe a brisk walk home would settle this blaze that was ripping through him like a wildfire.

But as they walked back into the house and he closed the door behind them a few minutes later, all he was aware of was the emptiness of the house closing around them like a prison cell.

They were entirely alone, no one to save them from this madness. No Pete to send Emily a text, no Zach to cry out, no little Tilly to appear at the top of the stairs and demand another story, or make him sing 'Twinkle, Twinkle, Little Star' for the fourth time.

'Do you want a drink?' Em asked him, but he shook his head.

'No, I've got work to do. I'll just change out of this lot and I'll sort myself out.'

He ran upstairs, and the landing light slanted across her room and fell on Pete's face. Jean's words came back to him, the fact that Pete had leant on Emily, that he'd never loved her as she'd deserved to be loved.

Had she loved Pete? Or had she really just married him out of kindness? And was he about to use her in the same way Pete had?

He went into his room and closed the door, turning the key and throwing his jacket down on the chair, kicking off his shoes, unbuttoning his shirt—and then he heard the door handle rattle.

'Jake? Jake, let me in.'

'No.'

'Jake? Please don't do this. Please talk to me.'

'No. You've been drinking, Emily, and so have I, and I'm not doing this again. Just for God's sake leave it and go to bed.'

He held his breath then, heard the faint rattle of the handle as she let it go, then the creak of a board, the soft click of her bedroom door closing.

And then, moments later, the sound of a muffled sob that tore his heart in two.

He went out, crossed the landing to her room, rested his hand on the door, his palm flat against the wood, and cursed himself for hurting her, for doing this again, for letting the music and the atmosphere reel him in just as it had before fifteen years ago.

Jean had told him to tell Em that he loved her, but he didn't dare. Not tonight, when their emotions were running so high, when so much was riding on it.

He'd tell her tomorrow, when they were both sober and he'd had time to work out what to say. Not that he'd had much to drink. Hardly anything, because he'd wanted to make sure he stayed in control, but he hadn't, had he, and neither had Em, but he'd pretty much accused her of being drunk and sent her away in the only way he knew how, and now she was breaking her heart.

He hadn't wanted to do that to her. He'd never meant to hurt her, not now, not ever—but he had, and maybe more than once. He rested his head against his hand on her door, and felt something wet fall on his wrist.

Tears.

Tears that were refusing to stay unshed, sobs that were rising in his throat and tearing it apart.

He went downstairs to his study, shut the door and sat down, his hand clamped over his mouth as he finally gave in to the outpouring of grief that he'd bottled up since the day she married Pete.

All the chances he'd wasted, all the opportunities to tell her he loved her, to ask her out properly, to risk the ridicule he'd been afraid of and lay his heart on the line—dammit, he'd had her in that hotel room and OK, she'd been going out with Pete by then, but only just. They didn't mean that much to each other then, he could have told Em how he really felt, stopped her relationship with Pete from developing any further, made love to her.

But he hadn't. He'd said nothing, and she'd left his room, and three years down the line she'd married Pete and he'd lost her then for ever.

Except he hadn't, because he'd always been there for her, and now she was back in his life, giving up everything to help him, and if he did nothing then he'd risk the chance that she'd marry him for the same reason she'd married Pete. Out of kindness, and selflessness.

And he didn't want that. He wanted all of it. He wanted Emily, heart and soul and mind and body, and he didn't have the slightest clue if that was even a possibility…

Why wouldn't he talk to her?

She wasn't drunk. OK, she'd had a couple of glasses of Prosecco and she wouldn't want to operate, but she wasn't *drunk*, and she didn't believe he was, either.

But the way he'd looked at her on the dance floor, the way he'd kissed her, the burning longing in his eyes— was that a man who didn't want her? Unless he was just doing what she'd accused him of before and letting his lust get the better of him?

Did he lust after her? She didn't know. She didn't think so, but there had been times—like when they'd been watching *Titanic* and she'd snatched the popcorn. And when she'd caught him naked in the kitchen. And that night when he'd come home late. He'd kissed her then, and if he hadn't been so tired maybe— She didn't know, but there'd been something there in his eyes, and it hadn't looked like lust to her, it had looked like—

Love?

No. If he'd loved her, he would have said so. He did, all the time, and he meant it, but not in *that* way. Not in the way she wanted him to mean it.

Unless…

No. Maybe she *was* drunk. Drunk and deluded and trying to convince herself he really cared when he was just a normal man with needs and desires, stuck in a house with a passable woman and with no other relationship on the go.

Idiot. She was an idiot, but she was too tired and too emotional to tackle him again tonight. She'd talk to him tomorrow in the cold light of day and make him talk to her. It was time she got her feelings for him out into the open.

She swiped the tears off her face, rolled onto her side and fell into an uneasy and restless sleep.

She found him in the kitchen.

She'd woken in a tangled heap of dress, her hair knotted, but his bedroom door had been open and his bed hadn't been slept in, so she'd gone downstairs and found him slouched back in a chair, his eyes red-rimmed and bloodshot seeking her out like lasers.

She didn't suppose she looked any better.

'I'm sorry,' he said heavily. 'I didn't mean to make you cry, I just—'

'Didn't want to talk to me?'

'No. I *did* want to talk to you, but if I'd let you into my room, we wouldn't have talked, Emily. Not last night, not after that dance.'

'Why wouldn't we have talked?'

A humourless little laugh escaped from his chest. 'You really need me to spell it out?'

She walked round the table and sat down next to him, hitching one foot up and resting it on the edge of her chair, wrapping her arms around it as she sought out his eyes again.

'Maybe, because I really thought you wanted me, and then you shut the door and suddenly I didn't know any more.'

He let out a ragged sigh and raked his hand through his hair, then looked back at her. 'I did want you. I do— but I can't do this anymore. I can't live a lie. I can't let you marry me just for the children, trap you into a sham of a marriage when you could be free to find someone you really love, instead of yet another compromise that has to be doomed to failure! And I can't do it to you, my love. I can't.'

'Why, if it's what I want?'

'Because I love you too much to do that to you!'

Emily stared at him, stunned by his outburst.

She'd thought her love was one-sided, because apart from the occasional awkwardness he'd been nothing but her best friend, but now all that was stripped away and she could see the truth in his distraught face, his wild eyes, the love she could see so clearly written all over him.

'Why is it doomed to failure?' she asked numbly, wondering if she'd totally missed the point.

'Oh, God, Em, of course it is! I'd do anything for you, anything—but not this. I can't let you do this again, I can't let you marry the wrong man for the wrong reasons, even if we have to find another way to guarantee security for the children, because it would just be wrong and you deserve more than that. You said nothing would change, but it has, because I've finally realised just how much I love you, how much I've always loved you, and I love you way, way too much to ask this of you. You mean everything to me, and I want it all, and that's not fair on you.'

His hand reached out, trembling, and cupped her cheek, his thumb brushing away a tear she hadn't even known she'd shed.

She lifted her hand and laid it over his against her cheek, turning her face to press a kiss into his palm. 'I wouldn't be marrying the wrong man, or for the wrong reasons,' she said softly. 'I'd be marrying the right man, the man I should have married years and years ago.'

She reached out, resting a hand against his chest, feeling the pounding of his heart beneath her fingers.

'I love you, Jacob Stratton. I think I've probably loved you for ever. I just never let myself admit it because it was never the right time. I started to realise years ago, after that wedding, but there was a bit of me that didn't want to be one of the endless women who spent one night with you and then got dumped.'

'I only dumped them because they weren't you,' he said softly, and she stared at him, searching his eyes and finding nothing but sincerity.

'But—you'd never looked at me like that before, and I thought it was just because of the drink and the atmosphere and the dancing, so when I got the text from Pete I got cold feet. I should have stayed, and then who knows what would have happened?'

'Who knows? I just know that there's never been another woman who made me feel like you do.'

She sat up straighter. 'Really? Is that why you've never married, never settled down with anyone in all this time? Because of me?'

He reached out a hand and laid his palm against her cheek again, his fingers curling under her jaw, his thumb idly tracing her lips. 'Maybe. I think it must be. I didn't realise, perhaps, but no one's ever measured up to you, and by the time I realised how I felt, you were with Pete, and then he was diagnosed with cancer and I had to walk you down the aisle so you could give your life to him for what was left of his, and it broke my heart, Em. That's why I was always there for you, doing what I could to help, supporting you while you supported him, being there for you in the only way I could.'

A tear trickled out of the corner of his eye, and she reached out and wiped it away tenderly. 'Oh, Jake. I'm so sorry. I wish I'd known, but if I'd ended it with Pete, do you think we'd still have been together?'

He gave a slow, ragged sigh and shook his head. 'I don't know, but I couldn't wish now that things had been any different because that would mean you didn't have Zach and I didn't have Matilda, and I couldn't wish them away.'

'No. No, neither could I, but we've got two beautiful, wonderful little children, and fate's given us a second chance and maybe it's time to take it. Maybe now's our time, at last? I've waited long enough for you, Jake. Please don't make me wait any longer. Take me to bed? Do what you should have done fifteen years ago, and make love to me?'

She saw the hope flare in his eyes, the realisation that she meant it, and with a ragged groan he closed his eyes and let his breath out on a long, shaky sigh.

'Emily,' he said, his voice cracking, and then he cupped her cheeks between his trembling hands and kissed her as if she was the most precious thing in the world.

And then he lifted his head and stared into her eyes, and she felt as if she could see to the bottom of his soul. 'You're right, Em,' he said softly. 'It is our time now, and we're meant to be together. Will you marry me? Not because of the children, but because you love me, and I love you? We've waited far, far too long and I need you. I need you so, so much. Marry me, Emily—please? Make us a proper family?'

'Oh, Jake, yes, my love, yes—' Her eyes filled, his face blurring as she reached up and touched it, felt the rasp of stubble against her palm, the warmth of his skin, the dampness of tears on his cheek.

She drew his head down and touched her lips to his.

'Make love to me, Jake,' she murmured. 'Show me how much you want me.'

He lifted his head and stared into her eyes, and then he stood up and pulled her to her feet and led her upstairs to his room and closed the door.

'I love you, Em. Don't ever forget that,' he murmured, and then, his hands gentle, he turned her round. She felt the soft huff of his breath against her skin as he pulled the last of the pins out of her hair and sifted it through his hands, easing out the tangles, and then he swept it aside and pressed his lips to her shoulders, nuzzling against her. She felt his mouth trail down, felt his fingers on the zip, his lips following the line of it down her spine to the small of her back, his breath leaving a trail of heat that threatened to engulf her.

The dress slipped off her shoulders, cascading to the floor in a heap of crumpled silk and petticoats, and she stepped out of it and turned to watch him as he kicked away the last of his clothes and reached for her.

'I love you,' he said again, cradling her face in his hands and touching his lips to hers. 'I want you.' Her mouth caught fire, and she gasped, opening to him, feeling the sweep of his tongue, the tender bites as he toyed with her lips, the heat spreading low as his hands moved, tracing her body, unerringly seeking out the places that made her legs tremble and her mind go numb.

'Jake, please—'

He lifted her, laying her on the bed and moving over her, one leg wedged between hers as his mouth moved down her body and found her breasts.

'Do you have any idea,' he said unsteadily, 'how erotic it is watching you breastfeed?' And then his mouth closed over her nipple, his tongue teasing it until it peaked, then sharing the love with the other one while his hand tracked lower, sliding over her hip, across the bowl of her pelvis, down—

'Jake!'

'Shh,' he murmured, his fingers touching her with devastating accuracy, seeking out all those hidden places that were weeping for him.

'Jake, please—'

He moved over her then, his hands cradling her face as he stared down into her eyes. 'I love you, Emily,' he said again, and then he was there with her, moving slowly, wringing every last ounce of torment out of her until finally, finally he let her free, driving into her, taking her over the edge and falling with her, sobbing her name against her shoulder as his body shuddered with the force of his climax.

And as the last shock wave died away, he lifted his head and kissed her tenderly, and it felt as if she'd finally come home.

He lay on his back, Emily draped over him, their hands clasped on his chest.

'I love you,' he said softly, for what must be the hundredth time or more, and she lifted her head and kissed him, her mouth warm and gentle against his.

'I think I've got that now,' she said, and he could feel her smile against his lips. 'You've been saying it for years, but I never dreamt you meant this way. I wish I had, because I've loved you so long, I've leant on you so hard, and you've never failed me, never let me down, never questioned it.'

'How could I, Em? You were in an impossible situation with Pete. Jean told me how he leant on you, and that you just took it on your shoulders without a murmur. How could I do any less than that for you, especially by the end?' He sighed unsteadily. 'Did you know Pete asked me to look after you and keep you safe?'

'No, I didn't. I wonder if he realised how we both felt? He asked me more than once how come I hadn't ended up with you instead of him.'

'Really?'

'Really. I just laughed it off, said I couldn't live with your untidiness, but maybe he saw through that. Maybe he saw how much you cared for me, and how much I needed you. Perhaps that why he asked you to look after me and the baby at the end, because he knew we belonged together. Maybe he had a fit of conscience, who knows? And we never will, but I wouldn't be surprised. He wasn't a bad man, just terrified of what was to come and too scared to tackle it alone. I can't blame him.'

'No. Who knows what any of us would be like in that situation? I felt so sorry for him, and I've been feeling racked with guilt every time I've seen that picture of him in your room, every time I've seen Zach look at me with Pete's eyes, knowing how I felt about you, what I wanted. Yes, I was keeping you safe, but not for his sake, and maybe not even for the children's. Perhaps they were just a convenient excuse, a way I could justify keeping you by my side.'

She shook her head. 'You would never do that. You've been worried about Tilly for over two years. I had nothing to do with that.'

'Not in that way, no, but maybe I *was* guilty of using you.'

'No. No more than I was using you. Everything we've set up so far, like the job and the childcare and so forth, has all been for the right reasons. Even if we hadn't loved each other in this way, Jake, we would have done it. I would have married you for their security, and you would have married me, and it would have been fine. And instead of that, it's going to be amazing.'

He shifted his head so he could look into her eyes. 'Can I tell you what's amazing? To hold you like this, to touch you, to learn your body, to feel you touching mine, to know how much you care, how much you love me, how much you want me. I didn't believe in love—not like this. And making love to you—I've never felt anything remotely like this before and I don't quite know how to handle it.'

'Neither do I, but you've done a pretty good job so far,' she said, a smile teasing her lips.

He smiled back at her and ran his hand through her hair, sifting the pale gold strands through his fingers. 'Your hair's so soft. I've had fantasies about you trailing it all over my chest—'

'Like this?' she murmured, moving over him and sending his pulse rate into orbit.

'Just like that,' he breathed, and then her mouth found his again and silenced him.

They were married two months later, in a quiet ceremony in the register office in Yoxburgh with only close family and friends present.

Jean and Duncan were there, of course, together with his parents and brother, and of course the close-knit friends who'd supported them all the way—Ben and Daisy, Nick and Liv, the others from the coffee group with their husbands—and afterwards they went back to their house for drinks and a wonderful spread put on by the coffee ladies at their insistence.

She was wearing a simple dress in a soft oyster cream—not a traditional wedding dress by any stretch of the imagination, but it suited her, and he thought he'd never seen her look so radiant.

He slipped his arm round her and gave her a quick squeeze, and she turned her head and kissed him. 'I think they want you to make a speech,' she said, but he just shook his head.

'No way,' he began, but then he changed his mind and found a spoon to tap against a glass.

'Ladies and gentlemen,' he said, his arm still firmly round her waist, 'I don't know how much any of you know about us, so I thought it might be time to fill you in, starting with how we met.'

'Jake, you can't!' she squealed, but he just laughed and carried on.

'It was freshers' week, and I'd been led astray by some guys who thought it would be really funny to take all my clothes off and handcuff me to the railings outside the halls of residence. And there I was, at six o'clock in the morning, when this gorgeous girl came running out of halls dressed in skin-tight Lycra, her blonde hair flying. And she ran towards me, slowed right down and stopped, and then she laughed.'

A chuckle ripped through their guests, and Emily groaned as he went on.

'She gave me a lecture, laughed a bit more, then she took the key which was taped to the fence and unlocked me, handed me my clothes and took me for breakfast. We were eighteen, and for the last—wow—almost twenty-one years we've been the best of friends. She's so good a friend she dropped everything to help me when I needed her, and then she suggested we should get married and I said no, because she's too generous, too kind, too selfless—'

His voice cracked, and she took his hand and squeezed it, and he carried on.

'But then things changed, and we finally both came to our senses and realised just how much we love each other. There are people here partly responsible for that change, so I have some people to thank, and I want to start with Jean. You know why, Jean. You know what for, and how much I owe you for that. How much we both owe you, so thank you, from the bottom of my heart. And I want to thank our colleagues, for making Em so welcome in a really difficult situation, especially Ben, who moved heaven and earth to fix our job share and make it all possible. Although actually, Ben, we need to talk about that,' he added, with a wink at Emily, 'because there will have to be some changes in a few months' time and Daisy might have to come out of retirement and pick up a little of the slack.'

'You can't tell them yet,' Em said, laughing, but Ben was heckling them from the crowd.

'Too late, Emily, you're rumbled. You've been drinking fizzy water, and no one's seen you with a coffee for weeks. Did you really think you'd get away with that?'

Everybody laughed, but it was laughter that was filled with warmth and affection, and as a light breeze off the sea caught the climbing rose and drifted petals over them like confetti, Jake turned his bride into his arms, bent his head and kissed her…

* * * * *

A MUMMY FOR HIS DAUGHTER

AMY RUTTAN

MILLS & BOON

This book is dedicated to everyone who has been lost
and has found their way home.

CHAPTER ONE

I HATE FLYING. I hate flying.

Evelyn closed her eyes and gripped the armrests tighter as the Cessna C207 Skycraft she was flying in was jostled by turbulence. And being in a small plane that only seated seven people meant that the turbulence *really* rattled her around, making her stomach twist and knot in apprehension.

Although it wasn't just the turbulence that was doing that to her.

She'd thought in the twenty years since she'd been here that her hometown might have built a road from Sitka to Wolf's Harbor, but no.

Nothing seemed to have changed. Wolf's Harbor was still relying on the service of bush pilots and a small airport and harbor to service the larger hub of Sitka. Although there was a ferry service to Juneau, it took three hours to drive to the ferry terminal and another four hours to cross the channel. That was if the ferry was running. The fastest way was still by air.

Evelyn would have preferred a boat excursion from Sitka to Wolf's Harbor, but there were no vessels departing on the eight-hour journey from Sitka through Cross Sound and into the small inlet of Wolf's Harbor. The Cessna had been her only option.

She didn't like airplanes, even though she was used to flying. Her grandmother had loved taking trips all over the world, but even though air travel was second nature to her she didn't like it any better.

The plane rocked again but the other people who were on the same flight didn't pay any attention to it. They were calm and just rocking with the turbulence as if it was nothing. Of course they were probably used to it.

Evelyn was not. She was used to first class. She wasn't used to a bush plane way of life, nor to this level of turbulence where the pilot would probably have to crab land on the Tarmac because of the wind shear.

The first time she'd flown on a Cessna had been when she'd left Wolf's Harbor—or rather when she'd been taken from Wolf's Harbor.

She'd never got to go back.

Of course she'd been only ten when she'd gone to live in Boston. Her father had been killed by a runaway logging truck when he'd gone out one evening. Her mother—who'd died when Evelyn was four—had been Tlingit, and her maternal grandmother and uncle had lived in Wolf's Harbor, but Evelyn hadn't heard from them in twenty years.

When she'd first left she'd written letters to them, but nothing had ever come back. She'd been devastated, but her paternal grandmother had taught her to be tough. To harden her heart against disappointment.

Besides, it was really *her* fault that her father had died. It was no wonder her mother's family had written her off. Her father had been the beloved town doctor for years until that accident. It had been for the best that she'd left.

Still, it had torn a hole in her soul. She'd got world experience, and a great education, but as a child she hadn't wanted to leave Wolf's Harbor.

A social service worker from Juneau had come to take her away. Her father's estranged mother in Boston had got custody of her. And, as a child, she really hadn't had a say....

"I don't want to leave," Evelyn protested, clutching her small rag doll and looking back at her father's log cabin with longing.

She loved her cozy home in the forest, where she'd used to wait for her father to come home. But he was never coming back. Her father was gone—and all because he had been on his way to see that woman. The woman who wanted to replace her mother.

"You have no choice," the social worker said, kneeling in front of her.

She could see the pain in the woman's eyes.

"I'm sorry, Evelyn, but your grandmother in Boston is looking forward to your arrival and she's your legal guardian now. Your father didn't have a will and a judge has ruled in your paternal grandmother's favor. You have to go live with her."

"I don't want to go to Boston."

"I know." The social worker squeezed her shoulder. "I wish you could stay too."

Evelyn picked up her knapsack, which held all her belongings, and took the social worker's hand as they climbed into the taxi cab which drove them to the airport.

The Cessna was waiting and there were other passengers climbing on board. She gripped the social worker's hand as she looked back at the town.

The taxi cab driver—Uncle Yazzie—had tears in his eyes as he waved goodbye to her.

"Why can't I stay with my uncle? Why can't I stay with my grandmother? They can take care of me. I want to stay with them."

"Your grandmother in Boston has guardianship over you. The court has decided that you have to go to Boston, Evelyn. I'm so sorry. I know that you want to stay, but you have to be a brave girl. It will be okay."

A lump formed in Evelyn's throat. She was leaving everything she knew, everything she loved, to live with a stranger.

Uncle Yazzie scrubbed a hand over his face. "Don't worry. We'll see each other again soon."

Evelyn nodded and tried to fight back the tears as she walked away from the only family she'd known.

She would never forgive herself for not stopping her father from going out that night to see Jocelyn—the woman he'd wanted to marry. If she'd stopped him he'd still be alive...

"Ladies and gents, we're now making our descent into Wolf's Harbor. Please fasten your seatbelt."

The pilot made the same announcement in Tlingit and Evelyn felt sad that she'd almost forgotten her mother's language. She understood it still, but when was the last time she'd spoken it?

Evelyn couldn't remember. Her grandmother had banned all talk of Alaska and anything of her past because it had been too painful for her, and Evelyn hadn't wanted to make her grandmother upset. Her grandmother had blamed Alaska for taking her son away, for her having had to disinherit him. Alaska had ruined her father's promising surgical career.

Evelyn had still loved Alaska, but had said nothing to her grandmother about her love for her former home. She had always been worried her grandmother would send her away, so she'd just tried to please the woman.

She hadn't wanted to be alone. She hadn't wanted to be sent away again.

That trip to Boston… She'd known then what alone felt like. It had been terrible, and she'd never wanted to feel that way again.

Except now you are alone!

And it was her fault again this time.

She'd been with Nathan for two years, but her career had always been more important to her. Nathan had a great surgical practice in Minnesota, and he wanted to settle down and get married. Only that was the last thing that Evelyn wanted.

She didn't want a family. One that could be taken away from her in an instant. One she didn't deserve.

There was a part of her that should have felt sorrow over losing Nathan, but she felt numb and a little bit relieved.

He'd accused her once of being cold. And maybe she was.

Of course being cold meant that you kept your heart intact. Not feeling was her armor. Her protection against pain. Her grandmother had taught her to guard her heart in order to avoid pain. Emotions were for the weak. And it served her well as a surgeon.

She took a deep breath and looked out through the small window to see Wolf's Harbor come into view through the misty summer rain that was clinging to the mountains.

Her heart skipped a beat and her palms were sweaty, but she wasn't sure if that was from the turbulence or from seeing the place where she'd been born. A place she'd never thought she'd see again.

The sight of the boats moored at the town dock and even the vessels that were out on the eerily calm water made her stomach flip in anticipation. It was just as beautiful as she remembered.

For the first year of her life in Boston she'd dreamed about Wolf's Harbor, dreamed about her father, and then what she remembered had begun to fade as she'd integrated into life in Boston.

Her grandmother had been distant and mourning her son's decision to head to Alaska, and her grandmother's grief and bitterness had seeped into their life in Boston. So they'd traveled a lot. Boston had been their home base, but she had always felt her grandmother had traveled so she wouldn't have a moment to grieve for her son. Boston might have been a base, but it had never felt like home.

She'd excelled in school, to please her grandmother, and had gone to Dartmouth and then Harvard Medical School. During her last year at Harvard her grandmother had died, but Evelyn's time there had seemed to please her. The more Evelyn had excelled, the more her grandmother had seemed happy with her.

She'd done her residency in Seattle, and earned a fellowship in obstetrics and neonatal medicine. She'd been searching for a new challenge when she'd been contacted by a surgeon friend in Sitka, who had begged her to come and take over her practice while she went on a three-month honeymoon.

Evelyn had thought it would be good—she just hadn't had any idea that part of the practice was a rotation in Wolf's Harbor that her friend shared with a couple other OB/GYNs and that she worked there every three months. And the day Evelyn had landed in Sitka had been the day she was to start her three-month rotation in Wolf's Harbor.

At first she'd thought of not going, of letting her friend down, but she longed to see Wolf's Harbor again. To help where she hadn't been able to help before.

She owed it to her father.

To her home.

Not your home.

She had to remind herself of that. There was no place for her here. Not anymore. All she had to do was step in for the next three months and then she could leave with a lighter conscience.

Dr. Pearson, the OB/GYN who was finishing his rotation in Wolf's Harbor, would be waiting for her at the town's clinic, where he'd hand over the keys to the clinic, and the furnished apartment they used during rotation, and would show her around before he drove back to Juneau.

The plane landed with a bump on the small gravel airstrip and the props slowed down as the Cessna taxied to the terminal. When it had come to a stop and shut down, the pilot hopped into gear, opening the door as the ground crew pushed over the stairwell, and Evelyn could feel the hatches being opened to unload the cargo.

The two other occupants—both men—grabbed their duffel bags and headed off the plane.

Evelyn took a deep breath. *You got this.*

She slung her laptop bag over her shoulder and unbuckled. When she stepped out of the Cessna she was hit by the scent of salt water, rain and damp. There was a clanging from the buoys out on the mist-shrouded water. It hadn't changed.

Home.

Evelyn closed her eyes to stop the tears that were threatening.

"Come here, Evie."

Her father held open his arms and she ran to him, pressing her face against the soft flannel jacket he wore.

"I love you, Daddy."

Her dad kissed the top of her head and smiled, his blue-gray eyes twinkling.

"I love you, too, Evie."

"Do you need help, miss?"

Evelyn shook the memory away and glanced down to see the pilot, in a flannel jacket that was similar to the one her father had used to wear, holding out his hand to her.

She straightened her spine and beamed brightly at him, taking his hand as he helped her down onto the Tarmac.

"Do you need help with your luggage?" the pilot asked.

"No, thank you. I'm okay." Evelyn shifted the weight of her carry-on bag on her shoulder as she walked onto the chip-sealed portion of the airstrip. She picked up her suitcase from outside the plane, where it had been unloaded, and popped up the handle to roll it.

A gust of wind tossed her hair in her face and she cursed herself for not tying it back before she headed for the small terminal.

I wonder if anyone will remember who I am?

A knot formed in her stomach—because it had been twenty years since she had been taken away…twenty years since her father died. She remembered some faces, but she was sure most folks were long gone.

Like her maternal grandmother.

And her classmates at the small village school wouldn't remember her.

It was for the best that they didn't.

It was *her* fault her father had left that night in the rain and died. She should have stopped him.

She'd taken away Wolf's Harbor's finest doctor. Now she was here to make it right.

Or as right as she could in the limited amount of time she was here.

The terminal was quiet. Everyone was dealing with

cargo, rather than the few passengers. The other two who had been on her plane were long gone. They had somewhere to go. Loved ones to see.

She had no one.

"Can I help you?"

Evelyn turned to the young woman who was manning the counter at the Wolf's Harbor terminal.

"I'm looking for directions to the town clinic."

The young woman smiled brightly. "It's about a fifteen-minute walk from here. Do you want me to call you a taxi?"

"That would be great. Thank you," Evelyn said, smiling back.

The young woman nodded, but didn't pick up the phone. Instead she got up off her stool, and Evelyn saw the round belly of a pregnant woman under her hoodie.

The young woman opened the back door and shouted. "I have a fare for you!"

Evelyn's pulse kicked up a notch, and she couldn't help but wonder if it would be her Uncle Yazzie.

His had been the only taxi cab in town twenty years ago. When her father had been working endless hours at the clinic, or in Juneau at the hospital, Uncle Yazzie would come and pick her up every day in his taxi cab and take her to school. She'd often stay with him and her grandmother. Her mother's people.

A young man of about twenty, who looked very familiar, came out from the back.

He beamed at her and held out his hand. "Can I take you someplace, miss?"

She didn't answer as she racked her brain for how she knew this man.

"Are you okay, miss?" he asked, appearing slightly uncomfortable with her staring.

"Sorry, you look so familiar," she said, before catching herself.

"Really? I look like my dad—or so they tell me."

"Then it must be jet lag messing with me." She rubbed her eyes. "I didn't mean to gawk at you. Just déjà vu."

The young man smiled. "It happens. Don't worry. Unless you know my dad?"

"Who is your dad?" she asked.

"Joe—Yazzie Sr. I'm Joe Jr. Do you know him?"

Evelyn's heart skipped a beat as she saw it now. Saw the younger version of her uncle in this young man. Obviously Uncle Yazzie's son had been born after she'd left. For a moment she had a pang of homesickness. She'd missed Joe Jr.'s birth. Her *cousin's* birth.

Evelyn's heart stopped its racing and she took his hand. "The name sounds familiar..."

She wasn't lying—she just wasn't telling him the whole story. There would be time for that later...that was if his father was interested in seeing her again.

"Not surprising. He doesn't leave Wolf's Harbor."

"Well, I'm Dr. Evelyn Saunders. I'm looking for a ride to the medical clinic."

"Of course—you're the new OB/GYN in town for the next three months, yeah?" He picked up her suitcase.

"I am," Evelyn answered.

"My wife..." He pointed over his shoulder at the young woman behind the counter. "Jennifer—she's due in a month."

Jennifer beamed and nodded. "I have an appointment with you tomorrow afternoon, Dr. Saunders."

"Well, I look forward to seeing you then."

Evelyn quickly reassessed the small bump under her hoodie and some red flags went up. It could be nothing. Some woman were known to carry very small until right near the end. But Evelyn would be sure to check out Jennifer Yazzie's file as soon as she got access to the patient records.

She followed Joe Jr. out of the terminal and to a blue and orange cab that was painted exactly the same as the old cab she remembered, but a new model of the vehicle.

She slipped into the passenger seat in the front and after Joe had got her luggage in the back he took the driver's seat and started the cab.

"Is this your first time in Wolf's Harbor, Dr. Saunders?"

"No." She wanted to say yes—to serve her three-month rotation and maybe go unnoticed, so she could leave the painful memories of her past behind her—but she couldn't lie.

She'd lost a piece of herself when she'd been taken away from Wolf's Harbor, and even though she was only going to be here for a short time perhaps she could lay to rest some of the ghosts that continued to haunt her. Stop the restless feeling she often got. The night terrors which sometimes still plagued her.

"Really?" Joe asked. "I don't remember seeing your face before."

"How old are you, Joe?" she asked.

"Twenty—which I know is young to be a father…"

"I wasn't going to judge you for your age, or tell you that you're too young to be a father—it's just that the last time I was in Wolf's Harbor I was ten, which was twenty years ago."

Joe beamed. "No kidding? Well, welcome home."

He didn't pry further, for which she was glad, but she was sure that he'd soon be getting the word out that she was back.

It would be better this way. To let everyone know that

she had come back instead of facing a constant stream of questioning shock. She just hoped they wouldn't all give her the cold shoulder as they had done for the past twenty years.

Twenty years with no word from her family up here.

Twenty years of silence.

Joe pulled up in front of the clinic and she paid the fare, insisting that he keep the change. The clinic was a new building with red siding. It reminded her of a barn, but it was very clean, with the sign freshly painted. It sat on the main road downtown, and through the gaps in the buildings across from her she could see the tall masts and onboard hoists of the fishing boats in the harbor. Her father had practiced medicine out of a small storefront. This looked so much better than that cramped old space.

Joe set her luggage down beside her.

"I guess I'll see you tomorrow, Dr. Saunders."

Evelyn grinned. "See you tomorrow, Joe."

She picked up her luggage as Joe drove away. The clinic sign said "Closed" and there was no sign of Dr. Pearson anywhere. It began to drizzle and Evelyn tried the handle. The door was unlocked and she stepped inside.

There was no nurse behind the reception desk. It was quiet. Deserted.

Great.

She wandered past the reception desk, looking for someone. Anyone.

"Dr. Pearson?" she called out. She was met with only silence.

Just great.

She peeked into an exam room and flicked on the light. It was modern and well stocked, which surprised her for such a small community. She wandered through the room, taking it all in. She couldn't believe that she was back here. Back in Wolf's Harbor.

Home.

Evelyn cursed under her breath. She had to stop thinking about this place as her home. This was not her home. It hadn't been for some time.

Still, it was hard not to think of those days. And all the time that had been taken away from her.

And whose fault was that?

"Who are you?" a harsh voice demanded.

Evelyn spun round and was taken aback by the sight of the most handsome man she'd ever seen. She felt a bit stunned, and all she could do was stare at him in awe. He was tall, broad-shouldered. He wore a flannel shirt stretched a little tight over his strong, muscular upper arms. His dark hair was close-cropped and his skin was a warm, deep tawny brown. He had a neatly kept beard. But it was his eyes, a green-gray-blue, which were really stunning. Clear, bright—and focused on *her.*

They held her rooted to the spot.

"You're not supposed to be in here," he growled.

"Are you Dr. Pearson?" she asked, finally finding her voice.

His eyes narrowed. "No. He's gone back to Juneau."

"What?" Evelyn frowned. "You've got to be kidding me!"

Derek had been in the back. He had been waiting for the new doctor to arrive, annoyed that Dr. Pearson had left for Juneau early and saddled him with the new OB/GYN when he had a full caseload as general practitioner to handle.

He hadn't left for a bigger city even though he could have.

His mother had begged him to return to Chicago when

Vivian died. She'd even offered to retire from her catering business to help him raise his daughter, but he couldn't leave Alaska.

He might have been born in Chicago but, like his parents—one of whom came from Haiti and one from the Ukraine—he needed to forge his own path. Put down his own roots. And Wolf's Harbor had been the place to do that.

He loved it here. Loved the people. Loved his life.

Even though as a widower it was slightly lonely.

Whose fault is that?

It had been his choice to be alone after his wife had died from a uterine rupture when their daughter was born. His life was his practice and his daughter.

Still, he was annoyed that he had to deal with these rotating doctors. Doctors who came in and left him with more work in the end. Doctors who saw the patients of Wolf's Harbor as an inconvenience. He was tired of the extra burden, but he'd gladly bear it for his patients.

Dr. Pearson had left him high and dry by leaving before the new OB/GYN showed up, and Mo was still getting over a bug she'd picked up, so he had to relieve the sitter. He would be glad when school started again. He had no time to deal with another rotation doctor and Dr. Pearson had just dumped this one in his lap.

So like Dr. Pearson. So like *all* these doctors who came through the town, never staying longer than they had too. Never willing to help him out or put in a good word to get a hospital built in town. These big city doctors were all selfish—if it wouldn't further their career they didn't lend a hand.

Okay, you're sounding like a curmudgeon now.

He stuck it out all year in this isolated community, while these specialists fluttered in and out, never staying long enough to get to know the people. There was no real trust between these doctors and the patients. It was a dangerous thing.

He tried not to think about how the lack of a specialist during one of these rotations had cost him everything. How his late wife had hemorrhaged and bled out before they could get her on an air ambulance to Sitka. And the fact that it had happened during a storm that had grounded all the planes had made it so much worse. There had been nothing he could do. But if there had been a hospital here in Wolf's Harbor maybe she would have had a fighting chance.

He focused on this fiery, auburn-haired woman, who thought it was okay just to waltz into his closed office. He'd been taken back by the beautiful, tall, polished woman who was now standing in his exam room. *So* like Dr. Pearson to have his girlfriends and paramours just show up unannounced.

Although he was a bit jealous that this one was one of Dr. Pearson's girlfriends…

He'd seen many of them go through this clinic when Dr. Pearson had been here on rotation, but this one—this one actually made him jealous of Dr. Pearson.

It had been a long time since he'd been attracted to someone. If he didn't have Mo, or the practice to run—if he was the same man he had been before he'd come to Wolf's Harbor—he would pursue a woman just like this.

You're lonely. Face it.

"Pearson has gone back to Juneau," Derek said again, and moved from the doorway to encourage her to leave. "Sorry for your trouble. I can call you a cab…"

"I'm the new OB/GYN. I'm Dr. Saunders."

Derek frowned. "What? I thought that this was Dr. Merritt's rotation?"

"Dr. Merritt just went on an extended honeymoon," Dr. Saunders said. "I'm covering her practice."

"What?" Derek asked, scowling. So now Dr. Merritt had just got a replacement without consulting him? Not that Dr. Merritt *had* to consult him, but it would have been considerate of her to do so.

At least she sent someone else.

Although he knew nothing about this Dr. Saunders. "Well, that's unacceptable. Just because we're a small town, it doesn't mean we'll take *anyone*."

She crossed her arms. "Why is it unacceptable?"

"I know nothing about you."

"So?" she replied firmly. "You need an OB/GYN and there are appointments tomorrow."

"How do you know there are appointments tomorrow? You obviously don't know Dr. Pearson, because you thought I was him."

"First, I know there are appointments here tomorrow because Joe Yazzie Jr. and his wife are expected for prenatal. I introduced myself to them when I landed from Sitka. And second I assumed you were a doctor—was I mistaken?"

The nerve of her.

Of course he was pleased that she'd already made a connection with one of his patients. She had one up on every other doctor who'd waltzed through here.

But why were redheads always like this? Every one he'd ever encountered in Chicago had been like this. And of course he was a complete sucker for them.

You can't have her.

He had to keep reminding himself of that fact. He wanted nothing to do with someone who would leave after her rotation was done. He wanted nothing to do with *anyone* ever again.

Not since Vivian had died.

He was not going to go through anything like that again. Besides, he had Mo to think of, and his practice, his patients. That was what was important.

"I *am* a doctor," he said tersely. "I'm the general practitioner of Wolf's Harbor."

"Are you on rotation too?" she asked.

"No," he snapped. "Unlike you and Dr. Pearson, I am here all the time. Wolf's Harbor is my home. I actually *care* about my patients and their medical care enough to stay."

Her eyes narrowed and a strange expression crossed her face, but only briefly.

"If you truly cared about your patients then you wouldn't object to me being here. I'm here to stay."

His eyes widened. He was surprised. "Stay? As in permanently?"

She blushed. "Well…no."

Of course not. He knew better than to get his hopes up. *Who was this woman?*

"I'm just as capable as Dr. Merritt," she said, breaking the tension.

"Are you?" he asked, raising an eyebrow. "I at least *know* Dr. Merritt. I know nothing about you. Not even your first name."

She smiled tightly. "Dr. Evelyn Saunders. I just completed my fellowship in fetal surgery at Richler Medicine in Seattle. I'm one of the few people in this country who can perform delicate fetal surgeries. I'm also a board-certified obstetrical and gynecological fellow, and a pediatric fellow specializing in premature infants. I completed that fellowship and practiced for three years at the Mayo Clinic in Rochester, Minnesota. You can check my credentials, but they speak for themselves. I am more experienced than Dr. Merritt and I will be an asset to your patients."

Damn. She was right.

And he was completely impressed by her résumé and where she'd studied. She had every right to be confident to the point of obnoxiousness.

She was a triple threat and he'd be an absolute idiot to turn her away—but he couldn't help but wonder why someone with so much experience didn't have a thriving practice of her own.

Who cares? She can help your patients even if it's only for a short time.

He couldn't help but wonder if someone like her had been here that horrific night five years ago Vivian would still be here and he wouldn't be alone. Mo would have her mother. He'd still have that piece of his heart and soul that had been torn away the night he'd lost Vivian. The night Mo had lost her mother. His patients needed her.

"Fine." He sighed and he ran a hand over his head. "I'll show you to the apartment and get you a clinic key, then give you all the information you need to start tomorrow."

"Thank you, Dr...?" she asked, extending a hand.

"Dr. Taylor. Dr. Derek Taylor." He ignored her hand, afraid to touch her and still not wanting her to feel too welcome. "Come on, I'll show you to your place."

His mother would *totally* be slapping him upside the head if she could see how he was being such a jerk to this woman, but he couldn't get attached. Dr. Saunders would be gone in three months and he had no interest in getting attached to someone who wasn't going to stick it out for the long run.

It was so much easier on his heart this way. Better for Mo too. He didn't want her to get hurt. He'd promised Vivian he'd protect Mo. So he planned to treat Evelyn like every other physician who passed through Wolf's Harbor on rotation. Even if she *was* easy on the eye and had a spirited personality—the kind which always drew him in when it came to members of the opposite sex…

He was a professional above all else. His patients came first. And even though he knew nothing about her—even though training a new doctor about the ins and outs of Wolf's Harbor Medical would be an extra burden on him—he'd gladly do it.

Unlike all the other doctors who came and went, *he* was here for the long haul.

CHAPTER TWO

HE'S A BIT cool and stand-offish.

Evelyn waited outside with her rolling suitcase as Dr. Taylor—Derek—locked up the clinic. It was beginning to drizzle and it was dusk, but since it was summer it would stay light pretty late.

She glanced at her watch and remembered she hadn't switched it over to Alaska daylight time.

Derek whistled. "That's some fancy watch you have there!"

Heat bloomed in her cheeks, because she'd caught the undertone of his sarcasm. Yeah it was flashy and out of place here, but he didn't have to point it out. "It was my grandmother's. She left it to me when she passed."

His expression softened. "Sorry."

"She had a good life. She was ninety-nine when I lost her to cancer. I miss her—she was the only family I had."

No, she wasn't, a little whisper said in her mind, but she ignored it. She knew now that Uncle Yazzie was still around, but Léelk'w probably wasn't. Still, she'd been gone for twenty years and had had no contact with any of them. It was apparent that they hadn't thought of her. Joe Jr. hadn't even blinked an eye when she'd told him her last name.

So she had no family left. Not really.

"I understand," he muttered, but then shook his head as if he felt bad about what he'd said. "Look, let's get out of this drizzle before it turns to full-out rain."

"That's fine with me. Is the apartment far?"

"Nope." Derek shoved his hands in his hoodie and headed up an alleyway behind the clinic.

Evelyn rolled her eyes and followed him. It wasn't really an alleyway after all, but a steep slope up to a set of wooden stairs that were at the back of the clinic.

"This is the place," Derek said. "There's no connection to the clinic on the inside, however."

"Great—well, at least it's summer." Evelyn would hate to climb those open wooden steps to the second floor in the winter. She wouldn't be here then.

A shudder ran down her spine as she thought of those cold Alaska nights. How the sun had set early, the northern lights had shone and there had been hot chocolate by the fire with her father in the cabin.

He had read to her for hours, until her eyes were so heavy that he'd had to carry her to bed and tuck her in while the snowstorms had raged outside her window.

She'd been safe in her father's arms.

"Come on, then," Derek said, interrupting her thoughts as he jogged up the steps, not even offering to take her suitcase for her.

Evelyn cursed under her breath and lugged the case up, bumping it with each step. So much for her new luggage.

At the top Derek was waiting, and he was smirking. She wanted to wipe it off his face.

"You okay there?" he asked, a hint of humor in his voice.

"Perfectly," Evelyn said through gritted teeth.

Derek opened the door and stepped inside. She dragged her suitcase in. The apartment was a mess.

Derek was annoyed. "Yeah, sorry about this. I forgot. Dr. Pearson is a bit of a slob."

"It's fine," Evelyn said. She could clean it up, no problem. She was definitely not a fan of Dr. Pearson, though. First the jerk had left without waiting for her, leaving her to the mercy of Dr. Derek Taylor, and now this.

Derek handed her a key ring. "The clinic key is this large one and the other is the apartment."

"Is there a car that's available for me while I'm here?"

"Unless you drove one in from the ferry terminal that connects to Juneau then, no, but everything is in walking distance."

Great.

She'd been hoping a car would be available because she wanted to see if her father's place was still standing. She was wondering if it had changed. From going through what had been left to her after her grandmother had died, she knew that the property had been sold shortly after she'd left Wolf's Harbor.

Grandma hadn't want any part of Wolf's Harbor. She hadn't wanted any reminders of her son's worst mistake.

"Your father could've been a great surgeon, but he left for Alaska and took up with your mother and I never saw him again. He could've been great, Evelyn, but he threw it all away for a woman who was not part of the world he was brought up in."

Evelyn shook her grandmother's voice from her head.

Her father might not have become the kind of surgical god her grandmother always envisioned, but he'd been a respected general practitioner in Wolf's Harbor. People had looked up to him. He'd saved lives and her grandmother had never got to see it.

Now she, Evelyn, would finish what he'd started and

lay the memories of her father to rest. Maybe then she could move on.

"I flew in from Sitka," she said as she pocketed the keys. "So if I want to order in a pizza I just say the back of the clinic?"

"Yeah—they'll know," Derek said. "The clinic opens at nine."

"And how do I access patients' records? Is there a computer password?"

"No password—and you can access the patients' records by opening the filing cabinet. Your schedule is on the receptionist's calendar."

There was that smug sense of humor again. As if he was trying to shock her with the fact that they still had hard copies of their records.

"Okay. Well, I'll be there earlier than nine to get myself acquainted with everything."

Derek reached out, grabbing the arm with the fancy watch, and stared at its face. "Not if you don't set your alarm to Alaska Daylight Savings, you won't."

Just that simple touch caused a shiver of anticipation to run down her spine. He was annoying, but there was something about him which drew her in.

He was dangerous.

She had no interest in any relationship. Every relationship she'd been in had ended with her being dumped because she could never commit—because she was never there and was too focused on her career. Or so those men had believed. She'd actually pushed them away because she knew she didn't deserve what she secretly wanted.

A family of her own.

She shook him off. "I'm well aware of the time-change."

He smirked and raised an eyebrow, then moved past

her through the open door. "Okay, then. I'll see you to-morrow—bright and early. Good night, Dr. Saunders."

Evelyn shut the door after him and was glad to be rid of him. For now.

She'd see him tomorrow, but after a good night's rest she knew that she would be better suited to dealing with him.

She could handle guys like Derek. Guys who were arrogant and used to being the lone wolf. They saw every new arrival as a threat.

Nathan had been nothing like Derek. When she'd first met him he'd been nice and almost too accommodating. Still, look where that had got her. It had got her nowhere. She'd spent two years of her life with Nathan and he'd left her.

You really gave him nothing, though. Remember?

She locked the door and scrubbed a hand over her face, staring at the apartment and feeling completely exhausted and hungry.

There was a clock that was showing Alaska time, so she quickly set her watch even as her stomach growled, reminding her that she hadn't had much to eat since leaving Sitka. While she'd been dragging her bag up the stairs she'd noticed a pub across the road, and it had looked like the kind of bar that might serve a quick meal. She was starving. She didn't feel like waiting for pizza. She felt antsy, trapped in this messy apartment. It would be better for her to get out of there and grab a breath of fresh air.

She grabbed her purse and her keys. First she'd eat and then she'd tackle this mess—even though she was still running on East Coast time and needed to sleep.

The drizzle had dissipated and a damp mist hung in the air. Outside it was quiet, with only a couple of trucks slowly puttering through down town. She knew that it was at least three hours to the nearest ferry terminal, and then four hours to Juneau. Wolf's Harbor was remote, and surrounded by the dense, mountainous forests of the Inside Passage.

She remembered when her father had used to drive her to the far side of the island, to the ferry terminal, so she could watch the large ferry bringing people to the island and sometimes a cruise ship on its way to Skagway. And sometimes she'd see the orcas.

For the most part Wolf's Harbor relied on logging and fishing, and it was only fishing vessels or large logging trucks that would go by.

A shiver ran down her spine as she thought of her father's death. How he'd been hit by that runaway logging truck that had been going too fast through town. And how a ring had been in his pocket.

"Evelyn, your mother has been gone a long time now. Jocelyn isn't going to replace her. She makes me happy. Be good. I won't be long at Jocelyn's."

That had been the last time she'd seen her father alive. The last words he'd said.

Don't think about it.

She dashed across the road and straight into the pub.

As soon as she took a step inside the murmur of hushed talking stopped and people stared at her. There'd never been a lot of visitors when she was a kid.

"Hi," she said, waving uneasily. "I'm the new doctor in town."

There was another few seconds of stares, which felt like an eternity, but then most people returned to their food, their conversations or their drinks.

Except one.

Derek.

He was positively glowering at her from the far side

of the bar. And he was next to the only empty seat in the place.

Great.

Maybe it would be better to wait for pizza? But of course now that she'd made her entrance and he was staring at her she couldn't really back down.

So she pretended to ignore him and sat down, picking up one of the vinyl-covered menus and pretending to study it, ignoring the sensation of his staring at her.

"I thought you would be cleaning," Derek said gruffly.

She glanced at him. "Usually a gentleman would introduce himself or offer to buy a woman a drink before trying to strike up a conversation with her."

Derek snickered, staring ahead at the bar. She could see his reflection in the mirror.

"I'm no gentleman. And you know who I am."

"Do I?" she muttered.

He got up and just stood there, saying nothing until she turned and looked at him.

"What?" she asked.

"Hi, I'm Derek Taylor. Can I buy you a drink?"

"Not interested." And she turned back to her menu, trying not to smile.

"Oh, for the love of…"

"Sit down." She chuckled. "I don't need a drink."

Derek sat down, setting his mug of beer back on the bar. "I'm surprised to see you out and about."

"Why is that?" she asked.

"Because usually the specialists who come into town to do their rotation don't bother with the locals. They order in, keep to themselves—it's somewhat of a burden."

"Well, the cleaning of that apartment is 'somewhat of a burden.'"

She set down the menu. She was hungry, but she

wasn't sure she really wanted to eat at this moment. Her stomach was twisting and turning from being back here. And as she glanced around the dim bar she had faint memories of this place.

Her father and Uncle Yazzie playing pool here, and her mother singing up on that stage. Her last gig before she'd got sick with the cancer that had killed her. And as she studied the room further she remembered the booth that was reserved for live entertainment. It had seemed so much bigger when she'd been curled up in it, eating ice cream.

"Daddy, what're you doing?" Evelyn asked, seeing her father with another woman.

Her dad stood up, shocked. "Evie, what're you doing here?"

Her eyes brimmed with tears. "I saw your truck outside. I was running an errand for Léelk'w. Who is that woman?"

"This is Jocelyn. She's my girlfriend."

Jocelyn smiled and waved. She was pretty, blonde and young—and not her mother.

"No!" Evelyn screamed. "No!"

And she turned and ran out of the bar.

Her father yelled for her to come back.

"Hey, you okay?" Derek asked, interrupting her memory.

"Yeah," she said, and ran her hand through her hair in the nervous twitch she'd always had. "Yeah, I'm fine."

"You totally zoned out," Derek said. "Tired?"

"A bit."

"Where did you say you were from?" he asked, trying to draw her into conversation.

"Boston, but I've been in Sitka a couple of days."

"Still, the change is a bit jarring if you're not used to it."

"I'm used to it," she whispered. "It's just been a long time."

Derek cocked an eyebrow. "Pardon?"

The door opened and the hair on the back of her neck stood on end. She slowly turned around in her seat, because instinctively she knew what to expect and she wasn't sure she was ready for it.

She wasn't ready to face a ghost from her past.

Taking a deep breath, she stood and looked up at the man who had been her family. A man she'd never thought she'd see again because her grandmother had cut off all ties to Evelyn's life here in Alaska.

The man her father had thought of as a brother, because he had estranged himself from his WASP mother back in Boston, "throwing his life away" to live in the wilderness.

It had been Uncle Yazzie who had introduced her parents. Her mother's loveable, goofball little brother. A man who had represented everything her grandmother had hated about her son's life and his wife in Alaska.

Tears stung her eyes as she stared into the dark eyes of Joe Yazzie Sr. She could still see him standing on the Tarmac of the airport all those years ago when she'd been forced to move to Boston.

"I had to see with my own eyes," Yazzie whispered. "I thought my son was bluffing me."

Her stomach twisted into a knot as she wondered if he would turn his back on her. She wanted to run. She was afraid of his rejection in person, because his silence had hurt her as a child.

No. You have to face him. Good or bad.

"Uncle Yazzie…" she whispered, her voice faltering.

Derek was highly confused. "What's going on here?"

Evelyn sighed and turned back to Derek. "I'm from Wolf's Harbor. I'm a local."

She's a local?

If Evelyn Saunders was a local he would know that. He'd lived here for fifteen years and he knew everyone in this town because he was the general practitioner.

And he would remember her.

She was local?

He was still in a bit of disbelief over it all, but there was no denying it when he saw Joe Yazzie Sr.'s reaction to her.

The man who was usually stone-cold and emotionless had his arms wrapped around her, holding her and crying.

Crying?

Derek did a double-take. He'd never seen Joe Sr. cry. *Ever.*

"Am I missing something?" Derek asked.

Joe took a step back, tears glistening in his eyes as he spoke some words in Tlingit.

Derek could only make out a piece of what he was saying. Something about someone being home?

Joe turned to him. "Dr. Taylor, this is my sister's child. She's been missing for over twenty years."

"Missing?" Derek asked, confused.

Evelyn smiled up at Joe and then looked back at Derek. "My father died when I was ten and my guardian was my grandmother in Boston. A social worker came and—"

"Took her away," Joe interrupted. "We were her family. Her father left her care to me and my mother. Evelyn is half-Tlingit and we would've cared for her, but we lost out to the Matriarch Saunders in Boston. There was no will, and a judge determined Georgina Saunders a better fit. She had the finances…we didn't and couldn't afford to fight. Georgina had sole custody. It broke my mother's heart, being separated from her. We tried to call, but Georgina changed her number and blocked us at every turn."

"I see." Derek was in shock.

Joe turned back to Evelyn. "We tried to get in touch with you, Evie. I swear!"

Evelyn nodded, only Derek noticed a strange expression on her face, as if she didn't quite believe it. "I know."

"So you're related to the Yazzie family? You didn't mention it before," Derek said.

Evelyn shot him a warning look. "It didn't come up naturally in conversation."

"I asked where you were from."

"I am from Boston."

Joe frowned. "Well, I'm glad you're back, Evie. We have a lot to catch up on."

"I think that's my cue to go," Derek said as he stood up.

"You don't have to," Evelyn said.

"I have things to do. I'll see you tomorrow." He quickly slapped down money for his beer.

He had to get out of this place. He had to put some distance between him and Evelyn. *Fast*. He'd overstayed anyways. He'd only come for a quick drink before he had to head home to relieve the sitter and deal with a cranky, fussy five-year-old who wanted the sitter to stay longer because Jessica read stories better than Daddy.

Derek looked back at the reunion scene. He smiled and for one brief moment wished he could stay. Evelyn's smile made his heart skip a beat. It made him feel like his old self.

Seeing Evelyn with Joe Yazzie made him feel lonely.

She was from here.
She had family.
He frowned at the realization.

Evelyn had a reason to stay, and if she stayed…

He didn't want to get his hopes up that another doctor would stay. They never did. So he was going to carry on believing she was like every other doctor before her. A doctor with a time limit.

Even if secretly he wouldn't mind if she stayed, because he was so drawn to her and it would be nice to share the load—

That thought scared him.

There was no room in his heart for anyone else.

His heart was too broken, too damaged, for him to make room for someone again.

CHAPTER THREE

EVELYN GOT UP before her alarm in the morning. Of course it had been hard to sleep, because her emotions were all over the place.

The reunion with Uncle Yazzie had wrung her out completely, even if she *had* managed to keep it all together. And every time she'd closed her eyes she'd seen her father, her mother or Derek. And the fact that Derek had invaded her thoughts irritated her greatly.

He shouldn't be in her thoughts.

She was here to serve Stefanie's rotation in Wolf's Harbor and then she'd return to Sitka. And then... She didn't know where.

There were so many opportunities.

Nathan hadn't understood that about her. She wanted to keep learning and expanding her curriculum vitae. She wanted to learn from the very best in her field of work. And all Nathan had wanted to do was stay put, have kids and settle down.

You want those things too. You're just afraid.

Evelyn ignored those thoughts. They were dangerous to have, and she was never going to entertain them. She was never going to have a husband or kids. She didn't want to put her heart at risk or, worse, have her kids go through the traumatic experience that she had.

Evelyn swore she would never do that. Even if she wanted it badly.

"You're restless, Evelyn."

Nathan's words echoed in her head.

Maybe she was, but she could protect herself better this way.

She took a sip of the instant coffee she'd made from the powder she'd found in a cupboard and winced.

It was awful. Bitter.

She dumped the coffee down the sink before gathering up her things and heading outside. She shivered, even though it was summer. It was brisk compared to Boston, and she was glad she'd brought her sweater.

Down the steps and through the alleyway beside the clinic was a small coffee shop, and she could smell coffee brewing.

The bell above the door jingled as she walked in and a sudden rush of being there before, washed over her. The scent of coffee and the sugary sweet smell of pies wafted in from the back.

She'd been here before, but she was having a hard time remembering it.

A middle-aged woman looked up from cleaning the counter and beamed. "Well, I'll be…"

"Hi," Evelyn said unsurely.

"Joe told me that you had come home."

The woman came out from behind the counter and before Evelyn could stop her she was being wrapped up in the woman's arms and crushed in a bear hug.

"You don't remember me, do you?" the woman asked, her smile not disappearing.

"No, I'm sorry."

"That's okay." The proprietor walked back behind the

counter. "You left so long ago. Your father used to come in here every day to get coffee. I'm Sally."

Evelyn smiled at Sally. "Nice to meet you…again."

Sally grinned. "No worries. What will it be, Evie…? I mean, Dr. Saunders. *That's* going to be hard for me to get used to saying. I can't believe you're a doctor. Your dad would be so proud."

Just the simple mention of her father caused Evelyn a pang of longing. And then the memory came back to her.

Yellow curtains filtering in the bright sunlight on those odd days when the sun would peek through the clouds. Chocolate milk and her father blowing the steam across the top of his coffee before he took a sip. And *her*. That woman Jocelyn with her bright smile and golden hair. The one who'd tried to take her mother's place.

Evelyn shook the memory away. She had to focus on today.

"Can I have a coffee, please?"

"Of course, Dr. Saunders." Sally turned and picked up a carafe of coffee. It smelled heavenly. "Would you like it to go?"

"Yes, that would be great, Sally."

Evelyn took a seat at the counter, her pulse thundering in her ears because nothing had changed. The drapes were faded, but everything was the same. She'd forgotten about this place, but the moment Sally had mentioned her father it had come flooding back to her.

And the pain was just as raw as it had been twenty years ago.

She hated feeling it again.

You knew this would be hard. That's why you're here.

The door chimed again and Derek walked in, pulling down the hood of his hoodie.

"Brisk out there today, Sally. Can I get…?" He trailed

off as those brilliant gray-green eyes locked onto her, sending a shiver of the dreams from the night before through her.

His eyes were the most intense she'd ever seen.

"Good morning," she said, breaking the gaze so she could look away and try not to let him see her blush by hiding behind her long hair.

"Good morning," Derek said carefully, and took the stool next to her at the counter. "I see you got up early."

"I told you that I would." She held out her arm and pointed to her watch. "See—it's set on Alaska time."

A brief smile flitted across Derek's face. "So it is."

"And I have my key. So I'm not going to be a burden for you."

Sally handed her a coffee. "There you go, Dr. Saunders."

"Thanks, Sally. How much do I owe you?"

Sally shook her head. "Not today. It's on the house. A welcome back gift from me."

"Thank you!"

"Hey, I've been your physician for fifteen years—how come *I* don't get a free coffee every now and again?" Derek complained.

Sally frowned. "You're not local."

"I've been here longer than *she* has," Derek teased.

Evelyn playfully stuck out her tongue and beamed at Sally. "I'll see you later, Sally. Thanks for the coffee."

She felt like skipping out of that coffee shop, but she refrained.

She didn't get very far before Derek, carrying his own paper cup, came jogging up beside her. "You won over Sally pretty fast," he said, sounding impressed. "Not many people do."

"She seems cheerful enough."

Derek's eyes narrowed. "She knows you—but you don't remember her, do you?"

"I told her that," Evelyn said. "I was young when I left. Are you telling me she's usually a grump?"

Derek frowned and took a pull of his coffee. "Maybe she's only a grump with me. She said once that she didn't like doctors."

"I hate to break it to you, but *I'm* a doctor," she said lightly.

"Yeah, but you're Thorne Saunders' daughter, and those who remember you have a warm fuzzy feeling when it comes to you. Which will change when you leave again."

"What's that supposed to mean?" Evelyn asked as Derek sidestepped her to open the door of the clinic. "And how do you know my father's name? I never told you."

"Come on—you're not going to be here forever, Saunders," he said as he stepped through the door and flicked on the fluorescent lights. "It's just a phase. And I did some research last night. Your father was the first general practitioner to stay in Wolf's Harbor. He was the first to stay and help the people here. I'm impressed."

That gave her a punch in the gut that she hadn't been expecting, because he was right. They remembered her father with fondness, but really they were just being kind. These weren't *her* people.

She'd been gone too long.

And you're the reason why your father's dead.

"I'm just here to do my job. I can't control people's re-actions to me. But if I instill some kind of trust in them while I'm here, then all the better."

"Don't get your feathers ruffled," Derek said as he set his coffee cup on the counter. "I'm just stating a fact."

"Yeah, because you're annoyed by the townspeople's

reaction to me. My guess is they never really warm up to the other doctors that rotate through here. Am I right? And that gives you some sort of power."

Those intense eyes flickered with something close to anger and she realized she'd struck a nerve.

Good.

"You have use of exam rooms three and four. One and two are mine for today." He picked up his coffee cup and stormed away to the first exam room.

Evelyn was going to ask him more when the clinic's door chimed and a young woman in scrubs came in, stopping dead in her tracks as she looked up at Evelyn.

"Oh, you're not Dr. Merritt," she said.

Evelyn sighed and plastered a fake smile on her face, bracing herself to explain who she was again. Hopefully the nurse wouldn't gave the same contempt for her that Derek did, but she wasn't going to hold her breath just yet.

Derek had been managing to avoid Evelyn all morning, but to give her credit she was taking good care of her patients and they genuinely looked happy to see her. Or at least that was what Janet, his nurse and current spy, had said.

He picked up the next file in his pile.

Great.

He always had trouble with this patient, and he couldn't even begin to think why she was here today.

"Katlian Yazzie?"

The venerable old woman stood up and fixed him with a stare that meant business. "Well, it's about time. I'm not getting any younger."

Derek tried not to roll his eyes—and then a thought crept through his head. If Evelyn was related to Mrs. Yazzie's son Joe, then she was probably familiar with

Katlian Yazzie. For one brief moment he thought about palming her off on Evelyn.

Mrs. Yazzie made it clear time and time again that she didn't trust doctors. *"I like you, Dr. Taylor. I just don't trust you. I don't trust any of you."* And he couldn't help but wonder if she'd trusted Thorne Saunders. Most had.

Thorne was a bit of legend. He had been the first doctor to stay and after his death no one had stayed. Not until *he* came.

Of course the Yazzies didn't speak of Thorne the way the other locals did, and now he understood why. Thorne had been family, and he understood how grief could devastate. How it was too painful to talk and just easier to bottle it up.

"It's good to see you again," Derek said, grinning at her.

"Don't *even*!" she teased. "I know you're not thrilled to see me, but I'm not here to see *you*. I'm here to see the OB/GYN. This Dr. Merritt."

"Dr. Merritt isn't here, Katlian."

"Joe Jr.'s wife is supposed to see her this afternoon and I wanted to talk to her about Jennifer's birthing plan. I didn't trust that Dr. Pearson."

"That I can agree with you on, but Dr. Merritt got married and sent in a replacement. Have you talked to your son?" he asked gently.

Katlian's brow furrowed. "What does it matter if I talked to Joe. He knows nothing. Why would I…?" The words died in her throat as Evelyn stepped out of one of the examination rooms.

Evelyn wasn't paying attention to them at first—she was flipping through a file before she stepped back into the exam room. Not even noticing them.

Katlian turned away and covered her mouth with her hand. She'd gone pale, as if she'd seen a ghost.

Derek reached out and held her shoulders, steadying her. "That's why I was wondering if you'd talked to your son."

"Is that…?" Katlian's voice wavered.

"Dr. Evelyn Saunders," Derek answered. Then he guided Katlian toward exam room number one, away from some of the curious onlookers in the waiting room. He helped Katlian take a seat and then shut the door.

Katlian was wide-eyed. "I haven't talked to Joe since the day before yesterday. I've been staying with Joe Jr. and Jennifer. They didn't tell me."

"Joe Jr. didn't know who Dr. Saunders was. But I think he told his father, because Joe Sr. and Dr. Saunders had a reunion last night."

He'd seen the love there in Joe Sr.'s eyes when he'd looked at Evelyn, but he'd seen fear in hers. The way she'd held herself, her body rigid, her smile fixed—she had been throwing up walls.

Derek knew the art of going through the motions. He'd practiced that art so many times after Vivian had died, when all people had done was offer him condolences and feel sorry for him. What he'd needed was help. So he'd learned to put on that act. Worn that armor to shield his heart from pain.

He wondered why Evelyn felt she needed to do that.

What had happened when her parents died?

He knew she'd been taken away, but there must be more to the story.

Is it really your business?

No, it wasn't and he was annoyed with himself for caring so much, but for some reason he couldn't help himself when it came to Evelyn.

She drew him in. Just this short time of getting to know her and he was completely drawn to her. He wanted to know more about her, and that was a dangerous thing indeed.

Katlian Yazzie smiled. "Evie's mother was my daughter. Evie…"

Katlian wept.

Derek was taken aback by the usually stoic woman's crying and was at a loss as to what to do. He slipped his arm around the old woman. "Joe mentioned she was taken away?"

Katlian nodded. "By Thorne's mother. Because a judge deemed that *she* was better for Evelyn. That Boston was better than Wolf's Harbor."

"Why would a judge decide that? Evelyn knew Wolf's Harbor not Boston," said Derek.

"Because Boston had access to more healthcare. Thorne was our only doctor… Well, you know no one replaced him after he died. Not until you came. So the judge decided in favor of Boston and not here."

Derek's stomach twisted in a knot. He understood that. If there had been a local hospital on the day of that storm that had grounded all the planes to Sitka, Vivian would have had a chance of survival, instead of bleeding to death.

"Thorne died at the scene—no hospital could've saved him. Joe and I fought. We fought hard—spent money that we didn't have—but we lost. We didn't have the money or the power that Georgina Saunders in Boston had. We had to walk away. I wrote to Evie constantly, but my letters were returned to sender. Once Joe went down there to see her, but Georgina had taken Evelyn away on a long vacation so he had to come back. Georgina had sole custody. We had nothing."

"I'm sure if you explain…"

Katlian sighed. "I need a moment."

"Do you still want to talk to her about Jennifer?"

Katlian shook her head. "I don't know if she would want to see me. I don't know if I'm ready to see her or even if she'll remember me."

Derek was moved by Katlian Yazzie. There was a heart in there. Everyone in Wolf's Harbor loved Katlian Yazzie, even Mo, but with Derek she'd always been untrusting and a bit cold. This was a different side to her.

"She's a doctor!" Katlian said in disbelief. "A doctor!"

"Maybe you'll have to change your stance on doctors now, eh?" he teased.

Katlian's dark eyes glittered as she frowned, but then she smiled. "Perhaps."

"Do you want me to get her?"

Katlian shook her head. "No, you let her work today. She's going to see Jennifer and I want her to be focused on her work. I will see her later."

Katlian stood up and Derek opened the door for her. She walked out of the clinic, past a few people who were still concerned about the always strong and steadfast Katlian Yazzie breaking down in the waiting room.

Derek ran a hand over his head.

Was this what his rotation with Evelyn Saunders was going to be like? All these relatives coming out of the woodwork and daily emotional reunions? As much as he was all for family coming together, he couldn't let this keep happening.

The office door chimed and a pregnant woman hunched over came in.

"I need help!" she cried out. "I'm in labor and my husband is out in the bush on a logging run."

"Evelyn!" Derek shouted over his shoulder as he dashed toward the woman.

He held on to her as she breathed through a contraction.

"Christina..." Derek said in a soothing tone. "Don't worry we have an OB/GYN here."

Christina nodded. "But it's too soon. Dr. Pearson said last week my baby was breech and he was going to try and turn it this week."

Damn Dr. Pearson.

"He didn't turn it?" Derek asked as he helped Christina toward the exam room while the receptionist worked to rebook the couple of patients who were waiting. She knew the drill when an emergency patient came in.

"He was supposed to turn it today," Christina said. "I was coming here to have it done, but labor started..."

This was why Wolf's Harbor needed a hospital. The air ambulance to take her to Sitka would be ready in thirty minutes, but this baby might be born before they got there.

Evelyn came out of the exam room where she had been going through case files. Her eyes widened as she saw the woman, but it didn't take long before she was helping Derek get the woman up on a stretcher in exam room two, which sometimes acted as an operating room.

"I'm Dr. Saunders and I'm an obstetrician. How far along are you...?"

"Christina," Derek said as he handed Evelyn a box of rubber gloves as if it was second nature.

"Thirty-seven weeks," Christina panted.

"Well, if the baby needs to come anything over thirty-six weeks is safe, Christina. Let's get you draped and then I can see how far along you are."

Derek helped drape Christina while Evelyn helped her remove her clothes.

"Is this your first baby?" Evelyn asked gently.

Christina nodded.

"How far apart are your contractions?"

"Two minutes. They started hard and fast."

She gripped the sides of the gurney and Evelyn reached out and laid her hand on Christina's belly, closing her eyes.

"Derek…" Evelyn said.

"What do you need?" he asked.

Evelyn stood up, pulling off the rubber gloves and dumping them in the waste receptacle. "Can we talk briefly outside?"

"Is everything okay?" Christina asked.

Evelyn smiled. "Perfectly. You're seven centimeters dilated. Still a bit to go, okay? Your water is intact and I'm going to send the nurse in to set up an IV to get some fluids into you and make you more comfortable."

Christina nodded and smiled. "Thank you, Doctor."

Evelyn motioned for them both to leave the exam room. "Can you get Janet in here? Get her to set up an IV and stay with Christina?"

"Sure." Derek went to the front desk and relayed the instructions to Janet, who went straight to work.

Nancy the receptionist had locked the front door and closed the blinds.

"All your patients and Dr. Saunders' patients have been rescheduled," Nancy said. "I'll man the phones. And I'm still trying to get hold of Christina's husband in the logging camp."

"Thanks, Nancy. How about that air ambulance?"

"It'll be ready in thirty minutes, but there's a storm brewing off the coast."

Great.

Derek scrubbed a hand over his face. "Keep them on standby, okay?"

Nancy nodded. "Will do, Dr. Taylor."

Derek turned to Evelyn, who had come out of the exam room.

"Well?" he asked.

"The baby is breech. Frank breech. The baby should've been turned last week."

Derek cursed under his breath. "What do we do?"

Evelyn bit her lip. "Her contractions are strong. Janet is getting a read-out, and it doesn't appear that the baby is in distress. It's just happening so fast."

"So taking them in an air ambulance to Sitka is out of the question?"

"Yeah, that baby is going to move soon, if the contractions and her dilation progress have any say in the matter. As it's a frank breech I may be able to deliver the child vaginally. But it'll be hard and she'll have to work…"

"Your other option?" Although Derek already knew, and it terrified him to the core.

"You have surgical equipment. I've seen it. And I have taken courses in anesthesiology."

"So have I," Derek said. "Do you think it will come to that?"

"I don't know." Evelyn tied her hair back. "Do you have any spare scrubs in the back?"

"Yes. What do you need me to do?"

"Prep surgical supplies, just in case, but I'm hoping that it doesn't result in a crash C-section. Janet has the patient's care in hand. You didn't tell me she was a nurse who had skill in midwifery."

"Well, we never got around to that." Derek took a deep breath. "I'll help any way I can."

Evelyn nodded. "I appreciate it. I've delivered frank breech babies before. It can be done. Protocols have changed. It's not an automatic C-section."

Derek nodded. "I know."

"Good, because it looks like there's going to be a baby born. Today." Evelyn headed off to the storage room to change into scrubs.

He went to collect the surgical supplies, his insides twisting, and tried to shake away all those dark memories that were threatening to bubble up.

There's a supply of blood in the fridge. You're prepared this time.

He had this. This was his patient. He had control. He was prepared for anything.

Vivian's death had taught him to be prepared so more lives could be saved and fewer lives lost. Vivian's death was the reason why he fought so hard for a hospital in Wolf's Harbor. And it wasn't just for crash C-sections, but other traumatic injuries. They needed more room. They needed surgeons here. Qualified people.

But no one ever stayed.

Except him.

And Evelyn?

She could handle it. She was trained for this and he was glad she was here. They were the only hope and he had to pull himself together. There was no time to think about Vivian. Right now he had to help Evelyn save two lives. They needed to be a team and he needed his A-game. Which was exactly what he'd give.

CHAPTER FOUR

DEREK JUMPED INTO the fray and seemed to anticipate her every move. It was nice. It could take time for two doctors to learn each other's cues and timings and work seamlessly together, but with Derek it was as if they had been working together for years.

And that put her at ease about delivering a frank breech baby on her first day back in Wolf's Harbor.

The receptionist, Nancy, helped her into a gown and gloves.

"She's ten centimeters dilated, Dr. Saunders, and her water broke," said Janet. and showed Evelyn the read-out. The baby's heartbeat was strong and everything was going smoothly—except the fact that the baby was heading out upside down. "The contractions are close and strong."

Evelyn nodded. "Thank you, Janet. Christina, I think we're ready to have this baby."

"Tom isn't here," Christina panted. "I can't have this baby without Tom!"

"I don't think the baby is going to wait for Tom," Evelyn said as she took a seat at the end of the bed. She bent down and could see the baby's backside crowning. "In fact I *know* we can't wait for Tom. You're going to have push and push hard, Christina. This baby is breech. But we'll be with you all the way and at the end you'll have your baby, yes?"

Christina nodded, but she was crying.

Derek stepped up and held Christina's shoulders. "I'm here in Tom's place, okay? I'm here for you, and you know I've done this before."

Christina nodded, and Evelyn couldn't help but melt slightly, watching the care and tenderness Derek showed his patient. The gruff exterior was gone and replaced by something tender and compassionate.

It made her heart skip a beat.

She shrugged it off and watched the monitor as another contraction went off. "Come on—now, *push*, Christina. Hard. That's it. Push to ten."

Evelyn kept one eye on the monitors and one eye on the baby. Twenty years ago she'd have been putting Christina under and delivering the baby via C-section, but a frank breech—if the mother and baby were healthy—could be delivered the old-fashioned way. If the baby had been a footling breech it would be a different story.

Still, this was going to be a hard birth.

Janet continued encouraging Christina, and Derek supported their patient as Evelyn guided a beautiful baby girl into the world—bum first.

The baby didn't cry right away, but that wasn't unusual, and Evelyn suctioned the mouth while Janet rubbed the baby vigorously.

There was a fraction of a moment when Evelyn worried, just for a second, that the baby wouldn't cry and she'd have to resuscitate. She shifted her brain to focus on the protocol for that—especially since they weren't in a hospital. But it was only for a fleeting moment, because then the baby took a breath and cried out at the indignity of being cold and pestered.

Evelyn's heart swelled and she smiled behind her surgical mask. This was her favorite part. Life. A healthy baby. She held the little one carefully to get a closer look. Her heart raced as a secret pang of longing coursed through her.

So wonderful. Pure. A new life safely arrived in the world.

The possibilities for this baby were endless. It was thrilling, as always, to be there on day one of a child's life.

"It's a girl!" she announced. "Do you want me to cut the cord?"

Christina nodded. "Tom was going to do it…but, yeah."

Evelyn cut the cord and the placenta was delivered soon after. Janet took the baby to the warmer to rub ointment in her eyes, weigh her and do the heel stick. Everything that needed to be done. But it wasn't long before the baby was brought back to Christina, to be held skin to skin with the relieved mother.

"Excellent work, Dr. Saunders," Derek said as Evelyn finished cleaning up. He was beaming at her. Those intense eyes sparkling with pride. "Seriously—excellent job."

"Thanks to you, as well," she said. "I couldn't have done that without you."

He looked stunned. "I did nothing."

"What do you mean nothing? You have a well-stocked clinic and I didn't have to give you instructions. You knew what to do."

"Still, *you* did all the work," he whispered.

"I don't do much," Evelyn said. "I just catch them."

Derek chuckled and then left the room.

Evelyn passed on the post-op care to Janet. If all went

well Christina and the baby could go home today. For a breech birth, it had been almost textbook. And she was relieved that the first birth she'd had to attend to in Wolf's Harbor had been easy.

As she peeled off her gown and gloves Nancy opened the door to the exam room. "Look who I found!" she announced.

A man in flannel and denim, who looked a bit wide-eyed and dazed, stumbled in. "Did I miss it?"

"Tom, I presume?" Evelyn asked with a smile.

"Yeah. I missed it, didn't I?" He rubbed his hand over his head. "I *knew* I shouldn't have gone to work today."

"Everything is fine, Tom. Go meet your daughter."

Tom grinned. "A girl?"

Evelyn watched as Tom went to Christina and bent down to see his newborn daughter. A happy family.

That pang of longing for something she could never have washed over her again.

But you could have it if you want.

She forced that thought away and left the exam room to clean up. The birth had happened so fast. It was only lunch time and they could see their patients in the afternoon. She could still get Jennifer Yazzie in.

Evelyn went to find her file, worried suddenly, because if Dr. Pearson hadn't tried to turn Christina's baby before he left, what was going on with Jennifer and her small measurements?

Nancy was back at the front desk.

"Can you reschedule Jennifer Yazzie for later this afternoon, Nancy?"

"Sure, Dr. Saunders."

Evelyn thanked Nancy and headed to exam room three, which had a desk and was obviously the office for a rotating specialist. It was cramped, and a bit dark, but it worked and that was where she set up her computer.

There weren't many pregnant women in Wolf's Harbor, but there were a couple of six-week check-ups and everyday women's health stuff to deal with. For the most part it was going to be an easy job.

Evelyn fired up her laptop and frowned because the clinic did not appear to have high-speed internet access.

"Have I gone back to the time of dial-up?" she murmured under her breath.

"Yeah, the Wi-Fi here is really not reliable."

Evelyn looked up and saw Derek standing in the doorway. Her cheeks flushed with warmth at being caught muttering to herself.

"It's okay," she said.

"It's just a fact of life at the clinic and in these parts. Life can move a bit slower around here."

"Not for Christina," Evelyn teased. "Thank you again for your help."

Derek nodded. "Like I said, I didn't do anything. You did fantastic, though. You really calmed her down."

"Thanks. Textbook frank breech birth, though. Nothing to it."

She turned back to her computer, embarrassed by the compliment. She knew that she was good—one of the best—but it was always hard for her to take praise when she was just doing her job.

"I was going to head to Sally's next door and grab a quick bite. Do you want to join me?"

The question caught Evelyn off guard. "No, thank you. I want to look up some information, and I have a quick email I want to send to a colleague before I see Jennifer Yazzie this afternoon."

"Anything I can help with?"

"Did the other OB/GYNs confide in you about their patients?"

"No. Not really. They didn't like to talk to a general practitioner who knows nothing."

Evelyn rolled her eyes. "Why does *that* not surprise me?"

Derek shrugged. "You get used to it. Still, it angered me. The people in Wolf's Harbor are my patients long after any temporary specialist is gone." He crossed his arms. "When I came to town fifteen years ago Jennifer was my first patient. She was five years old. I know her medical history pretty well."

"You've been here a long time."

"I like it here. This is home."

"It must be weird, seeing your patients having families of their own. Makes you feel a bit old, doesn't it?"

"Well...*now* it does."

Then Derek smiled, which totally caught her off guard, and she couldn't help but laugh with him.

"So *you're* not opposed to talking over stuff with me?" he asked.

"No. I work better sometimes after talking it out."

"Not surprising. I'm the same. Fire away."

"It's about Jennifer Yazzie."

"What's eating you about Jennifer?"

"I met her when I arrived, and she told me how far along she is, but she's awfully small."

Derek's brow furrowed. "What're you thinking?"

"Anything in her past I should know about? Beyond the obstetrical records?"

"No. She's been healthy. Non-smoker and non-drinker.

Are you thinking it's intrauterine growth restriction accounting for her small measurements?"

She was impressed that his mind had immediately gone there.

"I'm hoping it's not, but I'm worried about that. We'd have to get her to Juneau—to a larger hospital to deliver the baby. But I'm hoping she's just carrying small. Some women will do that right until the baby is about to be born. But if not, it could be very dangerous for Jennifer and her baby."

A strange expression crossed Derek's face. "I hope it's not, too. I'm going to grab a bite. You should try and have something to eat."

He left quickly, and Evelyn couldn't help but wonder what had gotten into him. She'd thought he wanted to talk more.

She shrugged it off. She couldn't worry about it right now. She opened Jennifer's file and starting skimming through the various notes made over the course of her pregnancy. Her heart sank as it became apparent that she wasn't the only one who was thinking intrauterine growth restriction.

Damn.

Derek didn't head to Sally's. He didn't feel hungry all of a sudden. Instead he headed down the street to daycare.

It wasn't a bustling daycare center. His daughter was currently the only child in town who needed continuous daycare service during the summer. It was convenient, as she was still a bit sick, and he knew if they'd been in a big city he would have had to arrange for another sitter or taken time off.

Of course if they *had* decided to move to Chicago he would have had his mother there to help—plus most likely he wouldn't have been the only doctor in his practice as he wouldn't have been able to afford to buy a solo practice.

But he loved Wolf's Harbor.

Vivian had been from here, and though she'd had parents elsewhere in Alaska she'd been on her own, and they'd made a vow to raise their children here.

Perhaps if another doctor would come and permanently settle here they could trade off, but that was unlikely.

No one ever stayed.

He opened the door to the daycare center, making the bell jingle as he walked in, and slipped off his shoes. Mo was sitting on the couch. Her round gray-green eyes that were so like his lit up when she saw him. His heart melted. He loved her. She was his world. The only thing besides his practice that kept him going.

"Daddy!"

Derek went over and sat down next to her. "How are you feeling?" he asked.

"Better," Mo chirped.

"Monica's fever has broken this morning," said Edna the daycare owner as she came into the room.

"Good."

"You off for the day, Dr. Taylor, or is this just a visit?" Edna asked.

"Just a visit."

Edna smiled and left the room.

Mo curled up next to him, holding her blanket, completely fascinated by the crazy cartoon that was on the television.

Derek ran his hand over her forehead. It was clammy, but no sign of a fever.

"I'm fine, Daddy," Mo said, pushing his hand away, annoyed that he was interrupting her show.

So like Vivian.

Everything about Mo reminded him of his late wife. Her personality. Her attitude. Vivian would have loved everything about Mo, and instead of Edna it would have been Vivian taking care of her.

Edna had been helping him take care of Mo since she was born, and she was a warm, loving caretaker, but it wasn't the same as having a mother. And in that Derek thought he was failing Mo. That he wasn't enough for her.

He sat next to her and mindlessly watched the cartoon, laughing with her at the parts she thought were funny and wishing he could give her more. But he wasn't sure that he could ever put his heart in jeopardy like that again.

He was frozen.

It had been five years since Vivian died, and he was lonely, but remembering the agony he'd gone through losing her, he knew he could never do that again. Mo didn't remember her mother. Didn't know the pain of losing her. He never wanted to put her through that. He could handle the pain, but he never wanted Mo to feel it.

Mo drifted off to sleep and Derek slid off the couch, helping her lie down and then covering her with the blanket that Vivian had made for her when she was pregnant. The blanket was ratty and worn, but Mo wouldn't be parted with it and Derek wouldn't even try.

Edna came into the room and Derek motioned to her that Mo was sleeping. He waved goodbye to her from the door, put on his shoes and strode out into the drizzly afternoon.

He stopped by Sally's and grabbed a sandwich, and then grabbed one for Evelyn. He didn't know what she'd like, so he stuck with egg salad just in case she was vegetarian.

He'd been impressed with Evelyn's performance in helping Christina and her baby. Maybe if she'd been here when Mo was born Vivian would still be here.

He shook his head, because he couldn't dwell on the what-ifs. Those what-ifs that haunted him nightly.

He rounded the corner to the clinic, and his heart skipped a beat when he saw the town ambulance waiting outside.

He ran into the clinic and saw Nancy looking pale.

"What's going on?" Derek asked.

"Christina started bleeding. Heavily. Dr. Saunders had to transfuse her, but it's not stopping. The air ambulance is waiting to take her to Sitka."

Derek glanced over and saw Tom, looking stunned, holding the baby. He knew that expression all too well.

No. Evelyn has this handled.

They'd been like one being in surgery.

Surgery was not his strong suit. He could get by, but being with Evelyn had made him feel completely at ease. It had been like a beautiful dance, and he couldn't have done it without her.

"Dr. Taylor…?" Tom said.

Derek knelt down in front of Tom. "It'll be okay, Tom. Dr. Saunders is a pro."

There was a commotion from the back and he saw Evelyn helping the paramedics wheel out Christina, who was on oxygen and getting blood.

Derek helped Tom up. "Go with your wife. Take your baby. The nurses in Sitka will help."

"I'm going with Christina, Tom," Janet said as Evelyn and the paramedics loaded Christina into the ambulance.

Derek nodded in acknowledgement and Janet took Tom and led him to the back of the vehicle.

Derek walked back to the exam room where not that

long ago they had delivered Christina and Tom's baby.
A frank breech that Evelyn had said was "textbook."

He opened the door and saw the blood on the floor.
His stomach twisted in a knot—not because of the sight
of it, but because all he could see was Vivian on the floor
of their home, his arms around her as he tried in futility
to help her, begging her to stay with him.

A life was saved today. Two lives.

A sense of pride overcame him.

It was all thanks to Evelyn.

There had been no tragedy here. There could have
been. There might have been. But she had brought hope.

He grabbed a mop, started cleaning up the mess.

Saving lives was all that mattered.

And who will save yours?

CHAPTER FIVE

EVELYN BREATHED A sigh of relief as she watched the air ambulance take off. Christina was stable, and that bleeding might have been the result of anything. It might have been a tear, or a clot, but Evelyn didn't have the means to examine it herself. There was no anesthesiologist on hand. Derek had stocked blood in his clinic, but not enough to do a surgical repair. It was better that the Sitka hospital take care of it. There were more people in Sitka. There were more supplies and specialized instruments that weren't here.

At least Christina was still awake… She must remember to praise Derek later for having that small stock of universal blood on hand. If there hadn't been any it might have been disastrous. Derek's smart thinking in stocking the clinic had probably saved Christina's life.

"Need a lift, Dr. Saunders?"

Evelyn turned to see Joe Yazzie Jr. sitting in the airport.

"I would like that—but I have to confess I left my purse at the clinic."

Joe chuckled. "It's on me. Family and everything."

Evelyn's heart skipped a beat. "I guess you're right. We're cousins, I suppose."

Joe scratched his head. "Yeah, no 'suppose' about it.

We are. That's what Léelk'w and my father say. It's nice to meet you, cousin."

Evelyn felt like she'd been sucker-punched. "Did you say Léelk'w? Is she still…?"

Joe beamed. "Alive? Yeah, Léelk'w is still alive and kicking. I don't know if she knows you're back in town. Dad hasn't gotten around to seeing her since he ran into you last night."

There were so many emotions that were swirling around inside Evelyn. Her maternal grandmother was *still alive*? She'd thought she'd died. In fact she'd been led to believe that she'd died. Evelyn had mourned her so long ago, but Léelk'w was still alive.

She felt angry for all the time that had gone by.

All the time she'd missed.

And whose fault was that?

She'd written so many letters and never heard back. After a time Evelyn had felt as if Léelk'w must have forgotten her, and as more time went on she assumed that Léelk'w had died.

How had anyone thought that was the best thing for her? How was being separated from you family and not knowing about them *better*? How was Boston better than Wolf's Harbor and not vice versa?

No one had ever taken into account *her* feelings. No one had ever asked her what *she* wanted.

Because you didn't deserve it. Your father didn't get what he wanted so why should you?

She really hated that voice inside her. That internal dialogue that never let her forgive, never let her forget what happened.

"You okay, Dr. Saunders?" Joe Jr. asked.

Evelyn nodded and plastered a brave smile on her

face. "Yeah, I'm great—and you know what, Joe? You might as well call me Evelyn. We're cousins, after all."

Joe grinned. "Okay."

Evelyn climbed into his cab and he whisked her back to the clinic.

"Will I see you later with Jennifer?"

"Jennifer couldn't get time off for the afternoon, but we're coming tomorrow first thing."

Evelyn nodded. "Good. I look forward to seeing you both."

Joe parked the cab out front. "We'll see you tomorrow."

She got out and walked back into the clinic. Nancy looked up from the reception desk.

"I tried to get Jennifer Yazzie in…"

"It's okay, Nancy. I spoke with her husband and I know she couldn't get the time off. I'll see her tomorrow."

"I'm headed home. Dr. Taylor hasn't rescheduled his appointments. He said to take the rest of the day off."

Evelyn frowned. "But there's still time left."

"Well, he'll stay here in case there's an emergency, but no regular patients. Do you need me to stay, Dr. Saunders?"

"No, it's fine, Nancy. If Dr. Taylor gave you the rest of the day off, go. It's been one heck of a first day for me, anyways. Thanks for your help."

Nancy smiled. "See you tomorrow, Dr. Saunders."

Evelyn walked back to the exam room, to clean up the mess, and walked in on Derek, mopping the floor. He glanced up as if only just noticing her.

"Need help?" she asked.

"Nope—I got it," he said, not looking up at her. He seemed sad, distant, and she hoped he wasn't mad at her for not cleaning up right away.

"I was coming back to clean." Evelyn grabbed another mop.

"Don't worry about it." Derek sighed. "I've got it mostly cleaned up. But, honestly, a mess like that shouldn't be left."

"And was I supposed to stop trying to save Christina's life and clean the floor?"

Derek rubbed his temple. "No, you're right. Sorry."

"What's wrong?"

"Nothing. Just concerned about my patient."

"She'll be fine. I wanted to congratulate you for having universal blood on hand. That probably saved her life."

"Thanks, but it was you too. Your skills which saved her life."

She helped with the mopping, then glanced up at him. "You're really connected to the people in this town, aren't you?"

He fixed her with a piercing stare—one that made her blood heat with the intensity of it. She was always attracted to stand-offish alpha males, but usually they never wanted anything more to do with her than a quick fling. Just sex. And she could tell this was no exception.

Nathan had wanted more.

The problem was, she hadn't wanted more from Nathan.

Did she want something from Derek? Yeah, she did. It was alarming how much she was attracted to him. How he made her nervous and yet excited. How much he affected her.

No man had ever made her feel this way before, and she wondered if Derek might be the kind of guy who might cure her of her restless nature.

But even if she wished it, it wasn't that way—because she didn't want any of that. It was way too risky.

You're not here to stay. You don't have time for a relationship.

He shrugged. "They're like family, and someone has to be."

She understood that. He was protective of his practice just like her father had been. Where her grandmother had loathed his dedication to Wolf's Harbor, Evelyn had admired him for it.

"Are you okay?" he asked.

"Of course," she said, hoping he didn't detect the nervousness she was feeling.

He cocked his head to the side, as if he didn't quite believe her. As if he knew what she'd been thinking about only moments before.

"It was an intense first day for you," he remarked before going back to his mopping.

Whew.

"Yes," Evelyn replied, relieved.

"It's usually not like this here. It's a quiet town."

"Oh, you *know* that's not a word you should utter after an emergency situation. Especially to a surgeon."

Derek cocked an eyebrow. "Why?"

"'Quiet' means anything but in the emergency room. It'll get busy again now. You just watch."

"I hope you're wrong. We've had enough for one day. Heck, we've had enough for a *month*!"

They laughed together at that.

Just as she had finished disposing of the trash and placing the instruments on a tray to be sterilized she heard the distinct cry of a child in pain.

Derek's head snapped up and he dashed out of the room as if he'd been struck by lightning.

What in the world...?

Evelyn peeled off her rubber gloves and followed him.

An older woman was holding a gauze bandage to a little girl's head, and Evelyn could tell it was soaked through with blood. The girl was clinging to Derek, who was rubbing her back, and as the little girl stopped crying to speak to him she could see brilliant gray-green eyes—*Derek's eyes*—looking up at him.

Now she understood what was keeping him in Wolf's Harbor. It wasn't just his patients who were his family.

He *had* a family. A *real* family.

Great. You're lusting after a married man.

"Is everything okay?" Evelyn asked.

Derek looked at her defeatedly. There was worry etched on his face.

The older woman spoke up, "She was feeling better and running around the house, but then she had a dizzy spell and slipped, hitting her head against a cupboard door. It was a deep gash, so I've brought her here."

"She's my daughter," Derek said. "This is Monica. Mo for short."

She was surprised. Derek didn't wear a wedding ring, and had never mentioned his daughter before, but then again he didn't chat much about his personal life.

She looked at the little girl, bleeding from her head wound, crying and clinging to her father. She had once been that little girl in her father's arms.

Her heart melted. She loved kids.

"Well, why don't you bring her into exam room two and I can look at the gash?" Evelyn suggested gently.

"I can do it," Derek said, not looking at her but holding his daughter close and rubbing her back.

"No, you can't. You're her father. I will do it."

"You're an OB/GYN."

"I'm a surgeon, first and foremost. I think I can suture a wound."

Derek nodded, and then turned to the older woman. "I've got it from here, Edna. Thank you for bringing her in. I'll see you tomorrow."

Edna nodded, but looked worried all the same as she left the clinic.

Derek followed Evelyn into exam room two. His daughter had calmed down and was staring at her, with her head pressed against her father's shoulder. She had the same beautiful eyes and tawny skin, and the most beautiful curly sandy-colored hair that Evelyn had ever seen.

Derek set her down on the paper-covered exam table and Monica still watched her.

"Who's that, Daddy?" she asked.

"I'm Dr. Evelyn Saunders, but you can call me Evie."

Monica smiled. "I'm Monica, but you can call me Mo."

Evelyn smiled at her. "Well, Mo, can I take a look at your head?"

Mo looked at her father, unsure.

"It's okay. Dr. Saunders is nice."

"Evie, Daddy," Mo corrected.

"Oh, I don't let *him* call me Evie. He's too grumpy," Evelyn teased, and Mo's eyes twinkled and she laughed.

Derek smiled tenderly at his daughter, but didn't look at her.

"How old are you, Mo?" Evelyn asked.

"Five—well, I just turned five."

"It was your birthday recently?"

"In March," Derek said. "Not *that* recent."

"I wasn't talking to you," Evelyn teased.

Mo laughed, and then winced.

"Can I look at your head?"

Mo still looked uncertain, but Derek gently prompted her and Evelyn was able to remove the gauze from her head.

"Ouch—you're being super-brave, Mo."

Evelyn brought over a suture kit and Mo eyed it with worry.

"What's that?" she asked.

"This is going to fix that nasty cut on your head and make you feel a lot better." Evelyn got some numbing agent out. "In fact, looking at it, I don't even think I'll have to stitch that. I think we can get away with cleaning and some paper sutures—which is a fancy word for a plaster."

"Really?" Mo asked.

Evelyn nodded. "Yep."

"Edna said I would have to get stitches cause it bled so much. I got blood on my blankie." Mo held up a ratty old crocheted afghan.

"Who made that for you?" Evelyn asked.

"My mommy."

"I'm sure your mommy can clean it for you."

"Mommy is dead."

She saw Derek stiffen and she looked up at him quickly. Now she understood. All the pain in his eyes was the same pain that she'd seen in her father's.

Evelyn's heart melted even more. Sure, Derek was sexy, and she was highly attracted to him physically, but this was something more. This was something far more dangerous. She felt sorry for him handling this alone.

She remembered all those times she'd snuck downstairs and caught her father crying, mourning her mother. She knew the keen sense of loneliness he'd felt.

"I'm sorry to hear that," Evelyn said gently. "How about your daddy? He can clean it for you, right?"

Mo nodded. "He can."

"That's good. He'll get it all cleaned up and you'll forget that this even happened." Evelyn pulled out the antibacterial cleaner and some gauze.

"Will this hurt?" Mo asked.

"Truth?"

Mo nodded.

"A little bit," Evelyn said. "But if we get this cleaned out and fixed up then it won't hurt later and it will heal right up. Kids have an amazing super-power."

"Oh?"

"They heal super-fast." Evelyn smiled. "If *I'd* cut my head that bad I would probably need stitches, and it wouldn't heal as fast as your cut will heal. Plus, I think this would be an awesome opportunity to get some ice cream out of your dad."

Mo's eyes lit up. "Okay!"

"Thanks." Derek chuckled.

Evelyn grinned. "Can you lie back for me? I'll get that cleaned out. It's going to sting a little bit, but it'll be over with soon—I promise."

Mo lay down and closed her eyes as Evelyn began.

"Why did it bleed so much, Evie?" Mo asked.

"Your head always bleeds a lot because there are tons of blood vessels in your scalp that are close to the surface—so when you get a cut it bleeds a lot."

Evelyn finished cleaning the wound and then placed Steri-strips over the wound and a bandage.

"There—all done, and you were incredibly brave."

Evelyn helped her sit up. Mo's little hand slipped into hers, and in the little girl so attached to her father Evelyn saw herself.

She had once been Mo.

The only difference was that she'd remembered bits

and pieces about her mother, and she'd had her mother's extended family reminding her of who her mother was.

"You can take her home now," Evelyn said to Derek. "You know the drill. I can manage closing up the clinic."

"Thank you, Evelyn." Derek scooped up his daughter, but didn't look at her.

"Thanks, Evie," Mo chirped. "Daddy, can Evie come over for dinner? Evie, do you want to come over for dinner?"

Evelyn was taken aback by the sweet, heartfelt invitation. But Derek's eyes were wide as he tried to come up with an excuse and she knew that she couldn't intrude on their dinner. Derek was clearly uncomfortable, and now she understood. He had a daughter to protect.

Evelyn wasn't going to be here in Wolf's Harbor permanently, and Mo had lost her mother. The last thing Mo needed was some strange woman coming over to the house and getting attached. Evelyn didn't want things to be harder on Mo. She knew personally how that could feel, and she didn't want this poor little girl to have any more trauma.

It wouldn't be fair.

"That's very sweet of you to invite me, Mo," Evelyn started. "Maybe another night?"

Mo looked sad, and Derek looked at her. "Tonight is fine, Evelyn—if you're available. Mo is right. You *should* come over for dinner. It's the least we can do to say thank you for helping us."

Mo looked so hopeful that Evelyn didn't want to disappoint her. And she didn't really have any other plans, except continuing to clean that atrocious apartment.

Make an excuse. Don't go.

Only Evelyn couldn't break that sweet little girl's

heart. She knew what that girl was feeling deep down. She felt a connection to her.

"Sure. I can come for dinner."

"Great!" Mo beamed.

"Will Joe Jr. know where you live?" Evelyn asked, her stomach swirling as every fiber of her being told her she was foolish for agreeing to have dinner with a widower and his daughter.

Derek nodded. "Yes, he'll know. We'll see you at seven?"

"Bye, Evie!" Mo chirped happily as Derek walked out of the exam room with his daughter in his arms.

Evelyn let out a breath she hadn't known she was holding as she tried to figure out a way to get out of it without hurting Mo's feelings, but the more she thought about it the more she realized she was stuck.

What harm can come from one little dinner?

She sighed, thinking those were famous last words—because she knew exactly what the harm could be. How it could tear someone's heart apart.

She needed to find a way out of this. Not only for her sake, but for little Mo's heart too.

CHAPTER SIX

WHAT DO YOU bring to dinner with a man who probably hates you and his cute five-year-old daughter? That was the crux of the matter.

And *that* was an overreaction. Derek didn't hate her. He didn't know her. He tolerated her, and that was something different.

She couldn't blame him for being a bit cool.

She *got* why he was defensive about his practice—especially in light of Dr. Pearson messing up earlier. It was hard trying to protect your patients and raise a child on your own. She'd seen her father struggle. And if she was in the same position she would be untrusting of temporary doctors creating more work for her or jeopardizing her patients.

So, she was not really looking forward to this dinner, but she'd put on her best face and get through it.

And if there was one thing her grandmother had taught her about attending dinner parties it was that you didn't go empty-handed, but Evelyn had no idea what to bring. She finally settled on a bottle of wine that she'd found in the apartment and then went next door to Sally's before the bakery closed and bought the cupcakes that Sally told her Mo particularly liked.

Joe Jr. picked her up in the cab.

"Hey, Evie, I was surprised to get your call."

Evelyn slid in beside him. "Why is that?"

Joe shrugged. "The other doctors never went out. Never really socialized. Well, except Dr. Pearson—but he had his own car and usually he went to Hoonah or a bigger community to socialize."

"I guess I'm the exception."

"Where are you headed?" Joe asked.

"Dr. Taylor's place. He said you would know the directions."

"I sure do," Joe said, nodding. "It's just outside of town."

"Great."

Joe headed down the main street and they chatted easily about things, but when they turned off the main road toward a gravel road that wound its way through the forest Evelyn's pulse kicked up a notch.

The trees were denser, but she recognized each curve and bend in the road.

It can't be.

Her stomach flip-flopped and then bottomed out when Joe pulled up at the end of the road and she found herself staring at the little log house that was set in the forest near the water.

She *knew* this road.

She'd memorized it in her dreams, though as the years had gone on it had faded, but now, as she gazed at the little cabin, she knew without a doubt where she was.

The place she'd dreamed about. The place she'd longed for. One of the last places she'd truly been happy because her father had been alive and they had been happy together.

Home.

Except it wasn't home. Not *her* home. Not anymore.

"Here we are!" Joe said.

"Thanks, Joe." Evelyn paid him and then slipped out of the taxi. She waved as Joe drove away and then just stood in front of the place she'd once called home. If she closed her eyes she could almost see herself running from the front door and down toward the water to greet her father.

She could still smell the scent of pine in the wood stove on those cold winter nights.

And she could remember how empty the house had felt when she'd realized that her father was never coming home.

The door opened and Derek stepped out.

"Evelyn? Have you been standing out here long?"

"Not long." Evelyn smiled and held out the box of cupcakes. "For Mo. How is she feeling?"

"She's asleep," Derek said, taking the cupcakes.

"Do you want me to come back? I can call Joe…" In fact she was slightly relieved that maybe she'd be able to get out of this dinner and she wouldn't have to spend any time in this house.

"No, come in."

"I'm not sure I can," she said.

"Why?" Derek asked, confused. "Is it because of me?"

"No."

He cocked an eyebrow. "Then what is it? It was Mo's invitation, wasn't it? It freaked you out. Look, it shocked me too. She's never really taken to someone like that before."

"It's not Mo's invitation. It's complicated."

A warm smile tugged at his lips and it sent a zing of electricity through her. His smile made her weak in the knees, and he was so much more tempting when that smile was directed at her. It was a potent smile.

"Complicated I get," he said gently.

Evelyn chuckled and tucked her hair behind her ear in a nervous twitch. "I just didn't expect… I didn't expect you to live *here*."

Derek turned and looked back at his house. "Something wrong with my house?"

Evelyn bit her lip and then sighed. "I used to live here, Derek. This used to be my home before I was taken away."

There were a lot of excuses that Derek had been expecting to hear from her.

Before Vivian, women had come on to him all the time, even if he hadn't been interested in them, but they'd soon lost interest in him when he'd told them his plans to move to Alaska.

He tried once to date, a couple of years after Vivian had died, but the woman had learned he had a daughter, emotional baggage in the form of a deceased wife, and a practice that took up a lot of his time. It had been enough to scare her away and had soured him on dating anyone.

Which had always been fine with him. Until now.

He'd seen the look of shock in Evelyn's eyes when he'd explained that Mo was his daughter and that he was a widower. He'd seen that pity and he didn't want it. Not from her.

He wanted something completely different from her. Derek didn't want Evelyn just to see him as a single dad and a widower. He enjoyed working with her. It felt natural and she kept him focused. She chased away the nightmares. The numbness. He wanted her to see him as just himself.

Who he really was.

And who is that?

He wasn't sure he knew anymore.

All he knew was that look of pity with the head-tilt, and he didn't want to see it from her.

He'd honestly been expecting her to call and cancel the dinner, even though such a call would have absolutely devastated Mo. So he was happy she was here, because of Mo's feelings, but when she hadn't come in right away he'd been pretty sure she was going to bolt.

He hadn't been expecting her to say that his home had once been hers. And he'd had no idea that he was living in Dr. Thorne Saunders' home. Evelyn's childhood home. He'd bought it from a logger who'd worked here in Wolf's Harbor for a few summers and then decided to join a crab fishing boat. He'd sold the home to Derek when he'd first arrived and then Vivian had moved in.

He knew about Evelyn's past—sort of. Different people had told him about her parents dying and her having to leave Wolf's Harbor, but that was it.

People didn't talk about Thorne Saunders besides saying he'd been an excellent doctor. And no one had told him this was Thorne's former home. The name on the deed before the man he'd bought this house from was L. Yazzie, and he'd assumed it had belonged to the Yazzie family at one point. He hadn't known the connection between the Yazzies and Thorne until recently.

Now it made perfect sense. He just hadn't seen it before, even though Evelyn had had that emotional reunion with Joe Yazzie when she'd first arrived.

He could only imagine what she was going through, but though he knew he should tell her it would be OK to leave or call Joe to come get her, he didn't want her leaving.

He was lonely, and Evelyn was someone bright, vibrant. Someone who excited him. And he wanted her to stay. He wanted to talk to an adult. To have a conversation and enjoy a glass of wine.

"Come inside," he said, surprising himself.

This was not treating Evelyn like all the other doctors who'd come through town. He'd never invited *them* over. They'd never known he had a daughter.

Yeah, but none of them had really cared about this place beyond serving their time.

Evelyn came from Wolf's Harbor. She had an emotional investment in the people. She cared. And it was nice to have that in common with another physician in town.

Derek wanted her to stay, even if he knew it would be hard for her *and* for him. He liked working with her. He liked talking with her about medicine. He was lonely for that.

Evelyn coming here was like a breath of fresh air—one he didn't want to end.

He'd felt as if he was suffocating before.

Evelyn nodded and he gently placed his hand on the small of her back to guide her in. Just that simple touch did something to him. It sent a zing of anticipation, of electricity through him and he was taken aback by it.

It made him think things that weren't chaste.

Don't think of her like that.

Only around her, it seemed, he couldn't help himself, and constantly thought about her *like that*. He thought about what it would be like to run his hands through her hair, to taste her lips and feel her body flush against his.

You're treading on dangerous ground.

Derek snatched his hand back as quickly as he'd placed it there. Then shut the door as Evelyn stood in the foyer and stared up at the exposed beams.

"Wow, it's brighter in here. I don't remember the exposed beams."

"Yeah, I did some renovations when I first bought the place. It was a bit dark…" He closed his eyes, cursing himself inwardly. Maybe her father had built this home and he was insulting it.

Evelyn smiled at him and unwound the scarf she was wearing to hang it up on the hook by the door. "Yes, it was. It was cozy, but I like the exposed beams and the skylights. That's a nice touch."

"Thanks. The kitchen is in the back still." Derek started walking toward the kitchen that he'd updated as well.

Evelyn followed him silently and it was awkward. You could cut the tension with a knife.

Why couldn't this be easier?

You know why. It's because you find her attractive and you hate yourself just a little right now.

There was no time for him to think of his selfish wants or desires. He was a dad first and a doctor second. That was all.

He didn't deserve anything else.

He couldn't get involved with someone who would leave town in a couple of months, and he certainly didn't want Mo to get attached to someone who was leaving soon.

He set the box of cupcakes down on the counter and ran a hand over his head, unsure of what to do. It had been long time since he'd been on a date.

This is not a date. It's a dinner for a colleague. It's a thank-you dinner.

"Is everything okay with you?" Evelyn asked, standing in the kitchen door.

"Yeah. I… I didn't think that you would come," he admitted.

Evelyn chuckled. "Truth?"

"Yeah."

"I almost didn't," she said.

He smiled and then they both laughed nervously, the tension melting away.

"I will say it's not because of Mo. That's not the reason why I almost didn't come."

"Then what is it?" he asked, shocked but secretly pleased. Usually it was his status as a single dad that threw women off.

"You haven't exactly been friendly or welcoming to me since I arrived. Though if you had to deal with Dr. Pearson for the last month I can understand a fraction of that and I don't even know the man."

"Ah, yes. I have to apologize about that."

She cocked an eyebrow. "Really?"

He nodded. "I have control issues when it comes to my clinic."

She laughed gently. She had a beautiful smile.

"I hadn't noticed."

"I care a lot about my patients."

"I have noticed that, and I admire it."

His pulse kicked up a notch at the compliment. "You do? Most people…they don't understand that."

"I do."

"I know. It's refreshing."

"How so?" she asked.

"Most doctors who come through here don't care. They do their time, don't interact and move on. You seem to care. You put yourself out there to get to know your patients."

"I love my job, and an important part of the job is trust.

I give it my all. And Wolf's Harbor was my home once.
My father loved his patients too. Coming here is a way to
honor him." She looked away, pink coloring her cheeks,
as if she was afraid of him seeing her get emotional.

It touched him. Deeply.

There was much to admire about Evelyn Saunders.

Dammit. It was going to be hard to treat her like all
the others who'd come before her.

"Well, I'm truly sorry if I've been cold to you. Thank
you for coming here and making Mo's night—despite
the fact you think I'm an intolerable grump."

"You're welcome."

"Would you like a glass of wine?" he asked.

"Sure."

"Take a seat in the living room and I'll bring it out."

Evelyn nodded and headed to the living room while
Derek pulled down two wineglasses from a cupboard.
He opened the red wine she'd brought and poured two
glasses. He looked at the label and was surprised she'd
been able to get such an expensive bottle of wine in
Wolf's Harbor.

He picked up the glasses and set them on a tray that
also held some cheese and crackers.

Evelyn was sitting on the large sectional couch that
was set in front of the fire that he'd started. She was staring up at the wooden beams in awe. Or at least he hoped
it was awe and not something like boredom.

He thought again how it really had been a while since
he was on a date.

This isn't a date. Remember that.

He cringed inwardly. This wasn't a date. He was *not*
on a date.

"This still looks the same," she remarked. "I'm glad
you kept this the same."

"I didn't really change this room. I liked it cozy," he said as he set the tray on the coffee table and then handed her a glass.

"Wow," she said.

"What?" he asked, sitting down next to her.

"You are so neat and organized. Your house is immaculate. Very smooth compared to what Dr. Pearson left me."

He breathed a sigh of relief and chuckled.

"Well, my mom has a very successful catering company in Chicago so I grew up learning how to entertain, I suppose. I was a waiter for many years when I was working my way through college. As for the cleanliness—that's thanks to a cleaning lady and the fact that Mo and I don't spend much time here. I'm sure if I were a stay-at-home dad this place would be a lot more disorganized."

"Order is something you can control."

He cocked an eyebrow. "What do you mean?"

"The clinic is immaculate too. You like to be able to control things, and when things are out of your hands you don't like it. I get it. I respect it. Because I'm the same way."

"I'm glad," Derek said quietly, and they sat in silence, listening to the fire crackle and trying to ignore the awkward silence between them.

"Thanks for your help today and for cleaning up the mess I left," she said.

"It's okay. It's just…it was intense today, but you were there for Christina and you were amazing."

"Yeah, she's stable now, and they fixed the tear in her uterine wall. She had a fibroid, and with the force of her labor and a frank breech birth it tore. I didn't know she had fibroids. Of course, she was supposed to have the baby turned by Dr. Pearson and that never happened."

"Yeah, well, I'm not too impressed with him."

"There's something else." Evelyn set her wineglass down on the table. "Jennifer Yazzie's measurements have been small."

"Are you still concerned about intrauterine growth restriction?"

"Yeah." She sighed sadly.

"I'm sorry. I don't know a lot about that. You don't encounter it much up here."

"It's okay. It's just that you seemed bothered by it before when I brought it up," she said.

"Well, I worry about... My wife died here after giving birth to Mo. If she'd been in a city she would've survived."

"I'm sorry."

And she reached out to touch him, placing her delicate hand on his thigh. There was no pity in her beautiful deep brown eyes. Just heartfelt sympathy.

He shrugged, but said nothing else. It still ate at him. He should've got Vivian to a hospital, but her pregnancy had been textbook and she'd wanted a home birth.

It's your fault. You should've convinced her to go to Juneau.

"So is there anything else?" he asked, ignoring that voice in his head—the voice that kept him up at night, reminding him how he'd failed Vivian.

"Well, I see that Dr. Pearson suspected intrauterine growth restriction, but I don't think he told her."

"No, he probably didn't." Derek rolled his eyes.

"Well, I'm going to speak to the medical board, because that's two patients here that were not dealt with properly. What else has been missed?"

"He was here for three months, but Jennifer is getting close to term now, so how many other people didn't see it. Now you understand why I'm mad that I'm the only one who stays. This constant rotation of doctors is not good for the people here. Sometimes it does more harm than good. And we need a hospital. Even if it's small. We need a hospital with regular staff so that when situations like what happened to Christina or Mo arise then they can be taken care of right away. I've been fighting for years to make it happen, but money is tight."

She nodded. "A hospital would be great, but it wouldn't have saved my father's life."

"What happened to your father?" he asked. "I know that he passed, but no one has told me how."

"He was walking through town to..." She trailed off. "To visit someone and it was foggy. A logging truck that was speeding came through the fog and my father was hit. He was killed instantly. There was nothing to be done. Even if there had been a hospital the damage was too great. No doctor could've saved him."

Derek could see the hint of tears in her eyes, but there was something else there. Something she was not telling him. Just as he wasn't telling *her* the whole truth. How he'd redone the kitchen because that was where Vivian had died and he didn't want to see the wooden floors that were stained after her death. He wanted no part of that room to remind him that she'd collapsed there. That she'd died there.

"I'm sorry, Evelyn. I'm sorry that happened to you."

She smiled. "I'm sorry about your wife. And I'm sorry that I'm only here for a short time, just like everyone else."

Their gazes locked and in her eyes he could see pain just like his pain, reflected back at him. They had so much in common when it came to that, but he also felt something else and his pulse kicked up a notch.

His gaze turned to her pink full lips, the flood of color that was in her smooth tan cheeks and her long slender neck. He had the urge to reach out and touch her. To kiss those lips and feel the silkiness of her long red hair.

It shocked him, but also thrilled him that he was feeling this way.

Get a hold of yourself.

"I'm glad you were there today." He looked away. "For both Christina and Mo."

"Thank you. I'm glad I was there too." She looked down at her empty wineglass.

Tension hung in the air, electric and crackling. How long had it been since he'd felt this way? It had been too long. He'd forgotten what it was like. He'd forgotten what it was like to feel so alive.

He looked back at her. "I'm sorry I get so possessive over my patients and my home. Even though I wasn't born here, Wolf's Harbor *is* my home."

"I understand," she whispered. "That this is your home."

"Isn't this *your* home?" he asked.

"No," she whispered. "It hasn't been my home for some time."

He wanted to tell her it could be. Because they needed her medical skill.

He didn't want her to stay for any other reason.

Liar.

He had to put some physical distance between them before he did something he would regret.

Would you regret it?

"Would you like another…?" He leaned forward, but he was gripping the glass too tight and it shattered and cut his hand. "Dammit!"

He got up and ran to the kitchen to inspect the damage.

Evelyn followed him. "Let me see."

"It's fine. It's small and superficial."

"Let me see," she repeated, taking his hand.

Her touch sent a shiver through him. Her skin was soft, but her grip firm. A surgeon's hand. Delicate, long fingers. They were hands that had been taken care of.

"See," he murmured. "Superficial."

"Not even a shard of glass in there."

She looked up at him. They were close and he could see how long her lashes really were.

Evelyn cleared her throat. "Do you have a first aid kit?"

"Yeah, in the powder room over there—under the sink."

She disappeared and Derek took a deep breath. He had to get control. He was made of stronger stuff than this.

She returned with the kit and opened it, pulling out gauze and ointment. She bent over his hand and went to work. He could smell the scent of her shampoo. It was coconut. It reminded him of summer. Hot summers with his friends on the beaches of Lake Michigan, swimming and trying not to get too burnt.

"There," she said, wrapping his hand because the cut was on his palm. "You had some Steri-strips, so I put a couple on just to make it easier on you."

"Thank you," he said, his voice hitching.

Their eyes locked and they didn't say anything. Against every rational thought in his head he reached out and touched her cheek. She sighed when he touched her, closing her eyes, and he bent down, his lips barely grazing hers. His pulse thundered between his ears…

"Daddy?"

Evelyn jumped back, as did Derek when he heard Mo call from the other room.

She came into the kitchen. "Evie! You came!"

Evelyn smiled and cleared her throat nervously. "You bet I did. A promise is a promise."

Mo looked at his hand. "What happened, Daddy?"

"I cut it. Just an accident. Dr. Saunders fixed it for me."

Mo beamed. "Good job, Evie."

Evelyn picked up the box of cupcakes. "I brought you these from Sally's. How's your head?"

"Ooh, yum! My head hurts a little. Do you want to come see my room?"

Evelyn looked at him, as if asking for permission. He appreciated that. He nodded. "Go ahead."

"Sure," Evelyn said.

Mo took her hand and led her out of the kitchen while Derek tried to regain some of his composure.

It had just been a light kiss, barely a kiss, but it had seared his soul. Then Mo had almost walked in on them, and that was a scary thought indeed.

He couldn't let that happen again.

Even if he wanted it to happen again.

Badly.

CHAPTER SEVEN

EVELYN DID NOT sleep a wink that night.

The rest of the evening had been completely awkward, but little Mo hadn't seemed to notice at all. She'd been happy as a lark as they'd had a dinner of macaroni and cheese with a side of chicken fingers.

Derek had barely looked at her, and when he had talked to her he'd referred to her as "Dr. Saunders." Still, there had been some stolen, heated glances which had made her pulse quicken, her blood burn and her guilt to go into overdrive.

Mo had almost caught them kissing.

She didn't even want to *think* of what it would have done to Mo if she'd seen them. She remembered when she'd walked in on her father kissing Jocelyn and how it had made her feel to see her father with someone who was not her mother.

Evelyn didn't want Mo to go through that confusion. Or feel guilty later for destroying her father's happiness. She would never forgive herself for ruining her father's happily-ever-after.

As much as she had wanted that kiss to continue, it was good that it had been interrupted. It was good that it hadn't continued for Mo's sake.

And she did really like Mo.

Mo was the sweetest, most darling girl Evelyn had ever met. When she pictured having a daughter, someone like Mo was what she pictured.

But being with Mo just reminded her of what she would never have. Of course she didn't deserve to have it.

Finally her alarm went off and she rolled over and shut it off, groaning because she'd spent the night tossing and turning.

She just hoped Derek and their almost kiss didn't make things awkward.

Evelyn dragged herself out of bed. She got ready as quickly as she could and saw that it was still early. She could probably beat Derek into the office and then lock herself away in an exam room until Jennifer came.

Even though it meant that she would have to drink the horrible instant coffee that had been left in the apartment because she hadn't had a chance to go shopping yet.

It would be worth it.

She didn't want to run into Derek at Sally's and have some weird, tension-filled meet-up that Sally would be privy to and that would soon become the talk of the town. She might have been away for a long time, but she still knew how these towns worked.

As she rounded the corner she ran smack-dab into something hard and warm.

Arms came around her to steady her. "Hey, watch out… Evelyn."

Evelyn winced and looked up to see that Derek was the warm, hard wall she'd managed to run into.

"Derek," she said uneasily. "I was about to start my day. How's your hand?"

She knew she was babbling, but it couldn't be helped. This was exactly what she'd wanted to avoid. It didn't have to be awkward. They were professionals.

"Me too—and good," he responded, slightly stunned.

"You were trying to avoid me, weren't you?" she teased. "Just like I was trying to avoid you. Unsuccessfully, I might add, as we're in such a small town."

"Yeah…" He chuckled and rubbed a hand over his head. "I suppose I was."

"Look, what almost happened was a mistake. It doesn't have to happen again. It *won't* happen again."

He nodded. "It's not that I… I have Mo to think about. But I want you to know that I don't regret what almost happened. Just that with Mo I have to be careful."

"I know. I agree. I wouldn't want her to get hurt. I just want us to work together without it being weird."

Derek sighed. "Me too."

"Good. I'll see you in there, then?"

"Yeah." He started to walk back to Sally's and then stopped. "Look, don't drink that horrible stuff from the apartment. I'll get you a coffee."

"You don't have to do that," she said. Even though she was secretly pleased that he was offering to buy her a coffee. It was a sweet thing to do. What colleagues did.

"Hey, it's what coworkers do. You can get the next round." He turned back around and then headed down the alley toward Sally's.

Evelyn breathed a sigh of relief. She was glad they were going to try and work together, but there was a part of her that was kind of sad that that was all it could ever be.

Why do you want more? You never want more.

Which was true.

She never wanted more out of a relationship. Her relationships never lasted because she wasn't sure that she ever wanted to settle down or have kids. She loved kids, but she knew what it was like to lose both parents. To be taken away from everyone and everything you'd ever known and be sent to the other side of the country.

She knew that pain and she was sure that she never wanted to put a child through that—because there were no guarantees in life and that wasn't a risk she was willing to take.

It was better this way, and she was glad that Derek was on board with it. That they could be professional about their almost-kiss.

The non-kiss.

Just thinking about the almost-kiss caused her heart to kick up a notch, her blood to heat and her body to react as she thought about his arms around her. His lips brushing over hers. All she could think about was him, and she couldn't remember the last time a man had made her feel this way.

Certainly not Nathan.

There had been an attraction with Nathan, but nothing like this mooning, consuming desire that she seemed to be having for Derek.

Get a grip, Evelyn. Seriously.

This was going to be a long, long day if she didn't get her mind off Derek and focused on something else. Anything else.

She unlocked the clinic and flicked on the lights, setting her travel coffee mug on the counter in order to pick up the first file in the small stack that was waiting for her.

Jennifer Yazzie was coming in for the first appointment today, after having to miss yesterday's due to the excitement Christina had caused.

The bell over the door jingled and Janet came in.

"Good morning, Dr. Saunders."

"Good morning, Janet. When did your flight get in from Sitka?"

"Late last night."

"Shouldn't you be home, resting?" Evelyn asked. "I can't begrudge you that after your amazing work with Christina yesterday and flying to Sitka."

Janet beamed. "Thank you, Dr. Saunders, but I'm fine really. It's only an hour flight, gate to gate, and I'm a bit of a night hawk anyways."

Evelyn grinned. "How *is* Christina?"

"Stable when I left her last night. They named the baby Evie, by the way. Not Evelyn, but Evie. Close to your name."

She blushed and felt very honored. "That's very sweet of them, but Christina did all the work."

Janet handed her an envelope. "Her post-op notes and information from the surgeon in Sitka for Christina's file. Do you need anything particular prepped for this morning, Dr. Saunders?"

"The ultrasound would be great. I'm having Jennifer Yazzie in and I want to check her measurements."

Janet nodded. "Of course, Dr. Saunders. I'll prime the machine now."

Evelyn turned back to Jennifer's chart, reading over all the notes and information about her pregnancy. She wanted to formulate a plan now, since Jennifer was so far along. She didn't want this baby or Jennifer to die because of lack of healthcare.

Besides, Jennifer was sort of family, even though Evelyn didn't know her particularly well. She would hate for something to happen to the next generation of Yazzies. She wasn't going to lose anyone on her watch during her stay in Wolf's Harbor. She was here to save lives, just like her father had.

She smiled to herself, and when the bell jingled at

the front door she didn't look up. It was probably Derek with the coffee.

"I hope you didn't let Sally overload it with sugar. Yesterday she added so much to my coffee my back teeth got a sugar rush."

"I don't have coffee," a frail voice responded, barely a whisper.

The hair on the back of Evelyn's neck stood on end and her hand shook as she turned around slowly.

The woman before her was someone she'd thought she'd never see again. She had osteoporosis, and the once-ebony hair was white, with a few strands of black woven through. Her face was wrinkled, and she still wore the traditional abalone earrings that had always fascinated her as a child when she was in her arms.

And although she tried to hold back the rush of emotion she just couldn't.

"Léelk'w…" Evelyn whispered, tears stinging her eyes.

Léelk'w smiled at her brightly. "You *do* remember me, then?"

Evelyn laughed and ran into her arms.

Léelk'w whispered words in her mother's language but Evelyn couldn't find the words to speak back. It was too hard.

"You must speak English first here, Evelyn. No one knows Tlingit."

Evelyn sighed and stared up at her grandmother, annoyed that another note had been sent home from the principal about her using what he assumed were curse words in another language directed to other kids.

"I'll try, Grandma. I'm just so used to speaking—"

Her grandmother cut her off. "You're doing it again. English, please."

Evelyn began to cry. Tears rolled down her cheek.

"Ladies don't cry, Evelyn. You are a Saunders woman and we are strong. Resilient. Never show your tears."

"Yes. I'll try to fit in better, Grandma."

Her grandmother smiled. "I know you will."

She swallowed down the tears, hearing her grandmother's words in her head.

Evelyn broke the connection and took a step back. "Joe Jr. told me that you were still in town."

Léelk'w cocked an eyebrow. "You mean he told you that I was still *alive*. You're just putting it nicely."

Evelyn chuckled. "I suppose so."

She wanted to ask why Léelk'w had never written to her, never called, but she was too afraid. Too afraid of being hurt. Because she really hadn't fitted into Boston well and maybe she'd never really fitted in to Wolf's Harbor either.

You need to know.

"Why didn't you write or call?" Evelyn asked.

Léelk'w was stunned. "Your grandmother had a private number that was blocked. I wrote, but all my letters were returned to sender."

It should have shocked Evelyn, but it didn't. It sounded exactly like her grandmother.

Which made her angry.

"Are you okay, Evie?" Léelk'w asked.

"I'm fine. I'm glad to see that you're still here."

Léelk'w grinned. "I'm in my nineties. My life expectancy is not the best."

Evelyn frowned. "Are you ill? Is that why you're here?"

"No, I came to talk to you about Jennifer."

"I can't do that. It's doctor-patient confidentiality."

Léelk'w snorted. "We're family."

"Well, yes…sort of." She instantly regretted the words as she said them.

Great way of mending fences, Evelyn.

Léelk'w didn't look fazed. "I *knew* that your father's mother would try to erase all you'd learned up here. I knew that she would turn you into the kind of person your father was when he first arrived in Wolf's Harbor."

Evelyn sighed and walked back to her pile of charts. "It has nothing to do with my late grandmother."

"I hadn't heard that she'd passed. I'm sorry."

There was genuine regret there. Evelyn nodded, but couldn't look Léelk'w in the eye. "It's regulations. I'm bound by certain laws, and discussing Jennifer's file without her presence is against them."

Léelk'w crossed her arms. "I can wait until Jennifer comes. She wants me there when the baby is born. Just like I was there when your mother had you. We're blood."

Evelyn's stomach twisted in a knot. They might be related by DNA, but she wasn't sure that they were family. Not anymore. It was her fault that her father had died and she'd been was sent away.

They'd been estranged for so long.

She wasn't sure she could ever go back.

You're scared to try.

"That's fine." Evelyn turned back to her work and tried not to think about her mother or about her childhood.

If she hadn't agreed to take over Stefanie's practice she wouldn't be here in Wolf's Harbor. She'd thought that while she was here she might be able to lay some ghosts to rest, but she was finding it particularly difficult to do that.

It seemed that the ghosts of her past didn't want to be laid to rest. They seemed to pop up unexpectedly and at the most inconvenient times.

"You have closed your heart," Léelk'w said out loud.

"What?" Evelyn asked, stunned.

Léelk'w sighed. "I can't fault you for that. You never got to grieve for your father and I don't think you forgave him for almost marrying Jocelyn."

That struck a chord, but she was about to make her excuses, because she didn't want to talk about Jocelyn. If Jocelyn hadn't existed then her father would never have gone out that night to visit her. But she'd ruined Jocelyn's life, and there was no way Evelyn could make it up to her.

Maybe if you did you wouldn't be so afraid of settling down and having a family.

She was going to say something to respond to that, but the door chimed and Derek walked in, carrying two coffees.

"Dr. Taylor," Léelk'w said stiffly which caused Evelyn to raise an eyebrow in question.

"Katlian, good to see you."

"Liar," Léelk'w muttered, but there was a twinkle in the old woman's eyes.

Evelyn shook her head and Derek set a coffee in front of her. "For you."

"Thanks. I appreciate it."

"I felt bad that you were avoiding Sally's because of possibly running into me," he said.

Evelyn was going to respond, but she saw that Léelk'w was craning her neck, trying to listen. And she couldn't help but laugh.

"Thanks," Evelyn said. "I was just in a rush. I wanted to look over my charts for the day. Janet is back as well."

Derek nodded, understanding that she didn't want to talk about last night in front of Léelk'w. "Good. Well, I'd better start my day."

He lingered, as if he wanted to say something more,

but then looked over his shoulder at Léelk'w and walked into his room.

Evelyn made sure that he'd closed his door before she turned back to Léelk'w. "You chased him off."

Léelk'w snorted. "He doesn't like me much, but he's a good doctor."

"Why do you give him a hard time, then?"

"I give *all* doctors a hard time." Léelk'w fixed her with a serious gaze, but there was a twinkle in her eyes. "I gave your father a hard time at first."

"I see." Evelyn ignored that, trying not to think of her father, and picked up Jennifer's chart just as Jennifer and Joe Jr. came into the clinic.

"Dr. Saunders! No laboring women today?" Jennifer teased good-naturedly.

Evelyn smiled. "Not today. I'm all yours."

"Léelk'w, I wasn't expecting to see you here," Jennifer said in surprise.

"I am here, and you will give Dr. Saunders permission to speak with me, yes?"

"Of course," Jennifer said, and then turned to Evelyn. "It's okay if Léelk'w knows about my file."

"Okay, but I'll only discuss your file with her in front of you. I'm bound by rules of doctor-patient confidentiality."

Jennifer winked and Evelyn saw Joe Jr. was trying not to laugh.

"Okay, let's get you to the exam room. I want to take another look at your baby and see how he or she is growing."

"Sounds good!" Jennifer said excitedly as she got up and walked toward Evelyn.

They knew where they were going, and Janet was waiting for them in the exam room that held the ultrasound.

As Léelk'w passed Evelyn she squeezed her shoulder.

Evelyn took a deep breath.

You can do this. This is no different from any other patient with intrauterine growth restriction. This isn't your family.

Not anymore.

Only it was. This was her cousin's wife.

This was technically her family, but solely by genetics.

Evelyn had been on her own too long.

She didn't have family. She just had herself.

And that was all she deserved.

Derek had wanted to get to work early so as to avoid Evelyn, but then he'd run smack-dab into her. He felt like a fool, thinking that perhaps he'd led her on and now she'd be clingy, but of course she wasn't. She was trying to avoid him just as much as he'd been trying to avoid her.

Even though he should be relieved he was quite upset by that, because he wanted her. He didn't want Evelyn to have to avoid him or vice versa.

He wanted more and that thought scared him.

What is wrong with you? Isn't that what you wanted?

Except maybe it wasn't.

When they'd collided this morning he'd been glad to see her, his body instantly reacting to her.

When he was younger and had felt that way he would usually sleep with the woman to work her out of his system. Then he'd met Vivian and those roguish ways of his youth had disappeared. Vivian had been the only one for him.

Yeah, and she's dead. She's been gone for five years.

Derek groaned and scrubbed a hand over his face. He'd sworn when Vivian had died and torn open his heart that he would never allow himself ever to think of another woman that way again. Yet here he was, doing just the opposite. What was wrong with him?

Well, whatever was going on with him he had to get control of it.

There was a knock at his office door.

"Come," he said, regaining his composure.

Evelyn opened the door. That glorious dark auburn hair that was just as soft as he'd imagined it to be was tied back.

Seriously, dude. Get a grip.

"Do you have a moment?" she asked.

"Yeah, sure."

She slipped inside and shut the door, crossing her arms and frowning as she stood there. "It's Jennifer Yazzie."

Derek's heart sank. "She has intrauterine growth restriction, doesn't she?"

Evelyn closed her head and nodded.

"Damn," he cursed. "What's your course of action?"

"Monitor weekly. I explained kick counts and put her on bed-rest. So far the baby looks to be doing well, but it is small for gestational age. I don't think it would survive the stress of a vaginal delivery, so at thirty-five weeks I want to get to her Sitka and do a C-section. In the Sitka hospital they have a great NICU and that's the baby's best chance. Did she ever have rubella as a child?"

"Jennifer? No, she didn't have rubella. She was vaccinated."

"And all the tox screens come back clean?"

Derek frowned. "She's a good kid…er…woman. She doesn't smoke or drink or anything like that—as we discussed before."

"I know, but I'm trying to rule out reasons for intrauterine growth restriction. I think there might be something chromosomal going on, and it could be the baby."

"You want to do an amniocentesis, don't you?"

Evelyn nodded. "I want to test the baby's lung maturity and whether the baby will require blood transfusions. Also, Jennifer is RH negative. I would like to administer Rhogam as she lost her first pregnancy at twenty weeks."

"Right, I do remember that."

Evelyn nodded. "So there are a lot of factors that put her in the high-risk category. Not to mention the intrauterine growth restriction."

"Has she given permission for you to do an amniocentesis."

"She has, but you don't have the right gauge needle in stock. Nor do you have Rhogam. Sitka can't take her—their genetic department is overloaded and they don't currently have any Rhogam. But Juneau does, so I want to go to Juneau and get what I need, then fly the sample to Sitka, where they'll test it. I'm hoping you'll let me off for a day or so to get to Juneau and back. Joe Jr. has a car I can borrow."

Derek couldn't believe he was about to offer, but he didn't want Evelyn driving to Juneau and getting lost. And he had an "in" at the Juneau hospital. He could get everything she needed—including a place to do the procedure.

"I'll take you to Juneau. I'm going there on Saturday."

"You don't have to do that. I can arrange my own transportation. I don't want you to go out of your way."

"I'm not going out of my way. I was going there anyways. Tell Joe Jr. to get Jennifer to Juneau by Sunday and I can get you access to a safe site to do the procedure. Sunday is an off day, and you'll have access to the lab."

"You can get access to the Juneau hospital?"

"Yeah, an old schoolfriend of mine is Chief of Surgery at Juneau General. I can make a call."

"What about Mo?" Evelyn asked.

"She's the reason I'm going to Juneau. My late wife's parents are there and they take Mo every other month for a couple of days. So, do you want to go? Shall I make a call to the chief?"

Evelyn grinned from ear to ear. "I'll call Jennifer and Joe right now."

Derek nodded. "Okay. Tell them to be there Sunday evening and we'll get the amnio done. Then she can rest in the hospital for a couple of days while the results come. I know she won't want to stay there if you've made arrangements in Sitka. It's hard for her family to get there."

"Well, if it's a danger to the baby the Juneau obstetrician can handle it."

Derek cocked an eyebrow. "You mean Dr. Pearson? *He's* the head of obstetrics."

Evelyn frowned. "Well, I guess I will have to go back to deliver the baby, then, if she's told to stay put. I hope Dr. Pearson is around Sunday. I would like to speak to him. Thanks, Derek."

Evelyn left the room and he shook his head, chuckling to himself as he thought about the fire and brimstone that Evelyn was going rain down on Dr. Pearson's head if she ever got hold of him.

Another reason why he liked her so much. She didn't seem to back down or shy away from uncomfortable situations, and she was willing to go above and beyond the call of duty to help her patients. *His* patients.

If she had been any other obstetrician he knew that she would have just packed the patient off to Juneau or Sitka and had the obstetrical team there deal with it. But not Evelyn. She was so involved in taking care of her patients.

She would be the perfect physician for this town.

Come on—a surgeon of her caliber, specializing in maternal fetal medicine, is not going to stay in some rinky-dink town.

Janet opened the door. She looked panicked.

"Janet, what's wrong?"

"It's Mr. Schilling. He was out on his fishing trawler and there's been an accident. The trawler is about five minutes out and they're going to bring him here to get him stabilized before even attempting to fly him to Sitka."

Derek leapt up and grabbed his jacket. "What happened?"

"I don't know. They didn't say."

"I'm headed there, Janet. Tell Dispatch at the docks that I'm coming."

"I restocked the blood supply while I was in Sitka. Don't forget that," Janet said as she left the room.

Derek went into the supply room and began to grab things he might possibly need for a trauma. Including a cooler with the blood.

He couldn't think about Evelyn right now, or the fact that she'd be gone by the end of three months. One of his patients needed him.

And that was why he stayed.

It was what kept him going.

CHAPTER EIGHT

IT WAS EARLY Saturday morning, and even though Mo was extremely excited to be spending a couple of nights with her grandma and grandpa it was still too early in the morning for her. She was not an early riser, and for that Derek was extremely grateful.

It had made all those feedings in the middle of the night that much easier on him because she'd let him sleep in. Not that he'd got much sleep in the days after Vivian had died. He had just existed, because he'd had to for Mo, but sleep had been elusive and he'd only slept when his body had collapsed.

Still, Mo would fall asleep again today, which meant the three-hour trip to the ferry terminal would be so much easier. Right now she was chattering happily about Evie coming with them to Juneau.

"Will she come back with us when we come home, Daddy?"

"Of course. I'm her ride."

"Good. I like her. Do *you* like her?"

The question caught him off guard. "Yes, she's nice."

"Yes. She's super-nice."

"Mo, you barely know her—why do you like her so much?" he asked, curious.

"She's the same as me," Mo said.

"How so?"

"I don't know. She's just like me."

And that was the last thing Mo said before she fell asleep in her booster seat.

Derek was surprised at how easily Mo had taken to Evelyn. Mo was usually shy with strangers, but not Evelyn. It would hurt her when Evelyn left. He had to make sure Mo understood that Evelyn wasn't here to stay.

Evelyn was waiting in front of the clinic with a small bag for the overnight stay and a tray with two coffees from Sally and a small box.

Derek parked the car but left it running as he got out and took her bag from her, putting it in the trunk next to his and Mo's luggage.

Evelyn slipped into the front seat and Derek closed the trunk, returning to the driver's seat.

"She's asleep," Evelyn whispered, peering into the back seat.

"Yeah, she's not a morning person."

Evelyn set the coffee into the cup-holders, but held onto the box. "I bought her some chocolate chip cookies."

"Well, it's a long trip. They'll keep. Chocolate in the morning? Would you enjoy a three-hour car ride listening to an endless stream of shrieking?"

She laughed quietly. "Yeah, well, Sally said they were her favorite."

"Thanks—and for the coffee. It's appreciated, but unnecessary."

He pulled out onto the main road and headed out of town to the dense forest road that wound its way through the island and headed for the ferry terminal in Hoonah. From there it would be another three hours or so until the ferry docked in Jordan Springs and then it was a short drive to Juneau.

"So who is going to watch the practice for the couple days we're gone?"

"There's a young resident who flies in from Sitka when I need to make a Juneau run. I scheduled this trip long before you showed up. He arrived the same night as I set Mr. Schilling's leg. Dr. Vance has family here."

Evelyn winced. "I heard about Mr. Schilling's accident, but Janet didn't tell me everything and we've been so busy at the clinic since."

"Well, he got a hook in his hand, and just as he was about to get it out a wave struck the side of his trawler. A boom wasn't fastened properly and it came down on his leg. He's lucky it wasn't crushed. But it was a pretty simple break and I stitched up the hand."

"For a fish hook?"

Derek chuckled. "It's not some angler's fish hook you can buy at the store and use at the old fishing hole, Evelyn. It was a large commercial fish hook."

Evelyn winced again. "Okay. Got it. I don't need to hear anymore."

Derek chuckled. "That makes you queasy?"

"Yeah, your description of it *does* make me queasy. This is why I didn't pursue trauma surgery. It's not my forte. I can lend a hand in a trauma situation, but fish hooks…no, thanks."

He grinned and then shook his head. "It's a way of life up here."

"I know. My dad was the doctor here and… I remember some interesting accidents."

"Like what?"

Evelyn shook her head. "I'm really not going to talk about them."

"Come on," he teased.

She shuddered. "Fish hooks were some, I guess. But the most interesting one was a bear mauling."

"I've had one of those."

"Oh. Was it a tourist?"

"Yes," he said in surprise. "How did you know?"

"They get in too close to the wildlife. I remember Dad talking about it. It used to frustrate him, because once a bear loses its fear of a human it ends up getting destroyed. It was a pet peeve of his."

"I get that."

They didn't say anything else, but he knew that Evelyn understood the way of life up here. It was nice that she *got* it. That he didn't have to explain things to her. She just *knew* and he could talk to her openly about life up close to the sixtieth parallel. Which was so different from anywhere else—except further north, perhaps.

I wish she'd stay.

And that thought caught him off guard.

"Anyways, Mr. Schilling will make a full recovery. He's at home for the rest of the season and Dr. Vance will check in on him while we're gone," Derek said, changing the subject.

"Your replacement?"

Derek nodded. "I was hoping he'd take a permanent position in Wolf's Harbor, but I don't think he will. He has a girlfriend in Sitka. I just need a couple of regular doctors to help with my bid to get funding for a hospital in Wolf's Harbor."

"If you had a hospital I wouldn't have to go to Juneau to run this test, or send Jennifer so far away from Wolf's Harbor to have her baby."

"Exactly. Wolf's Harbor is right in the middle of the Inside Passage and we serve a lot of fishermen and loggers. I've been trying since I lost my first patient over a preventable injury when I first came here."

"What happened?" Evelyn asked.

"Cut his femoral artery in a logging accident. If I could've gotten him into surgery we might have saved him. But I can't get surgeons or nurses to stay in Wolf's Harbor."

Evelyn didn't respond to that, but he saw the bloom of color in her cheeks as she went back to looking out the window.

Great. This is going to be a fun three hours. What else can we talk about to make it completely awkward for her?

"Ever been to Juneau before?" he asked, trying to steer the conversation to something more chatty.

"No. I've never been to Juneau...well, other than to the airport when I was sent to live with my grandmother in Boston. I went to Sitka and then flew to Juneau and then to Boston, which was a long flight."

"You don't like flying?" he asked.

"No."

The silence fell between them again. He felt awkward, nervous around her.

Then Derek chuckled. "I'm sorry."

"For what?"

"I can't seem to start a conversation without it getting awkward."

Evelyn grinned. "I know. Let's stick to talking about Juneau, because I've been to Hoonah, and my dad would take me sometimes to watch the cruise ships come up the Inside Passage or we'd watch for whales, but I've never taken the ferry to Juneau."

"Never?"

"Never. Dad would take the ferry to Juneau if he

needed to go to the hospital, but I would always remain behind with Léelk'w."

"Léelk'w means grandmother?" he asked.

"It's what I called her. Or what she told me to call her. Do you know much Tlingit?"

"No. I don't know much. I've had people try to teach me, but no."

"You've been in Wolf's Harbor for—what?—fifteen years?—and you don't know much Tlingit?"

"Well, I haven't had much time to learn it, and languages are not my forte, much to my mother's chagrin."

"Your mother wanted you to speak a lot of languages?"

"She is Haitian and my dad was Ukrainian, but I couldn't pick up any of the languages my parents spoke— not Haitian Creole, not French, and certainly not Ukrainian or Russian. My Spanish grades in school were miserable too."

Evelyn chuckled. "Well, Léelk'w would speak to me when I was younger in Tlingit. Dad didn't know much. He did know Russian, though."

"Do *you* know Russian?"

"No," she said. "Just English, Tlingit, French and Spanish."

Derek snorted. "Show off."

Evelyn laughed, her eyes twinkling. He liked it when she smiled at him. It made him feel good. It made him feel at ease and relaxed. It made him feel alive again.

"You have a pretty smile, you know."

She smirked. "So do you. Although I was kind of used to your scowling."

Derek chuckled. "Thanks."

"So, tell me more about Juneau and this ferry ride. I mean, it's a three-hour ferry ride, yes?"

"Yep, but the views are incredible, and the ferry has

a cafeteria on board, a movie lounge and a lot of comfortable seating."

"Wow! I'm impressed."

"What did you think it was going to be like?"

"I thought it would be like a barge."

"Nah, we do things right here in Alaska—come on—it's a three-and-half-hour voyage."

"It's very good of your friend to offer us space to do this test. Really it should've been done ages ago. I really hope I *do* have a run-in with this Dr. Pearson."

Derek cocked an eyebrow. "What're you going to do to him?"

"What do you mean?" she asked, confused.

"You sound like some kind of cowboy character, out for revenge. Are you going to deck him or something?" he teased.

"Tempting, but, no. I am going to question his medical integrity."

"That's the same as shouting *Draw!* in the Old West."

Evelyn snorted. "Well, whatever, but he messed up when it came to two patients. Christina and Jennifer. At least Christina survived—as did her baby."

"And Jennifer's will survive. You're here."

Evelyn gave him hope. Something he hadn't felt in so long. And he wanted to pull her into his arms and tell her how alive she made him feel, but he couldn't.

And he didn't want to think about the next doctor coming in. One who wouldn't measure up to Evelyn, because none before had been like her.

Evelyn's expression softened. "Yes."

"Look, he didn't care. He was forced to go on that rotation, like most are. He didn't take it seriously. No one ever does. They just see a small town on a remote side of an island far from civilization."

"I know, but I still want to give him a piece of my mind."

"Okay, but don't step on any toes," Derek warned.

He didn't want to jeopardize the rotation of professionals to Wolf's Harbor, but honestly, if it came right down to it, he was going to back Evelyn every step of the way when it came to dealing with Dr. Pearson.

The rest of their trip to Hoonah passed peacefully. Mo slept the entire time until they got into the line-up of vehicles waiting for passage. That was when she woke up, and was more than happy to have the cookie that Evelyn offered her.

It wasn't a long wait before Derek drove his car into the vehicle hold of the ferry. Evelyn grabbed her bag out of the trunk, Derek grabbed what he needed for Mo and they headed to the upper decks.

Once they were in the solarium Mo ran straight for the lounge chairs that were closest to the prow of the ferry and overlooked the open water of the Inside Passage and the mountains that seemed completely to surround them.

"Wow," Evelyn whispered. "I forgot."

"What?" Derek asked, taking off his jacket and setting it down on one of the chairs.

"What it looked like." There was a sparkle in her eyes as she drank it all in. "I really forgot what it looked like. I think I'm going to head out on deck."

Derek nodded and watched her go. Mo wanted to stay in the comfy chairs, where she could stand and look out the window as she didn't like the wind blowing in her face. So he stayed with Mo and watched Evelyn through the window. He couldn't help but watch her as she leaned over the rail, the wind coming off the water tangling her hair around her face.

She was wiping tears away.

His heart melted for her and he was terrified by how much she moved him. How she was making him feel again.

Something he hadn't ever thought would ever happen again.

Something he didn't want to happen again.

Evelyn had to regain her composure.

She'd forgotten about this place.

She'd forgotten about the times her father had taken her to Hoonah and how she would stare for hours at the mountains and the water. She'd forgotten what it looked like. The picture in her mind hadn't done justice to what she was actually looking at.

She closed her eyes and drank in the salty smell of the water, the mist that clung in the air on this gray morning.

"Look, see that over there?" her father said, pointing as they stood on the pier.

"What, Daddy?" She glanced over, but could only see water.

"Watch for it."

A jet of water spouted from the surface and she saw a smooth, effortless black back just peek out of the water.

"Oh! What is that?"

"An orca pod. See—there are several of them. They travel together. They're a family."

Evelyn smiled and squeezed his hand. "Mommy loved orcas."

Her dad nodded solemnly. "She did. She loved them so much."

"I love them too. I will love them forever, and when I see them I'll think of Mommy."

Her dad hugged her tight and kissed the top of her head.

"Yes. Do that. That is what she would want you to do.

She dreamed of her spirit roaming free over these waters with them."

The horn from the ferry startled her. She quickly wiped away her tears and looked back.

Mo was in the window, waving at her and Derek was gazing at her, a strange look on his face. Their gaze locked for a brief moment and then he looked away.

Evelyn took a deep breath and headed back into the solarium as the ferry began to pull away from the docks, leaving Hoonah behind, headed to Juneau on the far side of the passage.

"Hey, Evie!" Mo shrieked, bouncing up and down in her seat.

Evelyn resisted the urge to hug her. She didn't want to overstep her boundaries with Derek. She knew he was protective of his daughter, and rightly so.

"Hi! Did you have a good sleep?"

"Yep!" Mo said, and then went back to her book, sitting with her legs crossed in the air as she read her alphabet story book.

Evelyn couldn't help but chuckle.

"You okay?" Derek asked.

"Fine. I just needed some fresh air, but it's kind of drizzly out there so I came back in. The water is a bit choppy today."

"Hopefully the sun will come out. After I get Mo settled with her grandparents we can take a trip up the gondola to the summit of Mount Roberts."

"A gondola ride?"

"Sure. You said you've never been to Juneau, and we have some time to kill before we meet with the chief for dinner and discuss our plan of attack at the hospital tomorrow."

"It's nice you want to entertain me, but I don't want to take you away from your family."

"You're not. You're doing me a favor. My in-laws are nice people, and great grandparents to Mo, but they were never fans of me."

Evelyn was intrigued. "Why is that?"

"I took their daughter away," he muttered under his breath. "Although truthfully she was already gone. She came to Wolf's Harbor. I didn't meet her in Juneau and whisk her away. She was trying to escape them. Vivian was a bit of a free spirit."

There was a pained sense of longing in his voice and Evelyn was envious, because she'd never felt that way about anyone ever—because she'd never let herself.

"Well, then, yes—I wouldn't mind a gondola ride to the summit of Mount Roberts. I think that might be fun. I've never been up a mountain."

He smirked. "You're born and raised in Alaska and you've never been up a mountain. Pathetic."

"Ha-ha."

"Don't fight," Mo chirped from behind her book.

They both laughed at that.

"Who's hungry?" Evelyn asked.

"Me!" Evie shouted, putting her book in her knapsack.

"Let's get some lunch. We can come back after and see if we can see some whales in the water."

Mo grinned and took Derek's hand. "Sounds good!"

Evelyn picked up her bag and they made their way to the cafeteria. Derek and Mo were walking ahead and her heart skipped a beat, aching with a sense of longing to belong. To have family.

She hadn't felt this way since she'd lost her father, and

even then it had been fleeting because her grandmother had taught her to harden her heart. To be emotionless.

"It's how I coped with my disappointment with your father."

Whatever, it had served her well.

Or had it?

Now, watching Derek and Mo, she wasn't so sure.

She wasn't sure *what* she wanted, but the part of herself she always relied on was telling her to run before she was hurt. To walk away from the family she so desperately wanted.

A family she didn't really deserve.

CHAPTER NINE

THE TIME PASSED faster than Ēvelyn had expected. Mo kept them both on their toes and Derek teased her about letting her have a chocolate chip cookie and chocolate milk on the ferry.

She was still pretty wound for sound when the ferry docked at Jordan Springs, just outside of Juneau, but by the time they got back down to Derek's car and Mo was settled into her booster seat she was out cold again.

"Your car is like a sleeping pill for this kid," Evelyn mentioned as she set Mo's bag in the trunk while Derek got her belted in.

Evelyn slipped into the passenger side and Derek got behind the wheel as they waited for the ferry to open and let them out. "She's always been a good sleeper. Of course letting her sleep this much means that she's probably not going to sleep well for my in-laws." He grinned.

"That's very devious, Dr. Taylor."

He chuckled. "They're nice people, but they were very strict with Vivian. At least they're a bit more relaxed with Mo, and Mo loves them both to death."

Evelyn smiled as she gazed at Mo. Her curly light brown hair fanned her round cheeks, and her lips were parted as she breathed in her sleep.

"She's a great kid."

Derek beamed proudly. "Thanks. I'm going to miss her while she's gone."

"She goes every other month?"

"In the summer. In the winter it's harder, and my in-laws usually go down south for the winter. I don't know how many more years they're going to be able to do this, or even if they'll stay in Alaska, so I want Mo to have as much time with them as possible. It's a connection to her mother."

Evelyn nodded sadly. "That's important. I had Léelk'w to remind me of *my* mother. I didn't even know about my father's mother until he passed and she gained custody of me."

"And she didn't let you keep in contact with your family up here?"

Evelyn sighed. "No, apparently not, according to Uncle Yazzie. And Grandma told me that they didn't want anything to do with me."

What she didn't say was that she'd thought they didn't want her because of her father's death. She'd taken away Wolf's Harbor's only doctor. Everyone had loved her dad. Now she wasn't sure that it was true. Still, it was hard to forgive herself…which was why she was here in Wolf's Harbor. To seek forgiveness.

The child in her had believed that they hadn't written. The adult knew they had. Her grandmother's hardened heart toward anything connected with her father's death meant she'd probably hidden the letters from her. Her grandmother had been so determined not to be reminded of her son in any way, Evelyn was surprised she'd tolerated *her* presence.

Derek started the engine and slowly drove out of the ferry. "She actually told you that?"

"Well, she put it politely. I wrote letters to Léelk'w

and I guess they were never sent—and of course I never received any letters. It hurt then, but now I understand. There were legal battles fought and lost. And after a time I forgot it all. Forgot about Wolf's Harbor *and* them."

Did you?

She wasn't sure that she had.

"You didn't forget. You just buried it deep down. I get that."

They shared a look, but then Evelyn broke the gaze to look out the window as they drove down the gangway and onto land. Once they were out of the ferry terminal they turned onto the Glacier Highway and headed toward Juneau.

Mo was snoring gently in the back.

"You know, Léelk'w told me I had built up walls," Evelyn remarked.

"I think we all have our own set of walls," Derek said offhandedly.

"You have walls?"

He gave her a look and she laughed at the absurdity of the comment. Of *course* Derek had walls. She could see them as she peered over from behind her own walls. Walls were for protection. They guarded the heart.

"I have Mo to protect, and my practice. It makes it easier to deal with the stress of it all."

"Yeah." Walls were good for that too.

"So why do you think your grandmother wanted to cut you off from Wolf's Harbor?" he asked absently.

"My grandmother hated Alaska. Hated that it took her son away, wrecked all her plans for him. The life she wanted for him. She was grieving, I suppose, in the only way she knew how. Talking about Alaska or Dad was frowned on. She only talked about my father when she expressed her disappointment in his life choices."

"Not fair to you."

Evelyn shrugged. "I know, but I get it. I get her grief."

"Grieving I get," Derek said. "Still, it must've been hard for you, not being able to talk about your family. Do you know much about your mother's family?"

"I don't remember much. Except one thing." She chuckled.

"Oh?" he asked, intrigued.

"There's a lot of Russian on my mother's side, on top of the Tlingit. My maternal grandmother had a torrid love affair with a Russian fisherman. My mother is my uncle Yazzie's half sister. So I have no idea about my maternal grandfather. Or at least my biological one."

"Hey, close to the Ukraine," he teased, and she laughed. "Torrid, eh?"

"Yeah, though I don't like to think about Léelk'w having any kind of torrid *anything*."

Derek laughed. "Yeah, I can't picture Katlian as a young woman, but it doesn't surprise me one bit that her and her sister were a bit of a… Well, they had fun."

Evelyn laughed. "I'm glad you're letting Mo still have a connection to her mother, and I hope for Mo's sake it continues for a while longer."

She knew all too well the pain of losing your connection with everything you knew. Your heritage, everyone you loved. It was horrible, and no one should ever have to go through the pain of losing a piece of their soul.

"Me too," Derek admitted.

It didn't take them long to reach Derek's in-laws. Evelyn stayed in the car and Derek made a couple of trips to bring in the luggage that Mo needed for her couple of nights with her grandparents.

Mo gave Evelyn a hug before she left, and Evelyn cherished those small arms wrapped around her neck in a hug that had completely caught her off guard but was appreciated all the same.

Once Mo was settled, Derek returned to the car. "You ready for a trip to the summit?"

"I suppose…"

"Come on! Your *léelk'w* has an adventurous spirit. You need to have one too."

"I do have an adventurous spirit."

"Then there's no problem," Derek teased.

It wasn't a long drive to the center of Juneau's cruise ship dock. There were a couple of large ships in the harbor, but Derek parked and was able to get tickets for the next trip up in the Goldbelt Mount Roberts Tramway.

They crammed onto the tram with all the other people on their trip. It was a bit of crush, and most of the people were tourists from the cruise ships. Evelyn found herself crammed in a corner, with Derek pressed against her.

Evelyn craned her neck and saw the cables disappear almost vertically up the side of the mountain into the mist.

"Oh, my God," she whispered. "We're going up *that*?"

Derek looked. "Yep. It's eighteen hundred feet up and it's one of the most vertical tramways in the world."

She closed her eyes. "Remind me to murder you if we survive this."

"You can hold on to me—or to the hand-holds."

Evelyn went to reach for one, but an older man in front of her grabbed it, not noticing her. Derek reached down and wrapped a strong arm around her, pulling her close as he held onto a hand-hold himself. His arm around her gave her a sense of security she hadn't felt in so long.

It was nice.

The door shut and the tram began to move out of the station and up through the mist and the rainforest that blanketed the lower elevation around the mountain, on their way to the subalpine eco system at the summit.

Evelyn opened her eyes and braved the view as Juneau disappeared below them and they rose above the mist that was clinging above the city. The sun came out, burning away the drizzle, and she couldn't help but stare at the beauty in wonder.

Derek chuckled. "See—it's worth it."

"If we survive to the upper station," she teased.

"Well, since we're almost there I think that's a safe bet."

Evelyn peered over to the front of the tram to see the upper tram station waiting for them. Once the tram was safely docked the doors opened. Derek and Evelyn lingered to let the other people get off first, so they weren't caught up in the mad crush of tourists.

"Want to go for a quick hike? John said he'd meet us at the Langstrom Grill at seven o'clock. We can head up to the alpine meadow and then take the tram back down."

"Sounds good. Lead the way. I don't think I have my footing yet."

"What?" Derek asked playfully. "Come on, you, goose. This is solid ground."

"It's a *cliff.* This station is hovering over a cliff."

Derek rolled his eyes and then stomped his foot. "See—it's solid… *Whoa!* Whoa! Oh, my God, I'm going to fall off the edge of this cliff."

Evelyn punched his arm. "Ha-ha. Funny."

Derek was shaking his head and still laughing as they left the tram and headed for a path that wound its way through two-hundred-foot-tall trees up to the alpine meadow. There were a lot of tourists going there and back, but Evelyn didn't find them as overwhelming as when they were riding the tram.

In fact as they picked their way through the zigzag path away from the upper station she found it quite relaxing, though it was a bit cooler up on the summit than it was down in the city.

They stopped halfway and sat down on a bench. Through the trees she could see Juneau below them. All the brightly colored homes, and the cruise ships that seemed like toys in the Gastineau Channel.

She sighed. "This is great."

"Got your footing back?" he teased again.

She elbowed him. "Yes. Thanks for bringing me up here."

"No problem. I haven't been up here in a long time. Usually I come by myself, because I have time to kill after dropping Mo off, waiting to catch the ferry back to Wolf's Harbor the next day. Sometimes I take a couple days off to myself and spend it in Juneau before I go back. A little mini-vacation."

"Your family is still in Chicago?"

"My mom is. My dad passed away two years ago."

"I'm surprised you didn't move back to Chicago."

Derek shrugged. "Well, I love it here, and Mo needs her grandparents."

"What about her grandma in Chicago?"

She didn't want Mo not to have contact with her loved ones—especially the ones who wanted her and made an effort to stay in her life.

"My mom is coming up next month to spend several months with me, and I have siblings in Chicago and they have kids. Mo is getting old enough that if I can get another general practitioner up here we can go back home for Christmas or something. Mom would like that."

"I hope you find someone. I wish I could help."

Derek nodded solemnly. "Yeah, I know. But you don't know where you'll end up."

"I have offers in Seattle and at the Mayo. Even in Boston. All good offers."

"So why haven't you taken one of them?" he asked.

"I'm helping out a friend."

Those gray-green eyes narrowed in disbelief. "I think it's more than that."

"Pardon?" she asked, annoyed.

"I'm sorry. I didn't mean to upset you. I didn't think it was a touchy subject."

She didn't respond to that. She didn't tell him that it was indeed a touchy subject and she didn't feel like discussing it right now.

"It's not. I'm helping out a friend. If I wasn't, I would've left the moment she said Wolf's Harbor."

"Um…didn't you find out after the fact? Like after she left?"

"Details, details." Evelyn smiled. "Come on. Show me this alpine meadow before we have to catch our tram back down to meet with this John."

She didn't want to talk anymore. She didn't want to talk about why she was there, seeking acceptance of the never-ending guilt over her father's death. It wasn't his business. He was just her colleague. Nothing more.

She had to remember that and protect herself.

Even if she wanted more.

Derek had a shower and changed his clothes into business casual for their meeting with John. When he'd called John his friend had been wary at first, thinking that Derek was going to bombard him with questions and talk about a hospital for Wolf's Harbor, but once Derek had name-dropped Dr. Evelyn Saunders, John had taken notice. He'd heard of her.

"Derek, how the heck did you land Dr. Evelyn Saunders in Wolf's Harbor?"

"She's covering for a friend."

"She's a hot commodity. What I wouldn't give to bring her on board at Juneau General, but the board wouldn't pay enough to keep her happy here."

"Well, she needs to run some tests on a patient..."

"She can use our facilities. Of course. When is she planning on coming to Juneau?"

"I'm bringing her Saturday."

"Great. We'll have dinner Saturday night at Langstrom's."

Derek had the distinct feeling that he was going to be a third wheel in this situation, but he was okay with that. This was about helping Jennifer and Joe's baby.

He waited in the lounge for Evelyn and glanced at his watch.

The elevator dinged and she walked off.

Derek had to take a step back.

He hadn't seen her dressed up before. Her dark auburn hair was swept up off her neck and a tight black shift dress clung to her curves. High heels accented her legs and her rear, and he couldn't help but tilt his head just so in order to check her out.

And although he was glad he had, as his temperature rose, suddenly he didn't feel like having dinner with a colleague. He wanted to keep her all to himself.

Hey! Get a hold of yourself.

"You look handsome," Evelyn said.

She seemed nervous too. She was wringing her hands and fidgeting.

Good.

He was glad he wasn't the only one, and it gave him a thrill to think that maybe he was affecting her just as much as she was affecting him.

At least he hoped it was that.

"I've never seen you in a suit and dress shirt. Usually you're lumbering around in a flannel shirt."

"I can say the same about you. Jeans, cotton shirts and flats. And my shirts are woolen plaid. It deals with the moisture and the rain better than flannel."

"Are you really starting a conversation about flannel right now?" she asked teasingly.

"I do believe that I am."

Evelyn laughed. "Well, this must be important. I take it Langstrom's is the nicest place in Juneau?"

"Something like that." Derek proffered his arm. "It's not far from the hotel—just down the street. We can walk."

Derek led her outside. Even though it was seven at night, the summer's midnight sun was out—which was too bad, because the twinkling lights down by the water were a sight to see. But it was nice to see the mountains and the water in the Gastineau Channel, which was like a mirror reflecting the mountains. At least it was early in the summer still. They wouldn't have sun till midnight quite yet.

A horn sounded from one of the cruise ships, and music was blasting from another onboard party, but it didn't ruin the beauty of the evening.

Summer in Alaska was his favorite time of year. Though there were times when he missed those endless summers in Chicago. He missed the heat, the beach, and the complete freedom he'd felt back then, when his heart had been open wide and not closed. Not so full of responsibility.

Still, he loved Mo with all his heart, and Alaska and his patients, but it would be nice not to carry the burden of all the things he was—to let loose and be who he used to be.

Derek held open the door and Evelyn stepped inside.

Langstrom's was dark. It had plush leather booths, and wide windows that overlooked the yacht club and the water. The walls were painted burgundy and the exposed beams only added to the ambiance.

He'd always liked this place. But if it had just been him coming to meet John for dinner he seriously doubted that they would've been dining here. They would've probably met at the hotel bar.

John was pulling out the big guns, and since dinner was on him and the hospital board, Derek wasn't going to object.

The maître d' led them toward a private booth tucked in the corner, and as they wound their way through happy diners Derek's heart sank as he saw that Dr. Mark Pearson was at the table.

Oh. No.

At first all he felt was a sense of dread at the thought of Evelyn and Mark meeting, but then he thought that this might be an interesting dinner indeed, and relished the idea of Evelyn putting Mark in his place.

John stood up and seemed practically giddy. Mark, the creep, was eyeing Evelyn as if she was the main course, and Derek instinctively put his hand in the small of her back, which made Evelyn take a tiny intake of breath.

And that little sound coming from her responding to his touch made his blood heat.

"Derek—so glad that you and Dr. Saunders could make it."

"I'm happy you're accommodating us, John." Derek

shook John's hand and then turned to Evelyn. "Evelyn, this is Dr. John Collins, Chief of Surgery at Juneau General."

"A pleasure," Evelyn said, gripping his hand and shaking it firmly.

"The pleasure is all mine, Dr. Saunders," John gushed.

"Please call me, Evelyn."

John grinned again and turned to Mark. "Derek, I know you're familiar with Mark—Evelyn, this is Dr. Mark Pearson, Head of Obstetrics at Juneau General."

The warm, friendly smile instantly disappeared from Evelyn's face as Mark, totally unaware, took her hand.

"A pleasure, Dr. Saunders. I've been reading your work for years."

Evelyn kept the cool, fake smile on her face. "Have you really? Could've fooled me."

Derek coughed, clearing his throat and trying not to laugh as Mark looked thoroughly confused and John seemed completely oblivious to the burn directed at his head of obstetrics.

"Let's take a seat, shall we?" Derek suggested, and slid into the booth next to Mark rather than letting Evelyn sit there, which he knew Pearson was not impressed about.

"We're absolutely thrilled, Evelyn, that you're going to be using our facilities on Sunday. Everything is at your disposal."

"Thank you, John. I really shouldn't have to be doing this testing so late in the patient's pregnancy, but the last doctor who was in charge of this case was lacking."

Mark's eyes narrowed and Derek stifled another laugh.

"Well, it is hard in these smaller communities to get proper assistance when needed," said John.

Now it was Derek's turn to grind his teeth as John gave him this jab.

"Oh, Dr. Taylor has been wonderful. I honestly don't know how he manages to run things so smoothly and skillfully on his own. The town needs a hospital and more staff for sure," Evelyn said. "No, the fault of this patient falling through the cracks lies solely with the rotating OB/GYNs."

"How did you come to *that* conclusion, Dr. Saunders?" Mark asked tersely.

"I came to that conclusion because I have a patient who is documented as having intrauterine growth restriction, and yet she was never informed of that suspicion and an amniocentesis wasn't performed at twenty weeks. She's now at thirty-two weeks."

John frowned and Mark gritted his teeth.

"Perhaps an amnio would've put the patient in danger—and perhaps that patient didn't follow doctor's orders and get herself to Sitka or Juneau to have it taken care of with proper genetic counsellors?"

Evelyn smiled and picked up her menu. "Perhaps. But something should've been done before this."

Derek was having the best time. He loved her sense of humor and he especially loved watching Dr. Mark Pearson squirm in his seat. Evelyn was smart, she had an edge, and he was really enjoying this interchange.

"What's good here?" Evelyn asked, directing her question to John, who looked relieved to turn the conversation away from talking about Mark's error.

It took every ounce of Evelyn's strength during that long dinner not to reach across the table and throttle Dr. Mark Pearson for so many reasons, but she didn't want to embarrass Derek or John, who was a lovely man.

She was very aware that she was being wooed by this hospital, but she wasn't interested in Juneau General.

Not if it meant that she had to work with Dr. Pearson. Perhaps he was a capable OB/GYN, but his mismanagement of two patients in Wolf's Harbor put a sour taste in her mouth.

The dinner was delicious, and she was glad to be treated to lobster and wine. She was even more glad that she would have the full run of all the hospital's facilities.

She'd received a text from Joe Jr. in the middle of the meal that stated he and Jennifer were in Hoonah for the night, so they wouldn't have to spend all day on the road, and Evelyn had texted back that it was a smart decision.

"Well, gentleman, it's been an absolute pleasure, but it's been a long day and I have to prepare for a very risky amniocentesis tomorrow." Evelyn stood up and the men followed suit.

"I look forward to seeing you tomorrow," John said, taking her hand.

"Thank you, John," said Derek, shaking John's hand next.

Mark just nodded, but didn't say anything as she slid out of the booth, completely satisfied that she'd put the pompous ass in his place.

Derek slid out after her and guided her through the restaurant.

They didn't say anything until they were outside, but when they were a few feet from the restaurant Evelyn started laughing uncontrollably, as did Derek. It eased the tension between them that had become almost palpable.

"Evelyn, that dinner...that was worth the drive to Juneau," Derek said through his laughing. "Mark's face, it was priceless. I love karma."

"It was good, wasn't it?" She giggled. "I didn't know he was going to be there."

"Neither did I. I swear. I was worried you were going to deck him."

"I wanted to, believe me," Evelyn muttered. "He was brought there as bait."

"Bait?"

"I'm a woman," she said astutely.

Derek grinned lazily. "I'm very well aware of *that*."

Heat bloomed in her cheeks. "I mean he's a very good-looking man and he was meant to entice me. This isn't been the first time this has happened and it probably won't be the last."

"How many times has this happened to you before?"

"Twice, really. And one time it *did* work. I was with Nathan for two years."

"You don't seem sad about it," Derek remarked.

She shrugged. "It was for the best."

"You wanted different things?"

She nodded. "I wanted a career and he wanted roots, so we ended our relationship."

"I'm sorry."

"Don't be. It's fine. I've learned not to be dazzled by the best in show at a hospital."

"I hadn't noticed that about Mark before, but I suppose he is. So, would you have been enticed if it hadn't been Dr. Pearson?"

"Nope. I'm not swayed that way. They can try, but I've learned my lesson."

"Good," he said, and slipped his arm around her. It felt natural.

It was darker out—the start of a few scant hours of darkness. It wasn't completely summer yet. The end of June would bring about the really long days.

Evelyn stared up at the sky. Just over the harbor there was the faint ripple of the northern lights, but the dwindling dusk and city lights obscured them, stopping the truly stunning display they could've made.

"Oh," she whispered, staring up at them in awe. "I'd forgotten about them too. It's been so long."

"They're beautiful. I never tire of them," he said dreamily.

"Léelk'w told me they're the spirits of the departed dancing."

"I heard you're supposed to whistle at them to make them dance."

Evelyn frowned. "But I heard that some Inuit in Canada believe whistling at them means the spirits will come down and grab you. Don't whistle."

"Okay. I wouldn't want to be grabbed."

Evelyn chuckled. "No, neither would I."

They stood there in silence, just staring up at the green ripple of northern lights, his arm still around her.

It had felt so good when he'd placed his arm around her, and when his hand had been in the small of her back. Maybe it was the wine talking, but if Derek had been the bait, and if she'd been a different person, then she would have jumped at the job John was so slyly offering her.

Evelyn took a step forward, and before she knew what was happening she was lost in those gray-green eyes and swept up into a kiss that was tender at first but then, as she melted into his arms, became more intense. It felt so right, so good.

What are you doing? This isn't smart.

She broke off the kiss and pushed him away. "Sorry," she said breathlessly.

Derek glanced down at her, saw her staring up at him. "What?"

Embarrassed, she looked away. "Nothing—just tired."

Chicken.

"Okay, let's get back to the hotel so you can get some rest. It'll be a busy day tomorrow."

Evelyn nodded and they walked back to the hotel. His arm was by his side, the magic of the moment broken, but it was good that it had been shattered.

Derek was off limits.

She just wished she could remember that and stop testing fate.

CHAPTER TEN

EVELYN SPENT THE day mostly by herself, getting ready for Jennifer's arrival at the hospital in the afternoon, because there were no staff in Patient Intake working on a Sunday and she had refused to let John call one in. She'd told Joe to text her when they arrived so that she could meet them in the lobby and explain everything.

She hadn't seen Derek in the morning, but she'd left him a note at the front desk to let him know that she'd taken a cab over to the hospital. That kiss was still burned onto her lips, but she was nervous about seeing him. She wasn't sure if she'd be able to control herself around him. His kiss had made her completely melt and she wanted more. So much more.

It was for the best that she ignored him and focused on work.

That was why she was here.

Dr. Pearson had made himself scarce, and she was glad for that. The resident she'd been assigned was more than capable.

She had the NICU team on standby, and an operating room available to her should she need it, but she was hoping that she wouldn't.

Sometimes there was no reason at all for intrauterine growth restriction, and even though the baby would be born prematurely, with some health complications, there was still a very high chance that the baby would grow up to be a healthy adult.

That was if there was no chromosomal inconsistencies in this amniotic fluid draw, and Evelyn was really hoping that there wasn't.

Her phone buzzed and she saw that Joe had sent a message to say that they were in the lobby. Evelyn took one last look around the exam room where she'd be doing the work and then made her way down.

As it was Sunday the main lobby of the hospital was pretty empty because there were no scheduled procedures. It was the other side of the hospital that housed the emergency room, and that was always busy.

Jennifer was in a wheelchair, and Evelyn breathed a sigh of relief when she saw that. It meant that Jennifer was taking her advice on bed-rest.

"Joe, Jennifer, I'm so glad you made it."

Joe nodded, and Jennifer was smiling, but Evelyn could tell she was scared out of her mind.

"Thanks for doing this, Evie," Joe said.

"It's no problem. I'm just glad we're able to do it—and so quickly. I'm sorry it's so far from Wolf's Harbor, but this is for the best."

"Well, I'm ready if the baby needs to be delivered today," Jennifer said nervously.

Evelyn took her hand and felt Jennifer's fingers tremble in hers. "I do this all the time. We'll check on the baby, and if he or she is doing well we'll try to keep him or her in there as long as we can. But I do plan on delivering your baby at thirty-five weeks. That's my current choice. So week thirty-four we'll get you to Sitka, yes?

You can wait it out in the hospital and then I'll come and perform a C-section."

"It *has* to be a C-section?" Jennifer asked with trepidation.

"Your baby is measuring very small, and I'm not sure it would survive the trauma of a vaginal birth. It's for the best, and I promise you it's not as bad as it seems."

Joe pushed the chair, following Evelyn through the hospital.

She could tell that Jennifer was nervous, and couldn't even begin to imagine what she was going through. Over a year ago Jennifer had lost a baby, quite far along, and now this.

Evelyn was going to do everything in her power to make sure this baby lived. As she did with all her patients.

"How long do we have to stay in Juneau?" Jennifer asked as they rode the elevator up to the obstetrical floor.

"Only a couple of days," Evelyn said. "We just want to make sure that you don't go into preterm labor. I'm sorry—this must be a hit to your business, Joe."

"Nah, Dad is covering for me."

"This is our room. Jennifer, there's a hospital gown. Change into it and I'll come back in a few minutes. This will be over before you know it, and then we'll get you into a hospital room and get you fed."

Jennifer nodded and Evelyn shut the door to give them privacy.

As she headed to the next room to get the chart she saw Dr. Pearson headed towards her. He had a scowl on his face.

She was secretly pleased he was so put out. He was

a dumb-ass and needed to be taken down a notch. She was annoyed that he was headed in her direction, though.

Great.

At least she knew how to deal with arrogant guys like him.

"Ah, Dr. Pearson. How can I help you this fine morning?" Evelyn asked sweetly, and crossed her arms to hold her ground.

"Dr. Saunders—I thought you might be a bit more gracious, given that *I* run this department. Your behavior last night—"

"Was justified," Evelyn snapped, cutting him off.

"And how do you figure *that*?" Mark growled under his breath.

"Christina. You were supposed to turn her baby the day I arrived, but you decided you wanted to head back to Juneau early. Thanks for leaving the apartment like a pigsty, by the way. I really appreciated that."

"I had more pressing matters to attend to!"

"You were supposed to wait for me and give me at least *some* information about the patients."

"Is that what you're bitter about? Because I didn't stick around and clean an apartment? You were late. I had to catch the last ferry from Hoonah."

"No, I couldn't really care less about the apartment, or the fact you're a slob. What I care about is the fact you didn't turn Christina's baby and a day later she went into labor. I had to deliver a frank breech in a clinic. Not in a hospital—in a *clinic*."

"She had time. It was her first, and the baby would've turned on its own."

"She was thirty-eight weeks. That's not a premature infant. That's almost full term."

"I couldn't have known she would go into labor early. It was her first," Mark snapped.

"That doesn't matter. It should've been done when you said you were going to do it. I delivered a frank breech and had a uterine tear. Thankfully both of them survived."

To give him credit Mark did look relieved about that fact. At least he wasn't a totally heartless jerk.

"Well, I'm glad—but the way you brought it up last night was totally unprofessional. That's not how we handle things around here."

"Alaska is no different from any other hospital I've worked in."

Mark rolled his eyes. "Please. Alaska is not the same as the rest of the country. And Wolf's Harbor is small town—completely backward. I'm surprised you're even bothering with those people…but then again the way you and Derek were making eyes at each other last night I maybe get why you're bothering so much."

The urge to reach out and slap Dr. Pearson was strong, but she kept it in check. Still, she was worried that he'd seen something. What had Derek seen? Maybe Derek thought she was giving him a signal.

Aren't you?

Whatever it was, she knew it couldn't continue—and if other people were noticing it then Mo might notice it, and she couldn't let that happen.

"I will not humiliate you further, Dr. Pearson, but be advised that I have reported your inaction to the Alaska Health Board and the College of Physicians and Surgeons. Small town or not, the people of Wolf's Harbor matter."

Mark opened his mouth to say something further, but instead spun around on his heel and stormed off.

Evelyn took a deep breath, trying to calm her ire. Her pulse was thundering in her ears and she was still fuming.

Mark had basically written off the people of Wolf's Harbor because he felt they were backward for wanting to live a simpler life. He obviously didn't know that he was messing with a Wolf's Harbor native.

And really he didn't need to know that.

It wouldn't make any difference anyway.

She took another deep calming breath. She needed to focus. She had a job to do. A delicate procedure. And she wasn't going to let someone like that get into her head and screw it up.

Derek purposely kept away from the hospital because he didn't want to distract Evelyn.

Oh, who are you kidding? You don't want to be distracted by her.

Last night, walking her home, when they had been staring up at the northern lights all he'd wanted to do was take her in his arms and kiss her. And he'd done just that because he hadn't been able to control himself.

The scent of her hair was still burned into his brain.

The feel of her soft lips against his.

The way his blood had burned with desire for her.

How he'd wanted her even more.

And for the life of him he couldn't remember the last time he'd had so much fun. When he'd felt unburdened and free.

It was nice.

It had been a long time since he'd cut loose.

Mo's grandparents took her a lot during the summer, but he never really enjoyed himself without her. Usually, he was lonely with her gone and would work to fill the void.

He was still missing Mo, but it had been nice spending the evening with Evelyn and watching her handle the two other surgeons. It was a side of her he quite liked.

Strong-willed, stubborn and headstrong.

She had backbone and integrity.

He admired that in her.

So what was he so afraid of?

Having his heart broken again and, worse, having Mo go through the pain of losing someone she loved.

It was better to keep his distance. He must have temporarily lost his mind last night, when he'd taken her in his arms and kissed her.

He went up to the hospital to see if Evelyn wanted to have some dinner and to ask how the procedure had gone. He found her in the obstetrical patients' wing at the charge station, charting and grinding her teeth.

Derek frowned, hoping that nothing had happened to Jennifer and Joe's baby.

"Evelyn?" he said cautiously.

She glanced up and then smiled, but the smile was brief. "Oh, hey. Where have you been all day?"

"Keeping out of your hair," he said. "Is everything okay?"

"Yes, why would you...? Oh." She shook her head and *tsked* under her breath. "Just a run-in with Mark before the procedure. It set me on edge."

"How is Jennifer doing?"

"Good. She came through with flying colors. The baby's heartbeat is strong. Now I'm just waiting on the testing of the fluid. Joe and Jennifer are staying here until Wednesday, but they're in good hands if she goes into labor. We can head back to Wolf's Harbor tomorrow."

"Yeah, I got a message from Janet that there's a new pregnant patient in town and she's quite nervous."

"They always are." Evelyn chuckled. "Not that I blame them. I'd be terrified."

The words surprised him. "You don't want kids?"

"No," she said. "I like kids but…it's terrifying."

He was disappointed in her response, and then he was annoyed with himself for caring and for thinking about her constantly. What was going *on* with him?

"I came by to see if you wanted some dinner."

"I would love some," she said. "Where are you thinking?"

"The hotel restaurant? You should really get some rest before the long drive back to Wolf's Harbor. And we have to pick up Mo on our way out of town."

"Okay, let me go and make one last check on Joe and Jennifer and then I'll change out of these scrubs. It's going to take a couple of days for the labs to run the amniotic fluid. I can't sit around here waiting, though I want to. I'll be back in a few minutes."

Derek was relieved that Jennifer Yazzie had come through the procedure with flying colors, but he had never doubted that she would—not with Evelyn taking care of it.

She was such a talented surgeon.

I wish she would stay.

He cursed under his breath, angry at himself for continuing to think that way. Evelyn wasn't going to stay and he couldn't get attached even if he wanted to do just that. Surgeons like Evelyn never stayed. And how much work could Wolf's Harbor pull in for a surgeon of her caliber? Not much. They were a town of just under a thousand people. Most of that population elderly or male.

Not a huge call for OB/GYNs, even though his clinic did also serve the surrounding area. There were a lot of small villages near Wolf's Harbor.

Maybe there *would* be enough work for her. That was if he could get his small hospital off the ground.

Stop trying to find reasons for her to stay. You'll only get hurt.

"There you are. I was wondering where you'd got too."

"Just wandering. Waiting," he responded gruffly.

He *had* to get control of these thoughts.

"Are you okay?" she asked.

No.

"Yeah, fine. Let's go get something to eat."

Derek couldn't remember when he'd got so good at pretending that he was okay. It was just something he'd learned to do. Learned to cope with the fact that he'd forgotten what it was like to feel.

It was his fault that dinner was so awkward. He'd thrown those walls back up, even though he wanted to let Evelyn in. He didn't blame her when she excused herself and went to bed early. It was for the best.

The next morning was no better, but when they picked up Mo from his in-laws whatever tension there was seemed to melt away.

Or at least Evelyn acted as if there was no awkwardness between them for the benefit of Mo, which he appreciated immensely.

She was so good with Mo, and Mo just adored her. Why did this have to be so complicated?

"I can't wait to get back home," Mo chirped from the back seat.

Derek smiled as he glanced back at her in the rearview mirror, and then he looked over at Evelyn, who was smiling too, but then she frowned.

"What's going on?" she asked as they approached the ferry terminal, which seemed to have a blockade around it.

"I don't know." Derek slowed down and one of the state troopers who had clearly set up the blockade came forward when Derek stopped and rolled down his window.

"Good morning, folks. Are you headed to Hoonah?"

"Yes," Derek said. "We're on the first ferry back."

"A fog bank has rolled in from Sitka. It's pretty bad and there are no ferries operating that way at the moment."

"So what do we do?" Derek asked. "Will the ferry service resume once the fog bank clears?"

"Tomorrow. hopefully," the trooper said. "Even the planes are grounded. If you have tickets you can head to the office. They've made arrangements for accommodation for all stranded passengers."

"Thank you, Officer."

The state trooper nodded and stepped back, directing Derek where to go.

"What do we do?" Evelyn asked.

"Well, we're stuck. We'll find out what accommodation they have for us and I'll call Dr. Vance and let him know about our delay."

"Aren't we going on the boat, Daddy?" Mo asked.

"Not at the moment." Derek pulled into a parking place. "I'll go in with the tickets and find out what's going on."

Evelyn nodded. "Sure."

"I'll be back."

The line wasn't too long. The ferry terminal had everything moving swiftly and accommodation had been set up at motel further up the road that was formed of a series of small cabins. The only problem was that the three of them would have to share a cabin. There wasn't a separate cabin for Evelyn. At least the cabin had two rooms. He could stay with Mo in her room and Evelyn could have the other one. But they were stuck until the fog bank cleared, and that wasn't likely to happen until the morning.

He headed back to the car and slid in the driver side. "We have a cabin."

"A cabin?" Evelyn asked.

"That sounds like fun!" Mo said excitedly.

"Nothing to do but wait it out."

"I hope they have television," Mo said.

Evelyn shared a secret smile with him.

"Well, I was thinking we'd check into our cabin and then maybe drive up the coast to where the road ends and see if we can spot the sea lions in Point Bridget State Park."

"That sounds like fun!" Evelyn said.

Derek turned back to Mo. "Is that okay?"

"Yes!"

"Okay, sea lions it is."

It was just a short drive to the cabin motel and they checked in, dropping off their bags. There was a small café in the motel, where they grabbed a quick bite to eat and Evelyn bought some sandwiches to eat later in the park.

Driving along the coast was amazing, but they were soon headed north, toward Skagway—and there was no road to Skagway. The road ended at the beautiful, rugged Point Bridget National Park.

It had been a long time since Derek had been there, and as they all laughed and chatted on the drive up he was actually excited to go there again.

He hadn't been there since he was dating Vivian. He had always meant to bring Mo here, but had never got the chance, and then it had slipped his mind. Of course

Vivian wasn't here, but he was glad he was bringing their daughter and he was glad he was sharing it with Evelyn.

When they got to the state park they took the easy three-and-a-half-kilometer trail that made its way down to the rocky shore of the Inside Passage. The mountains all around them were reflected in the crystal-clear water and it was enough to take his breath away.

Even though it was densely foggy toward Sitka, here at Point Bridget it was sunny, and as they approached the final bend down to the water they heard the barking call of the sea lions out on the large rocks, sunning themselves.

Mo squealed, but kept her distance as she picked her way across the rocky shore, with Evelyn following close behind her. They were searching for rocks—colorful rocks that had been smoothed by the tides.

Derek couldn't help but smile as he watched them.

He wanted her. He wanted Evelyn and he couldn't remember the last time he'd felt this way. It was a long time since he'd let himself feel and though he was terrified by the emotions coursing through him it was hard to ignore them. Especially now, watching her as she knelt down beside Mo, their heads together as Evelyn showed her how to skip a stone across the water.

He didn't deserve to be this happy. Only he couldn't help himself. Try as he might to stop her, Evelyn kept wiggling her way in. It was hard to push her away when she brought him to life again.

"Daddy, watch!" Mo shrieked.

Derek waved and watched as Evelyn bent over Mo and helped her skip a stone across the water. The stone bounced three times before disappearing under the water with a plop.

"Good job." Derek clapped.

"You try, Daddy," Mo said.

Derek chuckled. "Okay. I'll try."

He shook off whatever doubts were eating away at him. Right now he couldn't think about those things. Right now he was just going to enjoy this stolen moment in life, because it might be the only chance he would get before Evelyn left.

Evelyn sat down on the couch in the cabin. She felt a little sunburnt, but her shower had felt good and Derek had now retreated into the shower while Evelyn sat with Mo in the living room. Mo was in her pajamas and watching a cartoon movie. She was really quiet, and Evelyn had the feeling that Mo was exhausted.

She understood that because she was beat too. But the day had been wonderful. They'd hiked, had an impromptu picnic and watched the sea lions frolic down by the water.

All the awkwardness that had crept between her and Derek was gone. It had been as if they were a family today. Evelyn had forgotten what that was like. It was breaking her heart, knowing that this would probably be the only time she'd ever feel like she belonged.

You could change that.

She closed her eyes, trying to relax.

Tomorrow the fog would most likely lift and they would head back to Wolf's Harbor. Back to being doctors. And she would have to monitor Jennifer Yazzie like a hawk. She also knew she'd be on edge until those amnio results came in.

She opened her eyes and checked her phone, but there was nothing.

Dammit.

Mo giggled and Evelyn glanced at the television.

"What're you watching?"

"The Unicorn Princess," Mo said, not looking at her. "It's so funny. The unicorn is crazy."

"I can see," Evelyn said, and she *could* see, by the googly-eyed expression of the unicorn as it pranced after a very annoyed princess.

Mo yawned, and then to Evelyn's surprise curled up beside her.

"You smell nice, Evie. I like that," Mo said.

"You smell nice too," Evelyn whispered.

She reached down and tenderly ran her hand over Mo's curls. Mo snuggled in closer and it wasn't long before her laughter at the crazy antics of the unicorn disappeared and was replaced by a light snore.

Evelyn glanced down and saw that Mo was fast asleep, her head on her lap. Tears stung Evelyn's eyes and she stroked Mo's back.

Derek came out of the bathroom and his eyes widened in surprise. Then his expression softened as he looked at Mo.

"She's tired," Derek whispered, squatting down in front of them.

"She's not the only one." Evelyn smiled and then looked at Derek, whose eyes were sparkling the same way they had last night when they'd kissed.

She shivered as she recalled the way it had felt to be in his arms.

"I'll get her to bed," Derek said. He stood up and gently scooped Mo into his arms and carried her to the bedroom.

Evelyn shut off *The Unicorn Princess.*

Get control of yourself, Evelyn. He's off-limits.

Derek came out of the bedroom and shut the door.

He headed for the kitchen and then produced a small bottle of wine.

"Where did you get that?" Evelyn asked.

"In the café when we got dinner. We have a nice little kitchen here, and I thought that after today, and you having to endure *The Unicorn Princess* while I showered, you could do with an adult beverage."

Evelyn chuckled. "Thanks. Yes, I definitely could."

Derek poured white wine into two tumblers and joined Evelyn on the couch. "Cheers, then."

Their glasses clinked and they both took a sip.

"Hey, I want to thank you for watching Mo. I rarely get a chance to be away from her and I never have help... it was nice that she had someone else to focus on today."

"I don't mind. She's wonderful—tiring, but wonderful."

Derek laughed softly. "Did you never want to settle down and have kids? I mean, you mentioned not even picking another job."

"I never really thought about kids."

Liar.

"No serious relationships since Nathan?" he asked.

She downed the rest of her wine. "No. Still not ready."

Liar.

"Oh." Derek finished his own wine and settled back against the couch.

"And what about you? How long has Mo's mother been gone?"

"Five years."

"And?" Evelyn asked.

He shrugged. "I haven't had much time, what with raising a baby on my own and my work... My wife died during a snowstorm after giving birth to Mo in our kitchen. Uterine rupture and she bled out. There was nothing I could do to save her. She died in my arms. By the time we got her to Sitka she'd lost too much blood and she went into organ failure. And I was left with this tiny baby...this little girl...and I was alone." Derek clenched his fist. "I didn't get a chance to grieve. Mo was a newborn and I just had to keep going."

"I'm sorry."

And she was. Taking care of a practice and a newborn must've been hard. She'd watched her father for years doing the same and she'd been older. She was sympathetic.

"I understand," she said.

His expression softened to one of appreciation. "I know. You don't pity me and I appreciate it."

"Why would I pity you?"

"So many do." He sighed. "It's tiring."

"I admire you."

Their gazes locked and her cheeks flushed with warmth from the blush she was sure was there.

Derek cleared his throat. "This is why I fight constantly for a hospital—so other people don't have to feel the agony that I felt when I lost Vivian. When I wasn't a good enough doctor to save my own wife."

"It wasn't your fault, Derek. What happened to Vivian was rare, but it happens. I'm sorry that it did. I understand."

"I appreciate you listening to me," he said. "No one seems to want to listen. They just offer condolences, pity, and move on."

"No problem," she said gently. "I'm here."

"Yeah and it's been nice."

Her pulse quickened. "Yes. It has been nice."

So nice.

"It's not just that, though, that's been bothering me."

He took her glass and set it down. His eyes were intense again and she trembled as he moved closer to her.

"What else is bothering you?" she asked, blood thundering in her ears.

"It's wanting you. I want you, Evelyn, and even though I know you're leaving, and I shouldn't… I want you."

His admission caught her off guard, and made her head spin. "What…?"

"I have been numb for so long and you—you make me *feel* something again. Anger, frustration and yearning. Dammit, Evelyn, you're the most beautiful, stubborn, sexy woman who's walked into Wolf's Harbor in so long, and I've been trying to fight the urge to kiss you again."

The butterflies in her stomach were swirling around and her body burned with need. Something she'd never really felt before with any other man.

Don't let him in. Keep him at bay. You're leaving. You can't stay.

Only she didn't listen to that voice in her head. She wanted to feel as well. She'd been numb for so long too. Derek was the only man to evoke this kind of intense, burning desire in her and she wanted him too.

Even if it was for just one night.

She stood up and he touched her face, pushing back her hair before leaning down and kissing her.

Only this time there was no interruption. This time the light kiss which had ignited the flame when she'd first arrived burned hotter, deeper, as he pulled her tight against him, his arms around her as his tongue slipped past her lips, turning her legs to jelly.

She wanted to be close to him. Nothing between them. If she was going to have him only once she wanted to savor it, even if a part of her was telling her right now that once would never be enough.

She broke off the kiss, closing her eyes and reveling in the feeling of Derek's strong hands over her body.

"Don't stop," she whispered.

"I won't unless you want me to," Derek said against her ear, which caused a shiver of delight to course down her spine.

She wanted Derek to possess her.

His kisses trailed down from her ear to her neck and to her collarbone, his hands caressing her breasts under her scrub shirt.

"Too many clothes," Derek muttered.

"I can help with that."

Evelyn unbuttoned his shirt and ran her hands over his bare chest, then worked on his belt, pulling it out of the loops and snapping it as she tossed it over her shoulder. It caused his breath to hitch in his throat as she slipped her hands down the front of his jeans.

He slid his hand down her back and cupped her bottom. "You're taking too long," he moaned.

He pulled her close, kissing her, then pushed her away, pulling down his jeans so he was naked in front of her.

She ran her hands over him, felt his body stiffening under her touch.

"Your turn," he whispered.

She pulled off her shirt and shimmied out of her leggings. Derek stepped forward and removed her bra, leaving her in her pink cotton underwear.

"Beautiful," he murmured, sliding his hand down the front of her undies and stroking her. Making her moan in pleasure. Then he moved his hand and she took off her underwear, so she was standing there naked, exposed to him.

"You're blushing," he murmured, touching her cheek.

"It's been a while for me."

He smiled at her. "Me too."

He cupped her breast and the heat from his skin seared her flesh, making her body ache with need. Her body was so sensitive and she was completely lost to him. No man had ever had such control over her senses. It was scary and thrilling at the same time.

Derek scooped her up and carried her to the bed, pinning her to the mattress. Each time his fingers skimmed her flesh her body ignited. She wanted more from him. She wanted to catch fire and burn.

He stroked between her legs, making her wet with need, and her hips thrust up at him as he touched her.

"I need you, Evelyn."

"I want you too," she murmured. "There's a condom in my bag by the nightstand."

He rolled away and found the condom. She helped him put it on, stroking him.

Derek pressed her against the pillows and settled between her thighs, the tip of his erection pressing against her. He thrust into her quickly, filling her and making her cry out, cling to him.

"Did I hurt you?" he asked.

"No."

He made her feel like she'd never felt before.

"You feel so damn good."

Derek began to thrust and Evelyn urged him to go harder and faster. He unleashed something inside her. Something she'd never felt before. A coil of heat was unfurling in her, singeing her soul and possessing her.

Then it came—pleasure like she'd never had before. And she clung to Derek, crying out as she came. Derek quickened his pace and joined her, then held still over her, breathing heavily before slipping out of her and rolling to his side, his eyes closed.

Evelyn curled up next to him, felt his arm around her. They said nothing, because exhaustion had won over the euphoria, and as Evelyn drifted off to sleep she realized she was falling hard for Derek.

Heck, she'd already fallen hard for him.

She was angry at herself. He was vulnerable and she'd taken advantage of him. She was the worst. She didn't want a family because she didn't want to lose it. She knew that pain all too well.

But another part of her wanted it all. She was lonely and she was tired of running. She was tired of having no place to call home.

This could be your home?

She rolled on her side away from him.

She couldn't have it.

She couldn't risk it.

Why not?

And she rolled back to look at him, watching him sleep and recalling the way his lips had felt against hers, feeling the taste of him still branded there. She touched her lips, as if trying to imprint the feeling onto her fingertips.

Maybe she could stay?

There was nothing stopping her. Maybe, just maybe, she could be happy if she'd just take the chance.

CHAPTER ELEVEN

"I APPRECIATE YOU staying on, Tim," Derek said as he handed a file back to Dr. Vance.

They had gotten in late last night. And still all he could think about was what had happened in that cabin, the feeling that they were a family, and seeing Mo sleeping on Evelyn.

He couldn't help himself.

And even though he knew it shouldn't have happened, that night in the cabin had been wonderful. Amazing. It was hard not to think of the way her body had felt under his. The taste of her lips and the scent of her hair, the softness of her skin.

Focus.

He had to be careful.

He'd been lax in letting Evelyn in when he should've been guarding his heart. But it was difficult to do that around Evelyn. She got under all his defenses. But he couldn't let Mo get hurt.

She smells like coconut and tastes just as sweet.

He shook that thought out of his head.

"It's no problem, Derek," Tim replied. "I had some family stuff to attend to anyway. Besides, I enjoy my visits up here, and I wouldn't have given up the opportunity to watch Dr. Saunders in work."

Derek's stomach dropped as he saw the way that Tim was looking at Evelyn. Not that he could blame him in the least. Evelyn was beautiful, and a world-class doctor. Although Tim supposedly had a girlfriend in Sitka…

And even though he shouldn't let it bother him, because he had already made up his mind that he wasn't going to pursue Evelyn, he was jealous of another man looking at her. Because the simple fact of the matter was that he wished he was free to go after her. He wished she would stay. He wished he deserved her.

"It's not like I'll be doing much," Evelyn mumbled as she went through a chart at the front desk before the clinic opened, totally oblivious to Tim's interest in her.

Good.

"Still, Dr. Saunders, I would be keen to learn from you," Tim said eagerly.

Evelyn looked up. "Of course—and call me Evelyn. It's fine. We're all working together here. Now, if you'll both excuse me, I have to prep for a possible emergency C-section. We need to get a lot more blood stocked in the fridge here."

"Emergency C-section?" Tim asked, intrigued.

"Yes, one of my patients here has intrauterine growth restriction. She's on her way back from Juneau, where I performed an amniocentesis which I'm still waiting on results for. I have everything I need—including an incubator which was generously donated by Juneau General just in case."

"How nice of them," Derek teased and Evelyn grinned at him.

They both knew that it was a bribe to get her to consider working at Juneau when her time was up in Wolf's Harbor. Still, they weren't going to look a gift horse in the mouth.

"If I can help in any way, Evelyn. I'm here to assist you," Tim said eagerly. "I would *love* to assist you."

"I'm good for now—but, thanks." She wandered away, seemingly totally clueless about his compliments.

Derek chuckled to himself. She probably *wasn't* clueless to Tim's subtle flirting with her—she probably didn't care. And that was what he liked so much about her.

The phone rang and Tim answered it. "Wolf's Harbor Medical."

Evelyn blushed as Derek shared a look with her. They had both agreed in the morning that they wouldn't mention it anymore. That it had been just a weak moment. They would carry on as they always had. But still, watching her now in the clinic, being so close to her, it was hard not to think of her in his arms.

"How bad?" Tim asked, with an edge of concern in his voice.

Derek turned and watched as Tim took down information and then ended the call.

"What's wrong?" Derek asked.

"A young woman on the island up the channel—possible miscarriage and bleeding heavily." Tim handed the notes to Derek.

"Okay—you man the clinic and I'll get Evelyn out to Yashee Island."

"I can take Evelyn out to Yashee Island," Tim offered. "I would *love* to assist her."

Derek cocked any eyebrow. "Do you know where Yashee Island is? Do you have a boat?"

"Yes, I know where it is. I grew up here. But no boat."

"Then you stay here," Derek said.

Tim laughed. "I'm trying too hard, aren't I?"

"Just a bit. Stay here at the clinic and I'll get Evelyn out to the island."

"Okay, Derek." Tim chuckled.

Derek picked up his coat from the rack and went to exam room one, where Evelyn was preparing everything necessary for an emergency C-section.

"You're needed," Derek said.

She spun around. "Oh?"

"Possible miscarriage and heavy bleeding out on Yashee Island in the channel."

Evelyn frowned. "I'll get the gear ready. Is there a boat I can hire to take me out to the island?"

"I have a boat. Or rather the clinic has a boat for instances like this. I can take you and Tim will man the clinic."

"Great."

Evelyn went about packing everything she could need. She packed the Doppler, and Derek packed the cooler with some universal blood.

"Is there anything else we might need?" Derek asked as he loaded the last of the gear into his car to take down to the docks.

"Well, if it's early on in her pregnancy a Doppler might not be able to pick up a heartbeat under ten weeks. An ultrasound would be best—but we can't transport that."

"No, we'd have to get her to the clinic for that."

"If she's hemorrhaging I'll need to get the bleeding to stop, but if it's a miscarriage I can usually tell in the pathology." She frowned. "This is the worst part of my specialty. Or one of the worst parts. We'll get the bleeding controlled and if the pregnancy is lost we'll get her back to the clinic to do an ultrasound and a dilation and curettage."

It was a short ride to the docks and they'd soon loaded and secured all the gear and headed out of the harbor toward the bay where Yashee Island lay, about five miles off the coast.

"It's really choppy today," Evelyn shouted over the roar of the engine.

"Storm is brewing somewhere. I'll check the radar tonight. It'll probably miss us. Good thing Joe and Jennifer are heading back right now. I would hate for them to be delayed or stuck somewhere."

"Well, if she was stuck in Juneau she'd be in good hands, but Joe texted me early this morning to say that they were catching the first ferry from Jordan Springs to Hoonah. They'll be here by dinnertime. What I'm waiting for is the results of that amnio."

Derek nodded. He could tell she was worried. He wanted to tell her it would be okay, but he was concerned too. He didn't say anything, though, because with the roar of the boat engine and the rough water, and the cold wind whipping up, the best course for Evelyn was to hunker down and keep warm.

It took him about twenty minutes to navigate the channel and then head out into the bay and deteriorating conditions towards Yashee Island. There were only about four families who lived on the small island, but all the homes were within walking distance of each other, and there were people waiting at the docks when they moored the boat there.

"Robert!" Derek called out as Robert Marshall, one of the island residents, helped him tie up his boat and bring the gear off.

"I got my ATV with a wagon loaded for your gear. Saves lugging it over to the Washingtons' house."

Derek's stomach fell. "Martha?"

Robert nodded solemnly. "She came home from university about a month ago, pregnant, and this morning she woke up bleeding. Pretty bad too."

"This is Dr. Saunders, the OB/GYN currently on rotation in Wolf's Harbor."

Robert nodded curtly and then paused. "Thorne Saunders' girl?"

"Yes," Evelyn said, smiling. "Did you know him?"

"He was my doctor before.... A good man."

A strange expression passed over Robert's face as he helped carry the medical supplies up to his ATV. Derek couldn't help but wonder what that was all about.

He shook his head. He didn't have time to worry about it.

They secured the gear and then climbed into Robert's ATV. He drove them away from the docks, up the winding path to the house furthest from the landing: a log house high up the hill, hidden in the trees of Yashee Island. It boasted beautiful views.

The door opened and Derek saw Martha's mother Jocelyn standing there, waving.

"I'll bring up the rest of the gear, Docs. Go on and take care of your patient."

Robert handed Evelyn her medical bag and Derek led Evelyn up the path.

"So glad to see you, Dr. Taylor," Jocelyn said nervously. "I've been so worried. It hasn't stopped. The bleeding is so heavy."

"Well, thankfully our clinic has one of the best OB/GYNs from the eastern seaboard in service this month. Dr. Evelyn Saunders—this is Jocelyn Washington."

Jocelyn froze, her face paling, and Evelyn's mouth dropped open as they just stared at one another.

Derek was confused. They knew each other. Or it appeared that way.

Evelyn snapped her mouth shut and looked as if she was staring at a ghost. "I would like to see the patient now, if I could. If she's bleeding she needs medical attention."

"Of…of course. This way," Jocelyn said just as nervously as she led them into the house.

"You okay?" Derek asked.

"Leave it," Evelyn muttered under her breath as she took off her boots and followed Jocelyn upstairs.

Derek stood there, still confused. It was apparent that Jocelyn and Evelyn knew each other, but the tension simmering under the surface was thick.

What was going on? What had happened?

Evelyn felt as if she was going to throw up. It had never occurred to her that she would run into Jocelyn again. She'd always been afraid of running into her. She'd ruined Jocelyn's life too.

It figured that just when Evelyn had found some sort of small happiness in Derek, karma had to remind her of what she'd done all those years ago.

Her father had wanted to marry Jocelyn. Jocelyn had wanted to replace her mother. And when she was a kid she'd hated Jocelyn. Now she had a hard time looking at her. Evelyn was ashamed of her past behavior.

"My daughter is in here," Jocelyn said quietly.

Evelyn barely acknowledged Jocelyn—because she couldn't look at her. She was having a hard time keeping her composure and she needed to have control. There was a young girl suffering and she needed help. She couldn't let her guilt overpower her and stop her from doing her job.

That was why she was here in Wolf's Harbor.

Evelyn walked into the room and saw a young girl of about nineteen on the bed, sweating. Her skin was gray and she knew just from the glassy expression in the young woman's eyes that she was bleeding and a lot of blood had been lost.

"Martha, I'm Dr. Saunders. I've come to help you."

Martha nodded, but clearly couldn't speak.

Evelyn pulled off her jacket and sanitized her hands. "Do you know how far along your daughter is, Mrs. Washington?"

"Sixteen weeks," Jocelyn answered, sitting next to her daughter.

"She's nineteen?" Evelyn asked.

"Yes," Jocelyn responded.

Well, it didn't take Jocelyn long to move on from my father.

She pushed that bitter thought away. At least Jocelyn had got some happiness. She deserved it.

"I'm going to examine you—okay, Martha? I'll take care of everything and then I'm going to have Dr. Taylor set up an IV for fluid and pain relief, okay?"

Martha nodded and closed her eyes.

Evelyn ignored the fact that Jocelyn was in the room. There was no time to think about that. She had to help this poor girl.

She had a job to do.

Evelyn came down the stairs, carrying her equipment. She was exhausted, but she'd managed to stop the bleeding. Now she just wanted to put some distance between her and Jocelyn.

There was so much she wanted to say to Jocelyn but couldn't. She was terrified. Terrified of having her apology rejected. She couldn't deal with that today.

Derek was waiting for her.

"Well?" he asked.

"Bleeding has slowed down and she's hooked up to some packed cells, but I need to get her into the clinic and do an ultrasound."

"Why?"

"I think she was pregnant with twins and she only lost one, because the Doppler picked up a heartbeat. I couldn't do anything else because I didn't want to jeopardize the baby, but she definitely miscarried just one. Her father has a boat and they're going to get her down to the docks. We should get back to the clinic now and prepare for her arrival."

Derek nodded. "We can do that."

"Good." Evelyn slipped on her coat and then picked up a couple of boxes.

"Whoa, what's your rush?" Derek asked as he grabbed her by the arm and stopped her. "Aren't you going to say goodbye to Mrs. Washington?"

"I already have."

"You're so in a rush. Why?"

"I told you—we have to get the clinic ready." She walked out of the door.

Derek caught up to her as she made her way down the path toward the docks. "What're you running from?"

"I'm not running from anything."

Liar.

"Oh, come on, Evelyn, you were positively rude to Jocelyn Washington and you've never, not once, been rude to *anyone* in town."

Evelyn glared at him. "Derek, if the other twin is currently alive I have to prepare everything back at the clinic to make sure it stays that way. Martha was absolutely devastated that she lost one. I promised her and her mother I would do everything in my power to save the other twin. I'm not running from anything. Honestly? I'm still a bit tired from our trip to Juneau."

"Fine," Derek said, but she could tell from his tone that he wasn't fine.

Evelyn was relieved when he dropped it. He didn't need to know that Jocelyn had been going to marry her father. Or that her father had been killed on his way to visit her. Part of her felt guilty about the whole thing, because her father had gone out that night to propose and he'd died. But the adult version of her wanted to know more.

Her gut reaction to Jocelyn had been cold. Now she was ashamed with herself for her behavior. Would Jocelyn have said yes? Jocelyn had lost someone that night too.

They loaded the boat and headed back to Wolf's Harbor. There was a fog over the water so thick it was hard to see, and she hoped that Martha's family would be able to get her into the clinic.

Derek wasn't saying anything to her and that was for the best.

She really didn't want to talk about it.

When they got back to the clinic Evelyn dried off and got the exam room ready, prepping the ultrasound with Janet.

Thirty minutes later Martha Washington was brought in on a stretcher by the paramedics, who had been called and had been waiting for the Washingtons' boat when it moored at the town's docks.

Jocelyn followed Martha in, but didn't look at Evelyn.

Evelyn couldn't blame her. She was so embarrassed over her behavior. She'd acted badly. She deserved Jocelyn's cold shoulder.

They got Martha transferred to the exam table, and when the paramedics had left Evelyn examined Martha. The bleeding had subsided.

"Give her another unit of packed cells, Janet," Evelyn said as she covered Martha up and wheeled the ultrasound machine over.

"She's stopped bleeding?" Jocelyn asked.

Evelyn met Jocelyn's gaze and nodded. "Yes, you can see for yourself. Her color is returning to normal. Martha, how is your pain?"

"It's a five now, Dr. Saunders."

Evelyn smiled warmly. "Better than the ten it was before. I know your belly is tender, but I'm going to do an ultrasound. I heard a heartbeat on the Doppler and I want to confirm that you were indeed carrying twins and that the other twin is fine."

Martha nodded.

Evelyn got the gel ready. "It'll be cold… Here we go. Janet, can you get the lights?"

"Yes, Dr. Saunders."

Janet dimmed the lights and Evelyn placed the wand on Martha's belly. She soon found what she was looking for. There was the strong flutter of a heartbeat for the other twin. She grinned and turned the monitor.

"There you go, Martha. You *were* pregnant with twins. You lost one, but this one right here has a strong heartbeat."

Martha began to cry, and Jocelyn bent down and kissed her daughter on the head.

"Now what, Dr. Saunders?" Martha asked nervously. "I don't want to lose my other baby."

"Bed-rest, and I'll want to check on the baby tomorrow, so you guys should stay here for the night. I want to monitor your bleeding and do another ultrasound before you head back to the island. You'll have to come in for regular check-ups for a while."

"Can she do that on bed-rest?" Jocelyn asked.

"Yes, but she needs to take it easy and rest wherever possible."

"We can stay in town, Mom, at our old house."

Jocelyn bit her lip and then smiled nervously as she glanced at Evelyn. "Yes. Of course."

"Well, it's good you kept two residences."

"Well, Mom didn't marry my stepdad until I was ten. My real father was killed in an accident before I was born. In fact, come to think of it, we have the same last name, Dr. Saunders."

Jocelyn's eyes were wide with fear as Evelyn's world teetered out of control. And as she looked at Martha for the first time—*really* looked at Martha—she saw her father's eyes. Saw her father's ruddy hair and freckles.

Evelyn favored her mother, and had missed out on her father's freckles, but she'd inherited his hair. Except hers was auburn—red mixed with her mother's dark. Martha looked like pictures of her late grandmother when she was young.

This was her half sister.

Oh, God. I ruined this girl's life too.

She had to get out of here.

"Well, it's a common surname. Now, I have to check on something—Janet will make sure you're comfortable."

Evelyn peeled off her rubber gloves and disposed of them as she quickly left the room.

Jocelyn followed her. "Evelyn, wait!"

Evelyn spun around. "No. We're not talking about it."

"I think we *should* talk."

Evelyn was shaking—with anger, pain, and just about every raw emotion she could think of. She didn't know what to think. What to believe. Everything inside her was telling her to run, which would save her from getting hurt.

"No. I can't… I can't talk about it now. I'm sorry."

She grabbed her coat and walked out of the clinic and straight into the rain. She wandered along the main street, not really knowing where she was going.

Her mind was screaming at her, telling her to pack a bag and leave.

She needed to protect her heart. When her father had died and she'd lost her home and the only family she'd ever known she'd sworn to herself that she would never feel that kind of pain again.

She didn't want a family. Families got shattered, broken, and people ended up alone.

You have one, though. Why can't you see that?

Evelyn continued wandering until she was standing in front of a clapboard house that had used to be bright red, but was now faded and chipped. Everything was the same—including the covered porch with the rocking chair. Only no one was home. The lights were out. The car was gone…

"Evelyn?" Derek said in confusion. "You're soaked."

Evelyn turned. "How did you find me?"

"I had a hunch."

"Good hunch." She chuckled nervously.

"Come on—my car is over here. I'll take you back to your place."

He slipped his arm around her and led her the way to his car and out of the rain.

It was comforting.

It felt good that someone cared for her.

They didn't say much as he drove her back to the clinic

and led her to the apartment in the back. Once they were inside he took off her coat.

"Go get changed and I'll make some tea."

Evelyn nodded and went to change into dry clothes. By the time she was done the tea was ready.

"Thank you, Derek," she said, not knowing what else to say. She was appreciative of the fact that he'd found her standing in the rain before anyone else had seen her.

He nodded. "What would you like in your tea? Honey or lemon?"

"Something stronger?" she said dryly.

Derek laughed and pulled out some whiskey. "This do?"

"Yes!"

Derek poured them both tea with a shot of whiskey. "Do you want to talk about it?"

"No," she muttered. "Not really."

"Okay."

She scrubbed a hand over her face, because she needed to talk about it to *someone*.

"Martha Washington is my half sister."

His eyes widened briefly. "Oh. That I didn't know."

"That's all I'll say."

"Okay," he said.

"I know you think I have walls…"

"I told you—we all have walls, Evie. I'm just glad that you've decided to let me in."

Tears stung Evelyn's eyes. "What am I doing here?"

"You've come home to lay some ghosts to rest. It's obvious." Derek finished his tea. "And to practice medicine, obviously?"

"You think so?" she teased, and then sighed.

"Well, you *are* a doctor." He winked.

Evelyn laughed, felt her mood lifting.

"If I had just accepted that my father wanted to marry again I could've had a sister. I wouldn't have had to leave."

Derek sighed. "We can't look at the past. It's hard, but we just have to do what's right going forward."

She nodded. "I suppose you're right."

"I know I am. Now, I'm going to head back down to the clinic. I'll see you later."

He pulled her close into a warm hug and she tried not to cling to him, but it felt so good to be in his arms.

After he'd left her phone buzzed and she picked it up. It was an email from Juneau General Hospital and her heart skipped a beat.

It was Jennifer's results.

She had to get to her computer and analyze them.

She was hoping the baby didn't have any chromosomal defects. She was hoping the baby would be able to survive an emergency birth if it came down to it. But if the baby had issues she was going to put Jennifer on a plane to Sitka and deliver the child.

Then, when Martha was stable and Jennifer's baby was safe, she was going to get the heck out of Wolf's Harbor.

She'd done her duty to her father. She was tired of ghosts.

Forgive yourself.

Only she couldn't. She'd caused too much pain and she had to leave before she caused anymore.

And the only way she'd escape was if she ran—and that was what she planned to do as soon as she could.

CHAPTER TWELVE

"WHAT DO YOU MEAN, a hurricane is tracking toward us?" Derek asked.

Tim Vance showed him the emergency report that was flashing on his laptop. "It's rare, but a hurricane that cropped up off the coast of Hawaii is building strength and heading straight for us. They're warning all residents of southeast Alaska to brace for hurricane conditions."

"Is Juneau included?"

Tim nodded.

Derek's heart skipped a beat and he picked up the phone to call his in-laws. He owed Vivian that much.

"Hi, George, it's Derek. Yeah, Mo is okay... But have you and Melanie heard about the hurricane? Okay, good. Stay safe. I know. Thanks."

Derek ended the call. His in-laws had already heard about the hurricane barreling its way toward them and had taken precautions, boarding up their windows and stocking their house with supplies. And they'd reminded him to take care of Mo more than once. He knew they blamed him for Vivian's death, because they'd told him so—many times.

Mo would be okay with Edna at the house until he was able to get out there and collect her. It would be best if they all just hung out at the clinic until it blew over.

And he was positive that Evelyn would let them crash at her place.

"Do you know when it's supposed to hit?" Derek asked Tim.

"Tonight."

"I think we're going to stay here tonight, then. We have Martha still resting until Dr. Saunders discharges her. I'll have to go get Mo and bring her in here."

"I'll get her," Janet offered. "I have to check on my place and it's on the way."

"Are you sure, Janet? Edna is with her—do you think you can bring Edna back into town too?"

"Yeah, of course. I've watched Mo before, and I know she likes riding in my truck, and picking up Edna is no problem." Janet grabbed her coat. "I'll get your house locked up too, and get some supplies."

"Thanks, Janet. And if you see Dr. Saunders tell her I need her."

Janet nodded and left just as Evelyn walked in. There were dark circles under her eyes. She looked exhausted.

"What happened to you?" Derek asked.

"I got the results in from Jennifer's amnio. I spent all last night analyzing them." She scrubbed a hand over her face. "How's Martha?"

"Stable," Tim answered. "I just went to check on her. They're wondering when they can leave. Mrs. Washington wants to get their home stocked up before the hurricane hits."

Evelyn's eyes widened. "Hurricane?"

"Yeah—they're grounding all planes," Derek said.

"Right. Well, I just went to check on Jennifer Yazzie. Baby is strong and no signs of labor. Let's hope it stays that way until the planes have clearance to fly, and then I'm getting her to Sitka as soon as possible."

"Why? Is it bad?" Derek asked.

"No chromosomal abnormalities, but Jennifer has symptoms of the beginning stages of kidney failure and the baby has polycythemia."

"What's that?" Tim asked.

"A concentration of red blood cells," Derek answered. "Not fatal, but it can cause complications."

"I need to get that baby out of her." Evelyn hung up her jacket. "I'll go check on Martha and get her discharged."

Derek nodded. "Okay, and then we need to get this clinic ready for the hurricane."

She nodded and disappeared into the back room.

In all his fifteen years in Alaska he'd never encountered a hurricane. They were rare in Alaska, but not unheard of. Hopefully this hurricane would lose steam, or the jet stream would make it change direction so they didn't get slammed with one.

Alaska got storms, even tropical ones, and really bad winter storms, but this was the first time a hurricane was coming to batter his clinic.

"Nancy?" Derek called out to his receptionist, who was in the filing cabinet. "Do we have any protocols for hurricanes?"

"Yes, Dr. Taylor." Nancy went over to a drawer and pulled out a binder. "Every possible natural disaster is listed in there."

"Great—and now you're going home."

"Dr. Taylor, I can stay and help."

"No, Nancy. You go home. You've got kids, and you need to make sure your house is ready for this storm. Go—and that's an order. I would send Janet too, but we're going to need her once she gets back."

"Thank you, Dr. Taylor." Nancy collected up her things and left.

Derek sat down behind her desk with the binder and flipped to the page about hurricanes. They could hole up in here. After Evelyn had taken care of Martha and sent her on her way they'd raid Evelyn's apartment for food and supplies and then board up her windows before securing the clinic.

At least they had enough supplies. At least people could get to them for help. Unlike the night that big snow storm had hit and he'd lost his Vivian because she hadn't been able to get the emergency care she'd needed.

"We were called for a transfer?" said Dan, one of the paramedics, from the door.

Evelyn came out. "Yes, Martha Washington. You have the address. But she needs to lie flat for a bit longer."

Dan nodded and they followed her in with a stretcher.

It wasn't long before they were bringing Martha out. She didn't have an IV anymore and looked better.

"Don't try to come out if there's a hurricane. When it's all clear drive her over to the clinic and I'll do an ultrasound," Evelyn warned.

"Thank you, Dr. Saunders," Jocelyn said, not looking at her.

When Martha was loaded into the ambulance Evelyn came back inside.

"Okay, what do we have to do to get ready for this hurricane?"

"Supplies. Food and water. All of us are going to crash here tonight. I'm going to drive out to my place and secure it, also grab as much bottled water and food as I can, and Tim will help you with your apartment."

"Okay."

"Planes are grounded, as you know, and ferry service has stopped. All the roads out of town are closed except for emergency services. It's a complete shut-down."

"Yeah, we used to have hurricanes in Boston. I remember. I'll take what I can and we'll meet back here in a couple of hours."

"Sounds good."

Janet called to say she was delayed. The wind had picked up and there were trees that had been knocked over, blocking the road back into town.

Edna, Mo and Janet were at Janet's place while the trees were cleared by the volunteer fire department.

Derek was stressed, but he knew Mo was safe with Edna and Janet, so he focused on battening down the hatches at the clinic. They would need the generator when the power went out, so he took stock of the supplies he could grab and other essential items—including another generator.

Lives depended on those generators.

By the time he'd finished unloading everything into the storeroom Evelyn and Tim were bringing down boxes of food from her place.

The apartment was on higher ground, but it had more windows. The clinic didn't have as many interior windows and they would be safer there. He was glad that the clinic was high above the sea walls that surrounded the lower part of town and the downs. They were perfectly situated on the hill.

It was then that the rain hit. And it was heavy.

"What time is this hurricane coming?" Derek asked.

"I'll check the weather network." Tim pulled out his phone. "Two hours it'll make landfall. It's large. So when it makes landfall in Sitka it's going to hit us."

"This clinic has back-up generators, right?" Evelyn asked worriedly.

"Of course. We'll be fine. You seem agitated? I thought you were used to hurricanes."

"I have a bad feeling," she muttered, and she was twitching nervously.

Derek wanted to comfort her, but not in front of Tim. Besides, he was worried about Mo and hoped the road would be cleared soon.

He had to keep his distance from her. That was what they'd agreed upon. It was for the best. If he comforted her now, he wouldn't be able to stop himself. She'd draw him in again. Get through his defenses.

Who are you kidding? She already had. Evelyn had a way about her that just drew him in and he was a lost man.

"Where's Janet? I thought she'd be back with Mo," Evelyn asked, and there was concern in her voice.

"Tree fell, blocking the road. They'll be here as soon as it clears."

Evelyn still looked worried and it melted his heart, seeing her concern for his daughter.

She loved Mo too. It was obvious.

He wrapped his arm around her and gave her a hug. She rested her head on his shoulder. It was comforting, sharing this burden with someone else, with her. He didn't feel so alone.

Only you are.

He broke the connection.

"Come on—let's finish boarding up the windows of the clinic," Derek said.

They worked together in uneasy silence. Then Derek made a preliminary check on the generators. Outside it was growing dark, which was unusual it being summer time in Alaska.

It was eerie. He could hear the rain pelting the metal

roof and the sides of the clinic. It was harder than it had been before. Once that gale force wind picked up it wouldn't be safe for anyone out there on the street.

What was that old saying? It wasn't that the wind was blowing, but what the wind was blowing around? He glanced at the clock.

How long did it take to clear a tree from a road anyway?

"Help!"

Derek ran from the back as he saw Joe Jr. come in, supporting Jennifer. On her other side was Joe Sr.

Evelyn came rushing from the back room. "Jennifer!"

Jennifer was moaning in pain, doubled over, and Derek's chest tightened as he saw himself in Joe's shoes, holding Vivian as she cried out.

"She went into labor, Evie," Joe Jr. said. "It happened so fast. One minute she was fine and the next her water broke."

"Her water broke? Get her into exam room one," Evelyn said.

She was cursing under her breath as Joe Jr. scooped up his wife and carried her to the back.

Joe Sr. and Tim braced the door shut, locking it as the wind hit, trying to throw it open with a god-awful howl which made Derek's insides turn into ice. It reminded him of the night Mo was born. The storm that had hit then. The howl and groan of the wind as it had dumped snow, almost burying them alive and impeding the medical attention Vivian had needed. They hadn't been able to get out and by the time help came it had been too late.

That storm had cost Vivian her life, and he prayed that this storm wouldn't cost Jennifer hers.

Derek headed to the back room and helped Joe lie Jennifer on the operating table. Evelyn was in the next room, putting on scrubs. He could see the look of dread on her face as she did so.

Tim was prepping Jennifer, and was already in a set of scrubs. Jennifer was unconscious, the pain having overtaken her.

"What's going to happen, Dr. Taylor?" Joe asked with terror in his eyes. "I can't lose her!"

"Come on, Joe. Let's go sit with your dad. Let Evie take care of her."

Tim ran past him to lend a hand as Derek walked Joe Jr. back to his father.

"What do we do?" Joe Sr. asked.

"I have to go help, but Jennifer is in safe hands, Joe. Evie is a good doctor. A good surgeon. Evelyn is brilliant."

And he would be there, every step of the way.

It wasn't ideal, but they wouldn't lose Jennifer or the baby.

He had every confidence.

This time he would win out over death.

"It will be fine, Joe."

Joe nodded nervously and didn't respond, but Derek had a good feeling that Evelyn would save Jennifer's life.

He was willing to bet on it.

Evelyn gave him hope even though he was worried about the storm, about Mo—about a lot. The one thing he was sure of, that he believed in, was Evelyn.

She'd done it before and he knew she'd do it again.

She might have a complicated past, like him, but she didn't let it interfere with her work.

The past was in the past. That was what he'd told her the other day when she'd opened up about Martha.

He had never thought he'd say that.

Ever.

But he'd meant it. Evelyn had given him hope for so much more. If he could just let go…

"I know anesthetics," Tim said as he finished scrubbing and headed into exam room one, which was now an operating theater. "I can manage her airway."

"Great," Evelyn said as she got into a surgical gown and gloves. "We'll deliver this baby here and now. Tim, get the incubator ready when Jennifer's anesthesia is stable."

"Of course, Dr. Saunders."

Derek came into the scrub room and changed in front of her. She was grateful that he was going to assist. She needed Janet to manage the baby while Evelyn operated on Jennifer and got her stable. Then Evelyn could focus on keeping the baby alive.

"There was meconium in the water," Evelyn said to Derek as he finished scrubbing and got a gown on.

"That's bad," Derek said.

"Yeah, I'm worried the baby aspirated it, and that's a definite sign of distress. The baby's heart-rate is elevated. We need to get that baby out of there."

The wind howled and the clinic creaked. The lights flickered and Evelyn took a deep breath.

You got this. You can do this.

"Back-up generators are running. If we lose main power we have the back-ups, and the incubator has a battery pack that is charged." Derek smiled from behind his surgical mask. "I'm glad you're here."

"Thanks." She sighed. "Let's go."

Evelyn took a deep breath as she entered the makeshift operating room. She wasn't used to conditions like this. She was used to state-of-the-art facilities. Large operating theaters that were fully staffed, and a gallery full of eager interns and residents who wanted to learn.

She wasn't used to working in the wilds of Alaska, where situations like this meant life or death.

The lights flickered again, but came back on.

Just stay on. Please.

This was what her father had done every day. There had been no specialists flying in. It had just been him.

She could do this because she had Derek by her side. Because this baby and Jennifer were family. She had to make sure she didn't lose any more family members.

She'd ruined enough lives.

She took her spot and went to work. She washed Jennifer's abdomen with betadine and then picked a scalpel off the tray. She drowned out the sounds of the storm, of the monitors, and of everything else.

The only sound she focused on was her heart. The only voice she heard in her head was her own, telling her what move to make.

She'd done countless C-sections before.

This was no different.

Evelyn looked up and saw Derek across from her, holding the retractor. He nodded and she reached in and pulled out a tiny thirty-three-week-old baby boy. He wasn't breathing, but that was to be expected. She was prepared for that.

She quickly cut the cord and handed the baby over to Tim, who was holding out towels. Tim whisked him over to the warming table and there was a tiny cry, but it wasn't strong.

Still, it was a cry, and tears stung her eyes as she thought of her little third cousin—alive.

Family.

"Keep him ventilated, Tim—and warm."

"Yes, Dr. Saunders."

Evelyn finished her work on Jennifer and made sure she was stable. She closed her up and injected antibiotics into her IV. Jennifer was going to make it.

Thank goodness.

She wanted to cry for joy, but she kept her emotions in check.

"Take her into the other exam room, Derek—and, Tim, bring her out of the anesthetic."

Tim nodded, but Derek stayed by the incubator.

"Is something wrong, Derek?" Evelyn asked.

"Nothing. He's breathing with the vent and his stats are good."

Thank God.

"Good. That's good. And Jennifer will survive."

And that was the only answer she could give. It was a relief.

"The baby will need the services of a neonatal doctor. I hope this storm lets up soon. I'm going to stay here with him now."

"Dr. Saunders!" Tim shouted. "There's blood in the drainage tube of the IV line."

Evelyn whipped back around.

Oh, God.

"I need to open her up again. I think her uterus has ruptured. Hang blood. Lots of blood."

And she was glad the stock of blood she ordered, for this reason, had come in before the planes had all been grounded.

Evelyn quickly worked on getting back in there to try and fix the damage.

Derek was pale as he stepped back. "What's happening?"

"She's bleeding out. I need help, Derek!"

"Tell me what to do!" Derek said, jumping back into the fray with her.

Evelyn knew this was hard for him after what had happened to his wife, but she also knew he was strong. Stronger than he gave himself credit for. Stronger than her. He was there, by her side, ready to save a life. He was a doctor first and foremost, and a damn fine one that she could rely on.

The first man in a long time she could rely on.

Even though Mo was still out in that storm he didn't fold under pressure. And she wouldn't either. He gave her strength in this moment. Strength she hadn't thought she had.

And she was glad he was here.

With him she couldn't fail.

She *wouldn't* fail.

CHAPTER THIRTEEN

HURRICANE TINA LASTED for twelve hours before it moved over the mainland and lost steam. The tree on the road was cleared. Janet, Mo and Edna made it safely to the clinic. There was no way Edna could get home yet, but her family was safe and everyone was relieved that the three of them were okay. Derek had Mo resting in his office and Edna had taken one of the empty exam rooms.

Evelyn was exhausted. She'd managed to stop Jennifer's bleeding, but Jennifer would need a hysterectomy. They had to get her into Sitka.

The baby was still alive and she'd given him some saline and packed cells to try and dilute the packed red blood cells. His lungs were wet and underdeveloped still, even though Jennifer had been given a shot of steroids in Juneau to help quicken lung development.

Little Baby Boy Yazzie still had a long way to go. He needed to be in a neonatal intensive care unit.

Jennifer was still under sedation because of her blood loss and the major surgery.

Evelyn and Janet traded on watching the baby in the incubator. Just so they could have a break to stretch or eat or have coffee.

Evelyn's eyelids felt as if they were made of sandpaper now, as she sat next to the incubator, monitoring the tiny little infant.

Her third cousin was cute.

Evelyn smiled at him. She might have told herself she never wanted to have a family, or planned on it because she was too terrified, but she really did want one. A husband, kids, and to travel around the world.

That would be perfection.

Or you could just stay here.

"The planes are back up and running," Tim announced as he came in from the staff room. "The hurricane is over, just a tropical storm now, and the air ambulance is ready to take Jennifer and Joe the Third to Sitka."

Evelyn raised her eyebrows. "Joe the Third?"

Tim laughed and left the room.

She turned back to the baby. "Sorry, kid. I mean sorry about being Joe the Third."

Evelyn stood up, her body aching from being hunched over. She grabbed the chart she'd been keeping and stuck it under the incubator. The paramedics were already wheeling Jennifer out and Joe Jr. looked beside himself.

"She's not awake," he said when he saw Evelyn.

"I've kept her out—she's been through a lot. She'll wake up soon. She's stable, Joe. Remember? We talked about it? She'll need you when she wakes up."

Joe nodded and then looked at the incubator. Evelyn hadn't let him get too close to Joe the Third because she didn't want to put any strain on the baby.

Joe Jr. grinned and Joe Sr. came over.

"He'll be fine too," Evelyn said. "He needs to spend time in the neonatal intensive care unit, but he's made it this long."

"Thank you, Evie," said Joe Jr., and followed the paramedics outside with Jennifer.

Joe Sr. lingered behind and looked at his grandson. "Your parents would be so proud, Evelyn. If it wasn't for you I don't think Jennifer or the baby would be here. Thank you."

Evelyn nodded, but she didn't know how to respond to that at all. She wheeled Joe the Third out to the ambulance and the incubator was loaded in beside Jennifer and Joe Jr.

She stood there watching as they secured them and then shut the doors. The ambulance fired up and headed toward the airport, where the air ambulance was waiting to take them to Sitka.

Evelyn walked slowly back into the clinic.

She was wiped out.

"Have you seen Derek, Tim?"

Tim stretched where he was sitting behind the reception desk. "No, not since the surgeries."

Evelyn frowned. "I'm going to have a shower. Think you can man things here?"

Tim nodded. "I'm fine. I'll clean up and then lock up."

"Send Janet and Edna home too. It's been a long day and night. I'm sure they want to get home to check on their families."

Tim nodded. "Of course. Get some rest."

"You too."

Evelyn grabbed her coat and headed outside. There were a few fallen branches and some garbage littering the street. The damage wasn't bad. there was some flooding near the sea wall, and it might take some time to clear that, only she wouldn't be here to see it.

She couldn't stay here anymore.

Why not?

Evelyn cursed under her breath, annoyed at herself.

Being with Derek had been amazing, but what would he think of her if he knew the truth about her.

She'd ruined so many lives and now she was too hardened. Her grandmother had taught her well.

What if she ruined his life too? Or Mo's?

Derek and Mo deserved more than her. It had been a mistake coming here. She should've just turned down her friend's plea for help. Coming to Alaska had been a bad idea.

Had it, though?

Derek had dozed off with Mo. She'd been terrified of being separated from him, and when he'd got her settled down he hadn't been able to help drifting off.

He didn't sleep long before he woke with a start and remembered in crystal clarity everything that had happened. He reached over for Mo, worried that he'd lost her, but she was there.

Where was Evelyn?

And then he remembered Jennifer Yazzie.

He scrubbed his hands over his face, feeling emotionally drained because what had happened with Jennifer had reminded him of what he'd gone through with Vivian. Only for a moment, though. Jennifer was here still. The baby was stable. Strong. This was not a tragedy all because of Evelyn. She had brought light to the darkness.

Derek groaned and got up. He was angry at himself for sleeping with Evelyn, for giving in to the desire that he knew was wrong, but it had been worth it.

And, though he should feel worse than he did, he had loved being with Evelyn that way. He'd loved taking her in his arms. It had felt so natural to be with her and it had been so long since a woman had made him feel that way.

Evelyn made him *feel* again.

He wasn't Dr. Taylor and he wasn't Mo's dad when he was in her arms.

He was a hot-blooded man again.

What about Vivian?

Derek was confused about his feelings. All he knew right now, in this moment, was that one night with Evelyn would never be enough.

Maybe, just maybe, he could give this a shot?

He'd never thought he'd find anyone again after Vivian had died. He'd never thought he'd see hope in hopeless situations. He'd never thought he'd feel alive again, but Evelyn had changed that.

He was in love with Evelyn. He'd fallen in love with her.

He just wasn't sure if Evelyn reciprocated those feelings.

She was holding back. She was hiding something. And until she opened up he wasn't sure she'd let him in. And he had to protect Mo from getting hurt.

He got himself and Mo up and dressed and then drove to drop Mo at Edna's. As he walked back towards the front of the clinic he saw a person crossing the road. Before he could figure out who it was the person collapsed in a heap.

"Oh, my God!"

Derek ran over and saw it was Jocelyn Washington. She was unconscious.

"Hold on, Jocelyn!" He assessed her ABCs and saw there was a laceration to her head that was bleeding.

Tim ran out of the clinic, having been watching from the window. "What happened?"

"Jocelyn fainted. We need a backboard. Help Evelyn bring one out."

Tim nodded and ran off. Evelyn came outside within a few minutes, carrying a backboard with Tim.

"Great," Derek said.

"I saw the whole thing happen." Evelyn looked down at Jocelyn and paused. "She just collapsed."

"She's okay. I don't think she hit her head too hard. Now, *why* she fainted is another matter."

"This street is where my father died," she muttered as she helped Derek assess Jocelyn and then together they lifted her onto the backboard and carried her into the clinic.

"This is not your father, Evelyn. Jocelyn was not hit by a car."

Evelyn nodded and they carried Jocelyn into an exam room.

Jocelyn was coming to, groaning in pain.

"Jocelyn—it's Dr. Taylor. You fainted in the street and hit your head pretty bad."

Jocelyn didn't respond and Derek checked her pupils. They were reactive.

"She probably has a concussion," Evelyn said.

Tim came in and Evelyn stepped back, because Tim had more training in emergency medicine than she did.

"Abdomen is soft."

Jocelyn came around. "What happened?"

"You fainted in the street."

"Oh, my God." She tried to sit up.

"Don't move, Jocelyn. You hit your head hard and probably have a concussion. Lie still. We're going to get you taken care of."

Jocelyn nodded. She was in shock.

"Evelyn?" Jocelyn whispered.

Evelyn nodded, but Jocelyn still appeared stunned.

"Evelyn!" Jocelyn shouted as she stared at her with a dazed expression.

"Yes?" Evelyn said.

"I loved your father."

"I know," she said.

"He loved you more. That night he was distracted because you were upset about us. He wanted to get back to you and he didn't pay attention crossing the road. The ring he bought me—I had to sell it because I was alone and pregnant after he died. *You* were more important to him. It was *your* fault. *All* of it."

"Hey, now," Derek said to Jocelyn. "You need to stop talking."

Evelyn's cheeks were flushed with embarrassment as she left the exam room.

Jocelyn settled down and drifted off. Definitely a concussion.

"You got this, Tim?" Derek asked. "I'm going to call Jocelyn's family and let them know where she is."

Tim nodded. "Yep. I got this."

Derek left the room and found Evelyn in the storeroom, pacing.

"Hey, what she said…she has a concussion."

"I know, but it's got a lot of truth to it," Evelyn said. "I didn't know he'd asked her to marry him. But I knew he wanted to, and I was upset that night he left. I've blamed myself for so long for his death. I didn't realize she blamed me as well."

"I'm sorry."

Evelyn shrugged. "Well, it's not going to bring my father back."

"No."

She sighed. "I called Juneau General and they're going

to send a replacement OB/GYN out here to finish off my rotation."

Derek was stunned. "What?"

"I have to go," Evelyn said quickly. "I can't stay here."

"You can finish out your rotation."

"No, I can't. I have to get out of here. I can't live in the past. I have to move on. I have to forget about this place. I've done too much damage."

"What're you talking about?"

Evelyn sighed. "I told you that Martha Washington is my half sister. Because of me not wanting my dad to marry Jocelyn he was killed that night. It was always bad enough that I ruined two lives—but three? I have to leave before I hurt them further."

"What?" Derek was in shock, blocking her escape from the storeroom. "You're leaving?"

"I can't stay."

"Why? What about your family here?"

"What *about* them? They got along fine without me for twenty years."

"That's because your grandmother blocked them."

"My grandmother was grieving for her son."

"Evelyn, Wolf's Harbor needs you. I—" Only he couldn't finish that sentence. He couldn't finish what he wanted to say.

What about me? What about Mo?

"I can't stay. I can't deal with this. It's twenty years too late to mourn. I've got a good life and I have to put this place behind me. I can't…"

"You're afraid. You couldn't settle down with a man you'd been with for two years and you can't take a chance with your heart now."

"I'll ruin your life if I stay. I'm too hardened. I don't have the room or the capacity," she said stonily.

"You improved my life. You lit up this town. You have to stay."

"What's two more months going to do? Nothing will change."

The question caught him off guard and he realized that she'd never been going to stay. She'd never planned on staying.

"I *knew* it was a mistake. I knew it was a mistake getting close to you. I *told* myself that you weren't going to stay. You temporary doctors create more problems than you fix, coming through here."

"There was always a time limit on this, Derek. I can't stay any longer. Besides, if Mo changed her mind about sharing her father... Don't do what my father did to me. Don't do that to Mo."

Derek couldn't look at her. His heart was breaking but he couldn't figure out why. How could a heart love two people at once?

"Well," he said calmly, "you better get packed up. I'll check on your half sister."

"She's not my family, Derek. I lost my family a long time ago."

"No, you didn't lose them. They're right here. You're just too scared to find them again."

Evelyn's gaze narrowed. "I'm not the only one scared here, Derek. You're just as afraid of forgiveness as I am. You can't forgive yourself for Vivian, just like me and my father's death."

He stepped to the side and let her leave.

She slammed the door behind her and Derek kicked the wall.

Uncle Yazzie drove her to the airport. He'd been surprised when she called, but he'd come just the same.

He didn't say anything to her as he drove her away from the clinic.

Always running.

As she looked back at the clinic through the window she realized that she was tired of running, but she'd ruined more lives here than she'd saved.

That's not true.

Derek's words about her lighting up Wolf's Harbor resonated with her.

She was so hardened, like her grandmother. Her grandmother had been miserable and bitter all the years Evelyn had known her. But she could've been happy had she just accepted Thorne's life in Alaska. Her grandmother had deprived herself of happiness and Evelyn was doing the same.

She stared down at the box and the card on her lap that Uncle Yazzie had given to her from Léelk'w. Evelyn couldn't bring herself to open it.

"Are you sure about this, Evie?" Uncle Yazzie asked from the front seat.

No.

"Yes."

"This is your home." He parked the cab and turned around. "Don't leave. Stay. This is where you belong."

"I don't belong here, Uncle Yazzie. I did once, but..." There were so many pieces of her life that were missing. So much she'd missed out on. So much she'd lost.

She'd hardened her heart for so long that she wasn't sure that she could go back.

Ever.

"I think I'm going to take a job I've been offered in Seattle. I'll come to visit," Evelyn said, but they both knew that was a lie.

"You don't think that you fit in here, but you do, Evie.

I just wish you could see that." He climbed out of the cab and went to the trunk to get her bags.

Evelyn slipped out of the cab and took the bags from him. He hugged her and Evelyn closed her eyes, fighting tears.

Keep it together. Don't cry.

She turned and walked across the road to the airport. She looked back once, to see Uncle Yazzie standing there, just as he had all those years ago, waving after her sadly. The pain, the terror she'd felt walking into the unknown washed over her again. The loss of her family.

Oh, God.

She tore her gaze away and headed into the airport. There were a few other passengers waiting for the plane to Sitka. Evelyn checked in and then found a spot in the farthest corner of the airport. She stared down at the box and the card from Léelk'w.

She opened the card first.

> *Evie, you're scared of opening your heart again. You've suffered so much pain and loneliness. I understand the loss, but you cannot run from your ghosts. You need to embrace them, for they make up who you are. Your life will be empty if you don't accept who you are.*
>
> *These were your mother's. She made them herself and wanted you to have them when you became a woman. They're overdue coming into your possession. Wear them and remember us.*
>
> *And forgive, my love. Forgive yourself. Your family.*
>
> *Come back soon.*
> *Love, Léelk'w.*

Tears streamed down her face and she opened the box. There were the abalone earrings that shimmered and were smooth. Her mother's.

Like a long-forgotten memory she heard her mother's voice in her head, singing a traditional song and brushing her hair.

For so long Evelyn had locked all those memories away, making her restless. She'd forgotten who she was. She'd lost her family, herself. The pain had been unbearable, but now she had a chance to have it all back.

Love was worth the risk.

She loved Derek. She loved Mo.

She wanted to be in their life.

She deserved happiness.

She wasn't being selfish, pursuing happiness.

She wanted to stay in Wolf's Harbor—the place where she was born. It was in her blood. And she wanted to help Derek get a hospital here, so that women could safely have their children. So those who were severely injured could get treatment right away.

She wanted Wolf's Harbor to grow.

And she wanted to grow here.

She was tired of running. The way to make things right was to stay. To take her father's place and make amends with Jocelyn and Martha.

She wasn't her father, but she was their family too.

"Ladies and gentlemen, we'll now begin boarding for our non-stop flight to Sitka. Please have your boarding passes ready and line up at Gate One."

Evelyn pocketed the earrings and grabbed her bag, but instead of heading to the gate she ran outside.

Uncle Yazzie was still sitting there, gazing at the plane, and she could see tears in his eyes.

"Uncle Yazzie!" Evelyn shouted.

Joe Sr. turned around and grinned. "I thought my mother was crazy when she said you'd change your mind. You have a stubborn streak like your mother did and *she* never changed her mind."

Evelyn laughed and they hugged each other.

"Welcome home, Evie."

"It's good to be home, Uncle Yazzie."

She wasn't sure if Derek would have her, but she had to take the chance. Either way, she was staying in Wolf's Harbor and she was going to help Derek get that hospital—and if that was all her relationship with Derek could be, then so be it.

She wasn't going anywhere.

She was home.

Derek sat next to Jocelyn.

He was numb. He felt completely numb again.

"What happened?" Jocelyn moaned.

"You fainted and you have a concussion."

"Martha?"

"Frank is with her. She's okay, and Tim has checked on the baby. Still a strong heartbeat."

"Tim? I thought that Evelyn was your OB/GYN."

"Evelyn had to go to Seattle," Derek said stonily.

"Oh." Jocelyn closed her eyes. "I said something to her, didn't I?"

"Painkillers can lower inhibitions."

Jocelyn groaned. "Has she left? I need to apologize."

"Yes. She's left."

"She was a child and confused," Jocelyn said. "Thorne was distracted and the weather didn't help. You can't blame a kid. I feel terrible. Sure, I was the villain in her story as a child, but I see she doesn't think that way anymore. She's the villain in her own story. She blames herself."

Derek saw that. He recalled the things she'd said. She did blame herself. She said she'd ruin his life. But she wasn't to blame and she was denying herself any shot at love and happiness because she was punishing herself.

"You remind me of Thorne, Dr. Taylor."

"How so?"

"Widower, lonely with a child. Afraid... But I don't think you're too scared to move forward now. Thorne didn't forget his wife. He loved her. But he told me that his heart expanded."

"What?" Derek asked.

"I know it sounds silly, and I didn't get it until he died. There I was, devastated that the man I loved had died. I was left pregnant and alone. Thorne was the love of my life and I thought I'd never get over him. But a few years went by, and I just existed day to day, being a mother to Martha, and then I met Frank. I realized then what Thorne meant. A heart is not restricted to one person—it expands to encompass many people in your life. I will always love Thorne, but my heart has room for Frank too."

A tear slid down Derek's cheek and he wiped it away as Jocelyn's words sank in. He couldn't go on living this half-life. He was still alive and he had to *live*.

Even though he'd tried not to let it happen his heart had expanded and Evelyn had wormed her way in. He loved the way she was with his daughter. She said she didn't want kids, but he understood her fear. Evelyn had lost so much in her life—it was why she ran.

They were the same.

He loved her and he couldn't lose her. He'd convince her to stay. If she wouldn't he'd leave Wolf's Harbor—he would. He would follow her anywhere. He had to grieve. He had to forgive himself. He had to heal and move on.

He had to stop Evelyn from getting on that plane before it was too late.

"I've got to go, Jocelyn. Thanks."

Jocelyn nodded and smiled. "Tell her I'm sorry."

Derek nodded and left the exam room. He grabbed his jacket and checked his watch. He was hoping he would make it before the Sitka flight left.

He ran out of the clinic and stopped dead in his tracks when he saw Joe Yazzie's cab pull up on the other side of the street.

Evelyn got out and stood there. She crossed the street. His heart skipped a beat.

She stayed.

"What're you doing here?" Derek asked, stunned. "I thought you were going to Sitka."

"I was, but…" She was trembling. "I lost my family once and I blamed myself for that loss."

"You punished yourself," he said gently.

Tears welled in her eyes. "Yes."

"You don't need to punish yourself. It wasn't your fault. Jocelyn explained."

"She did?" Evelyn asked quizzically.

"You were a *child*, Evelyn. You didn't kill your father. A truck did."

She nodded. "I hardened my heart to love. I was so afraid of being hurt, of hurting someone or being left alone again. Having no feelings was easier. I thought so, but it's not. I love you. I love Mo. I thought I didn't deserve you both because I ruined so many lives. But I didn't ruin them. I was ruining just one—my own. I don't want to be bitter or emotionless anymore. I want to *feel* again."

Derek cut off her babbling by closing the gap between

them and cupping her face, kissing her. Her arms, shaking, came around him and she melted into him.

"I love you too, Evelyn."

She beamed up at him. "You do?"

"For so long I thought I couldn't love again. I thought you only got one love. But my heart has expanded and you're firmly in there. I can't lose you, Evelyn. Even if it means I have to leave here and go where you need to go, I will. You brought me back to life."

Tears slid down her cheeks. "You brought me back to life too."

They kissed again.

"So… Seattle?"

"What?" she asked.

"You said you were going there."

Evelyn grinned and then kissed him. "We're not going anywhere. I just came home and I want to stay here—if you think the clinic can use me."

Derek picked her up and spun her around, set her back down. "I love you, Evelyn Saunders, and I never thought I would feel this way again. You've brightened my life. You breathed life into me and Mo again. I was just existing. I wasn't alive. I was numb to it all. But you've given me purpose. I love you."

He kissed her again and wrapped his arms tightly around her, holding her tight.

He was finally awake.

He was alive again.

And although he would never forget Vivian, he felt as if he could feel, breathe and live again. For the first time in a long, long time.

He was whole once more.

EPILOGUE

One year later

EVELYN STOOD IN front of the construction site, staring up at the hospital that was being erected in Wolf's Harbor. Since she'd taken on the position as permanent OB/GYN there, Juneau General Hospital and the state of Alaska had invested funds to make Wolf's Harbor Community Health Center a reality.

Evelyn had to go to Juneau and teach classes a few times a year, but that was no problem for her. Or at least it hadn't been until last month.

She touched her round belly. Soon she'd have to stop traveling to Juneau and back, but there was another OB/GYN who'd come to work permanently at the clinic and would be taking over Evelyn's position while she was on maternity leave.

Tim Vance had also signed up to stay on permanently as another general practitioner, which meant Derek wasn't tied down so much.

More staff were being hired, and the small hospital was on schedule to open by the end of the month.

"What're you staring at?" Derek asked, coming to stand beside her.

"The sign is crooked."

Derek squinted up at the sign. "It is not. It's fine."

"Hmm…" She rubbed her belly as the baby kicked. "It's almost time to pick up Mo from school, isn't it?"

"Yep—you want to walk down together? I'm done for the day and I'm letting Janet handle the nurse interviews over Skype. She'll pick good ones."

Evelyn nodded and took Derek's hand as they walked down Main Street toward the school. "Martha is taking online courses to get her nursing degree."

"That's great. But I don't know how she's managing that and taking care of her little girl. Ever since her little one started walking she's been rambunctious. Do you know how many stitches I've had to put in that kid's head?"

Evelyn laughed. "Jocelyn said she keeps her on her toes. It'll be nice to have more young families here. This hospital is breathing new life into Wolf's Harbor."

Derek nodded. "I just hope no one makes fun of Joe the Third."

Evelyn laughed. "Why would they?"

"Joe *the Third*?"

Evelyn chuckled again. "Yeah, well, it's a tradition."

"I don't think Katlian was too pleased with having to hand you over to me, though."

"Léelk'w likes you—and she loves Mo."

"Mo loves her."

"Léelk'w's heart has always had room for all her family."

Derek kissed her hand. "I'm just glad she's not giving me too much of a hard time anymore."

They stopped at the school yard just as the bell rang and Mo came running out of the small community school, her purple backpack a dead giveaway as she ran toward them.

"Dad! Evie!"

Mo ran past Derek and went to greet the baby first, before kissing her father and then Evelyn.

"Did you have a good day?"

"Yep! And I ate all my lunch. Can we go to Sally's?"

"I think so," Derek said.

"Yes! Ice cream!" Mo said, pumping her fist.

"Not ice cream. Not before dinner," Derek said.

"I could do with some ice cream," Evelyn teased.

Derek rolled his eyes. "Fine. Ice cream."

"Yes! Ice cream!" Mo shouted again, fist-pumping harder.

"Who taught you to fist-pump?" Evelyn asked as they walked away from the school toward Sally's.

"Léelk'w," Mo said.

"Of course she did," Derek said dryly.

Mo skipped ahead and Derek followed close behind her, while Evelyn walked slowly, her heart swelling as she watched her little family run ahead. The baby in her belly kicked and she smiled, rubbed where the baby had kicked.

She wasn't sure what Mo was going to think about having a baby brother...

She was definitely not calling him Joe the Fourth.

Thorne was good option.

She smiled as Derek picked up Mo and swung her around.

Maybe Derek Jr.?

There was time still to name the baby.

She picked up her pace to catch up with her family.

She was glad that she had finally found her place.

She was glad that she was finally home.

* * * * *

MILLS & BOON

Coming next month

REUNITED BY THEIR SECRET SON
Louisa George

Finn walked through to the waiting room and was just about to call out the boy's name when he was struck completely dumb. His heart thudded against his ribcage as he watched the woman reading a story to her child. Her voice quiet and sing-song, dark hair tumbling over one shoulder, ivory skin. A gentle manner. Soft.

His brain rewound, flickering like an old film reel: dark curls on the pillow. Warm caramel eyes. A mouth that tasted so sweet. Laughter in the face of grief. One night.

That night…

A lifetime ago.

He snapped back to reality. He wasn't that man any more; he'd do well to remember that. He cleared his throat and glanced down at the notes file in his hand to remind himself of the name. 'Lachlan Harding?'

She froze, completely taken aback. For a second he saw fear flicker across her eyes then she stood up. The fear gone, she smiled hesitantly and tugged the boy closer to her leg, her voice a little wobbly and a little less soft. 'Wow. Finn, this is a surprise—'

'Sophie. Hello. Yes, I'm Finn. Long time, no see.' Glib, he knew, when there was so much he should say to explain what had happened, why he hadn't called, but telling her his excuses during a professional consultation wasn't the right time. Besides, she had a child now; she'd moved on from their one night together, clearly. He glanced at her left hand, the one that held her boy so close—no wedding ring. But that didn't mean a thing these days; she could be happily unmarried and in a relationship.

And why her marital status pinged into his head he just didn't know. He had no right to wonder after the silence he'd held for well over two years.

They were just two people who'd shared one night a long time ago.

Continue reading
REUNITED BY THEIR SECRET SON
Louisa George

Available next month
www.millsandboon.co.uk

LET'S TALK
Romance

For exclusive extracts, competitions
and special offers, find us online:

f facebook.com/millsandboon

⬚ @millsandboonuk

🐦 @millsandboon

Or get in touch on 0844 844 1351*

For all the latest titles coming soon, visit
millsandboon.co.uk/nextmonth